The Ox, the Horn, and the Sheaf

MEG DULY

ISBN 978-1-0980-0141-4 (paperback)
ISBN 978-1-0980-0142-1 (digital)

Christian Faith Publishing, Inc.
832 Park Avenue
Meadville, PA 16335
www.christianfaithpublishing.com

Printed in the United States of America

To my father, Reverend Dr. Harry A. Fifield. My father worked to bring people together across all areas of diversity despite the era of prejudice and bigotry in which he worked. My chosen paths as a wife, mother, clinical social worker, and writer come from his telling me and my brothers we could be anything we wanted to be as long as we took full responsibility for our choices.

Acknowledgment

I can never thank my mother, Margaret McIntosh Fifield, enough for her gift to me of the love of reading and writing.

I thank my dear friend Dr. Edward M. Gotlieb for his friendship since high school, for allowing me to work for him doing what I dreamed of doing since high school as a social worker, and for the vast bits of information and leads to research, which made this book possible.

Finally, I thank Christian Faith Publishing for their faith in my project.

Prologue

Secular and religious literature agree that sometime between 1050 and 930 BCE, the kingdom of Israel was divided into two kingdoms. The Northern Kingdom remained Israel, containing ten of the original twelve tribes. The Southern Kingdom held the remaining two tribes and became Judah. Both secular and religious literature also agree that in 732 BCE, the Assyrians, led by King Tiglath-Pileser III, attacked Israel and took those Israelite tribes east of the Jordan River into exile. Again, in 723 BCE, the Assyrians under the next king, Shalmaneser, swept the remaining tribes of the Northern Kingdom. At this point, all history of the ten tribes of Israel disappeared into oblivion.

Here, secular and religious historians disagree as to the *why* of these events. Most serious historians see the ambitious king of Judah, Ahaz, incurring favor with the powerful Assyrian king, thus giving Judah an opportunity to rid itself forever of their annoying cousins to the north. Sacred scripture states that the prophets of old warned of a wrathful God's vengeance against the wicked Israelite king, Jeroboam, who led his people into pagan worship. Perhaps, just perhaps, both are right.

And perhaps, just perhaps, not *all* history of those lost tribes disappeared into oblivion.

PART I

The word of Jehovah that came unto Hosea the son of Beeri, in the days of Uzziah, Jotham, Ahaz, and Hezekiah, kings of Judah, and in the days of Jeroboam the son of Joash, king of Israel.

When Jehovah spake at the first by Hosea, Jehovah said unto Hosea, Go, take unto thee a wife of whoredom and children of whoredom; for the land doth commit great whoredom, *departing* from Jehovah. So he went and took Gomer the daughter of Diblaim; and she conceived, and bare him a son. And Jehovah said unto him, Call his name Jezreel; for yet a little while, and I will avenge the blood of Jezreel upon the house of Jehu, and will cause the kingdom of the house of Israel to cease. And it shall come to pass at that day, that I will break the bow of Israel in the valley of Jezreel. And she conceived again, and bare a daughter. And *Jehovah* said unto him, Call her name Lo-ruhamah; for I will no more have mercy upon the house of Israel, that I should in any wise pardon them.

—Hosea 1:1–6 (King James Version)

Chapter 1

Edinburgh, Scotland
Hebrew year 5774 (2014 CE)

The long-forgotten passage ran off a tunnel that wound beneath the Royal Mile in Edinburgh. The leader explored many such places before finding this one. The damp, dripping passage stank of sewage and rot. However, it was the perfect place as no one there must ever be seen together, and the tunnel could be accessed from many different buildings above.

The leader got the attention of the recruits who just arrived at this designated area. Nothing about them justified faith in these people, but they were the only ones willingly to take the pledge.

"We tried previously to get hold of these artifacts. They represent the pagan Assyrians and the infidel Jews. Now they will be in one place. This will allow us to seize and destroy them." The leader's voice was soft but menacing. "Afterward, we call in our assassin, and the Israeli and his associates die, along with all their confederates. Then there will be nothing left of this blasphemy."

The leader's eyes wandered above the recruits' heads while imagining the future. *Despite these fools, I will succeed, and I will be honored for my efforts. No matter what, I will succeed.* With a sly grin, the leader gave the recruits orders for specific duties and warned them of the severe penalty for failure.

Then, once more, the passageway was dark and deserted.

* * * * *

Oban Airport in southwest Scotland is quiet at 5:00 a.m. The commuters to London and its airports left several hours earlier. Those headed to the big airports in Edinburgh or other Scottish cities would begin arriving in about an hour. This fact made it nearly impossible for Dunc to keep his eyes open. The only sounds he heard were the occasional ringing of the phone and the quiet voice of the woman answering the calls at the check-in counter. Other than that, the small waiting area was quiet.

Dr. Duncan McIntosh slumped down in his seat at the gate. He sat with arms crossed and one foot resting on the opposite knee. This lanky figure made the seat look like that of a child's. Fortunately, he only had a few more minutes to wait for the plane bearing his colleague and idol, Dr. Jacob Rubin. To keep his weary bones from falling out of the chair, he methodically went over the past week.

McIntosh arrived from Cambridge, Massachusetts, the previous Wednesday. He decided to extend his sabbatical to Scotland by one week so he could spend some time rooting through his own history. Dunc carefully planned his agenda, as he always does. His first stop was to visit the National Trust of Scotland. There he met an old friend from his undergraduate years. William Elder had a great deal of influence through the Scottish Natural Trust. Elder could help Dunc and his associates work with the Trust, vital for their pending archeological project. Dunc spent a full afternoon with Elder dotting i's and crossing t's for their dig. He left after a shared Scottish dinner and the understanding of reconnecting in five days.

McIntosh spent those days touring Inverness and every library, museum, and historic site he could access. He ended his weeklong quest back in the company of Elder for a promised visit to Moy Hall, the ancestral home of Chief MacKintosh of MacKintosh.

When Elder picked him up from his bed-and-breakfast, Dunc climbed into the car, in his mind, on the wrong side of the car, on the wrong side of the road.

"The chief and Lady MacKintosh are out of the country. However, being a very close friend of the chief, I arranged ahead of time to give you a tour. Lady MacKintosh is a historian herself. She recently updated the history of your clan, which, as I'm sure you are aware, goes all the way back to the twelfth century with the first chief, McDuff. She was delighted to accommodate the famous Dr. McIntosh," Elder explained.

"It sure is kind of you to go to all this trouble for me, Will." Dunc ignored the "famous Dr. McIntosh" statement because it embarrassed him.

"I was enormously pleased to hear from you. I didn't tell you this last week, laddie, but you were actually on my list to correspond with." Will smiled, quite pleased with himself and his good fortune. He explained that he just started his own book.

"It is a compilation of famous Scottish MacKintoshes and the American McIntoshes from the twentieth and twenty-first centuries. This is important to me personally," Will said, "because Elder is, as you also know, a sept of Clan Mackintosh."

Dunc heard the ego in Will's voice, remembering his many escapades, pranks, and off-color jokes back in school. Dunc laughed to himself and said, "Good heavens, I'm just looking for a little more of my history. What do I have to offer you?"

Elder smiled. "Dunc, my laddie, you happen to be the famous Dr. Duncan McIntosh of your prestigious Hammond University, who made one of the most valuable Neolithic discoveries in the Americas."

Elder teased Dunc with these accolades because he knew his friend would blush with embarrassments—which he did. Dunc never sought fame. He had a deep love of archeology that began with an inspiring teacher in the sixth grade. He knew then that it would be his life's work and passion.

Even though he was only thirty-two, McIntosh had amassed many backbreaking hours in study and actual archeological digs. After his postgraduate work, he remained as a consulting professor. All this led up to the dig in the California tar pits. There he found a child's body that dated almost a thousand years older than any previous find in America. He was sought after for the dig here in Scotland because of the device he developed for working in those tar pits.

"I have a deal for you," Will Elder said. "If you will tell me about your find in California and then about what you'll be up to here, I'll give you a tour of the Moy museum and a copy of Lady MacKintosh's updated history of Clan MacKintosh."

Dunc couldn't resist the deal, although he would have to be careful about his current project. Will Elder brought out a tape recorder, the likes of which Dunc hadn't seen in ten years. Dunc gave so many interviews after his California discovery that he knew what he was going to say by heart. He went into great detail about the California find.

Dunc then cautiously approached his current project. "Because of instructions from our funding sources, my university being one, I can't go into too much detail about this project. I can tell you that we will be working at the Moine Mhor, peat bog near Kilmartin. I will be joined by two other eminently qualified archeologists, Dr. Jacob Rubin from the Archeological Institute in Tel Aviv and Ms. Kathleen Wallace, who is studying at the College of Archeology in Edinburgh. All I can tell you about the project itself is that finds here may give us insight into mysteries of Israel and possibly Scotland. Will, I promise you that when I can talk more, it will be to you."

When they arrived at Moy Hall, the gatehouse, built much like the castles of old, immediately attracted Dunc. Then the long unpaved drive to the MacKintosh residence reminded Dunc of how different, though just as beautiful, the Scottish flora was from that of his Massachusetts home. The evergreens of Scotland made him think of fairy-tale princesses playing hide-and-seek among the lush upturned boughs of the stately British trees.

When he finally stood in front of the elegant massive manor house, he had a quizzical look. "After seeing the gatehouse, I was expecting a castle. Why the different architecture?"

"I've been told that two or three generations back, *Himself* made a very Scottish decision. It would appear that the ancient castle would cost the clan all its funds to keep it habitable. He therefore tore it down and used the stones to build this lovely home."

"Himself?"

"That is how we refer to our chiefs."

Dunc nodded in amusement as he gazed at the two-story gray-stone manor house. "Yes, how very *Scottish* of him."

Will explained that the house was the family home, and they did not allow tours of that; however, there was a great deal else to see. They proceeded to tour the grounds. A small flock of sheep could be heard braying in the pasture in front of the manor house. The pasture ran down to the shore of shimmering Loch Moy. In the middle of the small loch was a tiny island overgrown with the lush wildflowers and shrubs of Scotland in their many shades of color. The late chief's somber grave site, with its marble benches and metal memorial plaque, sat across Loch Moy.

After seeing all this up close, they then walked to the small outbuilding which housed the MacKintosh museum. Approaching the museum, Dunc stood stock-still, wide-eyed and amazed as he viewed the great tree in front of him.

"Is that…is that a California redwood?"

"Yes, it is. Have you heard of the Native American McIntoshes?"

"Yes, I studied them and met some of this generation…and am even distantly related to them. The ancestor of Chief William McIntosh of the Creek Nation came to Georgia with Oglethorpe. He married a Creek princess. Their son, Chief William, became the Creek chief. He was murdered by the Counsel of Chiefs for some untoward treaty he signed. His son took the tribe to Oklahoma, where they are today. I am descended from that part of the Clan."

"Yes, I guess you do know about them. Don't hold me to this, but I think it was the Creek chief Dode McIntosh, William's great-grandson, who gave this tree as a sapling to our late chief. The two old heads of tribes were quite good friends. They even died in the same year. Now, shall we go into the museum?"

Dunc was eager with anticipation. What hit him first was the smell of ancient wood and fabric with the dust that settled on these relics, most several centuries old. These items spread out into every corner and even up the walls. This included, as Will explained, ancient tapestries from the castle. Their colors muted with age, and even the bed in which Bonnie Prince Charlie slept the night before the Battle of Culloden.

"We have several of the beds which the prince supposedly slept in scattered around Scotland." Will laughed.

Dunc laughed as well. "In America, our famous beds were slept in by George Washington."

Dunc wandered around the room, daring not to touch the fragile remnants of his family's past. There were sets of ornate china, vases, century-old photographs, elaborate paintings, and significant documents, all having to do with the heads of Duncan's ancient clan.

Will, an excellent tour guide, made it through the extensive items before sunset. When they arrived back at his B and B, Dunc climbed out of the car and stuck his hand out to shake with his old friend.

"How can I ever thank you for this grand adventure?"

"By keeping your promise to tell me all about your upcoming adventure, *just* as soon as you can. Oh, I almost forgot." Will pulled a wrapped package out of his back seat. "I said this was part of the bargain, but actually, it was Lady MacKintosh's idea for me to secure this for you."

Dunc unwrapped the package. He held a signed copy of Lady MacKintosh's update of *his* heritage.

* * * * *

The dull sound of the incoming plane finally moved into Dunc's conscious mind. Other travelers were beginning to arrive, talking and jostling their luggage. Dunc stood, stretched, and looked out the window. The small plane landed and taxied through the early-morning mist. Dunc watched with quite some excitement to actually be meeting Dr. Rubin in person.

Five people got off the plane. The last to walk down the stairs was a slightly stooped man whom Dunc knew to be in his seventies. A raincoat was draped over the arm that carried an overstuffed valise. His wild white thinning hair and his dark tanned skin made him look like he had been in a desert windstorm rather than an airplane.

Dunc went out to meet him and grasped the outstretched hand of the elder archeologist in both of his. Dunc hoped he wasn't coming off like a child meeting Mickey Mouse in Disneyland. The warmth and sincerity that emanated from Jacob Rubin soon put the younger man at ease.

"I can't tell you how glad I am to finally meet you, Dr. Rubin."

"And I you, young man. For a youngster, you have amassed quite a reputation for yourself," Rubin said with his heavy Israeli accent. "Oh, and call me Jacob."

"Thank you, Jacob, I will. And I'm just Dunc. How was your trip?"

"Long, very long. I hate plane changes and their complications. That's why I always take carry-ons." Rubin held up his valise. "I've had my equipment sent by the university to the Kilmartin Museum."

"Yes, I did the same. Great idea. It saves all that worry over lost valuables," Dunc said and immediately tripped over his own two feet.

Dr. Rubin grabbed his arm. "You've driven all night, haven't you?"

Dunc nodded.

"Well, at least I had the opportunity to doze on the flight. If you haven't rented us too fancy a vehicle, I think I shall take over motoring."

"That would be great. With the way I feel and my not being used to this wrong-side-of-the-road thing, I think this is the best way to proceed."

Duncan wondered what passersby thought of this stooped older man supporting a much younger man. *It must look quite amusing.*

As the two traveled the relatively straight shot from Oban to Kilmartin, they discussed the upcoming dig.

"Other than showing off your new *thingamajig*, what has interested you so much about this project, Dunc?" Rubin asked, resting his right elbow on the open window. The sun was just rising over the low hills to the west. The air, though still chilly, felt good to both.

"I love archeology, and I love mysteries. Having the two together and possibly solving two of the greatest mysteries in history is like nirvana to me," Dunc said. "Working with you and, for that matter, Ms. Wallace is a dream come true. What brings you here other than the obvious Hebraic connection?"

"It would seem we are both mystery buffs," Jacob said. "I've asked questions about the lost tribes of Israel for as long as I can remember. There's also the fascinating Picts of Scotland and of course, our *shields*, with all they could mean." Jacob paused a few minutes and reacted to the last part of Dunc's statement. "What do you know of Ms. Wallace?" he asked.

"I know that despite her lack of *letters*, she is the most knowledgeable archeologist on bogs, Picts, and the area where we will be working. What do you know about her?"

The older man hesitated a brief instant. "I know she will be here to find and document more about the aboriginal people of Scotland. If we learn of eighth-century BCE Hebrews here, we may also learn of the Picts of the same time period. I also know that she is a freedom fighter. Her passion is working for the complete separation of Scotland from England. She has been in several demonstrations for her cause and even gone to jail for destroying property and resisting arrest in London."

Dunc furrowed his brow. "Is she a freedom fighter or a terrorist?"

Jacob laughed ironically. "My parents came to Israel soon after it was established. They fought the British for freedom, and my mother was killed doing so. My wife was killed five years ago by a Palestinian suicide bomber. I guess, depending on whom you talk to, my parents were either freedom fighters or terrorists. Similarly, that Palestinian woman who died with my wife was either a freedom fighter or a terrorist…and depending on whom you might have talked to two hundred and some years ago, the American revolutionists were either freedom fighters or terrorists.

"In answer to your question, her misdemeanors don't quite rank as terrorism, but her fervor just might. And at the same time, she is definitely a freedom fighter. Most importantly, her talents are very necessary to this project. I guess we'll just have to find out the rest."

Dunc was staring at the man in awe. "My God, you've been through so much loss. How do you stay sane?"

"I stopped hating. That's all—I just stopped hating."

Chapter 2

The tall, slender woman in her midtwenties stepped off the bus in Kilmartin. She had freckles and long curly red hair. Kathleen Wallace searched the crowd for someone who might have come for her. When she saw the young guy in jeans and a T-shirt leaning against the railing, arms crossed, she immediately felt hurt and anger. *The eminent doctors think so little of me that they sent their "gofer" to fetch me to them.* She squared her shoulders and walked to her perceived "gofer."

"I'm Kathleen Wallace. Have the *doctors* sent you to pick me up?"

The gofer had a confused look on his face. He stood, backing up a bit. "I guess you could say that one of the doctors sent me to meet you."

"Which one was so thoughtful?" she snapped.

The gofer smiled cautiously and said, "Dr. Rubin sent me to bring you to the motel. He is tied up with the National Trust group getting everything ready for the project."

She nodded and looked down. All the fight was gone, and what was left was hurt. She had no right to be rude to this kid. The many times she had been treated this way ran through her mind. Those she would love to call colleagues often treated her as though she existed for the sole purpose of making them tea.

She thought of her family, who had no money; and if they had, they wouldn't use it to send her to school. She worked so hard to get the education she did have. That PhD seemed light-years away to her. *Someday…someday I will be a doctor, sending gofers to pick up underlings.*

The gofer stepped forward and stuck out his hand. "Ms. Wallace, I'm Dr. Duncan McIntosh. I'm very glad to meet you. Both Jacob and I are so grateful that you agreed to add your considerable talents to our project."

Kathleen's eyes flew open wide. "Och jobby," she said just below a whisper. When she got her wits about her, she closed her mouth and said with her thick Scottish brogue, "I'm so sorry…I thought… I…I wasn't expecting someone so young. Dr. McIntosh, you must think I'm an eejit."

"On the contrary, I think I know what's going on. I get a lot of the same sort of stuff. You're young too. It seems no one will take us seriously until we get to be about Jacob's age."

"Or make one of the century's greatest finds, as you just did. I'm sure no one asks you to make them tea anymore."

Dunc laughed. "Actually, Jacob asked me to get him coffee this morning. He was terribly stiff after a long flight and driving here from Oban yesterday."

Kathleen had to smile. *Once again I'm taking myself way too seriously.* She hoped she might be able to redeem herself with gratitude. "Dr. McIntosh, thank you for taking me and my work seriously and for having enough faith in me to let me join this project."

"As Jacob said yesterday, you have talents and knowledge this project calls for…and it's *Dunc*," he said, emphasizing the name.

Misunderstanding what he said, Kathleen covered her head and cowered close to him. "What…what was it?"

"Oh gosh, I'm sorry. I didn't say 'duck.' I said *Dunc*. That's my name."

She closed her eyes tight, bit her lower lip, and bowed her head, blushing a bright red that almost matched her hair.

He again stuck his hand out and said, "I think we need to start this all over. You must be Ms. Wallace. I'm Dunc McIntosh. Jacob Rubin and I are very grateful that you could join us. He would be here but is tied up with the Trust group."

Kathleen looked up at him. He was very kind and funny—and nice-looking in an academic sort of way. She immediately gave herself a mental slap. She had no time or inclination for that sort of thing. She did allow herself a large amount of admiration for him for giving her a way to save face.

She took his hand and said, "Kate, please call me Kate. And thank you for coming to pick me up." She then smiled mischievously and continued, "May I *buy* you a cup of coffee?"

Dunc drove Kate to the tiny Kilmartin motel where they were staying. "It's not Buckingham Palace, but I've stayed in a lot worse," he said.

Kate looked around her new home for who knew how long. She assessed her lodging, which smelled of Lysol. It consisted of a single bed, a tiny bathroom, a bedside table, a cane-bottom chair, a dresser with four drawers, and a coatrack with several hangers. It looked as clean as it smelled.

Kate smiled and nodded. "A bed and a working loo is all I need. This will do fine." As she placed her only luggage, a backpack, on the table, she and Dunc heard a car pull into the gravel parking lot. They both walked out to greet Dr. Jacob Rubin.

Jacob immediately put her at ease. He took both her hands in his and said, "The Scottish Natural Trust is impressed with your work, Ms. Wallace. They are being cooperative because of your noted reverence for the ecology in Scotland. Oh yes, and you too, Dunc, for your new 'thingamajig.' They feel that between the two of you, we won't go about trashing their beautiful countryside. They loaned us a large tent and had it set up by the dig site. It will be invaluable to us both for comfort from the weather and for privacy. The funding universities have given us almost all the requested equipment needed. However, we need to go to the Kilmartin Museum and view the discoveries. I suggest we go there right away and lay out our plan of action."

The museum was a short distance away from the motel. The curator was there to greet them. Two large, quiet men who were local constables accompanied them into the museum. One or the other of them would remain at the entrance twenty-four hours a day. These men made Kate feel secure, considering the inestimable value of the items they were about to see. The three archeologists shared with one another their sense of excitement to actually be getting to work.

Jacob greeted the museum curator as an old friend and introduced him to Kate and Dunc. The curator then led the whole group into a private room. The special lighting there was suitable for viewing ancient artifacts while protecting them from harmful UV rays. The first thing on the agenda: viewing the two major finds, the basis for the whole project.

One was found in Southern Egypt six months prior. A close associate of Jacob's had notified him and made arrangements for him to study it in Israel. It spoke to Jacob's enormous prestige in the archeological community for him to be allowed by the Egyptians to take this one item from the dig in Egypt to Israel.

The second find was discovered in the bog outside of Kilmartin over ten years earlier. Locals digging for peat found it. This artifact was stored away in the Kilmartin Museum and all but forgotten by everyone but the curator. When the news from Egypt reached him, the curator got in touch with Jacob. In less than six months, the famous Israeli archeologist put this project together.

Jacob laid out the two heavy round packages, both about three feet in diameter. The packages were clearly marked as to the date and the location where they were found. Jacob carefully and even lovingly unwrapped the two articles and laid them gently on top of their labeled packaging. Dunc and Kate drew closer to inspect the items. They were ancient shields. They were identical except for the one from the nearby bog being darker in color, indicating longtime submersion in the bog water.

Dunc said, "The markings around the rims are definitely of the Assyrian Empire."

Jacob and Kate nodded in agreement.

Kate knew what the artifacts were, but seeing them in person nearly made her heart jump out of her chest. "Great Scott! To find this one here…" She couldn't finish her statement for the emotions.

Both of the younger archeologists knew in advance they would see these ancient shields, dating to the eighth or ninth century BCE. However, these shields both had markings in the center of them, which, though identical to each other, were unlike any Assyrian marks ever seen by either. Wheat sheaves scratched into the center of the shields with gold painted into the carvings.

Duncan McIntosh looked up at Jacob Rubin. He smiled and said. "Beit Yosef."

Rubin smiled back and nodded.

Kate had been very quiet after the three left the museum. These men showed her nothing but respect, but this was something else. Would they lose their respect for her if she said anything? She decided to venture forth anyway.

"I'm not schooled in biblical *myths* or Hebrew. What is 'Beit Yosef'?"

Both men looked at her, but Jacob quickly answered, "It means 'House of Joseph.' Tell me, what is your religious persuasion?"

She gasped at his blunt and personal question. "What's that to you?" She felt violated.

"I want to know how much you know of Bible or Torah stories," Jacob said in an intentionally calm and friendly voice.

Kate settled her anger down, remembering once again the respect shown her. "I was raised a Christian, but I don't remember much of it. As to your question about my religion, I don't think I have one. I'm fairly antireligion, even atheistic. I can't find sense in it. I see only war and bigotry with religion." She stared at the floor, waiting for a lecture.

"Good," Jacob said, "then you will keep us honest. Duncan, my good lad, what is your persuasion?"

Once again, Kate was given a chance to save face.

"Well…let's see," Dunc said. "I'm a Christian…a Presbyterian preacher's kid. My father was a good man who did a lot of good for a lot of people and never took credit for it. I guess with him as my guide, I accepted the faith from childhood. As an adult, I've questioned a lot but stayed with the Presbyterians because they don't seem to have a problem with questions. You know how I like to ask questions. Now that you've grilled us, it's your turn, Dr. Rubin."

"Yes, I suppose it is." Jacob laughed. "Well, it's a little different with us Jews. Our religion, race, and history are all wrapped up into one. And yet we come in all different colors, from different locations, and interpret the Torah in many different ways. But we all seem to be one. I don't hold to all the kosher rules, but I respect them. For that matter, I respect all of yours…your traditions *and* your doubts and questions." Jacob smiled as he looked around the car. "I think what the three of us have in common is that we all have questions."

Jacob then looked at Kate. "Tell me what you know of our project."

"I know that there were twelve tribes of Israel, ten of which were exiled by the Assyrians in 723 BCE. All history of those ten stopped at that point. I know that artifacts have been found in Africa and here in Scotland that possibly pertain to those tribes. The one found here was found in an area populated by the ancient Picts of Scotland. We are attempting to trace wanderings of the Hebrew people by their artifacts. We are also trying to understand their association with the Picts. What I don't understand right now is who this Joseph is and what he has to do with our project. He was not one of those lost Hebrew tribes as far as my studies have shown."

Jacob looked at Dunc, who was driving, and said, "Do you want to take this one?"

"Nope, this is on your side of the Bible. You can take it."

Jacob shook his head and chuckled. "Well, let's see. The Hebrew patriarch Jacob had twelve sons. These sons were heads of the original twelve tribes. Jacob's next to the youngest, Joseph, was by all accounts his favorite. This angered the other eleven so much that they got Joseph alone and sold him into slavery to Egyptian travelers. In Egypt, this slave found favor with Pharaoh by interpreting his dreams. The interpretation was seven years of plenty and seven of famine. Pharaoh made Joseph secretary of 'Getting Ready for the Famine.'"

Dunc and Kate, who had been listening intently, broke into laughter at Jacob's humor. This gave Jacob time to take a drink of his now cold coffee.

"When the famine hit, it went as far as Canaan," he continued. "Joseph's brothers came from there to Egypt to buy grain. Joseph recognized them and forgave the jerks. They, their families, and the now aged Jacob moved to Egypt. Three hundred years later, the prolific Hebrews were growing in such numbers that it frightened the Pharaoh. He turned the Jews into slaves.

"That's when Moses and his brother, Aaron, came into the picture. The Torah says God told them to bargain with Pharaoh. 'Let my people go, or you're going to get a plague.' Ten plagues later, Pharaoh let them go. They wandered in the desert for forty years. I've heard it said that after thirty-nine years and eleven months, Mrs. Moses finally asked for directions."

Once again the two young people were caught off guard with Jacob's humor.

"So why didn't Joseph's tribe get to Israel?" Kate asked.

"Ah, but it did," Jacob continued. "Moses and his brother, Aaron, were from the tribe of Levi. God ordained Aaron and all his decedents to be Kohens or priests. Once they arrived in the Holy Land, the land was divided up into twelve portions for the twelve tribes. As clergy, the Levites were spread out among all the other tribes and given cities within the tribes. Because twelve is a very important number to the Hebrews, the tribe of Joseph was divided in half, that of his two sons Ephraim and Manasseh, who had been blessed by Grandpa Jacob, pretty much making them sons also."

"And they were among the exiled tribes," Kate admitted. She was absorbing this abridged history lesson. After a while, she looked Jacob in the eyes, knowing that he would not lie to her. "Some secular scholars believe these two tribes were just a second wave of immigration from Egypt. There is no mention of any of this in secular studies. How much of this is history, and how much is myth?"

Jacob smiled at her. "I can't answer that. There is some thought that placing the Exodus in late Bronze Age was an error. In middle Bronze Age, there is scant archeological evidence of all this. An Egyptian manuscript of that era speaks of one plague: the Nile turning to blood. A hastily dug mass burial suggests another. There is, from that time, the remains of a Semitic town in Egypt where the population appears to vanish overnight. Also going back to middle Bronze, archeologists found remnants of a collapsed wall in Jericho that match the biblical accounts of that battle. Kate, history is merely the collective memory and the summary of legends of those who were there…and who won. I'm telling you what I believe. You are more than welcome to listen to secularists or others. This is the only way to get anywhere near the truth."

Kate realized that all her carefully built prejudices, beliefs, and disbeliefs were going to be brought into question by this honest man. He would demand from them to open their minds to what they might find.

Chapter 3

The next item on the group's agenda: to become familiar with Dunc's "thingamajig." He had his invention shipped to the museum in Kilmartin. Dunc picked it up while they were there. The little group drove right to the tent provided for them near the bog.

"If I can get some help, I think we can get everything needed from the trunk," Dunc said, getting out of the car.

"From the what?" Kate asked Jacob.

Jacob laughed. "By the end of our time together, we may all be speaking the same language. I believe you call a car trunk a motor boot in the UK."

Kate smiled and nodded.

They followed Dunc to the back of the car, and he handed each of his colleagues one of three packages. He carried the biggest and heaviest. Inside the tent on the long folding table, Dunc opened the packages and laid out a large coil of heavy wire, a small computer, a remote control, a much smaller device, and what looked like a toy drone. Kate looked at these items with excitement and a degree of humorous expectation. Jacob's grin and chuckles told Kate he must feel the same.

Dunc picked up the smallest device. "This is my baby," he said, smiling with pride. "I've managed to put together in one unit a spectrometer capable of nondestructive molecule analysis, a new form of a magnetometer, a sonar scanner, and an x-ray camera. It can be attached to this coil of wire, a modified plumber's snake, which has an electrical wire run through it. The wire is attached to a small but powerful motor, which is run by this," he said, pointing to one device that looked similar to a TV remote control. "Or," he continued, "my *thingamajig* can go into this, my radio-controlled drone, and flown with the same device that runs the wire."

Dunc handled his invention much the same way a parent would handle a newborn. "The main device, the detector, is waterproof and made with a nearly indestructible material, like that of a plane's black box. The material is also a highly stick-proof form of Teflon. This allowed me to use it in the viscous tar pit. I can reach about a hundred feet with the snake into the bog and then about three hundred more over it with the drone. The device will instantaneously transmit the information to this computer."

Kate and Jacob were familiar with all the different technologies that Dunc was talking about, but to see them combined in one compact unit was incredible. To find, identify, analyze, photograph, and possibly even date artifacts without damaging the environment or the artifacts, saved both time and labor. Very precious commodities to archeologists. Also, the use of a plumber's tool and a drone similar to a youngster's toy was very like Duncan McIntosh—practical, brilliant, and unassuming.

"Surely you've had all this patented. What do you call it?" Jacob asked.

"Oh yes, after urging from a colleague. I had a lot of trouble coming up with a name. McIntosh, in all things computer, was already in use, so I just went with my initials, DAM. And before you ask, *A* is for 'Arthur.' It's patented as a…DAM Detector." Dunc stared at the floor, waiting for the jokes.

Kate and Jacob just watched him, holding back their laughter. Finally, Jacob clapped Dunc on the back and said, "*Damn* good idea."

Later that evening, the three ate together at the small pub near their motel. Kate loved Scottish food, especially the haggis. She ate heartily. Duncan just plain liked food, so he did as well. Jacob was not used to the Scottish cuisine, and he was having problems with heartburn. He only picked at his food. This, however, allowed him time to continue the conversation from earlier in the car. "Did we cover all of your questions today?"

Duncan smiled and nodded. "Questions? Yes, but I've been dying to talk to you about something else. Jacob, I have read everything you have ever written. My favorite work of yours is on Hebrew literacy. I particularly wanted to ask you about the scribe you talked about from the Ephraim Hebrew tribe. Some of his correspondence was found in the ruins of the Assyrian Royal Library. Do you remember who I'm talking about?"

Jacob laughed. "First of all, thank you for reading all my boring stuff. You must have run out of sleeping pills. Yes, I do remember him well. He was one of the most interesting characters I've ever run across. His correspondence was about the ancient Mesopotamian epic of Gilgamesh. His name was, Tal…Talmai. That's right, Talmai."

Dunc smiled and nodded. "My understanding of scribes in the Bible is that they were in an exalted position in the Hebrew religious hierarchy. They were the irrefutable interpreters of, and sticklers for, the laws of the Torah. It's hard to believe that a scribe would be that interested in a pagan myth."

"So true, so true," Jacob answered. "The position of the scribe that you're talking about didn't come into existence until about two to three hundred years after our scribe Talmai was writing. Those scribes took the place of the prophets of old as the voice of Yahweh. Talmai was a *soferim*, literally 'one who can read and write.'"

"I have one more question," Kate said. She relaxed now, finding all things Hebrew very interesting.

"As many as you like, my dear lady," Jacob said.

Kate smiled and said, "In my research and in talking to you, I keep hearing the same numbers over and over. For instance, I hear twelve, and I hear forty."

Jacob nodded. "Ah yes, our obsession with numbers. Actually, we Jews have meanings for all of them, as far as you can count. However, the main numbers you will hear in studying our particular situation are far less. Three is for divinity or truth. Two children can tell you what happened, but you need at least a third to find the truth. Seven is for completion, spiritual perfection. Twelve represents authority given by God, governmental perfection. That's why they needed twelve governing tribes. The last important one for us is forty.

It represents trial or probation or words like *large, many*, and *a long time*. That's the reason for forty years wandering in the desert. Any more questions, Ms. Wallace?"

"No, not now, but I know where to find you." Kate smiled. She would have gone to the moon and back to get tea for these guys.

The archeologists knew they would have no trouble getting all the help they would need for their project. There was an abundance of archeological schools with hundreds of willing students eager to earn extra credit by being on a dig, particularly ones with these noted archeologists. The nice thing about using student labor was that the young people actually pay to have this opportunity, as they would pay for their courses.

Jacob contacted archeological schools of universities in Scotland and England. Seven top students would arrive the following day. All were in their postgraduate studies, specializing in areas pertaining to this particular project. They were picked for their expertise in the areas of archeological technique and Middle Eastern and biblical archeology.

Since the lower schools were out for summer break, the universities arranged for the interns to sleep in a nearby schools' classrooms-turned-dorms. Duncan picked up the students and got them to the school with a bus donated by the school. After they got luggage settled in, the interns were then shuttled to the tent by the great bog Moine Mhor.

They stood on the hill overlooking the magnificent natural feature. All seven were wide-eyed, taking in the sight before them. Beyond the bog itself, the plateau dropped down to salt marshes by the Atlantic with its finger inlets. The inlets and isles intermingled, like fingers of a mighty hand in prayer. They stretched all the way to the pink and blue morning haze that covered the far hills on the Isle of Jura. To the south were the swampy woodlands where water-loving alder trees had invaded the bog. A rocky outcropping in front of them boarded acidic oak woodlands.

The initial investigation would be centered in the bog by the rocky shore where the first shield was found ten years earlier. The tent stood close to the bog itself. That part of the quagmire was dark and brooding, partially bordered by the water grass intermingled with a rainbow of brilliant water plants. To one side stood the huge mound of moss, the reason for the name *Moine Mohr*, "great moss."

The moss contained over two hundred identified spices of lichens, though it was primarily sphagnum. For this reason, the mountain of moss was itself full of a variety of shades and hues from the light-green matter on top, to the near black green of the water-logged area at the bottom. The students could hear in and among the flora the chirping and croaking of the birds and reptiles that made their homes, strangely enough, in such an inhospitable place.

The seven students stood silently taking in the cacophony of colors, views, sounds, and smells that overwhelmed their senses. In decades past, a majority of what was the bog was destroyed by industry dredging it for the peat and developers draining it for farmland. There was now even danger from natural invaders, like the alders and, further away, the evergreens. Kate stood behind the students, so very grateful that there seemed to be reverence among the students for this national treasure. The life of Moine Mhor would depend on such reverence.

However, she had mixed feelings about this group, being aware that an acquaintance of hers was among the seven—an acquaintance she could well do without.

Inside the tent, the students sat around the long table. Charts, maps, and photographs sat on easels around the canvas room. Carefully stacked boxes held the tools of trade for archeologists. At the head of the table stood Jacob, with Duncan and Kate on either side. Behind him stood an easel with a blank pad of poster paper, opened to the first page. The seven students, three women and four men, took their seats around the table.

"Welcome, welcome all of you. I am Jacob Rubin. This is Kate Wallace, and this is Dunc McIntosh." Jacob nodded to each of his colleagues with a warm smile.

Kate immediately heard that he had not included titles in his introductions and knew it was for her sake.

Jacob continued, "We, like you, have been chosen to be a part of this project, both as individuals and as a team, for what each of us brings to the job. In saying that, I would like to hear from each of you—who you are and why you're here." He pointed to the first young man on his left.

The student stood, knocking over his folding chair. He tangled with the chair, pinching a finger, which he sucked on, while nearly dismantling the metal seat. Finally, both he and the chair were upright. The others stared at him, transfixed. He didn't seem to be aware of anything out of the ordinary.

He rocked back and forth, continually pushing his glasses up his nose, and began to answer, "Well, I'm Henry Campbell. Well, they call me Henry, but I'm really Harry. Henry's a…well, it's a nickname. Which doesn't make a lot of sense because it's the same number of letters, but that's the way it is…and…what else did you want to know?"

With a level of patience and good humor in his voice that no one else in the room could have managed, Jacob answered, "Tell me what you're studying and what interests you about this project."

"I'm studying Middle Eastern archeology, and that really interests me, and besides that, I clean and prepare artifacts for transport better than anybody." Henry then sat down, almost tipping his chair over again. The other students wondered how much would be left of the artifact after he finished with it.

"Thank you, Henry. I'm well aware of your talents." Jacob then nodded to the woman on Henry's left.

Hannah Sinclair was a large woman with a deep commanding voice. Her passion was developing archeological equipment that could recover artifacts from difficult-to-reach areas. Next to Hannah was Sara Ross. She could not have created a greater contrast to Hannah, with her petite figure and dark hair and eyes. She was working on her own technique for treatment of artifacts.

The third woman stood and smiled, her head held high, displaying enormous self-confidence. Kate's lips tightened when the woman stood. "I'm Bonnie McGregor. I'm in the doctoral program at Edinburgh. I only have my thesis to go, and that's almost finished.

I've headed up the analysis for several digs and would be glad to do that here." She ended with a smug smile that said no one could possibly resist her magnanimous offer.

She then looked at Kate. "Kate, what fun working with you again. Are you any bit closer to that PhD?"

Kate could feel the blush rising up her cheeks. Bonnie's voice sounded of mock regret for *poor little Kate.*

"Closer and closer every day," Kate said. She was rubbing her hands together behind her back as she always did when embarrassed or uncomfortable.

"Thank you, Ms. McGregor. Except for Dunc running his detector, all areas of our project will be a collaborative effort," Jacob said. "Before we go further, I need to talk about my two associates. Duncan McIntosh has developed one of the most brilliant devices for locating, analyzing, and even dating items. This device is especially valuable in that it can go into the harshest environments and protect that environment.

"When I asked my Scottish colleagues for suggestions in putting together this team, every last one recommended Kate Wallace because of her extensive knowledge and experience in local archeology. More than that, her renowned reverence for the ecology opened doors for us that no one else could do."

Bonnie lost her smile—Kate regained hers.

Jacob then nodded to the three men sitting across from Henry and the three women. Clint Farquharson stood with a less-than-congenial look on his face. "I'm Clint Farquharson. I study biblical archeology. I intend to keep this project true to the Bible. That's why I'm here." Clint then sat down.

A room full of scientists turned to Jacob with one very readable question on their faces. Jacob answered it, "Clinton has a photographic memory. He can quote scripture and verse, as well as biblical archeological information from that memory. This is valuable to us since a large part of our work is based in biblical literature."

The sixth was a dark-haired swarthy man who showed no emotion whatsoever. He looked directly at Jacob and said, "I'm Bartholomew Guthrie. I do recovery."

"Thank you, Bartholomew," Jacob said.

Kate picked up on an ever-so-slight darkening in Jacob's tone.

The seventh student was Matthew Douglas. He participated in several digs in Israel and other areas of the Middle East. Matthew, though a man of few words, unnerved Kate when he scanned her frame from head to foot and then smiled at her with a leering grin. He then looked at Dunc and Jacob and said, "I am so grateful to be in such influential, acclaimed company. Dr. Rubin and Dr. McIntosh, you are both legends in our field." He continued to stand, waiting for a response.

Both Jacob and Dunc nodded briefly. "Thank you. You can be seated, young man." Jacob was smiling, but his change in tone was even more pronounced to Kate. She was stung by this last student's slight in not mentioning her.

Jacob turned to the blank poster pad behind him. In emphasizing and demonstrating collaboration, he led a brainstorming session to set up a schedule for activity. This was efficiently and effectively done. Jacob then moved through the pictures of the artifacts, the dates and places where they were found, and of the area of the bog where they would be working.

Recognizing when enough was enough, Jacob dismissed the team with instructions to enjoy the rest of their day, ask what questions they had, and then get a good night's sleep. They were to return by 5:00 a.m.

The students would eat in their dorm. Dunc, Jacob, and Kate had dinner at the same pub where they ate the night before. After dinner, they sat around in Jacob's room. They were exhausted but too excited to go right to bed.

Jacob told the two that he noted those who participated and those who didn't and that it was his goal to have each member of the team begin to "own" the project.

"Well, what do you think of our students?" Jacob asked, his voice conveying to both that he knew full well what his colleagues were thinking.

"A lot of ego," Dunc ventured.

"Well, yes, but a lot of talent also," Kate said, knowing she didn't feel as generous as she hoped this sounded.

Jacob smiled. "The main egotists either embarrassed or ignored you, Kate. But I think they will fall in line," he said. "This will be a very tough job. They will have to grow up quite a bit to handle the hard work. How did you know Ms. McGregor, Kate?"

"She and I were roommates when we first started at university. I was older because I had to work for several years to afford to go to university. I also wanted to afford dorm fees. Bonnie immediately started a competition with me. Not being very competitive, I never won. I couldn't even figure out what we were competing for. Most of the time, I just did my best to avoid her. Running out of funds actually was a blessing, even though I had to move home and commute. I have been on two digs with her. In both, she muscled her way into control. It took all my patience to stick it out at the digs."

"People who find it necessary to try and one-up someone usually pick people they are afraid are better than they are. I think she envies you. But don't let it worry you. It will be much different here," Jacob said.

"I'll say," Dunc said with a big grin. "Jacob, you really put McGregor in her place. I thought about punching Matthew in the nose, but it looked to me like everybody else in the room felt the same way. Kate, I saw your résumé. Despite your late start and lack of funds, you're only a couple of classes behind McGregor."

Kate smiled. "I ken it's going to be different this time, with you two."

The group turned in early. After Kate got ready for bed, she realized she had no ice for her water. The tap water in this part of Scotland was only tolerable if very cold. She took the bowl, which she assumed was to be used as an ice bucket. She threw on her robe and walked along the lighted outside walkway to the shed that held the soda and ice machines. When she passed the two men's rooms, she noticed Dunc's was dark, but Jacob's had a light on. She heard voices and assumed Jacob was watching TV.

While Kate was struggling with the door of the ice machine and scooping the ice, it hit her that the rooms didn't have TVs. She stopped for a moment, rather shocked. *Who would be visiting at this hour?* She stopped what she was doing and walked back to Jacob's room.

Because there were lights along the outdoor walkway, Kate held back away from the closed curtained window of Jacob's room. She pressed her ear to the wall, feeling guilt for doing something as onerous as eavesdropping on Jacob Rubin. But she couldn't stop herself.

The other voice was fairly familiar, and probably one of the students. But it was so low she couldn't place it. It was also angry. Kate felt a sense of fear. She had yet to hear Jacob, and that also frightened her.

Should I knock? Should I get Dunc?

Suddenly she heard the clear, strong voice of the man she had come to admire so much.

"If you get in my way, I will get in yours. I did not want you here. I will not put up with any interference. Play your part, do what you have to, and get out."

The other voice got lower, harder, and more terrifying to Kate. She could not understand him nor identify him. But she could tell that he was getting closer to the door. She jumped and ran past the door on tiptoes. Passing Dunc's room, she ran into hers and locked the door. She went to the window, straining to see who was leaving Jacob's room.

The man stayed so close to the building that Kate could only see a shadow, and then it was gone. She sat on the bed and tried to sort out her feelings. The ugliness of the conversation on both men's part was bewildering to her. Words like "I didn't want you here" and "play your part" spoke of deceit. And deceit was not a part of her understanding of Jacob Rubin. She sat for a while before weariness took over. Kate slipped into bed and turned off the light.

Chapter 4

The morning light had a calming effect on Kate, not to mention the excitement of beginning the dig. She was up and dressed when the sun first filtered through her curtains. Her uniform for all summer digs was a generous covering of sunscreen, a safari hat, shorts, T-shirt, and tennis shoes. The first two were vital for a redhead with freckles. She stuck her wallet and cell phone in her back pockets, grabbed her sunglasses, and headed for the car. Dunc was just opening his door, in fairly similar apparel and similar mood. He met her with a smile, and together they hurried to the parking lot.

Jacob stood by the van with a cardboard tray holding two large Styrofoam cups, one of tea and one of coffee. Jacob held a third and sipped on its contents. With huge grins on all three faces, the caffeine-sated group set off for the bog. While waiting for the school bus to arrive, the three ran through preparations for the day. Despite knowing and working together for such a short time, they had begun to act and perform as a unit.

Kate had only fleeting thoughts of the previous night. She decided she had way too dramatic a reaction to overhearing a minor tiff.

When the bus arrived, the archeologists watched as the seven students got off. Though all were adults, most were awake and bright. But some of the youngest ones looked to Kate like they had pulled an all-nighter. *They probably did, doing whatever young people did when not hampered with studies. Well, at least all arrived on time.*

Jacob stepped forward. "This morning, we are going to watch. Kate and I will pore over the computer while Dunc uses his remote control detector to see what we can find. I want each of you to spend time watching Dunc and then us. There may be times when you may have to work either machine."

Both Kate and Dunc were wearing Bluetooth earpieces. Because of injuries to his eardrums, Jacob could not use a Bluetooth. The two, with Jacob, walked to the edge of the bog, where the museum curator said the shield had been found ten years earlier. Kate and Jacob sat cross-legged on the ground. Kate got there with a great deal more agility. They positioned the computer screen between them. Dunc stood in front of them. He attached the detector to the drone and switched it on. The computer came to life with x-ray pictures of the ground beneath Dunc.

Dunc set his devices on the ground and took the remote control out of his pocket. He looked at Kate and asked, "Okay?"

"Go ahead. We're ready."

The drone began to come to life, wavering back and forth, and then rose straight up. Dunc moved it over to water's edge. Very slowly, the detector attached to the drone was moved back and forth across the great bog. The liquid of the top layer of the bog was nearly invisible. The second layer of developing moss was little more than a shadow. The harder layer of peat was itself penetrated by the probing eye of Dunc's DAM Detector. All the students hovered transfixed, some behind Kate and Jacob, others behind Dunc.

Often at high tide, the bog was washed by the sea. Therefore, it was no surprise that they saw ancient shells and fish bones. Kate related this to Dunc. He nodded with a smile, never taking his eyes off the detector. He had to pay close attention to the pattern of his sweep.

Jacob leaned closer to Kate. "These probably have all flesh preserved."

Kate nodded and then jumped a little. "Several larger bones," she said.

"I don't think they're human, but I can't identify," said Jacob loud enough to be heard through her Bluetooth.

"Mark!" said Dunc.

This was a prearranged direction. Kate immediately hit a tab, which took a snapshot and gave precise coordinates of the bones. Both the snapshots and the moving pictures were being recorded for as long as needed. Kate kept a watch on the numbers in the small box at the top left of the computer. They gave a percentage of the life left in the lithium-battery-charged equipment.

The process was very slow going as the sweeps moved over the wider areas of the bog. Students would occasionally peel off and go watch the others. More bones and fish were seen. If they couldn't be identified, or if they could and were thought to be extinct, they were marked.

After two hours, the students tended to be lying on the ground, some napping, others awake but just barely. The two exceptions to the bored crowd—other than Kate, Jacob, and Dunc—were Bonnie and Matthew. Bonnie sat directly behind Kate and Jacob so she could see the computer screen. Matthew sat next to Kate. He would occasionally point to bones or shells on the screens, having to lean against Kate to do so. Jacob seemed glad to have two extra pairs of eyes. Kate was uncomfortable with both, especially with Matt's closeness, but she never lost her concentration on the screen.

Suddenly Kate jumped just as Jacob pointed to a semicircle on the screen. Both Bonnie and Matt missed it.

"Stop!" Kate's voice was controlled and firm. "There is a semicircle at one o'clock. Move to three o'clock."

These commands told Dunc to move the detector just inches left, right, forward, or back.

"Three o'clock…three o'clock…twelve o'clock…twelve o'clock. We have a complete circle and there is another semicircle at two o'clock. You're at the center of the first circle, clarify," Kate said. She could feel both Jacob and Dunc's approval of her control, despite the overwhelming thrill she felt.

Dunc lowered the drone and activated a more intense viewing part of the detector. The picture that slowly came into view on the computer screen took the breath away from the four people watching. It was a round shield with Assyrian marking around the edge and the same golden sheaf symbol in the center. They were identical to the first two finds.

For the first time ever, Kate saw Bonnie speechless. Kate assumed it was her old roommate trying to grasp the immense significance of this find.

Kate smiled with tears in her eyes. "Dunc, *Beit Yosef*," she said. "I'll mark, and you come look."

As soon as Dunc got the drone back in his hands, he ran over to Kate and Jacob. Bonnie quickly scooted over, and Dunc knelt in her place. He placed one hand on Jacob's shoulder and the other on Kate's. He leaned in to see the screen as Kate lifted it for him to see. Dunc was chewing his lower lip with enormous expectation. His hands were trembling after over two hours of holding them so steady. Kate wasn't trying to hide her tears, looking up at Dunc. Jacob was watching the two with near paternal pride.

Bonnie and Matt showed irritation at being left out. Dunc, seeing this, took them both by an arm, pulling them closer to see the screen.

Matt was the one who finally called to the others, "Hey, everybody, up! We found it! We found it!"

Within seconds, all the students were gathered around the computer. A loud cheer went up with all clapping one another on the back.

By midafternoon, they had found and identified three other shields. And they were certain that these four were all that were there in the large area that was searched.

Dunc activated his spectrometer. After a several minutes, a rectangle appeared in the left top corner of the computer. It went in and out of view and finally showed some symbols. Jacob leaned into Kate's Bluetooth and said, "Dunc, it is an alloy, most likely iron. There also seems to be something corrupting what it does recognize."

"I was afraid of that," Dunc said. "Yes, it is most likely iron. The type of black paint or ink used in the era we're considering does corrupt the readings."

Kate watched Jacob. She was concerned for his disappointment. Jacob saw her worried look and shook his head. He smiled at her and

THE OX, THE HORN, AND THE SHEAF

said, "No, no, my dear, this is actually good news. It all but proves that this *is* Iron Age armament."

There were no other pieces of armament.

Dunc made one final sweep over the outer perimeter of the area searched. Kate was still manning the computer, but Jacob was busy on his phone talking to Natural Trust. They would have a great deal to say about the recovery of the artifacts. This was such an incredible find that even those highest up in the Scottish government were closely following this dig.

Everyone was gathering their stuff to get on the bus, each knowing that the next day would probably be the most important day of their careers as archeologists. Dunc looked exhausted, showing his mind was more than likely on the glass of ale that he intended to order very soon. He was jarred back to what he was doing when Kate yelled.

"Stop, there's a body. Clarify!" she shouted.

Dunc again moved the detector as Kate directed and then lowered it. The entire team had gathered behind her, and Jacob had resumed his place beside her.

"We've just found human remains. It's quite a ways away from the artifacts, closer to the rocks. Duncan is bringing the detector in closer," Jacob said into the phone.

Moine Mhor had been developing for millennia, long before the bearers of the shields had carried them out of Israel and over to Scotland. This could be anyone from anywhere along the bog's timeline. The amazing mummifying quality of the acidic waters could give these archeologists an understanding of humanity from long, long ago. Everybody there knew this.

However, the closer pictures told a very different story.

Kate's mouth dropped open as the crowd around her began to murmur. She marked the image and said in a quiet, shaken voice, "Dunc, there is a gun beside body."

Jacob said into the phone, "I'll have to hang up now. We need to call the authorities." He would later tell Kate that he had known his beloved project would inevitably get caught up in the indecent mess only he knew about. For an instant, Jacob's eyes met those of the man who was in his room the night before. Just as quickly, he turned away. It was all that was needed for Jacob to convey his anger.

Within an hour, the entire area was crawling with the Police Scotland. They confiscated Dunc's computer for the time being. They had brought in airboats, underwater divers, and grappling hooks. Jacob, Dunc, Kate, and each student were interviewed. The Natural Trust was on the scene also. They were asserting their authority. The Trust argued over what could be used to bring the body to the surface. And much to Kate and Jacob's relief, the Trust was winning.

Jacob had commanded enough control to have the students sent back to their dorms and for himself to be allowed to stand guard with the Police Scotland official manning the computer. Meanwhile, Dunc and Kate sat together off to the side, feeling somehow cheated that this powerful day had been diminished. They hadn't said much, just watching the drama taking place in front of them.

Both looked up as two black limousines pulled into the area. They pulled to a stop, and one man from the first car and two from the second got out. Dunc watched the rather impressive-looking men walk over to Detective Inspector Young, the detective in charge of the investigation.

"Who the heck are these guys?" Dunc said, not really expecting Kate to know.

"These are the *big guys* from Stirling. The man in the first car is Deputy Chief Constable Malcolm Frazier. He is over Crime and Operational Support for all of Scotland," Kate said without a hesitation.

Dunc turned his full attention to his surprisingly knowledgeable friend.

Kate continued, "The men in the second are Assistant Chief Constable McKinstry, in charge of the Western Command, and Assistant Chief Constable Gordon, in charge of Organized Crime and Counterterrorism." She never took her eyes off the police executives.

Dunc stared at her for an instant. He had two questions. The first seem to need immediate clarification. "Organized Crime and Counterterrorism?"

"Aye," she said with a degree of resignation.

"Then this dead body and possibly our project are somehow involved in…what? Antiquities theft by terrorists?"

"Very possibly."

Dunc carefully broached the second question. "How do you know these guys by name and rank? I'm not sure what my senator looks like, much less the guys on the police force."

She looked down and thought about her answer carefully. "When you're considered a terrorist, you get to know these folks."

"Jacob called you a freedom fighter. Will you tell me what you did to be called a terrorist?"

Kate smiled. She was pleased that Jacob thought of her in that light. "I participated in a separatist march in London. The police were pretty rough with us. They pushed an older woman, a friend of mine, to the ground and picked up metal barriers, using them to push us back. I was trying to get Margaret out of the way, but they just kept shoving us. I grabbed one of the barriers and threw it at the officer who pushed Margaret. I guess I hit him pretty hard.

"I spent three weeks in jail. My parents wanted to teach me a lesson and refused to pay bond. Finally, the barrister for our movement threatened to charge the officer who pushed Margaret with assault and battery, unless they dropped my case. They finally did." Kate looked over at Dunc, not certain what she'd see. He was smiling at her.

He patted her hand and said, "I'm from America. We demonstrate quite often for one group's rights or another. Remember, we were also freedom fighters against England 250 years ago. Had I been around, I hope I would have been as brave as you."

Kate stared at him. With great effort to keep from tearing up, she said in a whisper, "Thank you."

"I'm glad it was only three weeks for you in jail. I've heard people who irritate the establishment can get lost in there."

Kate's expression changed to one of deep seriousness. "It was the most terrifying three weeks of my life. I'm terribly claustrophobic. When you said I was brave, you were quite wrong. I was a sniveling coward. I would have sold myself into slavery to get out of there." She looked away with shame.

Dunc put his arm around her shoulder. "I'm so sorry. That was a flippant thing for me to say."

The conversation came to an abrupt end with excited activity at the edge of the bog. Dunc rose and offered a hand to Kate. She took it with a smile, and he helped her to her feet. They didn't have to get closer because they were on higher ground and could see that the diver had brought the body to the surface. Those in the airboat were getting the body on board. They then assisted the diver as he climbed in.

Kate and Dunc walked in closer as the airboat came ashore. Kate was curious but not anxious to see a corpse. However, being an archeologist, she'd seen hundreds of bodies, from well mummified all the way to fragments of bones and teeth. She was just thankful that the body was recovered and hopeful that this tangle of officials would soon leave the area. When the body was laid, faceup, on the ground, the archeologists gave a gasp.

"He was one of the guards at the museum," Dunc said.

Both could see the hole in the guard's forehead. And both knew that this murder and their dig were inextricably intertwined. They looked over at Jacob. His face showed the same understanding, along with a degree of controlled anger.

Dunc started toward him, but Kate grabbed his arm. "Dunc, Jacob already knows what's going on," she said. She proceeded to tell him what she heard the night before. "I'm ashamed of eavesdropping, but like this"—she pointed to the body—"I couldn't walk away."

Dunc stared at her, thinking through what he had just heard. Finally he nodded, took her hand, and said, "Let's go see him and find out the rest of the story."

Their immediate concern once they realized this was one of the museum guards was for the safety of the two shields at the museum. As they approached Jacob, Dunc asked, "That's the museum guard, right? Was he killed at the museum, and what about the two shields?"

Jacob was staring at the dead man. He answered softly, "I just asked those questions, and the sergeant explained that there was an attempted break-in at the museum, but the second guard arrived just in time to frighten the culprits away. They were already out of sight when he pulled up. Must have heard the second guard coming. This guard was nowhere to be seen. However, the museum was where the guard was killed. There was blood found there.

"Police Scotland was investigating the museum break-in and the missing guard when they were called here. To answer your most important question, the shields are safe and have been removed to Edinburgh for further safety." The strain and concern in Jacob's voice was palpable.

The sergeant standing next to Jacob was holding Duncan's computer. Dunc reached for it, but the sergeant pulled away.

"*Give Dr. McIntosh his computer,*" Jacob said, emphasizing each word. In a less threatening voice, he continued, "If there are more bodies in the bog, you'll have to find them for yourselves."

The sergeant started to object, but Jacob turned toward Deputy Chief Constable Frazier. "Chief Constable," he called. When Frazier turned toward him, Jacob said in a very pleasant voice, "Please ask the sergeant to return our computer. It is of no further use to you."

Jacob's authority was very evident in that the chief constable immediately smiled at him and then motioned for the sergeant to give up the computer.

"Thank you," Dunc said and cradled his computer to his chest. He then turned to Jacob and said, "Is there some place we can go and talk?"

Jacob smiled with resignation and nodded. "Let me make sure of one thing first." He walked over to Assistant Chief Constable Gordon. He forced a smile. "Can I be certain that the area will be secured so that no one will get to the artifacts?"

"Of course," Gordon said. "But you should probably let us keep the computer with all the coordinates of the shields."

"You're aware that we have protection. That won't be necessary," Jacob said and walked away.

It was already dark, and the three archeologists were exhausted. None of them, however, were the slightest bit hungry. They drove back to the motel in silence. When they arrived, there was a large group of detectives there. They were scouring the woods around the cottages.

Seeing the arrival of the group, the chief detective walked over to them. He immediately looked at Kate and asked if she owned a gun.

"Of course not," she answered curtly.

The chief looked at Jacob. Before the chief detective could ask, Jacob said emphatically, "No!"

The detective then looked at Duncan, and again, before he could ask, he was answered with, "Yes, I do. It was my grandfather's pistol. However, I left it in America."

Nothing more was said on either side. Several detectives went about their work looking for clues.

Dunc locked the cord, the drone, and the remotes in his car trunk but took the detector and the computer in with him. He had every intention of sleeping with his precious equipment. The detectives had gone through the archeologists' rooms in great detail. The three ran to their rooms, anxious over the destruction they might find. Though the police had left a mess, there was no destruction.

The weary trio filed into Jacob's room. Jacob slowly folded and replaced the items into the drawer, which had been pulled out and emptied on the floor. The other two sat watching him.

Dunc was the first to speak. "What's going on, Jacob?"

"I wasn't trying to hide anything. I just thought the fewer people who knew, the less likely it would be that we got involved. I know you're thinking that I'm an old fool sticking his head in the sand," the tired old man said.

Dunc looked at Kate and, seeing her compassion, said to Jacob, "I don't believe either of us is thinking anything of the kind." He looked at Kate again. She smiled with her agreement. "But now, we do need to know."

Jacob nodded. "Yes, of course you do. It would appear that we have a group of terrorists, from God knows where, whose main objective is to destroy all vestiges of pagan artifacts coming from the areas under Islamic rule. I suppose, if they achieve that goal, they will go on to destroy all vestiges of Judaism and Christianity. Our shields come from Assyria, which now contains several Islamic countries. To make matters worse, the shields now have Jewish symbols carved into them.

"When the shield was found in Egypt, the Kilmartin Museum curator put together the fact that they held a similar shield. Word got out. Egypt allowed me to take my shield back to Israel to study. And then to bring it here to study with the ten-year-old find. As I was putting together our team, I was contacted by Assistant Chief Constable Gordon. He had been in touch with the CIA, MI6, Interpol, and the Mossad. They were warning that the terrorists were after the shields. Police Scotland insists on having protection within the project. So they placed one of their own among the students. Kate, I know you heard me speaking to someone the other night."

"Oh, Jacob, please forgive me for eavesdropping on you, but the voice with you sounded so angry. I was fearful for you," Kate said.

"No, don't worry. I appreciate your concern," Jacob said, patting her hand. "I saw your shadow pass by my window at first and then hurry back by the second time."

"How did you know it was me?" she asked.

Jacob smiled at her. "There are only three of us at the motel. Even through curtains, I can tell the difference between you and Duncan. But there is an important question. I have to know if you recognized the person with me. This is *very* important."

"No, I thought the voice was vaguely familiar, but I couldn't place it," Kate said. "It was so low and so angry. I did try and see him when he left your room, but he stayed too close to the wall."

"Oh, good. You see, I have been forbidden to let anyone know who the police plant is. If I were to tell anyone, they will cancel the dig. I had to give my word."

Dunc furrowed his brow. "Why all the cloak and dagger? What difference would it make if any of us knew who this plant was? Isn't he here to protect us?"

Jacob took a deep breath and let it out. "Because they think that there is also one or more among our students who are terrorists."

"Why would they kill the guard before we found the shields?" Dunc said.

"The guard probably interrupted the break-in at the museum."

"Can you tell us who they suspect?" Dunc asked.

Again Jacob hesitated then finally said, with great sadness, "They don't know for sure, but their chief suspect is…you, Kate."

Chapter 5

Kate stared in stunned silence.

"What in God's name would give them that idea?" Dunc said, glowering in anger.

Jacob didn't answer. He was watching Kate. She slowly stood. She had a look of shock and sadness.

"I…I need…I need to…" She quit speaking and made her way to the door. Dunc stood and reached out his hand to her. She avoided his touch and left. Dunc looked at Jacob.

"I thought it best to just be out with it. But it was too cruel," Jacob said.

"Why would they accuse her of terrorism?" Dunc asked.

"In all fairness, you and I questioned it until we met her. But in this case, it's because the one who suspects her is a fool. He's looking for the easiest way out…the closest suspect, regardless of how irrational."

Dunc nodded. "How similar politicians are all over the world. I'm going to check on her," he said.

Jacob nodded.

Dunc knocked on Kate's door. He waited for a minute, but there was no answer. "Kate, please let me in. I'm worried about you."

Again he listened, and finally he heard the door lock click open. He slowly opened the door and walked in. Kate was sitting on the bed with her bathrobe around her. She was staring at the floor, hugging herself and rocking back and forth. The look on her face broke Dunc's heart.

"Kate, nobody believes you're a terrorist."

49

"These police, or should I say politicians, do. Dunc, I'm a danger to our project. They could shut it down because of me...I'm just going to pack up and go home." She looked up at him with a tear running down her cheek.

"No, no, you're not leaving. You're too valuable to me...to us. I've never had anybody who picked up on what I needed with the detector like you did. We did in two hours what has taken two days or even weeks before. You can't leave. You *can't* leave...*Jacob!*" Dunc yelled as he turned toward the door. Jacob, however, was standing right behind him, smiling at his anxious friend.

Kate was looking at Dunc eyes wide with surprise. She was totally shocked with his passion.

"She's going to leave, Jacob." Dunc was now close to tears.

Jacob observed both his colleagues' reactions to each other and was smiling broadly. He walked around Dunc and, putting his hands on Kate's arms, said, "No, Dunc, she isn't leaving. She's just figured out how much we need her and how silly it would be to let a fool get in the way of our project."

"Are you sure, Jacob? I do have a record," Kate said.

"Oh, I'm very sure...very sure. Your record is almost as silly as the politicians' suspicion. I think what we need to do now is concentrate on the project. Let's get busy and discuss our next phase, that of recovery. We have support from very high places. This find is that important to Scotland."

Kate stood and kissed Jacob on the cheek. Dunc had, at that moment, a most irrational feeling, one he hadn't had in years—he was jealous of Jacob.

The dig was allowed to continue because no other clues beyond the body were found at the bog. It was also indisputable that the guard was killed at the museum during a botched attempt to steal the shields. The next morning, the bus arrived on time. The students got out all with looks of serious curiosity. There was a small group of police still present guarding the artifacts.

The students gathered around the table in the tent. The excitement of the previous day's find had been replaced by the anxious concern over the murdered body. Jacob told Kate and Dunc that for this to be a successful day, he had to bring back the students' adventurous spirit. He very quickly and bluntly explained about the terrorists. The students were all adults and had always been under police protection. He then explained to all that they had the choice, with no hard feelings, to either leave if they felt threatened or remain if they felt challenged to continue their work despite the circumstances.

Everyone *was* an adult, and they and the schools would be thoroughly informed of everything going on. The schools knew about the situation as soon as Jacob did and agreed that the dig would go on with the planned protection. The students were not informed that the protector was one of them, nor that a terrorist might also be. But they were informed to be vigilant.

Jacob chose his words carefully, and his calculations paid off. Every person there chose to stay and finish the project.

With great pride showing in his smile, Jacob directed the planning of the day's work. Hannah and Bartholomew would be front and center in the recovery phase. All the material necessary for the scaffolding Hannah invented was delivered the day before.

The artifacts were found a little over thirty feet from the rocky shore. Hannah and Dunc worked out a plan to run Dunc's detector through the steel pipe attached to the bottom of the scaffolding's arm. It not only zeroed in on the exact coordinates of the shields but also directed the scoop that gathered the shields one by one. Dunc told Hannah his detector would be their eyes in the recovery.

The brilliance of the scaffold was the lightweight, strong arm that could reach out as far as needed, be moved up, down, and sideways, and not bend or break under great pressure. Sandbags were used at the back of the scaffold to keep it from tipping over into the bog. The six weighted legs were all on the shore. This meant that nothing but the scoop actually went into the bog.

Everyone spoke to Hannah of their appreciation for her work. Even those with haughty egos realized her genius. Jacob had known, the instant he read her credits, what an asset she would be. With everyone's help and Hannah's directions, the structure was completed in only four hours. Hannah was in high spirits as it began to do exactly what it was planned to do. Dunc, with Hannah at his side, guided the detector and scoop along the arm. Jacob and Kate again sat with the computer and directed Dunc's movements.

"Mark," Kate said into her Bluetooth.

The scoop was lowered, and in a very short time of maneuvering it, the first shield surfaced. Everyone cheered.

"Damn, damn, it works! It works!" Hannah yelled, driving her fist into her palm. Dunc was laughing at his colleague's enthusiasm. Kate looked at Jacob with a broad grin.

He smiled back. "Now, do you see why you were supposed to be here?"

"Yes," she said, all the time thanking her lucky stars that she was there.

Time after time, the detector moved the scoop out over the recovery site, lowering to each shield. As they were brought back to shore, Matthew and Bartholomew carried wooden trays and very carefully transferred the shields onto the trays. Matthew photographed and marked each shield as to where it rested in the bog. They were then carried into the tent to Henry and Sara, who began the delicate task of cleaning and preparing the shields for immediate transport.

They removed some of the bog mud and moss. These particles were placed in containers to be studied there. The two then placed the shields in individual airtight containers that Henry had created especially for the shields. He had developed this process on other artifacts he had worked with over the years. They then wrapped the containers in massive amounts of bubble wrap. These were placed carefully in the van which would transport them, under police guard, to the university lab in Edinburgh.

Archeologists and students alike couldn't help but compare Henry's delicate, patient work with the klutzy performance of his first day. Sara showed incredible admiration for Henry, despite her own excellent contributions to the work. Henry was far too busy and intent on his job to notice any of this.

By the time the fourth and final shield was placed in the van, Bonnie and Clint were studying the mud and moss that had been attached to the shields. These were placed in vials and labeled.

There was the possibility that the particles of matter could place the shields at their origin or places along their journey to Scotland. The particles would have to go back to the lab in Edinburgh for totally reliable analysis. However, one of Clint's vital contributions was to bring particles of sand from areas in Israel, Egypt, and of course, Scotland. He and Bonnie were checking for comparisons. The only similarities found so far were those of Scotland with vague possibilities of connections to Egypt.

Kate and Jacob were anxious to get to the tent. He was already headed there when Kate turned the computer off. As she did, she had a strange sensation, a tingling in her spine. *Did I do something wrong?* She carefully went over everything Dunc told her to do when closing the computer down. *No, everything was done correctly. The computer would have alerted me if not.*

Kate couldn't put a name to her discomfort, so she dismissed it and followed Jacob into the tent. Dunc and those in recovery would dismantle the scaffolding in the morning. They each found an opportunity to view, firsthand, the products of their hard work before Henry and Sara prepared them for transport. Jacob's smile and deep sigh of satisfaction showed he couldn't have been happier with those he had chosen for this project. He watched the entire team as they busied themselves with their phase of the project.

Matthew documented the entire project. Clint had quickly shown why he had been chosen for this team with his forethought of getting particles from ancient areas where the shields traveled. Sara was a perfect partner to work with Henry. Her experience and talents were vital. Bartholomew worked hand and hand with Hannah, which helped create the excellent results of recovery and then get the shields to Sara and Henry.

As each phase ended, those involved lifted their tired, stiff bodies and left their precious work. Hannah and Bartholomew were, of course, the first and, by early evening, were sound asleep sitting in a corner of the tent with heads resting against each other's. Henry and Sara followed soon after. They stretched out in an unused area of the tent next to each other. Dunc and Kate joined Bonnie and Clint, looking at the particles.

At some point, Dunc felt hunger pangs. Not looking up from the microscope, he said, "Can we order out for pizza?"

"Yes," Kate said with a laugh. "But I don't think you'll like it. Our pizzas come with mushy peas."

"Yuck," was all Dunc could manage to the laughter of everyone there—everyone still awake.

Jacob did manage—by ordering pizza, peas and all—to get them all fed, and everything was completed and closed up by a little after midnight. There were several guards on hand. The bus driver, who had eaten with them, woke to drive the students back.

The archeologists drove back to the motel in silence. They barely managed a smile rather than a spoken "good night" to one another. Kate could feel the sleep taking over before her head hit the pillow. She also felt the discomfort she felt as she turned Dunc's computer off. This led to a night of wild, abstract dreams. She was searching for something that was just out of reach. She was running from something that was just out of sight. Finally, she was trying to finish something but couldn't remember what or where it was.

In desperation, she reached out for help and grabbed the hand—*the hand!* Kate sat straight up in bed. She was covered with sweat. As she turned the computer off, something registered. It was so instantaneous that it hadn't registered in her conscious mind. It hadn't even registered that she had *seen* something. It was just a feeling, something left undone.

Kate looked at the clock: 5:00 a.m. Was it cruel to get them up after only four hours of sleep? Well, even so, it had to be done. She threw on her clothes, brushed her hair, and pounded on Dunc's door. "Dunc, you have to run the detector back out. I...I saw something...I think."

Dunc was standing in his underwear, rubbing his eyes. "We were sure there were only four shields. We got all of them."

"That's not what I saw," Kate said.

In a short time, Dunc moved the scaffold's arm out again and turned the detector on with his remote. He, Jacob, and Kate stared at the computer as the picture came into focus. All three gasped. There was absolutely no mistake. A human hand lay deep beneath the surface of the bog.

Dunc looked up at the other two. "This was a burial."

Chapter 6

The students arrived earlier than anyone of them wanted. What they found was, again, the site crawling with officials from Police Scotland. However, this time, Jacob had contacted both the National Trust and officials from the university before he contacted the police. Dunc was thankful to see Will Elder arrive. He had been so helpful to the team with the Natural Trust and the myriad of permits and other such paperwork. The pictures and the records from the detector proved to Will and those from the Trust that this was not a second crime scene, or at least not one that was less than two thousand years old. These officials were able to convince the constables. Although, Kate thought it had more to do with coercion by influence rather than intellectual persuasion. This was fine by her.

"Will, I can't tell you how much I appreciate your help. Some of these guys are already on my shit list for accusing Kate of being the murderer," Duncan said.

"Good Lord, what could possibly give them that idea?" Will replied with a frown.

"I guess it's her activity for the separation of Scotland from England."

"Ah well, you never know what the officials know about people that we 'lesser beings' don't," Will said, half-joking. "I didn't agree with her movement. I'm not sure those dedicated to separation quite understood the economics of such a move."

Dunc nodded at Will but was left with a slight feeling of discomfort by what he'd said. Dunc really didn't know Kate very well.

Jacob had done research into the charges against her, and there did seem to be only the one incident. But there may have been things done in secret that only the authorities knew about. He prayed this wasn't so and hated himself for not having faith in her.

Once the police were convinced that this was an ancient body, Dunc himself was chosen to go down to recover the body rather than a diver from the police. The water was about nine feet deep where the body was. Dunc was fitted in a wet suit and scuba gear. Kate had made sure the tank was filled and ready. Dunc knew that another part of her expertise was dealing with underwater gear. He strapped his detector onto his wrist to leave his hands free to maneuver the body onto a pallet that would lift it without damaging it. He also had a camera strapped to his head. Again, an airboat was used as it was less destructive to the moss than a motorboat.

Duncan's single concern at this point was this body. He thought to himself about the many other bog bodies in which the flesh and even inner soft tissues, though turned a dark tan and rubbery, were perfectly preserved because of the acidic material of the bog and the total lack of oxygen. *However*, he thought, *also due to the acid, the bones may be eaten away. I have to take enormous care in this recovery to keep the body from collapsing or falling apart.*

As Dunc walked to the boat, all the folks from the agencies, the ·police, and the students crowded around him. Kate followed him, explaining the special qualities of his air tank. She then sat down beside Jacob with the computer. She smiled broadly at Dunc. "We'll be watching you. Be careful," she said. His smile was strained as he nodded to her. Her brow furrowed as her expression changed to that of confusion. Dunc thought he should be kicked for being rude, but there was no time to make amends.

The police investigators, Will, other officials from the Trust, along with the ambulance, were ready to rush the body to the laboratory in Edinburgh. All waited on shore with Kate, Jacob, and five of the students. Constable Brownlee, who would propel the police airboat, Hannah, Bartholomew, and Dunc climbed on board. All the tools that might be necessary to recover the body were already there.

Dunc went over the communication procedures with Hannah and Bartholomew. He wouldn't be able to talk, but he had an earphone and could make hand signals for the camera. Kate had worked out the signals with him and could convey to those on the boat what he needed. She could also talk to him and tell him about the pictures he was transmitting back to the computer.

When they reached the coordinates of the body, Dunc got ready to fall backward off the craft. Hannah ran to him and gave him a bone-crushing hug. Then, as he got some breath back in his lungs, he smiled at her, inserted the mouthpiece of the scuba gear, and pushed over the side.

As he lowered to the body, the silence that surrounded him filled him with a serenity that he hadn't had in a long time. His mind went to Kate, and the thought was one of gratitude for their deep friendship. He knew at that moment that he must have faith in her. He would never again let those who didn't know her put doubts about her in his mind.

When he reached the level of the decaying moss, he could tell that almost all the body was covered by the rotting peat. He ran his detector over the area, and the full body came onto the computer. Kate and Jacob smiled at each other as the features came into view.

"Dunc, I'm almost certain this is a woman," Kate said. "Her hair is splayed out around her head. Her eyes are closed, and there is a band around her forehead."

Duncan ever so carefully moved the peat out of the way so he could see the face. Despite the effects of mummification, the face was beautiful.

He gestured into the camera that he agreed it was a female. She lay faceup with one hand on her chest and one on her stomach. He moved down the body, uncovering her breasts and then—finally, completely, and definitively—identifying gender by her genitals. He signaled this to the camera. The ancient woman was wearing a long tunic belted at her waist. There were intact sandals, probably leather, on her feet.

Duncan signaled that he was going to turn on different aspects of his detector. One was the spectroscope to analyze the metal band around her head, and one was a radiometer to date the remains. He switched on the spectrometer and ran it over the metal band on her forehead. The computer again formed a rectangle in the upper left-hand corner of the computer screen.

"It's gold, Duncan," Jacob said

Duncan made the universal sign for *okay*.

The radiometer dated the body at between one and three thousand years old. Kate read the results to Duncan and to those in the boat. Anything more definitive would be by carbon dating. Duncan then signaled the different tools he would need to free the body from the peat. Kate relayed his requests to Hannah and Bartholomew. The instruments were then lowered to Dunc, and he began the arduous work. After about a half hour, Dunc had freed the head of their "lady of the bog" and cut through the peat beneath her left side. By this time, Jacob and Kate could tell that Duncan was in some distress.

Jacob leaned into Kate's Bluetooth. "Dunc, my lad, it's time to come up for a spell."

At first, he objected but then realized that he was feeling drowsy, mildly dizzy, and his blood pressure was rising. He nodded and slowly rose to the surface. When they got him in the craft, Hannah told him she was concerned with his coloring and the fact that he seemed confused.

"We need to get him back," she said to those ashore.

"No, no, just let me rest. I'm over halfway there," Dunc protested.

No one paid him any attention. When they got to shore, Jacob and Kate, both with worry on their faces, helped him out.

He was very shaky but tried to deflect their worry by saying, "I guess this is what it feels like to come back to earth after a spaceflight."

Will had rushed over to check on his friend. "Are you okay?" he asked.

"Yes, yes, I'm fine. Just need a little break," Dunc said in a still wavering voice.

Kate and Jacob wouldn't let any of the anxious onlookers near him.

"I'm going to take it from here," Kate insisted.

"No, no," Dunc said. "It's too dangerous. I'll be okay. Just let me rest a minute."

"Duncan McIntosh, I've done this before in lochs all over Scotland and Europe. I'm the one who prepared the gear for you. I am completely capable of underwater recovery," Kate said. "Let's get this started." And she went to get into her wet suit.

She made it clear that though she wouldn't be stopped, just because she was a woman, from doing anything she was capable of, she still felt a little comforted that her friends worried about her. Neither Dunc nor Will, nor even Jacob, liked the idea of her dive, and they told her so.

"Too bad, you'll just have to accept my capabilities," she said.

Kate headed for the boat. Dunc stopped her and, placing the camera on her head and the detector on her wrist, said with a conciliatory smile, "Kate, I know you can do this. I have no doubt. Just be smarter than I was and come up before you get in trouble."

She smiled at her friend and nodded. "I'll behave. I promise."

Dunc then strapped the tank on her, and Kate boarded the boat. With a "You go, girl!" from Hannah, Kate pushed back overboard and descended to the body.

As she carefully picked some peat off the face, Kate laid her hand gently atop the "lady's" hand and gazed at the face. She was hit by an overwhelming sense of recognition of the "lady of the bog." With absolutely no idea of why, she said, "Miriam." Kate was stunned by what had just happened. She, however, knew without a shadow of a doubt that she had called the ancient woman by her name.

Her sense of responsibility took over, and Kate realized she had to get down to work. She was relieved to find that Dunc had cut away more of the peat than even he realized. The head and shoulder and the feet up to her knees were completely freed. Dunc had cut through the peat beneath her all but a few inches under her right side. All Kate had to do was cut those few inches away and call for the stretcher by way of hand signals.

She worked for only a few minutes and was ready for the stretcher. As she watched for the flat metal rectangle to be lowered, Kate began to feel very strange. She knelt beside the left of the ancient lady and aligned the stretcher with her. She unhooked the cords on the side of the stretcher next to the body. Kate then began to work the body onto the metal pallet. The job was slow and needed intense care. The problem was that, with each move she made, Kate felt sicker and sicker. She had trouble seeing and hearing and was having trouble getting enough air.

Kate willed herself to finish her job and to do it very carefully. When the body was squarely on the stretcher, with trembling hands, she clipped the cords onto the far side of the stretcher and pulled them. This alerted those above to raise the body. This was the last thing Kate remembered.

"Kate, Kate, what's going on? Kate!" Dunc yelled. He had seen the camera go haywire.

Hannah and Bartholomew were concentrating on raising the body when Duncan yelled.

"What's wrong?" Hannah asked into her Bluetooth.

"I don't know. She's in trouble. The camera is just floating around," Dunc said.

The police pilot was also in scuba gear. "I'll go down," he called as he dove backward off the boat.

Hannah and Bartholomew stopped what they were doing and just held the cords. It seemed like forever as the people on shore and those on the boat waited.

Jacob shook his head *I have to think strategically.* "Bring the body up and place the stretcher across the bow of the boat. Secure it as well as you can. You may need to come to shore the instant the constable brings Kate up," he said into the Bluetooth with all the calm he could muster. His heart was pounding in his ears.

The body was just below the surface, so the two students were able to follow Jacob's instructions very quickly. And as if on cue, Constable Brownlee reached the surface just as they finished securing the stretcher and its occupant. The constable was holding Kate's limp body in his arms. He pulled the gear out of her mouth and over her head. Brownlee lifted Kate up as best he could while treading water. Bartholomew reached down and took her from him. He laid her on the floor of the boat.

The constable threw her gear in the boat and climbed in. "Can either of you drive this?" he demanded of Hannah and Bartholomew.

"I can," Hannah said and took the controls.

The constable proceeded to do artificial respiration on Kate.

When the boat reached shore, Jacob directed the students to secure the "lady of the bog." He wanted more than anything to examine her but was desperate to see to Kate. He was extremely thankful for Bonnie's professionalism as she, Sara, and Henry took charge of the body. Matthew proved again to be an excellent photographer in documenting the artifacts. He was already busy doing just that with the body. Clint verified that the gold band was consistent with Jewish regal apparel of the eighth century BCE.

Matt seemed as concerned about Kate as was Jacob and Dunc. He, Jacob, and Dunc knelt beside Kate as Constable Brownlee continued to work on her. When the inspectors came over, the constable explained that the first danger was that she probably inhaled the bog liquid when she fainted. When he explained the second worry, Dunc, Matt, and Jacob were shocked.

"This tank can be a rebreather or a regular gas container," he said. To the blank stares, he explained, "A rebreather tank has a bag filled with barium hydroxide to scrub the breathed-out air of CO_2. It can then be reused. A regular tank just allows the diver to expel the CO_2 into the water. This was being used as a regular tank...but... the valve to allow the used air to be expelled had been closed, so Ms. Wallace and probably Dr. McIntosh by virtue of his symptoms were both being poisoned by CO_2."

Dunc, who was already feeling much better, and Jacob rode in the ambulance with Kate. Bonnie and Clint went with the bog body to Edinburgh. The other students would secure the archeological site. The people from the Trust, including Will Elder, and a presence of the police remained to be sure the site was safe.

Dunc and Jacob sat in the hospital waiting room with heads in hands. Dunc got a great deal of attention since he was still in his wet suit. Jacob felt irrationally guilty for not somehow...

Somehow what? Making everything perfect? Dunc said he felt guilty for not insisting she not go. "Like I could have stopped her."

The doctor walked in with an expression that told Kate's friends absolutely nothing.

"Are you here for Ms. Wallace?" he asked.

Both nodded.

"It would appear that she was poisoned by the CO_2. The constable said that the air tank had been tampered with. He also said that one other had used the tank before her. Can I assume by what you're wearing that, that was you?" He addressed this to Dunc, who was too worried about Kate to have the fact that the tank was tampered with sink in. However, it was already being processed by Jacob.

With a great deal of irritation, Dunc said, "Doctor, how is she?"

"Oh, of course, she will be fine, no permanent damage to her organs. You got her here just in time. She feels quite sick right now, but probably no lasting effects. Now again, did you use the same tank?"

Dunc kept looking toward Kate's door. "When can we see her?"

"Did you use the tank?"

"Yes, I did use it before she did. When can we see her?"

"I'll need to have you take a blood test," the doctor said, obviously not concerned with this man's worry about his friend.

Jacob was much relieved for Kate. He was also amused by this clash of cultures between an emotional American and an impassive Brit. He stood and put his hand on Dunc's shoulder. "It is necessary to see if you were badly affected also. From the way you looked and acted when you came up, I'm sure you were poisoned also. I'll go in and check on Kate. Which room is she in?" he asked the doctor. He got an immediate answer and went to the room.

Kate's voice, though very shaky, sounded so good to him after he knocked. "Come in."

Kate was lying on the examining table in a hospital gown. Her bare feet were crossed at her ankles. She had an IV going into her left arm and a breathing tube in her nostrils.

"Well, young lady, you've managed to add a great deal of excitement to our day."

Kate gave a short laugh and then became very serious. "Jacob, I'm the one who filled the tank. I know all about these tanks and that the valve to expel air *had* to stay open. I would never have closed it." Her voice was very weak.

"Of course not," Jacob said. "However, someone did close it."

There was silence.

"Do you think someone was trying to kill Dunc?" Kate was trembling.

"I don't know. I just don't know," Jacob said. "I can't think why they would want to."

At that point, there was another knock on the door. Jacob turned and opened the door for Duncan. He walked right over to Kate and took her right hand in his. "Are you all right?" he asked with a furrowed brow.

"Aye, I'm fine, just weak and shaky. The bronchoscope was worse than the symptoms. Dunc, I filled your tanks. You don't think I would hurt you, do you?"

With mischief in his grin, Dunc said, "Yeah, I figured you had it in for me all along."

Jacob leaned back against the wall. He was deep in thought. None of this made any sense. *The guard was probably killed because he saw the man who was trying to break into the museum. Trying to hurt these two would only make authorities look elsewhere for him... unless...*

The doctor walked in the room. "Oh, there you are, Dr. McIntosh. You do seem to have had dangerous levels of CO_2 in your blood. The only reason you didn't get sick any sooner is that, one, you had more unused air, and two, you are a much larger person than Ms. Wallace. Now, we need to get you in the examining room so we can look at your airways."

"Oh great. I just heard how much fun that's going to be." Dunc patted Kate's hand and left with the doctor. "Do I get a cute little gown like she has?" Jacob and Kate heard Dunc say as he and the doctor walked down the hall.

Kate thought of something she urgently wanted to ask Jacob about. "How's Miriam?"

"Miriam? Who's Miriam?" Jacob asked.

"Oh, I mean, how is the body from the bog? Did they get her up okay?" she said, eyes wide with eager concern.

"Our lady of the bog is wonderful. You did an incredible job of getting her on the pallet. The crew got her up perfectly, and Bonnie, Henry, and Sara got her in the ambulance. They are already in Edinburgh. Bonnie has called several times. She is very concerned about you," Jacob added.

"Yes, I was very surprised. I actually enjoyed working with her last night. I did want so to examine Mir—the body."

"Why have you named her? Do you do this with all your finds?" Jacob asked.

Kate wasn't sure he might not think she was crazy. *Oh well, what would one more thing do to my image?*

"No, I don't do it with each body I find. I've only done it once before, and I was proven right. Jacob, the woman's name was Miriam. I can't tell you how I know, but I'm sure of it."

"Have you ever studied ancient Hebrew dialect?" Jacob asked.

"No, why do you ask?"

"Because you are pronouncing the name as it would have been pronounced thousands of years ago," Jacob answered.

The two stared at each other with a sense of shared wonder, as well as an even deeper respect for each other.

The moment was interrupted by a knock on the door. Jacob opened it to find the lead inspector standing there.

"May I speak to you out here, Dr. Rubin?"

Jacob looked at Kate, who smiled and nodded.

"Yes, Inspector, what can I do for you?" Jacob asked after closing Kate's door.

The inspector started right in, "The lab has just finished going over the diving tank both Ms. Wallace and Dr. McIntosh used. We understand that Ms. Wallace filled the tanks to begin with. We found two different sets of fingerprints on the valve that was incorrectly closed. We can be sure of hers but not the other set. There are no records of them. Constable Brownlee, who motored the airboat, checked both his and Dr. McIntosh's tanks right after they were filled. The valves were in the correct position, open.

"We have concluded that even if Ms. Wallace closed the valve at a later date, intending Dr. McIntosh harm, she certainly would have reopened it when *she* used it. We also spoke to Mr. Bartholomew Guthrie. He said that Ms. Wallace is an expert with diving equipment and would never have made this kind of mistake. Furthermore, he heard her explaining the use and dangers of this kind of tank to Dr. McIntosh and that the valve must stay open.

"There is also the fact that the gun found on the murdered guard was not his and was the gun used to kill him. It was untraceable as to ownership. What I'm trying to say is: all this, and the fact that she was more gravely injured than anyone, leads us to conclude that Ms. Wallace is no longer under suspicion by the Police Scotland or our intelligence agency. Possibly someone was trying to throw blame on her."

The inspector finally stopped to take a breath. Jacob patted him on the shoulder and said with a huge grin, "My thoughts exactly. Do you have any other suspects in mind?"

"Not a one. Did you see anyone else around the tank after they were filled?" the inspector asked.

Jacob thought back. "No one person. Dr. McIntosh and I were so intent on the bog lady that we weren't paying attention to anything else. But everyone was close to both Duncan and to Kate at one time or another."

"Do you think I could ask Ms. Wallace a few questions?" the inspector said rather sheepishly.

Jacob nodded and went in to quickly explain the good news for her and ask if she could talk to the inspector. She was more than willing to help.

"I'm so sorry, Inspector. Before I started filling the tank, the students had arrived and were crowding around me to find out what we had discovered. Immediately after the students arrived, the gentlemen from the Trust and, for that matter, the police were there and were also gathered around.

"Constable Brownlee brought his tank in and used our generator to fill his. He and I talked about these tanks that can be converted from the usual type to a 'rebreather.' I suppose in the confusion, anyone could have turned that valve, but I feel sure it was open at least while I was explaining it to Duncan."

"Thank you, Ms. Wallace, and I hope you are feeling better soon." With that, he was on his way.

Being out from under the specter of suspicion gave Kate a whole new lease on life and joy in her work. Dunc, having suffered the indecencies of the bronchoscope, now had a sore throat. No serious damage was found in his airways. He and Kate had to stay a night in the hospital but were to be released early the next day with pills for discomfort.

Hannah and Sara had the good sense to realize that both needed clothes other than the wet suits they had on when taken to the hospital. After a call from Jacob, the manager of the motel allowed the two women in Kate's and Dunc's rooms to gather up their necessities. Dunc was up and dressed as soon as he got his clothes. Kate was still very wobbly, so Sara and Hannah stayed to help her.

"Now you sit right there while we go check on the guys," Hannah said.

Kate obeyed, holding on to the side of the bed. The girls hadn't been gone but a minute when Duncan came running into Kate's room. He had been so worried about her. She stood up as he came in, and her legs proceeded to give way. Dunc grabbed her and steadied her.

"I'm sorry. I'm still a little light-headed," Kate said, holding tight to his arm.

"That's okay. Do you want to lie down?" he said, now even more worried.

Jacob came in and immediately went to her other side to help hold her up. "I think we got you up too soon," he said.

"She almost fainted," Dunc said.

Sara and Hannah also came in and fussed over her. Kate was not feeling her usual "I can do it myself" attitude. Instead, she was realizing how good it felt to be cared for. Once they were sure Kate was okay, the women left to get Dunc and Kate's things in the van.

There had been something Kate had wanted to tell Jacob and Dunc, almost from the time she met them but hadn't known how. Now it just came flooding out.

"I have a child."

Chapter 7

Dunc and Jacob just stared at her. They were expecting her to link this blunt statement to the situation at hand. Finally, Dunc broke the silence.

"What?"

"I have a child, a little girl. She's three. She stays with my parents when I'm away."

"Did you want us to get you to her?" Jacob asked.

"No, she knows I'll be home soon. I just…thought…you ought to know." Kate wouldn't look at anyone. She had no idea what the response was from the one person she was really telling this to.

Jacob smiled, realizing this. He said, "I'll help the ladies." He then caught Dunc's eye and nodded toward Kate as though to tell him he had something to do. Dunc didn't have a clue.

When they were alone, he finally said, "Kate, why did you want to tell us this?"

"I just thought friends ought to know such things." She still hadn't looked at him.

Dunc thought of the question that he was afraid to ask. He might be told it wasn't his business, or worse, that she was happily married. "Where is her father?"

"She doesn't have one," Kate said with an edge to her voice. "Well, of course, she did have one. We dated for a short time, and he really pushed for the…um…physical part. I got pregnant, and he insisted I have an abortion. The feminist in me got angry. I told him off and that he needn't worry. I didn't want him or his money in mine or the baby's life. I haven't seen him since. Not having an abortion and not giving her up for adoption may have been to spite him at first. But…Dunc, she's my life. I adore her. It's hard to be away from her."

He was quiet for a long time, long enough for her to begin to worry. Finally, he tilted her chin up so she would have to look at him. "I bet she's beautiful," he said, hoping he didn't seem too happy about the absentee father.

By the next day, all equipment had been sent ahead to the university archeology department. Jacob and the other students had chartered a bus and were already in Edinburgh. The doctor had insisted that Kate take a week to recover before going back to work. Dunc used their rented van to drive her home. This gave them time to talk.

"Dunc, what on earth is going on? Dead guards…attempts on our lives. This whole bloody mess is terrifying."

"I know," Dunc said. "Jacob and I have been hashing this over and over. He thinks a real amateur is trying to get close to the shields so they can be stolen or destroyed."

"Why do you think he's an amateur?"

"In the first place, he let himself be seen, and we're sure that's why the guard was killed. Leaving the gun that shot the guard with the body was a big mistake. There is also the clumsy attempt with the air tank to throw suspicion on you."

Kate hesitated just a few seconds before asking, "Dunc, you were suspicious of me. I could see it in your eyes. Are you still?"

Duncan took a deep breath and frowned. "I did have my doubts. I didn't think I knew you. They were raised again when a good friend questioned what I knew about you. But when I was in the bog, it hit me. I do know you. I know all I need to know, and I have total faith in you. You are no more a murderer than I am or Jacob is."

Kate smiled. At least she could put that to rest.

Duncan was deep in thought. Finally, he asked, "Kate, you said you have worked on lots of projects in lochs. Have any of the other students worked with you on those projects?"

"No, why?"

"Whoever it was must have had knowledge about diving equipment to have known to close the valve," Dunc said.

"No, Bonnie is the only one I have worked with, and that wasn't in an underwater project. However, I'm fairly sure that she, Hannah, Matt, and I think even Clint have worked in lochs. That's not very helpful, is it? It doesn't narrow it down even a wee bit, does it?"

"You're right, it doesn't help a bit." Dunc laughed.

When they drove into the yard of the modest little house on the outskirts of Edinburgh, Dunc carried Kate's backpack in for her. Almost immediately, the front door opened, and a tiny redheaded girl flew out and into her mother's arms. Once again, Dunc had to steady Kate as she was still weak, and the impact of the child nearly knocked her over.

Kate was, however, delighted. The child babbled nonstop to her mother. That mother understood and answered back. Dunc couldn't understand a word, partly because of the speed they were uttered and partly because of the child's heavy brogue. An older woman with reddish-gray hair that hung limp around her face stood in the doorway. She was very thin, and her skin was quite weather-beaten. Dunc saw that she wore a look of abject disapproval as she watched Kate and the child joyfully catching up with each other.

Dunc also saw Kate's look of pure joy turn to one of somber gloom as she faced her mother. "Mother, this is Dr. McIntosh. He was kind enough to drive me home."

Her mother glanced at Dunc and, with the barest of smiles, nodded to him.

Dunc, in turn, nodded back. "Mrs. Wallace," he said in greeting.

Kate pushed past her mother and motioned for Dunc to come in. He carefully moved past Mrs. Wallace and placed Kate's pack on the floor. The room felt sparse and cold. There was nothing there to show the slightest touch of warmth. But when he looked at Kate, he saw her joy return as she turned her child to him.

"Mary, this is Dr. McIntosh. Can you say hello?"

The child grinned broadly but leaned her face against her mother's chest. "Hi," she said in a tiny shy voice.

"Hi, Mary, I'm glad to meet you. Your mother has told me a lot about you."

Again the child grinned, still pressing hard against her mother.

The mood was broken by the stern voice behind him. "Is he staying for dinner?"

Dunc quickly turned and said, "No, I have to get back." He immediately saw Kate's look of disappointment. "But I'll be back in a week to pick you up."

"Oh, Dunc, that's not necessary. I'll take the bus."

"No, I'll be back to get you. Goodbye, Mary, I'm glad to have met you. I hope to see you again soon." He turned back to Kate and said, "I'll be back in a week." Then to Kate's mother, he said, "Mrs. Wallace." And he was gone.

All the way back, he tried to sort out his feelings. He had absolutely no success in that.

Kate thought this was going to be the longest week of her life, waiting for Dunc to return. She was very wrong. The time with Mary went by terribly fast. She dreaded leaving her again. She stood in the front room of her parents' house holding Mary in her arms. Duncan McIntosh was to arrive in only ten minutes. He called a half hour earlier to say he was on the way. Kate was explaining to the sobbing child that she would be home next week and then stay for another week. "Next week" might as well have been ten years for Mary.

As Kate rocked Mary, feeling her usual guilt for leaving the child, Mrs. Wallace stepped up behind her. "Your father and I have talked. We're weary of caring for a three-year-old while her mother goes off with her gentlemen friends to get arrested for breaking the law. We intend to place the child in foster care."

Kate turned on her with eyes wide. She didn't know what to say. Kate would lose her child or her hard-fought-for career and education. She wasn't a criminal; she had fought for a cause that she believed in. And Dunc wasn't a "gentleman friend"; he was a colleague.

Before she could get her mind around what her mother was saying, Mrs. Wallace went on, "When you come back next weekend, be ready to take her with you—to a suitable home, I might add. Otherwise, we will have already made the arrangements for foster care."

Kate stopped herself from saying the angry words that had come to mind when she heard this last statement. She had a week to...*a week to do what?* Her head was spinning when she heard the knock on the door. Mary realized that it was the man to take her mother away and grabbed Kate around the neck in a death hold.

"My darling bairn, I'll be back for you very soon, and we'll stay together all the time." She untangled the child's arms and put her forcefully in her grandmother's arms. With something close to a snarl, Kate said, "For once in your life, show some kindness and compassion. This is your only grandchild. We'll both be out of your life forever in just a week."

Kate turned and opened the door for Dunc. He was stunned by Kate's angry tears, a child screaming and reaching for her mother, and the grandmother's bitter glare.

"We have to go quickly," Kate said. She charged past him toward the van.

Dunc picked up Kate's forgotten backpack and nodded to Mrs. Wallace, who ignored him. On the trip into Edinburgh, through sobs and gulps, Kate told Dunc what happened. Dunc listened with compassion. He began to realize the degree of loss this meant for Kate. She would have to quit school, leave archeology, and get a job to support her and her child. Those who funded the different projects did pay the archeologists. However, the fact that she didn't have her doctorate meant Kate was paid far less than him and Jacob. She couldn't make enough for her and Mary to exist on, much less provide adequate day care for her.

"We'll put our heads together with Jacob. Somehow he always comes up with something," Dunc said as they drove into the university complex. He didn't believe this himself.

"There's nothing anyone can do in a week," Kate said with resignation.

How wrong they both were. Jacob listened to her plight with rapt attention. He was drumming the fingers of his left hand on the chair of the arm. Dunc and Kate could almost see the thoughts rush through his mind. When he began to smile, so did Kate and Dunc.

"We will be here for several weeks until the DNA comes back, perhaps longer. We will be very busy during that time with our own testing and writing. They have guest housing here which includes those for families. The university also has day care for the faculty children. We are considered guest faculty. Kate, you might want to apply to teach a course for the upcoming semester. This would avail you of faculty housing. I can assure you, with your reputation, the university will jump at the chance to hire you.

"Oh, and one more thing. You might need a governess to assist you with little Miss Mary." Jacob smiled a very large smile. "You see, I also have a child, a beautiful daughter whom I miss terribly and who wants so very much to be a part of archeology. She loves children and is torn between my profession and her mother's, which was teaching. Would you do me the favor—no, the honor—of allowing my daughter to come help you?"

With tears of both joy and disbelief, Kate threw her arms around Jacob's neck and kissed his cheek. "Thank you," was all she could manage before breaking down in tears.

Within the week, Kate and Dunc had collected a very happy Mary. And Jacob had met his daughter at the airport. When he brought her into the front room in Kate and Mary's apartment, Kate was jarred by a strong sense of familiarity. This only increased when she took the hand of the lovely dark-haired, dark-eyed eighteen-year-old.

"Dunc McIntosh, Kate Wallace, and Ms. Mary Wallace"—Jacob nodded at the little girl—"I have the privilege to present my daughter, Miriam Rubin."

Kate was immediately struck with the same sensation of kinship to this Miriam as she was to the Miriam in the bog. She said nothing but reached her hands out to the young girl.

For the next few weeks, the band of archeologists was busy. They continued to collect specimens from the artifacts and test them to try and discover the journey they took to the Scotland bog. Kate had been accepted at the university to teach a course on Scottish archeology, so working on her curriculum took much of her time.

Many an evening, Jacob and Dunc would be let into the Wallaces' apartment by Miriam with a finger to her lips. They would find Kate hard at work preparing to teach, sitting in an armchair with a pad of paper and pencil on the arm, a textbook resting on her raised knees, and a sleeping three-year-old pressed against her chest. It didn't take a great deal of insight to tell that this had become the happiest time in Kate's entire life.

Kate would put away her work. Then Miriam, her father, and Dunc would gather around Kate and Mary and, in whispers, discuss the progress made at the labs. The shields were definitively identified as Assyrian, dating to the eighth century BCE, which was mid-Iron Age in that part of the world. They were almost certainly made in what is now southwestern Turkey. No other samples could be identified as to region of origin. The shields were an iron alloy that matched many other Assyrian artifacts of that period. Dunc found that it was definitely hammered as opposed to being cast, as was most often done in that period. The gold band on the forehead of the lady of the bog was also dated with 90 percent certainty to approximately the same period of time.

They were still waiting for the results of the DNA testing and carbon dating on the body, the pieces of cloth and leather sandals, and the leather straps on the back of the shields. All the artifacts, including the shields from Kilmartin and Egypt, came to the lab at the university and were under heavy security. The students were winding up their work and submitting their notes to Jacob. Most felt deep regret to be leaving this team. All but Bonnie would probably be back at university before these two major tests came in. Bonnie was going back to working on her thesis. She now wished she had chosen a less-challenging subject. It might well take her another year to complete.

This one evening, after Kate put Mary to bed, she, Dunc, Jacob, and Miriam (as a fascinated onlooker) were assessing where they were in their theory.

"We have evidence that people who were possibly of the House of Joseph and who had armament from Assyria were in North Africa and Scotland. The body and the artifacts appear to place them in the middle Iron Age, which coincides with the Assyrian dispersion of the ten lost tribes of Israel. Do we have anything else, and can we draw conclusions?" asked Jacob. He looked from one to the other of each of the young people in the room. He had a slightly saddened look.

Each one thought through the question.

"No…to both," Dunc said. "However, I want these questions asked to all the students."

And so they were brought to Kate's apartment and asked.

"The head band on the body speaks of high social status, if not royalty—as well as laying the shields on her body. It's quite possible that the two tribes of Ephraim and Manasseh put away their individual identity after their encounter with the Assyrians. It is also possible that placing the shields over their queen meant they would then take back those identities and again become two tribes. The reason for this might be that they had found their new 'promised land,'" Clint was speaking thoughtfully. He no longer felt the need to be defensive of his beliefs. He had been shown respect for his work. There seemed to be a lot of that going around.

This personalization of the lady of the bog seemed to invoke a new sense of excitement in everyone present.

Dunc looked at Jacob and then back at the students. "Then we need to be looking for royalty, don't we? Where would Jewish royalty go?"

A small voice spoke from beside Jacob. "By the sea. They would want to build their kingdom by the sea," Miriam said with a sense of confidence.

Jacob looked at his daughter with pride. The students stared at her, and then all began to nod in agreement.

"We need to follow the coast. I think farther north," Bonnie said. "Perhaps not as far as Orkney but certainly the Inner Hebrides."

"What ancient castles are there that we aren't *sure* of their dates?" Matthew asked.

"There are definitely some that are built on older ones that haven't been thoroughly studied," Kate said, feeling the excitement growing where before there was only depression.

"And the brochs? How about all those brochs? Nobody really knows what they are. And they are mostly in that area we're talking about."

Jacob sat back and smiled, watching his little group come back to life. Kate stood and took a sleeping Mary from Miriam. She smiled at Miriam and said, "Welcome to archeology."

Everyone's high was accentuated by three events that happened before the students left for their universities: First, the carbon-14 dating came back placing all the fibers attached to the shields and the body to within the range of time commiserate with the expulsion of the ten tribes from Israel. Second, the DNA testing arrived with encouraging results. The patrilineal (Y-DNA) study proved to be almost identical to those done on the Samaritans, those people in the area of ancient Israel who claim linage from the Ephraim and Manasseh tribes. The maternal ancestry (mitochondrial DNA) was less similar, but this was to be expected. One, the two lines of DNA are transmitted in different ways, and two, the lady of the bog was born before any assimilation with the Assyrians.

The third and most exciting event came as a call to Duncan from a dear friend and fellow classmate, Mamun Hakeem Al-Khaldi. Dr. Al-Khaldi was a renowned archeologist from Saudi Arabia. He and his students had just uncovered a mass grave in the southwest of his country. The site had been the scene of a huge massacre of Bedouins, known as Qedarites. It was certain that the killers were Assyrians. Most thrilling to Dunc was the fact that there were, here and there, amid the bodies, ancient Hebrew artifacts.

The arrows and broken lances and swords among the bodies were indisputably Assyrian. The well-preserved robes of the bodies were, with just as much certainty, identified as the ancient nomads of the area, the Qedarites. The bodies had been left to rot after the massacre. However, over millennia, the powerful shifting sands of the

Arabian Desert covered the bodies, giving them the dignity of graves that the Assyrians had denied them.

"Evidently, the Qedarites either were given or stole items from the Jews as they crossed paths," Mamun said.

"What were the Hebrew articles?" Dunc asked.

"Mostly coins. Many with King Hoseah on them, others that went further back. But, Dunc, the reason I knew I had to call you—Duncan, we found a crown. It had been flattened in order to hide it, but it had a symbol on it…Duncan, it had a horn. It had the sign of Manasseh. These Qedarites came in contact with your lost tribe."

"*Oh, my God,*" Dunc said. He was about to faint from excitement. When he got his breath back, he asked, "Why didn't the Assyrians steal the stash from them?"

"Ah, that was our question. It would appear that the Qedarites had very clever hiding places in their clothes. We only found the artifacts with metal detectors. They were hidden in well-disguised pockets and hems of the clothing. The attack was not one with intent of robbery, however. It was too brutal. It was one of revenge. If I didn't know of your finds in Egypt and Scotland, I would say that the Qedarites had stolen from the Assyrians and paid for their crimes with their and their families' lives."

"Why do you say that?" Dunc was beginning to put the puzzle pieces together.

"There were also Assyrian articles hidden on the corpses. These articles would have been jewelry or insignia of officers in the Assyrian army," Mamun explained.

"Okay, so putting our two theories together, the Israelites encounter the Assyrian troop, and they came out on top. They stripped the Assyrians of everything and probably left the bodies just lying there as the Assyrians did the Qedarites. At a later time, the Jews met up with the nomads. Either by theft or gift, the nomads ended up with both Israelite and Assyrian articles. When the dead Assyrians were found, their countrymen set out to find the killers. They assumed they found them when they saw the Assyrian articles and wiped out the Qedarites tribe. How does that sound?" Dunc was thinking as fast as he was talking.

"Duncan, it sounds like we are of the same mind. I will send you pictures. However, I wish you could come and see for yourself."

Dunc knew how carefully archeologists protect their work until it can be published. He was deeply honored that Mamun had enough trust in him to share these pictures, and he told him so. He also told Mamun that wild horses couldn't keep him away. "May I share the pictures with Dr. Rubin and Ms. Wallace? I will only do so if you agree," he asked.

"Yes, of course. After all you've told me about them and your project, I am seeing a cooperative effort between us," Mamun said.

"*Great Scott, man!* That would be wonderful."

"There are financial reasons. I have to be up-front with you. This is a massive project, and I'm nearly out of money already," Mamun confessed.

"All I can say to that, my dear friend, is, there *is* a God. Do you have any idea what your project will mean to ours?"

Within the hour, Dunc received the pictures and showed them to Kate and Jacob. He also talked about a joint project and his going to Saudi Arabia to view Mamun's site. With great excitement, the three talked way into the night. They discussed going to their funding schools for funding for Dr. Al-Khaldi's project. There was little doubt that the finds in Saudi Arabia would greatly enhance Jacob's finds. The consensus was that the schools would jump at the chance to sponsor them.

The conversation finally came back to Dunc's invitation.

"Jacob, Kate, you must go also," Dunc said enthusiastically.

"No, that isn't a good idea. The Saudis have the most restrictive travel policies in the world. It is very difficult for Jews to get the required advance visas. It is impossible for Israeli nationals, such as myself," Jacob said.

"I want to go," Kate said.

"My dear, it is just as difficult, if not more so, for an atheist." Jacob could see her disappointment.

"Am I going to have trouble as a Christian?" Dunc asked.

"Amazingly, no, but you need to be sure not to take any Christian items, especially a Bible," Jacob said.

He then turned to Kate. She had been wondering if her atheistic convictions still meant a great deal to her, and would she actually be able to check the Christian box? Jacob could almost read her mind.

"There are other problems as well, Kate," Jacob said. "The clothing restrictions for women are very strict. Another thing is that you must be accompanied at all times by a male relative when you are in public. There are groups of social police that rove the area and will arrest any woman not abiding by these rules."

Dunc could tell that Jacob was telling her this because he feared for her.

"Jacob, I can deal with the dress code. I can say honestly that I was raised a Christian…and can't Dunc adopt me?" Kate said.

Jacob smiled at her adoption question but was still very worried about her going. Dunc just rolled his eyes. He had wanted Kate to go until he heard Jacob. Now he felt a strong sense of foreboding about it. Kate saw his change of heart but was undeterred. She would not be kept from this incredible find.

"Dunc, before you take Jacob's side, please call your friend Dr. Al-Khaldi. Ask him if we can do something."

Duncan knew that his single-minded friend would not rest until she found a way to accompany him. He did call Mamun and had a long discussion with him. To Dunc's dismay, Mamun told him that it was done all the time with professionals. He would get a man from the UK embassy to sponsor her. This man would have to be with her every time she went out.

Kate was smiling from ear to ear and clapping her hands in joy. Jacob and Dunc stood stoic. They both had the same unnamed anxiety—this would not end well.

The ten-hour flight from Glasgow to Riyadh allowed Dunc and Kate to rest. Neither had fully recovered from the CO_2 poisoning. Kate also read the dress and behavior codes for women over and over, both that the airline had furnished her, as well as different travel guides.

Women, be they local or foreign, are all required to wear an *abaya*, a long and loose black robe. While a head scarf is optional for non-Saudi females (particularly in Jeddah), one should at least be brought along in order to avoid possible harassment from locals and the religious police or to be used as a means of deflecting attention from potentially aggravating men.

Saudi law prohibits women from *mingling with unrelated men.* Some family restaurants will go further and will not allow a married couple to dine together with a single man. Women may not drive cars. Women may not even be driven by unrelated men (e.g., taxi drivers).

A woman *may not* travel alone. They may not stay alone in hotels. Hotels *will* require the presence of a male guardian.

While all this legally applies to foreign women as well, in practice, foreign women are not restrained by their families in the way that Saudi women are and can have considerable leeway if they choose to take it. For example, a foreign woman and her boyfriend (or even male coworker) can simply *claim to be* husband and wife and thus mingle freely—although, if caught doing so, they will be subject to a stay in jail.

A single woman accosted by the police or the *muttawa* and requested to come with them *does not have to* (and for their own safety, should not) go with them alone: you have the right to call your male guardian and have him arrive. However, you may be required to surrender your ID, and you may not leave until the police/muttawa allows you to.

Kate was feeling high anxiety over all these rules. She was also feeling indignant that she should have such heavy restitutions when men had none. She, however, would not say a word to Duncan. He had been testy the whole trip. She knew he was worried about her, but she was sick of his sniping at her like a pesky big brother. Kate had borrowed clothes from a close friend who was Muslim. She was already dressed appropriately, including being wrapped in a traditional head scarf.

She and Dunc were barely speaking as they got off the plane. They were met by Dr. Al-Khaldi and the man from the embassy who would sponsor her, Mr. Frederick Bentley. Mr. Bentley was rather reserved and businesslike. He launched into all the rules, and Kate thought she would scream. Dunc looked on amused, which just made her angrier, but she held it in. She thought at some point that she would strangle him when he, smiling broadly, joined the other two men to walk in front of her.

He and Kate would only be there for that afternoon, the next day, and return to Scotland the following morning. Since this was such a short time, they were taken right to the site. It was massive. As far as you could see, there were skeletal remains. The flesh had deteriorated, but the dry desert sand had preserved much of the clothing. Because of this, one could tell male from female and child from adult. In and among the bones were various artifacts.

This had been a horrific massacre, an immense human tragedy almost beyond human belief. Kate and Dunc were professional archeologists, quite used to finding mass graves and the remains of war. Even so, this had shaken them by its proportions. Mamun's statement of this being revenge rather than robbery was almost certainly an understatement. As Kate put her personal feelings aside to begin her work, she felt that sense of familiarity with Miriam. The lady of the bog had not seen this, but she knew of it, and it had broken her heart.

Dunc realized quickly that to get all the data and pictures he needed, he would have to make nice to Kate, which he did. Kate was still angry, but Duncan's polite behavior did help them coordinate their work. Over the next two days, they were able to identify and document Assyrian medals and coins. There were also four shields that coincided with the finds in Egypt and Scotland. These did not have any sign of the symbol of Joseph, however. Dunc's detector was able to date these to between the seventh and ninth century BCE.

Most important to Dunc and Kate were the Hebrew artifacts: coins and jewelry. The coins had the image of the King Hoseah, the last king of Israel. The jewelry had one of the symbols they were there to see: the horn of Manasseh was on several medals. Another piece hidden in the hem of a robe was a pendant with the image of what looked like a unicorn, also most likely representing the horn of Manasseh. There were, however, no images of the ox of Ephraim. This was curious to the archeologists. But there was exhilaration over the significant finds. This even made Kate forget the indignity and inconvenience of her circumstances.

She sent hundreds of pictures with her and Dunc's comments to Jacob. He, in Scotland, was reviewing all this data with close to tears of joy. He was again pulling together his theory of the tribes' flight. Kate was right about the Qedarites being involved. But where was Ephraim?

Duncan and Kate had made arrangements with Dr. Al-Khaldi to meet them in Scotland once his artifacts had been secured. The entire site might become a memorial in the desert sands, if permitted by the authorities. In the meantime, they would arrange for dignitaries from their universities to be in contact with Mamun.

That last night, Mr. Bentley was looking very relieved that his babysitting duties were almost at an end. Dunc was still showing the exhilaration of the incredible finds. Kate was feeling both. The men stood at her door and wished her good night. Even though she would see them both in just a few hours, Kate shook Bentley's hand and kissed Dunc on the cheek. She went in and closed the door behind her, still not believing the incredible luck of their find. She was way too tired to do more than slip out of her abaya and into her short gown, turn off the light, and sink into bed.

Kate had only an instant to recognize that someone else was in her room. A heavy hand with a sharp-smelling cloth in it covered her face, and she lost consciousness.

Chapter 8

Northern Kingdom, Israel
Hebrew year 3038 (723 BCE)

The short, wiry little man bustled through the narrow streets of Shiloh. He was agitated, so he did what he always did in such a state: he talked to himself—himself and one other. Most who saw him just ignored or laughed. *We have a cave where we put people like that, do we not?* Very few took Neriah, the self-proclaimed prophet, seriously.

Neriah snorted and muttered, "I do not know why YHVH insists on these people, these particular people. They are as lazy and corrupt as the rest. I cannot do it all myself. But if I do not, it will not get done." He looked skyward. "Mighty YHVH, they are not going to—"

He abruptly paused, as if some *being*, perhaps YHVH Himself, only he could hear had interrupted him.

"Yes, yes, I know, but—"

Neriah sighed and smiled in compliance.

When he reached the door of the house, he took off his sandals and pounded on the door. He rubbed his blistered feet and wondered how he would make the thousands of miles journey required by YHVH when this ten-mile one from Shechem to Shiloh did this to him. *YHVH will provide…I hope.*

When Beulah opened the door, Neriah rushed in before she could slam it in his face.

"I told you before, you insane jackass, we are not going anywhere," Beulah said.

"That will be enough, wife. Go about your duties," came the voice from behind her. Talmai's voice matched the weariness of his face.

Beulah turned a look of disgust on her husband but, without further words, picked up the basket of filthy clothes and left. She and her daughters would go to the stream and spend the day scrubbing them and laying them out on the rocks to dry.

"What is it, Neriah?"

"Peleg has chosen his twelve, and they are gathering the wealth. They have also taken the required wagons and hidden them in the caves by the Jabbok River. Where are your twelve, and where is your treasure?"

Talmai ignored the question and asked one of his own, "How did you get Peleg to do your bidding? I think he would have little interest in YHVH." Talmai knew his far-distant cousin was allowing, if not practicing in, the pagan religion of his now dead wife.

"I lied to him and told him YHVH would make him king in the new land," the little prophet said with absolutely no shame.

"Thou shall not bear false witness against thy neighbor, Neriah," Talmai scolded.

"It was *to* him, not *against* him. Now answer my question," Neriah insisted.

"Picking the twelve most righteous men of the tribe of Ephraim was very difficult. You will be very disappointed in what I have found. As for the wealth, there is none to gather."

"Yes, there is. You are not looking. YHVH spoke and said that wicked King Ahaz of Judah wants to incur favor from the Assyrians and is going to their King Shalmaneser in one month. Shalmaneser is crueler than his father, Tiglath-Pileser. He will not just take us to be slaves, he will slaughter us and rape our women. We cannot stand against the Assyrians," Neriah said. He then turned and left as abruptly as he had arrived.

A month prior, this prophet of YHVH, Neriah, pronounced that because of the evil of its people, all of Israel was about to come to an end. Judah, the Southern Kingdom, contained only two tribes of the twelve originally in the lands of the Hebrews. Israel, the Northern Kingdom, held the remaining ten.

The little prophet quoted scripture to Talmai to the letter. The ten tribes of Israel would be destroyed. He declared he was then commanded to go to the most righteous man in both the tribes of Manasseh and of Ephraim. They were to each choose twelve families from their tribes who followed the laws of YHVH. They were to gather all the wealth they could and follow Neriah into the desert.

"It is not that the wrath of YHVH had abated toward Manasseh and Ephraim," Neriah stated with wrath of his own. "It is that centuries ago, YHVH proclaimed that the sons of Yosef, those from the tribes of Manasseh and Ephraim, will populate the greatest nations of the world. For this, they must leave Israel before the Assyrian hordes attack."

Talmai had been chosen as the most righteous of Ephraim and Peleg from Manasseh. For the life of him, Talmai could not see anything remotely righteous about his cousin, but he couldn't dismiss the scripture Neriah quoted. Talmai did respect and would follow the word of YHVH.

Peleg was not an evil man, but he was lazy. He found it far less trouble to just allow his wife to follow her pagan rituals. He quietly went about his own rituals, if they were not too difficult. He also had visions of grandeur and longed for fame and fortune. After promising him the crown of the tribe of Manasseh, it took little else to get him to follow Neriah's demands.

Most of the men of Manasseh had never forgiven their patriarch, Jacob, for passing over his firstborn grandson, Manasseh, and giving the firstborn blessing to his younger brother, Ephraim. Ephraim had become as much the name of the Northern Kingdom as was Israel. For millennia, the tribes had competed with, and even hated, one another. Neriah did not look forward to putting up with this animosity over the long, long journey ahead.

Talmai of Ephraim was a righteous man. He and his family followed the tenets of YHVH to the best of their ability. He found comfort in reading the Torah and in prayer. The problem for Neriah was Talmai's deep sense of defeat and fatalism. He knew well the scripture Neriah quoted; he just could not believe that *he* would lead his people to the lands promised them.

Talmai watched the little prophet shuttle down the narrow alleyways between the mud-brick houses. He thought of this man's unbending demands that seemed so far above his abilities. He then thought of his quarrelsome wife. Her rudeness to Neriah was a constant embarrassment to him. She was forever nagging Talmai and complaining about him and his children.

Ah, his children, a spark of joy in his life. Arieh was his oldest and his pride. The boy was well named as a lion. He was strong and very brave. He would be a great leader someday. Talmai secretly worried that Arieh would be ashamed of his father when that happened. Teman was his middle son and growing into a fine young man. He studied hard under his father and was as excellent a translator as Talmai. Ezer was his youngest, and the child that was not quite right. Perhaps if his mother showed him more love rather than constantly telling him how stupid he was, he might gain some wits about him.

His oldest daughter, Leah, was his second born. Talmai frowned at the thought of her. She was definitely becoming just like her mother: a critical, nagging gossip. His heavy sigh turned into a smile as he thought of his youngest daughter, Ester. She was a year younger than Ezer. Her name was "star," and she had all the loving brightness that her mother and her sister lacked.

Though he loved his children dearly, where Talmai truly found satisfaction was in his work. Talmai was a scribe, a soferim. He carefully and accurately wrote down the oral traditions of the Hebrew people. There was less and less of a call for his work as the kings of Israel in their lavish palaces in Samaria had become increasingly wicked. They were forever taking on the pagan debauchery of the heathen nations around Israel, deserting the faith of the patriarchs that led their people out of slavery and to the Promised Land.

There had been a few people who treasured his writings, and these were the families that he had chosen to follow Neriah into exile. Talmai believed that this pushy little man had spoken to YHVH. He had read the words of the famous and well-known prophet Hosea, threatening the same things as Neriah.

Thinking of all this made him very weary. He had been writing and realized he had made a mistake on the scroll. He would have to scrub the skins to correct this, and he felt far too morose to tend to the chore at that time. However, his eyes went to another scroll pushed way back into the alcove in the wall where he kept his work. He rolled it out and smiled. Talmai had a far greater gift than just reading and writing. He could very quickly pick up and translate any foreign language. The scroll he smiled over was just that: a translation.

A mentor of Talmai's had passed on a treasured stone tablet of his just before his death. This mentor, Zah-eil, was, strangely enough, an Assyrian. He had been a part of the army who had nine years before conquered the tribes of Israel west of the Jordan and carried them into slavery. Zah-eil had himself been a scribe and had access to the royal library in Nimrud, Assyria. He was conscripted into the army and forced to partake in the decimation of Eastern Israel.

Zah-eil had been wounded in battle and had deserted his post. He sought out Talmai, with whom he had a great deal of written communication, regarding the Akkadian language. He had carried with him into battle his most treasured possession. Zah-eil knew his wounds were serious and that he could not survive too much longer. He wanted his friend to have his treasure, knowing this man would truly appreciate it.

Talmai remembered the day the man came to his door. He immediately took the Assyrian into his arms and lowered him to the floor. Zah-eil, pale and near death, introduced himself, told Talmai of his circumstances, and placed his treasure in the Israelite's hands. He smiled, knowing it would now be safe, and he breathed his last.

Talmai remembered Beulah screaming about the unclean body in her house. He ignored her and said a prayer of blessing over his friend. He was, however, in a very precarious position. The Israelite authorities would imprison him for consorting with the enemy. And the Assyrians, if they came looking for Zah-eil, would kill him and his family for hiding a deserter. Talmai threatened Beulah with a beating if she did not shut up. He then told her his plan. She would have to go along or also suffer death or prison.

Husband and wife carried the body into their own bed and told the children this was a traveler from another tribe who had asked for their hospitality. No respectable Hebrew would refuse such hospitality. Late that night, Beulah and Talmai carried the shrouded body to their wagon and took the Assyrian to the banks of the Jabbok. Talmai had watched with sadness as his friend sank beneath the waters.

Now Talmai shook off this sad memory and reached over this scroll. He reached his hand farther back into the alcove and placed it lovingly on a clay tablet. His touch was no more than that of a feather, not wanting to cause the least bit of damage. This was the treasure that Zah-eil had brought him. It was one of the twelve tablets of the epic of Gilgamesh, king of Urik. It was an ancient story from Mesopotamia titled "He Who Saw the Deep."

These tablets had been written two to five centuries ago. As learned as he was, Talmai was well aware that there were earlier tablets that dated around eleven centuries earlier and even older Sumerian poems that were the inspiration for the adventures of Gilgamesh.

No one, not even Beulah, knew he had the tablet. Late at night, he would leave his bed and translate the words of the tablet from Akkadian to Hebrew and copy the translation onto the scroll. Talmai tried hard to forget that Zah-eil must have stolen it from the king's library. He also hoped that YHVH would not be angry with him for so enjoying this pagan story. But enjoy it he did.

In this tablet, King Gilgamesh did battle with Enkidu, a wild man sent by the gods to stop him from oppressing his people. Instead of becoming enemies, they became strong friends and set out to have wonderful adventures. Talmai had to laugh at himself for even one second of thought that he and Peleg would somehow duplicate the heroes in these adventures.

Chapter 9

It had been a mere four weeks since Neriah's last visit, and somehow Talmai had managed all of the little prophet's demands. His twelve families had packed their wagons and hidden them in the Jabbok caves with those of Peleg's families. Also, with their help, he had scrounged and begged quite a large sum of coins, gold, and jewelry.

"You have accomplished a great deal," Neriah said, hardly able to believe it himself. "Tonight you are to gather your family, tie their bedrolls on them, and meet us all at the river." The little man turned and left. Talmai felt a bit of excitement. He was actually going to participate in an *adventure*. Now the last and hardest job: tell Beulah they were about to leave their home forever.

"You are as stupid and crazy as that loony little fool," his wife said. "You will not take us on a wild trek to die in the desert."

The children were staring, confused and a bit afraid of what was to happen. Talmai had just told them of their coming adventure. They were standing in a row, watching their angry mother and allowing their father to tie their bedrolls on their backs. Leah was the only one who drew away, but only for a second. Even she knew better than to disobey her father, regardless of how much she agreed with her mother. When Talmai tried to put the bedroll on Beulah, she shoved him and marched out the door.

Talmai breathed a sigh of resignation. It was late, and he wanted to get his children to the meeting place. He went to his alcove and stared at his scrolls. Instructions were: absolutely nothing but the wealth, food, weapons, and bedding—*nothing more*. If he could take just one. How could he choose? He should be out finding Beulah.

No, no! He would not leave his treasure. Talmai laid his bedding on the floor and carefully laid on it the Gilgamesh tablet and then the scroll with its translation. Then to soothe his conscience for thinking first of his pagan work, he took the latest finished scroll of the Torah and placed it beside the other.

With his weighty hidden treasure strapped to his back, he gathered the children and rushed them to the meeting place.

"Father, you must go get mother," Leah said.

All the children were showing their concern. Talmai agreed and ran back through the alleyways of the sandstone boxy dwellings toward his home. Suddenly he heard heavy footsteps and the clank of metal. There were soldiers marching down the street. He flattened himself against the wall, hidden by the evening shadows. Almighty YHVH had led them out just in time. Some soldiers passed by, and they were definitely Assyrian.

Talmai heard a voice, a woman's voice, a very familiar woman's voice. "You there, you have to stop this terrible thing. You have to stop these people from leaving," Beulah called out to the soldiers.

The soldiers were as shocked, as was Talmai. They looked at one another and then at the woman waving her arms and yelling.

"I can show you where they have gone," she said, pointing almost directly at Talmai.

He pressed harder against the wall of the building. *How could my own wife betray me and our children like this?*

The soldiers were looking around, very wary of this loud woman and muttering to one another.

Beulah yelled for them to follow her and started down the very alleyway where Talmai stood frozen in place. She looked directly at him and stopped. He was certain she was going to reveal him to the men behind her, but she said nothing. As she stared at her husband, her eyes widened as if in shock; then they became vacant.

And...and what was that? Was there an arm growing out of her midsection?

Reality dawned as Talmai realized that what he had thought was an appendage was actually the blade of a sword. The soldier behind Beulah had run her through with his sword. She fell forward, stopped only when the tip of the sword stuck in the ground. Her head fell forward, her knees collapsed, and her hands drug on the ground. Her body slowly slid down the blade, leaving the sword above her blood red.

The soldier who had run her through stepped on her back and pulled his sword out. He cleaned his bloody sword by wiping it across the part of her tunic covering her buttocks. "Lead us into an ambush, will you, stupid whore?"

The other soldiers laughed, and the group walked on as if nothing more had happened than someone swatting a fly. Talmai stood in shock. He should go to her, bury her, and gather his family in mourning. He did none of these. He left her there and walked to the meeting place. Only Neriah guessed what had happened. He said nothing.

With little feeling, probably due to his being in shock, he told the children that their mother had chosen to stay, which was true.

The small band started out on their great journey. Hearing that Assyrians were already in Israel, Neriah picked two scouts: one he sent ahead and one he told to follow behind. They had traveled almost to daybreak when the latter scout rode up at high speed. He was very upset.

"The Assyrians have realized that we are gone. They are coming this way. They are not far behind me." He was shaking with fear.

Neriah rubbed his hand over his mouth, trying to decide what to do.

Before the prophet could say a word, Talmai stepped forward and, in actions that even surprised him, spoke in a loud, calm, and extremely commanding voice. "Get all women and children under twelve into the woods. Men, leave your bedrolls and follow me up onto the cliffs. Pick up rocks as you go."

Neriah smiled, finally realizing why YHWH had chosen this man.

All this was done very quickly. The women realized their lives depended on the men's actions. They held their children close. The daughter of Peleg, Miriam, watched Talmai with particular interest. She knew deep in her heart that this man would save their people.

The men readied themselves and waited. The scout had been right. The Assyrian troops rode into the pass in less than a half hour. The strategy had been set in place. When the soldiers got directly beneath the Israelites, they were pelted with a storm of rocks. Talmai, Peleg, and their sons scrambled down the cliff and grabbed the swords of the fallen Assyrians. They killed those who were still standing and then ensured the fallen were all dead.

Talmai stood over the leader, whom he recognized as the one who killed Beulah. As he ran the soldier through, he felt a degree of revenge, but most of all, enormous sorrow. He stood and stared for a moment. He then turned to the others. "Gather all the armor and the horses and leave the men where they are," he said and picked up the shield and sword of the leader.

Talmai, Peleg, and their sons would give to the others the armor they had brought; and the nine of them would, from that night on, carry that of the twelve slain Assyrians. The Israelites obeyed these commands. Everyone there, even Peleg, understood that Talmai was now their unopposed leader.

For the next month and a half, the little nation followed the eastern side of the Red Sea southward. They carefully skirted Dumat al-Jandal, fearing the people were in league with the Assyrians. They traveled at night and slept during the heat of the day, both to avoid the heat of day and the people of the area. They found oases or caves to protect them from the blazing sun. The food that they brought, though rationed, went fairly quickly; and the young men went out and hunted what game they could find, mostly longhair rabbits, which gave the crowd little more than a taste for the day. The women gathered the dates and fruits of the oases. The oases were becoming fewer and farther between, so water also became an urgent need.

Neriah and Talmai heard the cries and fears of the people. Neriah could hear the Israelites crying to Moses and felt deep kindred to the great leader of so long ago.

Talmai himself looked toward the heavens and asked, "Oh, YHVH, did you bring us out here to die of starvation and thirst?"

Neriah placed a hand on his shoulder. "I am going to the top of the hill and pray," the prophet said.

In a moment of humor, Talmai implored, "Please do not take forty days like Moses. I do not think this group can wait."

The little prophet smiled and nodded. He climbed the crest and knelt, raising both hands skyward. It did not take him forty days or even forty minutes. He suddenly rose and shaded his eyes with one hand. He was staring at something on the other side of the hill. With glee, he ran down the hill to Talmai, almost skipping with joy.

"Nomads! They must be the Qedarites," he shouted. "YHVH has answered! YHVH has answered!"

"How do you know they will not turn on us or that they are not with the Assyrians?" Talmai was very protective of his people, however quarrelsome they had become.

"No," Neriah said. "These are people of peace. And most important, they *live* the life we are struggling to just survive. They will feed us and teach us their ways. YHVH has sent them to us."

After much thought, Talmai approached Peleg and told him what Neriah had said.

"Perhaps it is better to die by an enemy's sword than of thirst and hunger," Peleg said with resignation.

He and Talmai gathered their sons and, armed with swords and shields, followed Neriah toward the nomad camp. The minute the Israelites appeared, so heavily armed, the men of the camp were also armed and formed a wall of protection, shielding their families.

"We have no quarrel with Assyria. We are humble folk who live off the land," the leader of the Qedarites said.

"They think we are Assyrians," Talmai said.

"Well, of course, they do. Look at our armor," Neriah answered in a whisper.

Talmai thought for a second and then gave the command for his entire band to lay down their arms. He said a quick prayer to YHVH that he was doing the right thing and walked forward to the leader who had spoken.

"We are not Assyrians. We are fleeing them. They followed us out of Israel, and we did battle with them. As you can see, we won."

Talmai gestured toward the armor lying on the ground. "We are from the Israelite tribes of Ephraim and Manasseh. My people thirst and are starving. All we ask of you is water and whatever food you can spare us. We will pay you."

"I am Ihsan," the leader said. His eyes were smiling with enormous esteem for this man who won in a battle with the Assyrians.

Talmai introduced himself, Peleg, their sons, and Neriah.

Ihsan bowed to the Israelites and said, "Bring all your tribes to us, and we will feed and give you drink."

There was great rejoicing as the Israelite families were brought into the Qedarite camp. There they were brought platter after platter of fruits and meat. There were given fresh water, all they could drink; and after the feast, they were served fine wine.

Ihsan sat with Talmai, Peleg, and Neriah. They spoke of the treachery of both the king of Judah and the king of Assyria. The conversation then turned to the practical matter of surviving long journeys through the desert.

"You can travel with us along the Red Sea. We will teach you everything from tent making, to raising grazing animals, to finding oases, to bartering for what you need in the villages you encounter," Ihsan said. "If you will send me your wife, I will introduce her to mine, and we can begin the many lessons of the chores the women can provide."

Talmai started to explain that he was a widower, but Neriah jumped in ahead of him. "That we will do in the morning. Talmai will bring his betrothed to you, and then we will begin the lesson." Neriah rose to leave. "It is rest we need now."

"My *what*?" Talmai asked with total astonishment.

Neriah grabbed him by the arm, pulling him to his feet. Ihsan realized the exhaustion of his newfound friends and bade them all a good night. The whole crowd rose and made ready for bed. When Talmai and Neriah were out of sight and sound of Ihsan, the little prophet pulled Talmai aside.

"The Qedarites have many wives, therefore, many children. Half of those children are girls. If their leader finds out that you are without a wife, you will be responsible for taking on several of his daughters for your harem as payment for their help. YHVH does not want this intermarriage."

"Several?" Talmai asked weakly.

"Yes, possibly twenty-five to fifty for a tribe's chief."

"Twenty-five to fifty?" Talmai thought he might be ill. He had not done so well with one wife, and the thought of a harem of fifty wives was more than he could bear.

"You are to go tonight to Peleg. Tell him what I have told you. No one has questioned his marital state as yet. You are to speak to him of his daughter, Miriam. You are then to ask for her hand in marriage. Now go. And close your mouth. You must always look strong even with these good people."

Talmai did what he was told and took Peleg aside. After he explained the circumstances, he cleared his throat and said, "I am asking you for your daughter's hand in marriage."

Peleg stared at his distant cousin. Actually, a harem did not sound too bad to him. However, if he had learned anything from traveling with Neriah, it was to trust him in proclaiming YHVH's commandments.

Peleg gave a shrug of his shoulders and said, "She could do worse." He went to Miriam and pulled her to her feet. He took her to Talmai and explained that she was now betrothed to him.

Miriam, with great shyness, bowed her head and then knelt before Talmai and said, "My Lord, you have done me great honor."

She remained on her knees with her head bowed. Talmai was flabbergasted at all this. This child could not be but a few years older than Leah. He had never been told by anyone, especially a woman, that he had honored them. He finally raised her to her feet and said something that later seemed so stupid to him, "That is fine. Now you can go back to bed."

"No," Peleg said with a wicked grin, "she goes to your bed."

Chapter 10

Talmai had taken his new wife and led her to where his daughters were lying. He handed her the bedding he had picked up for her, smiled, and said, "You can sleep here," pointing to a space by his daughters.

He had explained to his children that their mother was dead sometime back. The two older boys had reacted with anger toward the Assyrians. Leah had reacted with contained anger toward her father. She felt that, if he had not dragged them out to the YHVH-forsaken land, her mother would still be alive. Ezer and Ester had wept.

Now when he told the five that this was his betrothed wife, Arieh and Teman had smiled, knowing their father would no longer be alone. Leah was angry at her father and immediately despised his wife. The two little ones smiled because they felt they now had a mother again. And they did.

Neriah had made it clear that during their journey, the Hebrews' long-drawn-out betrothal, its ketubah contract, and its consummation rituals were not to be observed. Even proof of her virginity, though still important to the Israelites, was forgone during this journey. The minute the woman was given over by her father, she was the man's wife—and he was to bed her. Miriam knew this and was a bit surprised that she was left with the children. She would, however, do as her husband wished.

She set about that first night to be a mother to his children. It was quite easy with the little ones as they fell in love with her when they met her. The older boys showed her respect as their father's new wife despite the fact that Arieh was less than three years younger than she. Leah showed her resentment very openly. This saddened and worried Miriam, but she would not scold or tell on the girl, hoping she could win her over.

The very next day, Miriam took on the job of sitting with Ihsan's head wife to learn the ways of the wonderers. She, in turn, taught the women of Israel. Before long, the women were making tents and clothes and preparing foods for their families out of skins and plant materials they never believed they would find in the desert.

Miriam was admired by all who met her. She was caring and patient with her new children and carried herself as the wife of the great leader Talmai. She was kind and helpful to the Hebrew women and to the women of the Qedarites. She was, however, feeling more and more dismay over Talmai's lack of attention as well as Leah's hostility toward her.

Talmai did notice her and was very proud of her but had no idea how to express it. He felt guilt over Beulah and shame that he had left her dead or dying in the streets of Shiloh. He and Beulah were very young when they married. They had literally grown up together, at the same time growing apart. Having children was all they did together, and that had become more drudgery than pleasure. How could he take to his bed this beautiful young woman that he felt more fatherly toward than as a husband?

All this changed when Arieh came to his father and asked to take counsel with him. "Father, I am concerned about your wife. Leah has become crueler to her every day. I have found your wife weeping by herself after a vicious word from Leah." Arieh paused for a minute and finally said, "And, Father, there is some talk among the Qedarites that Miriam is really your daughter and not you wife. Forgive me, Father, for being so impertinent, but I felt it best to tell you quickly."

"No, my son, you are right to come to me with this. Two problems that I must deal with immediately."

But rather than scolding his daughter and taking his wife into his tent, he ran quickly to Neriah. Neriah, a bit irritated, said, "Even I have noticed both. In the first place, you should have beaten the girl who shows your wife such disrespect. I do, however, think I have another solution to this. Ihsan is noticing that Peleg is not with a woman. He shall immediately marry Leah. She then becomes his problem." The little prophet smiled at his ingenuity.

"The second problem is entirely of your making," Neriah scolded. "YHVH has given you a fine wife, far nicer than the last one. She is a woman of beauty, a hard worker, and kind to your children, even the one that does not deserve it. You have ignored this gift of YHVH and shown Him no gratitude. There have been no words of thanksgiving, and more than that, you have failed to take unto yourself this woman and make her your bride. She is shamed in the community. She should be great with your child by now."

With this, the little man picked himself up and walked away. Talmai closed his eyes and sighed. Neriah was the only one who knew he had left Beulah's body in the street. His response was, bluntly, that it was right to do so since she would have betrayed all the families, not just her own. Neriah told Talmai that his guilt was terribly misplaced. Perhaps it was, and perhaps he should stop worrying about it. But he went right on carrying this load.

Talmai did not have to think this over for very long. He walked to where his daughters and Miriam were readying for bed. He lifted Miriam up by her hands and then picked up her bedding. "Take these into *our* tent and wait for me," he said with a smile.

His words were met with a smile from Miriam but a scowl from his older daughter. He, however, reacted with a large smile for this daughter.

"And you, my dear daughter, come with me." He pulled her to her feet and all but dragged her to Peleg's tent. The leader of Manasseh turned with a surprise look.

"Lord Peleg, may I present you with your new wife or betrothed or whatever we are calling it now. I offer this marriage my blessing."

The new husband and wife stared at each other with surprise. Leah showed fear. But for Peleg, she was a rather beautiful young woman, and he had been without a woman for quite a while now. He turned to Talmai and nodded in agreement. This was an enormous relief to Talmai. He actually hugged his daughter, something he had not done since she was Ester's age.

He said, "Bless me with many grandchildren." He kissed her and quickly left to right things with Miriam.

When he got to the tent, he found Miriam sitting on the bedding, rocking Ester in her arms. The child was crying out of fear of being left outside alone.

"My lord, I hope you do not object. The child was afraid of being left alone," Miriam said with a bit of trepidation.

Talmai smiled at the beautiful sight of his wife mothering his child. "How could I, for an instant, object to your caring for my—*our* child? Here, let us hang this to give her a space."

He and Miriam managed to hang a blanket so as to partition off an area for the child to sleep. Talmai put his little girl to bed and turned his attention to Miriam.

Leading her to his bed, he said softly, "Can you ever forgive me for being an old fool? I did not know what to do with such a young and beautiful bride. Well, I…I do know. It is just that I would never shame you, and yet I…" He stopped talking, feeling ashamed and that he must really look and sound like the *old fool* that he felt himself to be.

Miriam smiled at his embarrassed babbling and placed a hand on his cheek. "I am quite sure you know, and I am eager to learn. Talmai, I have loved you since I saw you bravely leading our men to victory over the terrible Assyrians."

He smiled at her beauty and grace. For her young age, she had such wisdom about her. He took her in his arms and kissed her. That night, knowing full well what to do, he bedded her and felt completeness that he had never before known. Throughout the night, they would make love and then talk. Talmai told her about his love of language. He also told her about and showed her the Gilgamesh tablet. He even told her of his shame of leaving Beulah dead in the street.

Miriam was excited about his work as a scribe, and to his great surprise, she asked him to teach her to read and write so she could teach Ezer and Ester. He was shocked that a woman was interested in such but readily agreed. He also realized that with this woman's caring attention, there was now hope for Ezer. Miriam touched the side of the tablet with such care and such a sense of wonderment that it made Talmai melt. This woman understood his passion and would support him. He would never have to hide his work again.

He immediately regretted telling her about Beulah. What if it frightened her that he would leave her or not fight for her?

Miriam saw his concern and said, "YHVH chose you to lead us away from the Assyrians. Beulah was not only willing to betray you and all of us, she was betraying YHVH. You avenged her death by killing her murderer. In doing so, you saved all of us and fulfilled your duty to YHVH."

Even though Neriah had said almost the same thing to him, these words from his wife finally erased the guilt. For the first time, Talmai realized his *call* from YHVH.

The next morning, Talmai awoke to the softness of Miriam lying in his arms. He also woke to a six-year-old daughter standing beside their bed, looking at them curiously. Talmai covered his wife as best he could and suggested the child go help her older brothers ready food for morning repast.

Miriam chuckled at her husband's embarrassment. "That was quick thinking. I will get dressed and help the children," she said.

"Yes, you will, but not for a minute," Talmai said as he pulled his wife beneath him to one more time make love to her.

The exchange of each other's daughters cemented the relationship between Ephraim and Manasseh. However, the irony was not lost on the two women that not only had they become each other's stepdaughters; they had also become each other's stepmothers.

For the next year and a half, the two tribes followed along with and learned from the Qedarites. During this time, Miriam conceived and bore a child, a son Talmai named Yael, meaning "YHVH is G-d." Neriah gave his blessing on the newborn boy. Miriam had a difficult time, and Talmai thanked YHVH that the women of the Qedarites were there to help.

Giving birth while traveling great distances was difficult in itself. Miriam's delicate structure made it worse. The experienced Qedarite midwives were lifesaving in Miriam's case and with the many other births of the Hebrew women during that time. The two Hebrew tribes were growing in number. A fact Neriah knew was YHVH's will.

When Miriam regained her strength, she set about learning the skills of the midwives, knowing someday they would be leaving their gracious hosts. Miriam's first patient was her own stepdaughter, for whom she helped to deliver her and Talmai's first grandchild: a boy. This made a difference in Leah's feelings toward Miriam. They might even become friends. This also united the tribes for their long, long journey ahead.

Ihsan had explained to Talmai that their journey would follow one of the oldest and most heavily traveled trade routes in the world. This included travelers from all over the world. Talmai was thrilled that he would not only meet people from these faraway places, but he would come to know their literature. The scribe in Talmai would never die.

When the combined tribes of Hebrews and Qedarites reached the outskirts of Dedan, they were met with the most wondrous sight of what looked like a city carved out of the red sandstone cliffs. Ihsan laughed and explained, "Well, yes, it is a city of sorts—a city of the dead. These are all tombs. As you see, some are still under construction."

As they grew closer to the city of Dedan, they were met with a group of men. Both Peleg and Talmai immediately put their hands on the hilts of his swords. They had expected Ihsan to do the same. However, their host and guide did not. Ihsan smiled and ran into the arms of the large bearded man in front of him. After a few words together, he turned and led the man to Talmai and Peleg.

"Gentlemen, may I present to you my brave, courageous, and thoroughly wicked cousin Amro. He is chief of the Nabataean tribe."

Amro laughed a loud and deep laughter that all but shook the ground he stood on. He stepped forward and shook hands with the two Hebrew leaders.

After eating together, the two leaders of the Hebrews, Nabataean, and Qedarite tribes sat and talked. Talmai learned of the people of the Far East with their slanted eyes and yellow skin. They traded in beautiful silk and exotic incense. Amro told of their great wisdom and skill at healing. Talmai fell in love with the beautiful and wise people he had never seen. He finally grew the courage to ask about their literature. Amro again laughed and pulled from his wagon a scroll.

"Yes, you are a man who reads and writes. You would be interested in that sort of thing. Here," he said, "this is of no use to me. I am not a man of letters. However, I am not sure it will be of much use to you as these letters are like none I have ever seen."

It was true that the scroll held letters that Talmai had never seen before, but just being offered such a treasure made him wish to know more. One day he would read this. He thanked Amro profusely. Neriah scowled at what was surely pagan literature.

The evening ended with the Amro and Ihsan trading insults and barbs.

"For all your military might, I do not see you going up and getting rid of the Assyrians," Amro said to his distant cousin.

"Well, one day, if I have time from my *legitimate* vocation, I just might. Which reminds me, I have been hearing of your illegitimate business of pirating along the Red Sea."

Again Amro shook the ground with his laughter.

During the stay in Dedan, the Hebrews learned of the great value of items traded. There was value in sheep and very well-crafted pottery. The most highly prized of all traded items was frankincense. This seemed frivolous to the Hebrews, but the one trade that most disturbed Talmai and Neriah was that of sheep to the Qedarites and twenty young women to the Nabataeans. It would seem that they had a large crop of young Nabataean men who had come of age and not nearly enough girls to provide them with respectable harems. Both Neriah and Talmai stilled their tongues, knowing this was not their place to criticize.

And so the time of parting did arrive. During this journey together with their teachers and hosts, they had moved with the seasons and the calving and lambing of their herds. The Israelites learned these patterns well. Talmai had purchased both oxen and sheep from the Qedarites. They would use the many lessons taught them in times to come. The tribes of nomads traveled through upper and into lower Arabia and now passed into the land of Sheba, all the way to the very tip.

Ihsan's admiration for Talmai had increased to the point he thought of him as a brother. As they stood on the shore of the Straits of Bab-el-Mandeb, Ihsan placed his hands on Talmai's shoulders.

"My brother, you have a far greater journey ahead. From what the little prophet has told me, you will spend a generation in travel. Perhaps we will meet again in the land of the gods—or in your case, the land of your YHVH." Ihsan looked down, weighing what he was about to say next. "Talmai, your cousin is not evil, but he is a thief. He has stolen from me all along the way."

Talmai's eyes grew wide. "Why did you not tell me? I would have returned all and had him flogged."

"That would have done nothing but cause great divide and anger between your tribes. You need his loyalty in times to come," Ihsan said

"Why did you not stop him if you knew what he was up to?" Talmai asked.

"What was he going to do with it, all along the way? Anyway, last night, I…helped him repay me." Ihsan chuckled. "He was not as careful with his wealth as you are with yours. He will find his coffers quite empty the next time he looks. This includes the Assyrian shields he kept there. Do not be hard on him. He will have learned a valuable lesson. Do warn him that others he might journey with tend to cut off the hands of those who steal from them."

Talmai just shook his head. "My friend, what you have given us cannot be repaid. My prayer is that we do meet again in that land of YHVH you spoke of." Talmai looked toward the sky. He then took the leader of the Qedarites in a warm embrace and turned to lead his people on.

There were barges all along both shores of the straits. This was a very important trade route bringing goods from the Far East into Egypt and surrounding areas and taking their goods back again. The barges belonged to no one and everyone. There were watermen in the small villages on both sides of the straits, eager to earn their living by rowing the barges for the travelers. Trade was vital to the economies of all involved. Travelers were allowed, if not welcomed, to use the barges and hire the watermen.

Getting the large number of Israelites, plus cattle and sheep, across took days. Peleg and his family with Neriah had gone first, and Talmai, Miriam, and their children went last. Ihsan and his wife had waited with them. Miriam, holding Yael on her hip, fell into the arms of Ihsan's wife and held her. They said their tearful goodbyes and climbed aboard their barge. They turned for a last look and set off for their great journey. Ihsan and his tribe also turned to retrace their steps north in the great desert, just as all the other Qedarite tribes would do and had done for hundreds of years.

Chapter 11

As her barge passed the Perim Volcano, Miriam could not take her eyes off the angry steam of sulfur rising from its core. Was this an omen of evil to come? She felt a chill run through her that she could not explain.

The Israelites landed in an area far south of Egypt, known loosely as Nubia or Kush. They had been warned to avoid the cities and stay well away from Egypt. Kashta, the Kushite pharaoh of Egypt, was very skittish with the Assyrians conquering so much land and with their close ties to Judah. The tribes were, after all, Hebrew, and they carried Assyrian weapons. Ihsan explained that the Bedouins of Nubia were good people and would help them if needed; however, there were many marauding groups of thieves that they must guard against.

When Talmai's barge landed, he called Peleg and Neriah aside. He told them what Ihsan had said about the thefts. He also told Peleg that because of his thievery, he had lost all his wealth. Peleg was angry for his loss, relieved that he still had both his hands and ashamed that his guilt was now known.

Neriah, on the other hand, was very still. There was great anger in his face. However, he all but dismissed Peleg's sin of stealing from their hosts but brought down great judgment on Ihsan.

With a voice as stern as the two leaders had ever heard from him, Neriah said, "He did not just take back what was stolen from him. He has taken the wealth of the tribe of Manasseh. It was YHVH's command that you gather that wealth, and so that belonged to YHVH. He will not forgive the Qedarites." He then turned to Peleg. "You are the cause of this. You will also know His wrath. You must pray for forgiveness."

The little prophet walked away. Talmai and Peleg stared at each other. Somehow any admonishment Talmai could give to his cousin seemed trivial after Neriah's pronouncement.

The Hebrews had felt great comfort alongside the experienced Qedarites. Now they were on their own and had to put in place their lessons learned, or they would perish. To Neriah and Talmai's great relief, it only took a few weeks to adapt their own patterns of travel. They all felt more confident and were ready for the journey, however long it might take.

They traveled for several months, finding oases and cultivating their herds. It was then that they found the first Nubian nomads. The Bedouin men formed a line of protection much as Ihsan's men had with their armor and shields, ready for attack. Talmai approached cautiously. His tribesmen held their armor at their side, not wanting to look aggressive.

"We come as peaceful travelers. We only ask to use your watering hole," Talmai said.

The Bedouins stood stone-faced, not allowing any passage through their ranks.

"We will pass on if you will not allow us to drink and water our herds," Talmai said, very confused by the anger he saw in the faces of the men he had been told were most hospitable.

Finally, the man who must have been the leader stepped forward. He offered no signs of welcome but spoke in a loud and forceful voice. "We will be gone by sunset. You may use the water at that time. You must stay well away from us, or we will take up arms against you."

Talmai tried to explain, "We are not Assyrians or Egyptians. We are—"

"We know who you are. You are the Israelite tribes that traveled with Ihsan and his tribe. You slaughtered Assyrian soldiers when you left Israel, and the Assyrians have sought revenge. They found Ihsan with bags of Israelite coins and Assyrian armor like you carry with you today. The entire tribe was slaughtered, and Ihsan was staked to the ground and his eyes cut out. A few escaped and have warned us all of the curse you carry. The *curse* placed upon you by the gods. You are not welcome here or anywhere people roam the desert."

Talmai, Peleg, and Neriah stood side by side at the front of the Israelites. Peleg felt the full force of the guilt of his actions. It hit him like a fist. Talmai was shaken to his core, understanding the horror that had befallen his friend Ihsan and that friend's family. Neriah stood stoic. He realized the scope of YHVH's wrath. Miriam fell into a dead faint. Others revived her, but she would never completely recover from the shock of so horrendous a tragedy.

Talmai turned and led his people behind the slopes of the eastern hills. He commanded that all the shields be brought to him. He then set his sons and those of Peleg to work carving a certain design into the Assyrian shields. He called for all coins that bore the likeness of a Hebrew king. He melted them all to liquid and had the gold painted into the carvings in the shields. The rest of the gold was poured into small holes in the sand to dry and then be collected back to the coffers.

After all this was done, Talmai stood before his people. With a sadness that would never leave him, he said, "From this day forth, we are no longer of the tribes of Ephraim or Manasseh or even from Israel. We are and will be, until YHVH decides to restore us, from the House of Yosef." He lifted the shield with the golden wheat sheaf on it for all to see. Neriah stood beside him and nodded in agreement. Peleg stood off by himself, carrying the burden of his guilt.

For months and months, Beit Yosef wandered the desert sands. They fought off gangs of thieves and avoided tribes of nomads. They survived vicious sandstorms and plagues of nits that bore into their skin. Disease struck their cattle, and they lost half their herd. But through it all, they remained strong and drove forward, believing in YHVH's promise of a new land of plenty.

Leah had grown out of her disagreeable ways. She had come to love Peleg and wanted to help him. She had no idea how. She finally approached her stepmother. Things had changed greatly between these two women since Miriam had helped Leah through the birth of her children.

"I know my husband suffers terribly, and so does my father. There must be a reason we were spared, a reason the Qedarites were killed and not us. How can we help our men?" Leah said.

Miriam thought for a moment. "We must approach your father."

The women walked together to where Talmai sat in counsel with Neriah.

"Father," Leah ventured, "when you have finished with the priest, we wish to talk with you."

She then turned to leave. But Miriam took Leah's hand to stop her and said, "Husband, actually we would like to speak to both of you."

For one of his rare times lately, Talmai smiled. It was at his wife's presumption. He would have heard her out if she asked to speak before the pharaoh of Egypt. He motioned for them to sit with him and Neriah. The little prophet also smiled. He was very happy to see the changes in Leah and had long since understood the wisdom of Miriam.

Miriam started right in, "Peleg suffers more than any of us. Leah tells me of his constant pleas to YHVH to forgive him. He would never have brought such horror on anyone. There is a reason we were spared and not the Qedarites. Surely YHVH has work for us to do, and that must include Peleg. Is there nothing we can do to ease his pain?"

Neriah smiled and looked at Talmai, who was deep in thought. Talmai sighed and looked at his beautiful wife, then at his daughter, who had also grown into a lovely woman. He then glanced at the smiling prophet and smiled himself. "Yes," he said. "Yes, there is most certainly something that can be done, and I shall do it."

That evening, Talmai approached Peleg and put his arm around his cousin's shoulders. They walked out away from the camp and talked for quite some time. After that night, the mood of Beit Yosef change to one of determination and purpose. They acted as one because they were.

As the years were spent, the tribe moved westward, following the prophet Neriah's directions. They also moved with the seasons and birthing of their herds as they were taught by the Qedarites. Because they were shunned by all, they were a nation unto themselves. They had no way of knowing the plight of Israel, Judah, or even that of Egypt. They gave all this very little thought. They were the nation of Beit Yosef, and that nation was growing.

There were deaths, primarily of the elders of the tribe. Because they kept to the strict Levitical laws, there was very little illness. At the same time, there were many births tended to by Miriam and now Leah, along with those women that the two taught to be midwives. Leah, strong and lean, had given birth to four more children. Talmai's older sons had married and also blessed him with many more grandchildren. Miriam had struggled through her second pregnancy and, except for Leah's constant vigilance, would probably have died. But she lived and laid a daughter in her husband's arms to be blessed and named Elisheba, "YHVH is abundant."

Miriam's agony at birth terrified Talmai. He would die a thousand deaths before he would lose his beloved. He began to take her only when she was infertile. This was totally against the Levitical laws, which he knew only too well and that he insisted his people follow. Neriah knew of Talmai's transgression but said nothing. Miriam had become the heart and soul of this journey. Furthermore, Neriah felt that because he had no heirs, no other Levites to take his place, it would be Miriam's gentle spirit that would guide his people when he died. He could not bear the thought of losing her either.

When the wanderers stayed in camp for whatever reason, it gave Talmai time to write and read. Ezer was definitely the scribe of the next generation. The father wanted each of the families to have a copy of the Torah, and with his son's help, they did. Talmai also had time to read and to translate the Gilgamesh tablet. His son Teman had become almost as accomplished a translator as Talmai. However, it was young Yael who loved the mythical work and joined his father in learning the Gilgamesh tale. Neriah did not particularly approve of this but could not, or would not, find a specific rule to prohibit it.

Whether the tribe was in camp or traveling, the children were constantly taught the Torah. Miriam saw to that, having been taught herself to read and write by Talmai.

Beit Yosef—under Talmai, Peleg, and Neriah's leadership—kept the seven Levitical feasts, both spring and autumn. Because these people were again wanderers like their ancestors who had escaped slavery from Egypt, these feasts took on new meaning. Most of the tribes of Israel had forgotten the reason for them, if they practiced them at all. Talmai again instilled in his people the promises of YHVH through these special traditions. Ezer and Talmai had even copied Haggadahs for each family for use during Passover and the Feast of Unleavened Bread.

Those that required grain such as the Unleavened Feast and Firstfruits were still celebrated with the promise YHVH gave through Moses to the Israelites of long ago: "There would be a land of harvest again if the people of YHVH's kept their faith."

There were few attacks from marauding thieves. Possibly, it was because they also feared contact with the cursed tribe. But it was most likely because when they did attack, the thieves were dispensed with great efficiency by the young men of Beit Yosef, who were constantly practicing defensive and offensive maneuvers.

Though their warring skills had been honed, the tribe grew careless in their watchfulness. It was by the grace of YHVH that the lone watchman was awake that night. He was, however, engaged in playful talk with a young woman he hoped to marry. It was she who caught the movement on the hills to the north. When he turned to see what had startled her, the moon came out from behind a cloud. Its light ricocheted off metal.

A well-armed army moved very quickly toward the sleeping camp. The watchman's crises of warning brought the whole tribe to ready. The women knew to grab children and pull far back. The men, who fortunately still slept with their weapons close by, formed a strong front.

They charged the oncoming horde. This confused the attackers and gave the tribesmen an immediate advantage. The battle was over in minutes. Three tribesmen were killed; a dozen were seriously injured. The vast majority of the attackers were dead or dying. Several had run off, and a handful sat roped together. One lay quite still. He lay waiting for an opportunity for vengeance.

Talmai questioned the few survivors. They would do anything to save their lives, so they willingly spoke. This was the first news that the tribe heard from the outside. Years earlier, the Assyrians concurred Egypt and were brutal to their captives. There were many such groups fleeing into the desert. When scouts came across large groups of well-armed men, the Egyptian refugees attacked regardless of who they were rather than take the chance that the army might be Assyrians. Talmai determined that Beit Yosef would never again allow itself to become careless.

As the men talked to the prisoners and secured the camp, Miriam and the other women moved to injured tribesmen. They worked to do what they could to heal or at least ease the pain. When Miriam saw that she had done all she could for her kinsmen, she walked with compassion to a moaning enemy. As she stooped over him, the pretender saw his opportunity. Slowly his hand reached for his sword. And in an instant, he was on his feet and rushing with his weapon toward Miriam. Just as quickly, Peleg pushed his daughter, Miriam, to the ground and placed himself in the way. Peleg received the full force of the sword.

Though the pretender had accomplished his goal, he had no time to gloat. Peleg's sons and Talmai fell upon the pretender and killed him before he could withdraw his sword from Peleg's chest.

Talmai dropped to his knees and cradled his cousin in his arms. It was obvious that no one could survive this great a wound. Neriah, along with Peleg's sons, also knelt by the dying man. To all's amazement, Peleg smiled.

"Finally, I did something right. I saved my daughter," he said. He reached a bloody hand to Talmai's arm. "Care for your daughter Leah and her children. My only regret is that I must leave her."

By this time, Leah was holding on to Peleg with tears streaming down her cheeks. She leaned forward and kissed him. He reached his hand to her cheek and said with an even larger grin, "There is no more guilt, no more guilt." He smiled at Leah, at his children, Miriam, and at his dear friend and cousin Talmai. With this, he closed his eyes, and his body went limp in that friend's arms.

Miriam, sobbing uncontrollably, was clinging to Talmai. "My father, my father, if I had not gone over…"

"No!" said Neriah very forcefully. "This was YHVH's will. He gave Peleg the chance to show his courage and honor. He then took from him the terrible burden of guilt. In doing so, He has lifted the curse. We now walk in favor with YHVH."

Miriam held Leah in her arms as Peleg and the three dead tribesmen were buried that night. Peleg's eldest son, Aran, took his father's sword and shield and laid them over the grave. Each man brought a stone and placed it over the grave.

Under heavy guard, the Egyptian survivors were allowed to place their dead on a pyre and burn the bodies, as was their custom. They were again shackled and placed in a wagon. Beit Yosef broke camp that night and traveled on. The prisoners would be released far from Peleg's grave to make their way however they might.

As Talmai rode on, he could only think with irony of his treasured tablet. Like his dear friend, Peleg, Gilgamesh's dear friend and fellow adventurer Enkidu had been killed, leaving Gilgamesh to go on alone. Would the wound in the heart of this adventure that Peleg's death had left ever heal?

Talmai pronounced that the oasis, where they were attacked and Peleg killed would be forever known as "waters of the curse." Because of this, down through the centuries, the nomads and travelers would avoid this oasis, believing the waters to be poisoned.

Chapter 12

From the time the travelers left Israel until they reached the Great Sea, it had been exactly twenty years. Beit Yosef strained to see beyond the Great Sea to glimpse the mighty walls of the earth. They had been taught that these walls held all the waters and the lands together beneath the great arch of YHVH's heaven. Standing before the unending waters, Beit Yosef could only sing the praises of the Creator of all the seas and lands, Mighty YHVH.

Talmai's children by Beulah were all grown with families of their own. Miriam's two were nearly grown. Likewise, Leah's stepsons were adults with their own families, and her four in their late teens and early twenties. After Peleg's death, she had brought her family back to her father's house, vowing never to love again.

Talmai ached at his daughter's sadness, but he had enjoyed growing close to Peleg's sons, especially the eldest, Yehoshafat. He looked and acted so much like his father that Talmai could almost pretend that Peleg walked beside him once again. He was deeply proud of his own children and of his beautiful wife. Talmai was feeling his age though. Time was beginning to have its limits now. His youthful and loving wife by his side kept him from feeling morose about those limits.

Neriah, himself quite old, led the tribe north along the coast. As they traveled out of the lands south of Egypt, two major things happened: the desert sands evolved into lush forests, and the land became more populated. Talmai recognized that this was because they were now near ports of trade. Once the "curse" was lifted, the tribe began to interact with other travelers with whom they crossed paths and those in the few villages along the way. Talmai became very adept at trading and also at gathering news of the outside world. Now he began to feel enormous excitement about what he would hear from those who knew people who came from across the earth.

The tribe moved inland up into the hills. They kept their herds out of the cities but could still see the coast. When they began to see another coast, north across the sea, Neriah stopped them and raised his arms. The aged little prophet made very few pronouncements now. The entire tribe of Beit Yosef stood still, waiting for his words. Were they but across a small inlet from their new "promised land"?

No, that was not yet to be.

"My people," Neriah said with a strength most had never heard, "we have two more great bodies of water and two more great stretches of land to cross before YHVH will settle us. For that part of the journey, we shall travel, not just as tribes or even as a nation. We shall travel as a kingdom. We shall move through the people of these lands with pride and honor as the kingdom of Yosef. Your king has been chosen by YHVH himself."

Neriah turned toward Talmai. "Talmai, son of Ephraim, son of Yosef, son of Jacob, son of Isaac, son of Abraham, kneel before YHVH."

Talmai, as shocked as the rest of the tribe, did as he was told. Neriah pulled two golden bands from his tunic. He placed the larger over the head of Talmai and said, "Rise."

Again the stunned new king did as he was told. Neriah turned to the people and said, "Sons of Manasseh and Ephraim, bow to your king."

A great cheer went up as the kingdom fell on their knees.

Neriah then raised his hands to quiet them. He turned to Miriam and said, "Miriam, daughter of Peleg, son of Manasseh, son of Yosef, son of Jacob, son of Isaac, son of Abraham, wife of King Talmai, kneel before YHVH."

Miriam was just beginning to come out of her shock and realized the life-changing significance of what was happening. She too bowed to receive her crown. Once again, the royal couple was presented to their people. The crowd was mad with joy. Talmai, however, was well aware of the reluctance YHVH had in giving the people of Israel kings in the first place. He wondered if the people really knew what they were in for, becoming serfs of an all-powerful king. He also knew that the kings of Israel had slowly deteriorated into pagan tyrants. On the other hand, he had long since come to understand that Neriah spoke for YHVH and that to obey Neriah was to obey YHVH.

This coronation took only a few minutes, but the change in the people who had come out of Israel was immense. They were no longer weary travelers in a foreign land. They were citizens of a king-dom, and they were on their way home. Talmai and Miriam stared at each other in wonder, pondering what it meant to be rulers of this, as yet, unfound homeland. Talmai lifted the hands of his queen and kissed them. It was the regal beauty in her eyes that let him believe himself a king.

It did not take long for him to bring himself and his wife into the present. There was much work to be done. Miriam would remain the same caring woman who ministered to her family and her people. And except for the plain gold band around his head, Talmai acted as usual. That was to lead his people to the best of his ability to the new land of YHVH's choosing.

His first task was to take his sons and grandsons, which now included Peleg's male offspring, down from the hills into the Amazigh town of Tabnasset. He was surprised that the language was so easy for him to decipher. It had many words similar to the language spoken by fellow travelers and village folk he had met along the way. The Tabnassetians treated his people as equals and bowed and paid hom-age to his crown. This annoyed him, but he soon saw how to use it to his advantage. He quickly sold his herds, save for a few of his most fertile sheep. He used his profits to purchase fabric and goods for their journey into a far less arid and far colder land.

The king then chartered several great vessels and hired captains for each to carry all across from the great lands west of Egypt, to the land known as Iberia. He, Queen Miriam, and Neriah, with the first load of people, boarded the first ship. His and Peleg's sons, the new princes, led the other groups of families aboard their vessels.

They passed a giant rock that jutted out of the waters and seemed to Talmai to be pointing toward YHVH's heaven.

Talmai pointed to the great boulder. "Tell me about this impressive landmark," he said to the captain.

"Oh my king, yes, it is called Calpe, so named by the Phoenicians who traded with us some two hundred years ago. However, most now believe that it is the foot of one of the great pillars of Heracles," the captain said with obvious pride in the marvelous structure.

"Heracles?" the king questioned.

"Yes, yes, Heracles was the giant man-god who was tasked by the gods with dredging out these straits by hand to connect the eastern sea with the great one to the west. We learned of his mighty deeds from Carthaginians, people from the Aegean Sea, islands of Greece." The captain was obviously pleased with himself that he could inform a royal king of that which was of great pride to his countrymen.

Talmai nodded in understanding. He was in a quandary. He knew he should object to the captain's pagan beliefs, but instead he found himself enthralled, once again, by a fantastic pagan myth. Neriah, at his side, looked on with great disapproval and cleared his throat loudly so Talmai could hear. The king smiled at his little friend and patted him on the back.

"No need to make enemies. We will not be here long enough to change their ways, and we need their help," he whispered.

Neriah harrumphed, knowing full well that by nightfall, his king would own a scroll telling the story of this blasphemous creature.

As they neared Iberia, the land north of the strait, the captain was smiling as though he knew something the king did not. "Enjoy your stay, as I know you will. You have a beautiful adventure ahead. Do not, however, make the mistake of thinking you will stay. Only learn what these people have to teach and continue on," the captain said with a knowing smile.

Talmai, Miriam, and Neriah looked at him with confusion, but he would say no more.

When the great vessels landed, all came ashore with a sense of great wonder. The trees and plants were like none the people from Israel had ever seen. There were wild animals, some great and some small, all roaming the land together, neither threatening nor appearing threatened by one another. The streets and buildings were all a gleaming white.

Three men came out of the buildings and walked toward King Talmai's band. The three wore robes also of white, and each carried a golden staff as tall as they were. All three men were very tall and quite straight. This belied the fact that they were all three quite old. Approaching Talmai, they bowed from the hip.

"King Talmai, Queen Miriam, He Who Speaks to YHVH Neriah, and people of the kingdom of Yosef, we welcome you to our kingdom of Tartessus," the leader said in the Israelites' own tongue.

Talmai was taken back by these strangers who knew their names and that Neriah was a prophet on speaking terms with YHVH. He did not wish to appear as stupid as he felt, so he did not ask that question. Instead, he bowed to his greeters.

"Do I have the honor of speaking to the king of Tartessus?" he asked instead.

"Oh, dear me, no," the man who had stepped ahead of the other two said. "I am humbly Isokratis. This is my dear friend Pamphilos, and this is my other dear friend Chariton," Isokratis said, pointing to each of his fellow greeters. "We have not had a king in quite some time. We have not felt the need for one. Please be certain that we do not disparage kings, especially you. We are aware of your love and concern for all who follow you and of the daunting task of leading them to the land YHVH has chosen."

Talmai was bewildered. He had been crowned king less than a day, and yet these strangers knew all about him, even to the task assigned him by YHVH.

"How has so much knowledge of me and my people gotten to you, Isokratis?" Talmai asked.

"Well, we have travelers who pass through our land now and then from here and there. You are known to many. But that is of little concern. We have some very important people for you to meet. Chariton, will you take Neriah to meet his people?"

Chariton smiled and nodded. He then motioned for Neriah to follow him. Somehow Neriah knew that this was a gentle soul who could be trusted, so he smiled and went with Chariton.

Isokratis turned to Pamphilos and said, "Please take Queen Miriam and see that she and the entire tribe are cared for. I can only imagine how tired and hungry they must be."

Talmai grabbed Miriam, not sure he could trust anyone with his wife or his tribe. Miriam took his hand and looked into his eyes.

"No," she said, "it will be all right. These people have been put here to help us." Her wise and confident smile put Talmai at ease, and he let her go.

Not showing any sign of insult at Talmai's distrust, Isokratis took Talmai's arm and said, "And now for you, Your Majesty, I have someone for you to meet whom I feel you will have a great deal in common."

He led his royal guest down a wide street with many buildings on either side. All were white, except for the beautifully carved wooden doors. And they were all very different with strange and beautiful architecture. Isokratis stopped at one and knocked with his golden staff. A much younger man opened the door, smiled, and bowed from his hips.

"Isokratis, you did bring him. I am very honored, Your Majesty. Please come in."

Isokratis turned to the king and said, "King Talmai, this is Zotikos, our talented and well-read scribe. You have much to talk about. I will leave you to your interests." Isokratis then left, closing the door behind him.

Talmai grabbed the scribe's hand with both his. "My friend, my friend, this is such a great pleasure."

The two sat and could barely contain themselves with questions and answers about each other's work. Zotikos talked of philosophers and writers of the day. He showed Talmai maps and discussed how languages had evolved over the earth. Talmai talked of his copies of the Torah and showed Zotikos his tablet of Gilgamesh. Zotikos touched it with the same excitement and care that Talmai always showed toward it.

Finally, Talmai thought of his scroll written by the people of the Far East. This was the scroll given him by the Nabataean so long ago as the Hebrews traveled with the Qedarites. He asked Zotikos if he could translate. Much to Talmai's joy, Zotikos could not only translate, but he wrote down the translation. With this and Talmai's gift for foreign language, Talmai would learn the Far Eastern tongue and alphabet.

During this time, Zotikos's wife brought food and drink. Talmai noticed that this scribe spoke to his wife the way he talked to Miriam, with love and respect. She, in turn, showed the same excitement over his discoveries, as did Miriam.

Finally, Zotikos brought out his prize possession. "This is the story of Heracles. Few people know of it, and fewer still have read it. The writer is unknown, but I can assure you in less than one hundred years, some fellow will take credit for it and sell it as his work. They know enough of the story to have named our waterway after him." He handed the scroll to Talmai, who touched it with reverence.

Finally, Talmai spoke, "How much would such a treasure cost?"

Zotikos smiled at the king. "It is invaluable."

Talmai smiled in agreement. "Well, it would not matter if it could be bought. Our funds belong to YHVH and are not to be used for personal gain." He kept staring at the treasure.

"I said it was invaluable. I did not say it could not be acquired by another. My friend, would you do me the honor of accepting this scroll as a gift?"

"Zotikos, I could not take something so precious from you," Talmai said, not believing the generosity of his new friend.

"I have copied it in many languages, including my own. It would honor me and my family if you would accept my gift."

In turn, Talmai gave Zotikos his scroll on which he had copied the tablet of Gilgamesh.

Elsewhere in the city, Chariton led Neriah down another street. As they turned a corner, Neriah saw what looked like the temple in Jerusalem. It was far smaller and not the center of the city as was the original. Neriah still marveled at it. Chariton stopped at a huge oak door that had Hebrew letters on it. Neriah thought he must be dreaming.

The writing read:

Hear, O Israel: The Lord our G-d is one Lord: And thou shalt love the Lord thy G-d with all thine heart, and with all thy soul, and with all thy might. And these words, which I command thee this day, shall be in thine heart: And thou shalt teach them diligently unto thy children, and shalt talk of them when thou sittest in thine house, and when thou walkest by the way, and when thou liest down, and when thou risest up. And thou shalt bind them for a sign upon thine hand, and they shall be as frontlets between thine eyes. And thou shalt write them upon the posts of thy house, and on thy gates.

The little prophet read it over and over. He started to reach out and touch it but stopped and looked at Chariton for permission. His guide smiled and nodded in approval. As his hand brushed lovingly over the scripture so dear to the Israelites, the door slowly creaked open. At first, one would have thought Neriah was looking at a polished metal reflection of himself. But the reflection was smiling and opened his arms wide. Crying, the two men fell into a long embrace.

"Well, it is about time you got here, little brother. I have only been waiting thirty years," the look-alike said.

"Neriah, I shall leave you with your brother, Aaron. He has quite a large family for you to meet," Chariton said, quietly closing the door behind the joyous reunion.

"I thought the Assyrians had captured and enslaved you back when they took the eastern tribes," Neriah said, barely able to speak through his joy.

"Well, yes, they captured us. But they were fairly lenient with Levites. They allowed us to roam freely, hoping we would quiet the other captives. So we roamed freely right out of Assyria, all the way here to Iberia. We found these kind and wise people who gave us refuge and let us worship as we saw fit. We were even allowed to build a temple here.

"The fact is, little brother, they knew you would be arriving, and so we have waited. And here you are."

"Tell me about these people. Where do they come from? How did they know we were coming? They use YHVH. Do they use it for us, or do they also worship Him?" Neriah was tripping over words he was so happy to find his brother.

"Whoa, one question at a time. No one knows where they came from, although they appear to have kinship with the Greeks. I also do not know how they know that things will happen in the future. The important thing is, they always use these gifts of second sight to strengthen those of whom they have knowledge. As far as their religion, I cannot be quite sure of that either. They have deep respect for all religions. They are very learned people and do not seem to believe in the pantheon of gods their kin in Greece do. More than that, I cannot say."

Neriah could tell that his brother had long since stopped worrying over unanswered questions. He had simply learned to admire and appreciate these people.

Aaron explained that five Levite families left with his. He brought out his large family. Neriah's sister-in-law passed away several years before the brothers were parted. Now Aaron's five sons and four daughters were well grown with many children and even grandchildren of their own. Neriah marveled at his nieces and nephews into the second and third generations. Neriah learned to his great pleasure that his family and the other Levites would accompany the kingdom of Yosef into their new land, therefore giving his people Levite priests for many, many years to come.

All the Israelites were fed and given lodging. It was Isokratis's wife, Sophia, who took Miriam under her wing. Sophia saw weariness about her and let her rest. She then gave Miriam nourishment. They talked for a long time about the city of Tartessus, about the travels of the Israelites, and just about women things. Miriam realized how long she had been a wife and a mother and grandmother. These were wonderful things to be, but she missed having a woman friend. She had not had one to share secrets with since she was very young.

Sophia told her that the kingdom of Yosef was going into lands that had very harsh winters. "You give so much to others, and others will have health problems with the cold. You must also care for yourself," Sophia said.

"I will behave. Talmai tells me this quite often. I do not want to worry him, so I will behave." Miriam laughed, but the laugh was cut short by a coughing spell. "I am getting old," she said. "I get these often. Talmai says it is that I talk too much."

Sophia smiled at Miriam's humor, but there was a tinge of sadness in her eyes.

She then broke into a large smile. "I have a secret to tell you. One day, many, many generations from now, you will lead people to discover what a great leader King Talmai is today."

"Oh my goodness, I will be long gone by then. How can I do that when I am in my grave?" Miriam asked.

"I am not quite sure of how, but I am sure that you will."

Miriam assumed that her friend was teasing her and laughed it off.

"If you are feeling better, I have something to show you," Sophia said, pulling Miriam to her feet. They walked out into the bright sun. Sophia looked around and finally said, "Oh, there he is. Look over there."

Miriam looked the way Sophia pointed and, to her shock, saw a large male lion walking toward her. She had only seen drawn pictures of the beasts. Seeing one in real life was both terrifying and awe-inspiring. The lion was huge and powerful and very beautiful.

Miriam backed up to the door and clutched Sophia's arm.

"He will not hurt you. Here, I will show you."

Sophia walked over to the lion and rubbed his head. The lion nuzzled her hand. Mesmerized, Miriam walked over and cautiously patted the great beast on his head. He then rubbed against her leg. Sophia watched as Miriam lost all her fear and cuddled the lion as affectionately as one would a pet kitten.

Sophia and Miriam turned at the sound of another animal. A newborn lamb wobbled out into the street and toward the lion. As the lamb cried, the lion went to it, licked it, and then nosed it back the way it had come.

"Will he eat the lamb?" Miriam asked quite fearfully.

"Goodness, no, he is most likely carrying it back to its mother," Sophia responded.

"Talmai will never believe this," Miriam said, watching the lion and the lamb disappear into an alleyway.

"He will believe it when he sees it for himself," Sophia said as she put her arm around Miriam's waist.

And so Talmai did. He and Miriam spent many hours together walking hand in hand through the gleaming streets and into the beautiful forest that stood in the center of the town. It had once been a cemetery, but giant trees had grown up through the graves, leaving the stones pushed aside or toppled. There was nothing irreverent about this. All the king and queen thought about were the sayings of many wise men of Israel referring to the cycle of life.

"From the clay YHVH made man and when life is spent, he is put back into the earth," Talmai said.

Miriam smiled into his eyes, and he kissed her.

She could not wait to show him the animals getting along so well. When they found the lion, he was licking a small deer. Again Talmai looked to scripture.

"A great prophet of only a few years past, Hosea, was talking about a time when this would happen: 'And the leopard will lie down with the sheep.' Perhaps we have stepped into the end of times. If so, it is a lovely place to be and not one to fear."

This thought would carry them both till the end of their days.

Chapter 13

The people of Israel were made to feel at home. Talmai was given maps of the land they would travel. Isokratis and Zotikos talked of the geography and climate they were to expect. The young men of the tribe were taught the trades of masons, iron smiths, wood-carvers, and farmers. The women were shown how to make needles out of bone and to sow and weave garments in glorious patterns of plaids and herringbone, as well as dye these clothes vivid colors. In Israel, the only ones who wore such colors and patterns were royalty. *They* were also shown the wonderful plants, both edible and decorative, they would find in their new homeland.

Five years passed as though they were but a few months. King Talmai became very worried that his people had become so ensconced in Tartessus that they would never leave. He feared he had failed YHVH by allowing such a long visit to have happened. Neriah spoke to his king with the same concerns. It was then that Isokratis came to them.

He said, "My brothers, your fears are unnecessary. It *is* time for you to leave us. However, you will find that instead of being quite content here, your young men and women are only too excited about plying their newly learned trades in their own homeland."

And so the day of departure finally arrived. The kingdom of Yosef gathered north of Tartessus. The older Israelites would have stayed except that they knew their journey was ordained by YHVH. This included the king and the old prophet. However, the truth in what Isokratis said was very obvious. The youth of the kingdom were more than excited to be on their way.

Tartessus was no less a mystery after five years living among its people than it was the day they arrived. All the people seemed to stay the same age. To the knowledge of the people of Israel, there had been no births and no deaths among the residents of Tartessus. The Israelites had many births ministered to by the women of Tartessus. There were a few deaths; all were or nearly were centenarians. None of the Israelites can even remember severe illness while with their hosts. The travelers from Israel had learned, as Neriah's brother and his family had, to just accept their hosts' miraculous ways.

"If we survive this journey, it will be because of the knowledge and skills you have taught us. We owe you our future," King Talmai said, clasping Isokratis's hands in his.

"And you have given us great joy in watching your babies and children grow, in seeing your youth learn and experiment with their knowledge and fall in love with one another, and in watching all your generations give knowledge and joy and love to one another. You will be missed," Isokratis said with what Talmai thought was almost sorrow.

King Talmai and Queen Miriam said their goodbyes to Isokratis, Zotikos, their wives, and all who had meant so much to them. Talmai slipped his hand in Miriam's, put his arm around Neriah's shoulder, and walked with them before his people. He gave one long last look at Tartessus, turned, and led his people on.

They were barely out of sight of Tartessus when everyone began to feel the entire visit was only a dream. And so it may have been. The kingdom that had as yet no land traveled north along the coast of Iberia, across the Pyrenees Mountains, into Gaul. They traveled through Aquitania into the vast lands of Celtica. There they followed the long, long coast to finally arrive in Belgica.

All along the way, as they came to the small coastal villages, the young would build structures and make tools for the people. The women would sew and weave for the village, as well as share the medicines and foods of their former hosts. All felt the need to repay Tartessus by sharing the skills learned there. In turn, the villagers fed and housed them.

The kingdom never shared who they were or from where they came. And even though stories of the kind and generous people spread far and wide, their identity became more stories of mythical deities rather than the Israelite travelers they really were.

The travelers began to see land across the water and knew by the sun and the stars that they had turned to the east. They traveled briefly through Belgica until they arrived at Portus Itius outside the city of Morini. As the kingdom of Yosef stood on the shore looking across the channel, they knew they were almost home. This was the land that would be their home for centuries to come.

Again they secured passage across the channel, knowing that this would be the last of their many crossings. They set foot on the land called Pritania by its inhabitants. The kingdom of Yosef fell to their knees and praised YHVH for bringing them this far.

The king and Neriah, along with the princes of both Talmai and Peleg, sat together to discuss how they would undertake this last leg of their travel. It was decided: they set their course, no longer hugging the coast but traveling north, northwest through the center of the great island. There was renewed excitement and determination to reach their "promised land."

All along the way, they again shared their skills and knowledge. And again they never named themselves to the grateful people living in the primitive huts in the few villages they encountered. From those people, they acquired sheep for wool and goats for milk. Their trip was long and slow because, as they had done in the desert, they continued to follow the birthing schedule of their flocks.

The terrain was rugged and the climate much colder than they had ever known. There were many stops to allow the women to weave and sew garments for all to ward off that cold. They skinned the animals they slaughtered to eat and tanned the hides, leaving the wool on the outside. They then turned the wool inside and sewed boots for all to wear.

By the time they reached the land called by the people of the south Pictland (because of the strange and mysterious appearance of its inhabitants), another fourteen years had passed. This made it thirty-nine years from the day they left Israel.

Though the Israelites knew that they had no longer than one more year to travel, they had grown weary. Because of the climate and the terrain, there was a great deal of sickness. Many of their elders had died, along with way too many of their young children. Grief and hopelessness had set in. Neriah and Aaron prayed constantly for YHVH to help them stay the course. Talmai struggled at his age of nearly seventy to maintain his strength to lead and encourage his people.

What worried Talmai most was how frail and pale Miriam had grown. Whenever anyone was ill, she was there with her daughters and granddaughters to minister to them. She often fell sick herself. The king kept his queen close as they walked along. She would stumble, and he would grab her to him. Miriam would laugh it off as being clumsy, but Talmai knew that her balance was poor and her legs were weak. Often he would set her in a wagon or on a horse. She would object, wanting to be close to him.

On that day, when King Talmai felt his people could go no farther, they crested the plateau. Before them lay the great marsh, with its mountain of moss rising from dark-green waters. Beyond the marsh were ribbons of land and water. Beyond these was the mighty sea reflecting the brilliant red-and-orange sky as the golden orb sank into its waters.

"We are home, Talmai. We are home. I could stay here forever," Miriam said. "I have never seen such beauty with these islands and the great sea. This marsh is full of wonders. Look at all the colors of green."

Talmai smiled at her pleasure. He did not want to tell her that they still had a ways to go. She became very still and then began to nod.

She looked in his eyes and smiled. "I will stay here, my love, and wait for you."

Talmai looked confused. "No, my lady, it will not be that much farther. I will carry you in my arms."

There was sadness in her eyes, not for herself but for the grief she would cause him. "You have given me the most beautiful life. I could never have believed that such happiness was possible. We will not be parted long."

Talmai began to feel fear at what she was saying. He could feel her weight grow heavier against him. *No, no, Great YHVH, no, I cannot go on without her.* He picked her up in his arms and sank to his knees. His children and Neriah were gathering around him. The entire kingdom of Yosef looked on.

Miriam raised her hand to his face. "I will see you in the morning, my love." Her eyes closed, her hand fell to her breast, and she breathed no more.

Talmai bowed his head over her, and his whole body shook with silent sobs. His sons and daughters, also weeping, gathered close. The blanket of sorrow fell over the entire kingdom. Neriah, himself weeping, said a prayer to ease his and his people's heartbreak.

When he could again feel, Talmai rose to his feet with his beloved in his arms. He walked quietly but with great purpose to the marsh. He waded out waist-deep. Talmai raised Miriam's head to his lips and kissed her.

"In the morn, my love, in the morn." He then laid her to rest in the marsh she found so beautiful.

His four sons picked up their shields and waded out to Talmai. Each laid a shield over their mother. Talmai turned away, not able to bear the sight of her covered in death.

When the king was again on the shore, he turned to his oldest son, Arieh. As he started to remove his crown, he said, "My son, I have lost my heart. A king without a heart cannot lead. You must take the crown and lead my people home. For myself, I will return the long journey to Israel."

He started to place the crown on Arieh's head, but his son stayed the king's hands. He knelt before his father and said, "No, Father! You are and will remain our king. Your heart is broken, but it beats strong in your breast. If you are turning back, then as YHVH has ordained, I will follow you."

Talmai started to protest, but his other sons spoke, "And I, Father," they each said as they also knelt. And his daughters did the same. Peleg's sons followed suit, and soon the entire kingdom of Yosef was kneeling, vowing to follow their king. Only Neriah stood. He then walked before his king and, with great effort, got to his knees and said, "And I, my king."

Talmai looked at Neriah for a long time. He looked at his children and then at the masses that called him king. He looked back over his shoulder into the marsh. *In the morn, my love, in the morn.* He could barely see the glint of the shields beneath the murky waters. He turned back to his people, and with a nod, he replaced his crown. With a smile, he raised Neriah to his feet. The two old men embraced, and Talmai then pointed to the north. His voice was strong in tone but shrouded in sorrow.

"Let us journey on."

Chapter 14

King Arieh knelt beside his father's sarcophagus. The man who lay beneath the stone slab was the current king's greatest idol. Arieh was there to draw strength and, most of all, confidence from his father, the late King Talmai. Arieh allowed himself the tears that ran down his cheeks, knowing his father would be caring, not condemning, of this unmanly behavior.

His mind went back over the forty years in which the timid scribe became a mighty king, leading people from both the tribes of Ephraim and Manasseh out of Israel and to this promised land. The tears were not only for his own personal frustrations but for the memory of when the light in his father's eyes went out. King Talmai was carrying his dead queen, Arieh's stepmother, into the bog to bury her.

Arieh felt the pain of losing this loving woman too, but with her, he had also lost his father. He had stopped his father when Talmai tried to place his crown upon his son's head. It was only with the pledging of all his followers that Talmai determined to lead his people on. Arieh wore a crown now, but not the gold one belonging to his father. His was made of silver. As Talmai had buried Queen Miriam wearing her crown, so Arieh would bury his father wearing his.

* * * * *

Talmai led them on. Following the coast, they traveled another year after Miriam's death. Arieh remembered the point at which he and his father felt they were being watched. They saw no one and heard no one. The sea was to the west and deep forests to the east. The king and his sons instinctively kept watch among the trees.

That early morning, as they again broke camp, they were confronted with hundreds of dark savage-looking men. There were twice as many of these men as there were of all the men, women, and children of Beit Yosef. They were heavily armed, though their weapons were very crude. What was most terrifying was that they were naked, and their skin was covered head to foot with pictures, symbols, and strange shapes.

The men of the Hebrews stepped in front of the women and children with their weapons and shields at ready. The savages who had held their weapons at their sides now raised them to threaten their adversaries. Talmai immediately became the leader he had been.

"Lay down your weapons!" he ordered his men. And did just that himself.

There was a moment's hesitation, but the Hebrews did as they were ordered. One of the savages stepped forward. Talmai took as many steps toward him. Arieh remembered readying himself to rearm and jump forward to protect his father.

The Pict leader looked Talmai up and down. He focused on the king's forehead. Pointing at Talmai's crown, he asked, "Brode?"

Talmai answered with his brilliance for learning language, "King-Brode." He then returned the question, pointing at the leader, "Brode-King?"

There was the beginnings of a smile on the Pict's face. He nodded, slapped himself on the chest, and said, "Brode!"

Talmai amazed all watching on both sides by bowing from his hips toward the brode. He then touched his chest with his fingers and said, "Brode Talmai."

The leader of the Picts smiled at the man who had just honored him, bowed back, and again thumping his chest, said, "Brode Viporg."

Again Talmai bowed. He then got down to business. He knelt as best his age would allow and patted the ground. He then swept his hand across all his people standing behind him. Finally, he turned his hands, palms up, toward Viporg as a gesture of questioning. Viporg immediately understood. These two leaders were communicating with each other far better than many of the Hebrew tribesmen who spoke the same language. Talmai was asking for land for his people.

Viporg sent the majority of his men away and, with the rest, gestured to his newfound friend to follow him. In only a few miles, the group came to a shallow inlet. All carefully waded across. The waters were never more than waist deep. They ventured in, carrying the children and aiding the elderly. One question was answered when the tattoos on Viporg's people did not wash off in the waters. Some Hebrews questioned if these people were born this way. As they were now in closer proximity to the Picts, they made another startling discovery. Not all of them were men. Some were women; though small-breasted, they were definitely not men.

The kingdom of Joseph came ashore to a great windswept plain. They traveled on a few miles as the ground began to rise before them. They were headed in a more westerly direction away from the steep, sheer cliffs of the shore.

Viporg stopped and raised his hands. He swept his hand over the vast landscape and then, as if offering a gift, reached out both hands to Talmai. The king bowed in gratitude.

The aged prophet, Neriah, stepped forward, aided by his eldest nephew, Eldad. Neriah was smiling. There was a peace about him that King Talmai had never seen.

"We have arrived. YHVH has allowed me to see the promise land. We will be here for many generations. And one day some of us will return to Israel." With this, the frail man who was the voice of YHVH for his people sank against his king. Neriah knew no more.

Talmai held the fragile body of his dear friend close to his breast and wept. Arieh remembered aching for the pain in his father's eyes. The Pictish king also understood the pain and led Neriah's family, Arieh, and Talmai high up a hill to the entrance of a cave. In the depths of the cave, Neriah was buried, and King Talmai said a prayer over his dear friend.

When the group emerged from the cave, Talmai pulled a nautilus shell from his robe. He had picked it up by the bog where his beloved queen was buried. The shell had broken in half. It showed its inner ever-expanding vaults.

"We shall build our city on this order," Talmai said. "The walls will begin here upon this hill over the grave of Neriah. It will wind in ever greater circles until it opens there by the sea." He pointed toward the distant steep cliff at the foot of the hill.

After Beit Yosef set up camp, the women of the Pict tribe swarmed in, carrying baskets of food. These women were not tattooed and were totally clothed appropriate to the cool weather. The Hebrews would find out that only the king and his soldiers, men and women, were tattooed. They appeared to outsiders, naked and covered with tattoos to produce fear in potential adversaries.

In the days to come, the Picts showed their newfound friends where to hunt and where to gather. Brode Viporg discussed with Talmai that there were dozens of tribes of Picts. Viporg told the king of those who were friendly and those who were basically outlaws, even to other Picts. They were to be avoided at all costs. Talmai kept his four sons very close during all these talks.

* * * * *

"Here you are, *Your Majesty*," came the sarcastic voice from the passage of the burial cave behind Arieh.

The king quickly wiped his eyes and turned to his brother. He forced a smile and said jokingly, "What is it, *Royal Pain in the Ass*?"

Teman, Talmai's second son, had never taken the royalty of his family very seriously. What he did take very seriously was his brother's recent somber mood. He chuckled at his brother's insult and said, "We were all above ground wondering if you had crawled in with Father."

Arieh turned back to his father's sarcophagus. "I am not sure that would be such a bad idea," he said. "Our cousins from Manasseh are increasingly irritated that they must build with us and not form their own town. Even the men of our own tribe, Ephraim, are increasingly frustrated over the construction of this winding mess Father instructed us to build. Worst of all, I do not have father's ability to quickly learn a foreign language. I am embarrassed to continually ask Brode Viporg what he said."

"Well, *Exalted One*, I do have that ability, and all you have to do is ask, and I will either talk to Viporg for you or with you. As for our cousins, just let Manasseh leave. Give them some of the stones from our quarry and send them on their way. That is less mouths for us to feed. As for our masons, we have too many chief and not enough workers at our construction site. You know what Father wanted. You take charge, *O Noble Cave Sitter*."

Arieh looked at his brother with both amusement and gratitude. "I think I shall retire and hand the crown to you, dear *putrid prince*."

"Hell no, you will not. Father said you were anointed by YHVH. You cannot get out of that. Plus, I would look as silly as you do in that damn hat you have to wear. In case you have forgotten, not one of us have all of Father's skills. Each of us has one or more. That may exclude you, of course. Anyway, that is why he kept us all so close during those last days." With that, Teman's voice broke. He too missed his father, and despite his jocular attitude toward his brother, he loved his father as dearly as he loved Arieh.

Arieh rose and gave his brother a quick hug and then quickly went back to their teasing. "All right, *Prince Mouthpiece*, I will take you up on your talents, minimal though they may be. Now go away so I can continue *my kingly musing*."

Teman smiled more at his brother's heightened mood than anything. "Okay, but do not be long. Your wife is already beginning to fume, and she will not wait dinner."

Those musings took longer than the king had thought. He was very relieved at the thought of sending his bickering cousins on their way. He said a prayer thanking YHVH for his brother's offer to translate with Viporg. This helpful man was too valuable to the Hebrews to risk insulting by his misunderstanding.

What he wasn't sure of was if he really knew what his father wanted in building their city.

* * * * *

Talmai took the pearly half of a shell from his cloak. He turned it up to show his sons the inside. Starting at the center, he ran his finger around the coil, ending at the outer wall of the opening.

Making sure his sons were watching closely, he said, "In the center, over the cave, you will build a temple. It will be named for Neriah. A road will wind around inside a wall as many curves as that of this shell. It will lead from the temple to the opening. That wall that is on the outside of the city." He ran his finger around the outer edge of the shell. "It will be the height of seven men. Inside, the wall may be shorter, and between it and the road, we will build sturdy homes for our people and places for smithies, weavers, and for farmers to sell their foods. Adjoining the temple, we will build a modest palace for our family to live. There will also be space for the farmers to take refuge if we are ever attacked."

Talmai stopped to gauge the faces of his sons. The one who looked most confused was the very one he was entrusting with the oversight of building their city. He would go over this with Arieh many times, never quite sure he fully understood. Talmai would have to trust in YHVH to see this through.

Talmai was able to see to the groundbreaking of the temple himself with Arieh at his side.

* * * * *

"When I cannot even remember his directions, how am I to fulfil my father's wishes with this most important of tasks—building our people a city?" Arieh said this out loud.

"Well, I can remember. I had the sense to write it down," came a new voice behind Arieh.

Arieh had to smile at his younger brother. Ezer was the youngest brother of their birth mother, Beulah. Beulah had basically written him off as too stupid to bother with. It was his stepmother, Queen Miriam, who had seen the brilliance in the young man. Though he had not talked much as a child, under Miriam's tutelage, he had very quickly picked up his father's ability to read and write. Ezer kept complete records of their forty-year journey and all of King Talmai's instructions.

Although Ezer had never learned the skills of wooing the young maidens of Beit Yosef or even carrying on a casual conversation with other men his age, he had fit into the band of brothers like a glove. His skills were sought by them, as well as many others in the tribe.

Arieh put his hands on his brother's shoulders and, smiling down at him, said, "I am really beginning to feel the hands of YHVH upon me as a blessing, not a curse. What do you suppose Yael will bring me to get us through all this?"

"Oh, probably the curse of YHVH. He is already out with his new Pict friends studying their symbol stones. They are quite pagan, you know?"

"Ezer, do you forget your father's love of those fanciful stories from all different lands and religions? I never saw him lose favor with YHVH as he copied the tales of Heracles or Gilgamesh. Yael is helping us get to know our hosts, the Picts, better by studying their stories."

"Well, it's written that thou shalt not—never mind, you know what is written. What am I to tell your sisters and your wife? All three are very irritated with your long stay down here."

Arieh turned with a look on him that told his brother exactly what he could tell the women. Not usually good at catching subtleties, Ezer realized he should just go and avoid the women. The brothers hugged, and he was gone.

Arieh's two youngest sisters, Ester by Beulah and Elisheba by Miriam, had primarily been raised by Miriam and had her sweetness of character. His older sister, Leah, was Beulah from head to toe. But then again, his wife, Dinah, had much the same qualities. She nagged and yelled and stomped around the house. Had he married his mother? Thinking of the women in his life led him to that last chapter of his father's life.

* * * * *

Brode Viporg had wanted for weeks to show Talmai their very sacred spot. Talmai and his sons followed the brode to the coast only a few miles. Viporg stopped at one point and began his sacred tale. Talmai translated for his sons.

"There was a king of our people who lived here when the earth was young. He was a good and gracious king who kept his people fed and kept peace in the land. He was to be married to the sister of his cousin, as was the custom at that time. He met his bride for the first time on the union day. He feared the worst as he lifted her veil; his cousin had the face of a horse.

"Before him stood the most beautiful woman he had ever seen. He feared for a moment that this was a fairy who would disappear when he touched her. She was not. She was a real woman of such charm and beauty that he knew he had been blessed by the gods. And so he was for many years. The king and queen had two daughters as lovely as their mother.

"The queen had begged the king for years to take her north to visit her mother. She particularly wanted to show her daughters to their grandmother. Though the land was at peace, there was still those who would plot against the king. He dare not leave his kingdom. He knew his mother-in-law was growing old, and there was little time left for her to meet her beautiful granddaughters. He called the most trusted captain of his vast fleet and prepared him to take the queen and princesses to the lands north.

"On that day, the sun was shining bright. Only the captain knew that the sky had been red that dawn. He brushed it off as a sailor's superstition. The ship was packed with gifts for the king's mother-in-law. The king placed his ladies with all their luggage aboard his finest ship and kissed them goodbye. The king stood on shore, watching his beloved sail up the coast.

"They had not gone an hour's trip when a mighty gale blew up. The sky grew black, and wind knocked the king to his knees. The hail and rain pelted down with great fury. As quickly as it came, the storm was gone. The king searched feverishly over the choppy waters of the sea. A single trunk that was the queen's floated among broken boards and oars. There was no sign of life.

"The king fainted and was out of his head all through that night. As he rose the next morn, there were these pillars that stood to remind him forever of his wife and daughters." Viporg pointed out over the coast to one large pillar and two smaller ones jutting up out of the sea.

Talmai stared at the reminders of lost love. Tears streamed down his cheek. "I was once at the south of the Dead Sea. There is a pillar there that is told to be the wife of Lot, my ancestor. She was told not to turn around and look at the destruction of their wicked city. She did and was turned to a pillar of salt."

King Talmai turned to his son and said, "The throne is yours." He looked back at the stone pillars and whispered to the sky, "In the morn, my love. I will see you in the morn." He then sank lifeless into Arieh's arms.

* * * * *

The memory of this was always more than Arieh could bear. The tears flooded silently down his cheeks. Once again he heard a presence on the steps behind him. Once again, he quickly wiped his eyes. He turned to see his wife, Queen Dinah, standing on the first step of the passage. She had her hands on her hips and a scowl on her face.

"I know, I know, my dear wife. I have been a bad boy for staying down here so long."

"I told cook to throw out the rest of the food since it was long since cold." Her face was stern and full of disapproval.

"I am sure you did. But it does not matter. I do not think I could eat anything. This job weighs heavy on me. I will have to admit, my brothers have relieved a great deal of my worries," the king said rather absently.

"I know. Why do you think I sent them down here?" Dinah said with a touch of sarcasm.

Arieh turned to look at his wife. Somewhere deep inside, he had suspected that she was the reason his brothers had found him at this most difficult time. He began to smile as he walked toward her. He pulled her in his arms and kissed her with the passion he always felt when she was against him.

"Perhaps I shall just bed you right here. That sounds better than dinner anyway."

"Oh no, you will not. We are going back to the palace right now," she said.

"Well then, you will just need to brush up on your cooking skills and make me a new dinner," he said.

"No, I will not. I lied. Cook is keeping your dinner warm." She threw her arms around him and kissed him back. "Anyway," she said, "if you are going to bed me, it will be in our bed, not the dirty floor of a cave."

He laughed. *I was wrong. This is definitely not my mother.*

PART II

And now thy two sons Ephraim and Manasseh which were born unto thee in the land of Egypt before I came to thee into Egypt, are mine, as Reuben and Simeon they shall be mine.

—Genesis 48:5 (King James Version)

Chapter 15

Berber, Somalia
Hebrew year 5774 (2014 CE)

Kate woke to pitch-blackness. She turned her head to see the digital clock that she carried with her when she traveled. A pain shot through her head like the worst hangover she had ever had. She hadn't had one of those nights in years. For that matter, she couldn't remember any party or bar the night before. What was worse than the headache was the fact that she couldn't see her clock. She couldn't see anything. There was no light coming in from the hotel hallway or even from the windows.

She reached for the clock that should be on the bedside table, and her hand hit a stone wall. Panic began to set in. She reached for her covers and found that she was wearing the abaya she wore yesterday. She distinctly remembered being so relived to take it off and slip into the short nightgown. She got into bed and—

Oh my God, oh my God.

There had been someone in the room, and the hand went over her face and…and…

Her worst fear came from a movie she saw as a little girl. A man in Haiti was being punished by burying him alive. From that day on, she was terribly claustrophobic. The perspiration poured off Kate's face, her hands trembled, and the panic caused her heart to pound as though trying to escape her chest.

She slowly raised her hand directly above her. If she felt the lid of a coffin, she knew she would die. She was almost thankful

that she would, rather than feeling this terror until she slowly suffo-
cated. There was no coffin lid. She slowly sat up, continuing to reach
above her. There was nothing above her as far as she could reach. She
touched the stone wall and found that it also rose straight up without
a low ceiling.

She realized that she was lying on a rickety cot. She slowly
swung her legs over and let her bare feet touch the floor, also stone.
What if she walked away from the bed, and suddenly the floor fell
away, and she fell to her death?

Too many scary movies. Must never watch those again.

She was afraid to reach out too far or lean from side to side to
determine the other walls for fear the cot would collapse. She thought
that by now her eyes would be accustomed to the darkness, and she
would see some light. *Oh God, oh God! Am I blind?* She felt her eyes,
and some reason seeped through, letting her know they would probably hurt if she had been blinded.

She sat still, not knowing what to do. Who had put her here
and why? Tears streamed down her cheeks. She had never felt so
completely helpless. Even when she was in jail, there was light, and
people were humane to her. The weight of her terrifying situation
closed in on Kate. This wasn't a casket, but it was most definitely a
tomb—a cold black tomb. Tears flooded down her cheeks, and her
heart pounded with fear and grief.

"Oh God, oh God, somebody help me!" she screamed.

Suddenly a slit of light illuminated her cell. She knew instantly
that she was in a stone cell approximately ten by ten by ten. The cot
she was on was on one wall, and a bucket sat in the corner of the
far wall. The slit of light was a small opening in the door just wide
enough to pass a small tray through.

There was a hand in the slot, holding open the flap that kept
out the light. A woman yelled something to Kate in a language she
didn't understand. The voice was harsh and threatening, but to Kate,
it sounded like an angel from heaven spreading light to the world.

"You eat. You not make trouble. I slap you," the voice finally
said and pushed through a small loaf of bread and a bottle or Perrier
water. The irony of such a luxury under these circumstances would

hit Kate much later on. The hand withdrew, and the flap closed. Kate ran to the door and banged on it.

"Please, please don't go away. Please come back!" Kate sank to her knees, sobbing.

The woman banged on the door and said, "You make trouble, I slap you."

Kate leaned against the door, sobbing as she heard the woman's footsteps shuffle down the corridor. Then Kate reached her hand to where the flap was. To her surprise, she could open the flap as easily from the inside as it was from the out. She put her shoulder up under the flap to hold it open and reached for the bottle of water. She took the top off and drank almost the whole bottle in one gulp. Her mouth felt like it was stuffed with cotton. When that terrible thirst was satisfied, she closed the bottle and stuck it under the flap to keep it open.

It was then that she realized that she had a roommate. Two beady eyes stared at her as the large gray rat behind them devoured her bread. Kate screamed a bloodcurdling scream that could have been heard through several thicknesses of the stone wall. She immediately heard heavy footsteps, and the door swung open. Two men all in black with all but their eyes covered in black cloth walked in carrying guns. They were a lot scarier than the rat.

She pointed to the corner and said, "Rat!"

They both leveled their guns and fired. The blast was deafening, and Kate fell to the floor, covering her ears. The men were laughing and speaking in that foreign language. They closed her door, locked it, and walked away, chuckling to themselves. Kate slowly rose. She was still holding her ears because they were throbbing and ringing from the blast. She didn't know what she dreaded most: being in the dark or opening the flap that had closed when the bottle fell out as the men slammed the door; or if she opened the flap, she might have to look at the bloody carcass of the rat.

Never mind that; she had to have light. She found the bottle and again placed it in the opened flap. She hesitantly looked over where the men had fired. There were gashes in the stone but no dead body. Suddenly a small head popped up in the corner and looked around for the bread. Kate found it and held it in her hand. At that point, she made peace with the only other living thing in her world at the moment. She broke off a piece of bread and threw it to "Mr. Ratticus," as she named him. They were friends from then on.

Kate had no idea how long she was unconscious. She didn't know what day it was or what time of day it was. Through the slit in the door, she could see there were other cells on the other side of the corridor. She couldn't see either end of the corridor. There seemed to be one lightbulb hanging from the ceiling. That was the only source of light. There were no windows——no natural light from anywhere. However, that one bulb was the sun and moon and stars to Kate, her source of sanity.

She assumed, when she first saw it, that the bucket in the corner was her toilet. She used it only when she absolutely had to. She ripped a piece of her abaya. With that and some water from the bottles, she kept herself clean. No one came to empty it, so in very short time, the stench became nearly unbearable.

There didn't seem to be rhyme or reason to when the water and bread was pushed through the slot, so she couldn't gauge time by that. Kate ate very little, giving most of the bread to her little gray roommate. Her stomach ached, as did her head. Her lips were dry and parched. She felt nauseous from the smell of the bucket, and she feared sleep. When it overcame her, she woke with a start, sobbing and sick. She often added vomit to the bucket.

The hopelessness and helplessness weighed down on her like the lid of a coffin. She thought of her child and tried not to see her face. Kate had finally resigned herself to never seeing Mary again. She mourned that and the fact that she would not teach the course for which she worked so hard to prepare. Her friends and family passed through her mind like wax images at Madame Tussauds. When Dunc's, Jacob's, and Mary's faces came up, she bent over in heaving sobs and prayed to her friends' God to let her die. All she wanted was peace in death.

Kate wondered if she could come up with a way to kill herself. She might be able to fashion a noose out of the abaya, but there was no place to put it so she could hang. Neither was there anything she could use for poison. Even under these circumstances, she couldn't consider the contents of the bucket for that purpose. Possibly she could ground her wrist on the jagged stones where the men had shot at the rat. It was amazing how calming it was to plan for her death. Would she know if she actually went crazy?

The weariness of depression overtook her as she sat on the cot, staring into the darkness. When the door slammed opened and the men who had shot at the rat walked in, she just looked at them. Her first thought was that with their face covered, they could be anybody. She somehow thought that was funny.

They leveled their guns at her, and she thought this was the end. But the woman who had been feeding her and Mr. Ratticus walked in. The woman grabbed her arm and pulled her to her feet.

"You come. You make trouble, I slap you."

"Can't I just stay here and let them shoot me?" Kate asked.

To this, she received a resounding slap across her face. It was so hard that Kate saw stars. By the time her head cleared, she had been dragged out into the corridor and down a flight of stairs. They weren't in an area with cells now. Kate had little time to figure out where they were as a large iron door in front of her had been heaved open, and she saw starlight. Things were happening so quickly that Kate didn't even have time to rejoice at the incredible sight of stars and the quarter moon. There was a thin line of light at the horizon, which was all sand dunes. Having no idea where she was, Kate didn't know if that was sunrise or sunset.

The woman dragged her down two stone steps and on to a dirt pathway. Her bare feet immediately reacted to the pain of pebbles and chards under them.

"Ow, ow!" she yelled as she stubbed her toe and fell to the ground.

The woman started to slap her again, but this time, one of the men yelled at the woman and backhanded her so hard she fell to the ground, dazed. There was blood flowing from her nose. The man yelled something to the woman and took charge of Kate. He picked her up and carried her to an army-style jeep parked at the end of the path. Behind the jeep was a pickup truck with six men in the bed of the truck and two in the cab. Kate was put into the back seat of the jeep. The man who had carried her climbed in beside her. The other climbed in the driver's seat, and the two-vehicle caravan took off.

Surely, it doesn't take all these men and all this trouble to kill me. Kate was at a loss as to what was happening and couldn't shake the dread in the pit of her stomach.

It wasn't any time before the caravan reached the coast. What coast it was, Kate had no idea. The jeep and truck stopped by a small pier. All the men from the truck except the driver climbed out and into a small craft tethered to the dock. The man beside Kate picked her up and carried her to the boat. He handed her to one of the men in the boat, turned, got back in the jeep, and the jeep sped away.

The men in the boat had none of their faces hidden. They were swarthy with dark skin. They were short and angular in build and wore Arabic clothing of turbans and tunics. Once Kate was in the boat, they pointed to a seat and basically ignored her. Where she might feel that such fearsome-looking men as these were out to rape her, she felt in this case that there was some sort of a code of ethics about even touching her. She didn't want to touch them either.

The boat took off and headed straight out to sea. The horizon ahead was growing lighter, which of course let her know it was early morning, and they were headed east. This still didn't tell Kate where she was. She felt they took every wave head-on, and she was glad she hadn't eaten in some time. She was sure with this bumpy ride, she would have thrown up long before then. She was feeling very queasy and willed the boat to stop. It suddenly slowed, and Kate looked to see why.

Up ahead was a ship on the order of a large yacht. It had an upper and lower deck. There were two men standing on the lower one. One man held a rifle pointed down, and the other held a large sack. The way he was holding it out over the water told Kate it had to be very heavy. She could see from this distance that the man's arm was straining with the weight.

As they drew closer, Kate was trying to see what was in the sack. She knew by this time that she was being traded for whatever it was.

She was very intent on the sack, and her eyes only strayed once to the man holding it. When they did, her heart leaped into her throat. The dawning light let her see that the one standing, glowering at the men, and holding what she now realized had to be the shields of Beit Yosef, was Dr. Duncan McIntosh. For the first time in God knew how long, Kate felt a spark of hope. Dunc had come to get her.

The man standing next to Kate grabbed her up and put a knife to her throat. The other men in the boat raised their rifles, as did the man in uniform next to Dunc. Dunc took his eyes off Kate and stared at the man at the front of the small craft.

"You'll only get paid if you bring back everything that was demanded," Dunc said, his voice quiet but cold as steel. "Unless you want to go swimming for half of the ransom in shark-infested waters…" He motioned toward the sack he held out over the water and the fins gliding around the small craft. He then turned his eyes to the man holding the knife to Kate's neck. "Move that God-damned knife away from her throat, or I'll drop the sack and come over there and rip your fucking head off."

The leader looked at the sack, the fins, and Dunc. He made a strategic decision and motioned for the man to drop the knife. Kate let out the breath she was holding as the knife fell away.

"Now let her go," Dunc said.

"Not until we get everything and he puts his gun on the deck," the leader said with a heavy Middle-Eastern accent. He pointed to the man next to Dunc, who Kate realized for the first time was in a uniform that she assumed to be US Navy.

Dunc nodded to the sailor, who laid his gun on the deck. Dunc then leaned over and picked up another sac. "You put your guns down, and you get this," he said, holding up the other sac.

This was a game of chess that both had to win. The leader knew this and knew he had to play the game to get his payoff. He motioned for the men to put their guns down. They were not happy but did as they were told. The instant those guns hit the deck, Dunc threw the other sac of shield to the leader. He still held the first out over the water.

"I want to see you also have device," Dunc's adversary said.

Dunc reached in his pants' pocket and pulled out his detector. Kate had a quick intake of breath. This was Dunc's treasure. Surely he wouldn't trade it. What he held must be a fake, a replica.

"Let her go right now," Dunc demanded. "And you get it." Dunc could see they were not likely to give up their bargaining chip that easily. He leaned toward the man next to him. "Pick up your gun and throw it overboard," Dunc said in a stage whisper, loud enough for the leader in the boat to hear. The sailor hesitated but realized Dunc's wisdom and did as he was told.

"Now give her to me. You have the weapons, and if I drop this in the water, you will kill us."

The two men stared at each other with a modicum of admiration. For Dunc to get Kate and for the leader to get his massive reward, they both had to win. The leader lifted Kate under one arm as she climbed onto the gunwale. Kate swayed precariously as the small boat bobbed up and down.

The sailor next to Dunc leaned out to her. "Take my hands," he said with a relieved smile. As she did, she felt herself pulled to safety. Dunc moved closer, and when he did, the kidnapper lunged for the shields. Dunc pulled them up higher, and the man barely caught himself from going overboard. The terror in his eyes as he watched a fin glide between the two vessels told Dunc that he would never dive in after the shields. Dunc still had leverage.

"Take her below," Dunc said, never looking at Kate.

She wondered if he was still mad that she had insisted on coming along to Saudi Arabia. After all, if she hadn't, they wouldn't be in this mess. She saw Dunc throw the detector—or the fake, she hoped—to the leader of the men in the boat. As the sailor led her into the cabin, she heard Dunc make his final demand.

"Now throw your guns overboard. Once again, if I drop these in the water, you will kill us. If you throw the guns over and I still don't give them to you, you will come aboard and kill us. If I give you the shields and you still have the guns, you can still kill us. *Throw the guns overboard!*"

They threw their guns overboard, and Duncan threw the leader the last sack of shields. The leader turned to leave, and Dunc called out to him.

"Khalid!"

The leader turned, shocked that Dunc knew his name.

"You've gone to bed with the devil. When you get your money, leave and leave quickly."

Khalid stared in disbelief and then nodded to Dunc with understanding.

Chapter 16

Kate heard all this from below deck where she had been rushed. There was another sailor standing in what looked to Kate like a hole in the bottom of the yacht, something like a manhole.

"This way, Ms. Wallace," the sailor standing in the hole said.

"Duncan, I can't leave Duncan. They'll kill him," Kate said. She was worried about Dunc, but she was also trying to stall having to go into the hole with the sailor. Was this a ladder into some sort of engine room, or worse still, to a submarine?

"He'll be fine. He has more control over this situation than anyone in this whole darn crew. He was great up there."

Kate had much the same thoughts. The urgency of the two sailors also gave little time to object to going back into another black hole. The sailor who had been on deck guided her onto the ladder. The sailor on the ladder stayed one rung below her and kept his arms around her, holding on to the ladder. The ladder was rough, and it too hurt her bare feet.

As her feet hit the floor, she could hear Duncan's voice close to the opening into what she could now tell was a submarine. She wasn't allowed to wait for him. The sailor picked her up in his arms and rushed her starboard. He carried her through the door into what Kate could see was some sort of medical examining room. A woman also in uniform smiled at her, closed the door behind Kate and the sailor, and instructed the sailor to set Kate down and turn his back to her.

"I'm Medical Officer Jill Black, but you can call me Doc," the woman said as she very quickly stripped the abaya and head scarf off Kate. She was running her hands over the fabric.

She suddenly stopped and said to the sailor, "Aha, we were right."

She stepped around the sailor and showed him something in the abaya. The doctor and the sailor nodded to each other and he left with the hated clothes.

"What was that all about?" Kate asked.

"We suspected that they might attach a tracking device onto your clothes. I found it in the back of the abaya." The doctor was running her hands over the nightgown Kate wore under the abaya. "That seems to be all there was. The other clothes will be put back on the yacht."

She then turned her attention to Kate. "Ms. Wallace, I know you've been through hell. Did they harm you in anyway?"

Kate was trying to smile, but more than that, to breath. The "closed-in" feeling was making her light-headed. "No, not physical-ly...I...I can't breathe." Her voice was little more than a whisper.

"You're claustrophobic, aren't you?" Doc asked with enormous compassion. "I'm going to give you something to take the edge off."

"I...I don't want to be drugged. They drugged me when they kidnapped me." Kate was touched by the doctor's kindness but feared losing that much more control.

"It's a mild sedative. It won't put you to sleep. It will just help you calm down. You will stay clearheaded. But it will be totally up to you." All the while, the doctor was taking Kate's pulse, listening to her heart and checking her eyes.

There was a normalcy in Doc's procedures that engendered confidence and trust, as it was totally intended to do.

Kate began to relax, and in doing so, she took back control, the control that she lost, which seemed like ages ago. "Thank you, but I'm all right now. I won't need a sedative."

The doctor smiled and put the hypodermic away. Slowly Kate began to feel human for the first time since her capture. She told the doctor all she could remember about the ordeal. Since there was a period of time that she was unconscious, Kate let Doc Black give her a thorough examination. Though neither had thought so, they were both thankful that it revealed she had not been raped.

This doctor was chosen to accompany the submarine on this mission because she was very familiar with customs of the abductors involved. She explained to Kate that, as Muslims, Kate's abductors would have had the woman at the prison dress or undress her and attend to all her physical needs.

"Kate, you are a very strong woman. I can't tell you how much I admire you for making friends with a rat. You have handled both the black room and being in this tin can under the ocean with courage. You *will* get back to normal." Doc's words were strengthening, and Kate also knew she was going to be okay.

The doctor explained that they were, indeed, in a submarine and that the yacht was a decoy. The sub would be detached from the yacht, which would then be guided back to an aircraft carrier by remote control. This was because the terrorists could possibly send a missile to destroy the yacht. That missile would be guided by the tracking device the doctor found in Kate's abaya. Kate blew out a breath of relief at what might have happened.

The doctor continued to explain that this was a massive operation to rescue her but also to track the terrorist. The US Navy, the CIA, MI6, and the Mossad were all involved. There were even Muslim countries involved because this particular group of terrorists was out to destroy all vestiges of their pagan history. That would include the major museums in these countries and priceless structures like the Egyptian pyramids, structures precious to the whole world. They were also enormous revenue producers for their countries, coming from the tourist industry.

Doc talked about the specifics of this operation. Things had been planned to the smallest detail. For instance, raw meat had been scattered around the yacht to attract the sharks. She explained that Kate was kidnapped by Somali pirates, literally hired by the terrorist. They then traded her for the artifacts. They would now take those artifacts to the terrorists, who will pay quite a large sum for them.

"Dr. McIntosh has been invaluable to all the military and intelligence agencies. He was also very thoughtful on your behalf," the doctor said as she opened a drawer and brought out a pile of folded clothes with a pair of sneakers on top. "He remembered to bring your clothes from the hotel. You will never have to wear a black *tent* or even a head scarf again, unless you choose to do so. We are taking you to a US aircraft carrier. And from there, you and Dr. McIntosh will take a helicopter to Israel. You'll stay there overnight and take a plane from there to Scotland the next day."

Kate felt incredible comfort. Two days, and she would be in Scotland. She would be *home*. Getting her clothes back, especially her shoes, made Kate want to shout for joy. There was also a small travel pack of personal items like toothbrush and paste that the doctor put together for her. Kate planned to get dressed and throw away the last bit of memory from her captivity: her nightgown.

The doctor watched Kate's reactions very closely, especially when she talked about Dunc. She could see the smile broaden with Dunc's name. "I'll let you get dressed. Here are some protein bars. I would guess you haven't even had some stale bread this morning. I need to go tell Dr. McIntosh that you are going to be just fine. He has been very worried about you." She didn't need to watch Kate to know her reaction to this.

Dunc was leaning against the wall, arms crossed, outside the clinic. He jumped forward when Doc Black came out.

"How is she?"

"She is fine. No, she's better than fine. She is a very strong and a very brave lady. She's getting dressed right now and is extremely grateful you brought her clothes," the doctor said. She proceeded to tell Dunc the details of Kate's ordeal.

Dunc stared at the floor with furrowed brow. Quite often, he closed his eyes tight at particularly awful incidents.

"Despite all that, she is strong and refused any type of sedative." Doc Black watched Dunc for a second and then said, "She means a lot to you, doesn't she, Dunc?"

Dunc looked up, a little startled. His mood became a bit dark as he said, "She is a fantastic archeologist, the best I've ever worked with. She is a very good friend…and that's all, Jill."

The doctor smiled and nodded. She decided to let this alone. As she turned to go back in the clinic, Kate opened the door and walked out. As far as Kate and Dunc were concerned, the doctor may as well have disappeared. And the doctor was well aware of this.

"Are you okay?" Dunc said, stepping forward and grabbing hold of Kate's arms. He was searching her eyes.

"Yes, I am…thanks to you. You were rather impressive up there," Kate said with a smile.

Dunc just shrugged with a bit of embarrassment.

"Duncan, you yelled and…*cursed*. I've ne'er heard you do that before."

"I did it to cover the stark terror I was feeling."

"I don't believe you," she said with a laugh in her voice. "I think you were very brave."

Again he smiled and shrugged. He was relieved to find his friend joking and confident and not, as he feared, close to a nervous breakdown from being in a dark hole.

Kate got very serious. "Duncan, those weren't the real shields or your real detector, were they?"

"Of course, they were real. We couldn't take the chance that someone would be there who could tell the difference. We couldn't take a chance with your life."

"But, Dunc, your precious thingamajig…"

"I can make another detector."

His meaning was very clear to Kate. She just smiled.

"Dunc, you can't make new shields."

"There was no question in mine or anybody else's mind that you were more important than any artifact. Now let it go and come with me," he said, taking her hand and leading her toward a room down the corridor. "I have something to show you."

There was suddenly a shock wave that rocked the submarine. Dunc grabbed Kate around the waist and steadied both of them against the wall. The rocking was immediately followed by the muffled sound of an explosion. The fact that she was, as Doc Black said, in a "tin can" under the ocean hit Kate anew. She began to tremble and fight to catch her breath.

She gasped. "What was that?"

"The terrorists probably blew up the yacht. That's why we did it this way."

"Yes, I know. Doc found the tracker in that stinking abaya," Kate said as she hung her head and fought to calm herself down.

"Kate, you're safe. I promise you. I'm terrified of heights. A friend once told me if things get rocky on a plane to keep my eyes on the attendants. If they stay calm, then I should also. Of course, if I ever saw one screaming in fear, I would probably have a heart attack. Keep your eyes on me. I promise to let you know if it's time for a heart attack."

Kate had to laugh at Dunc. She'd never had a friend as caring as this man. She felt safe by just being near him.

When the sub's rocking settled down, Dunc again took her hand and led her into a cabin. This appeared to be a control center, not the bridge but a communication control center. There were four computers set up on long tables. Three were manned by sailors. One computer had a black screen with earth's coordinates, and the sailor was watching a blinking light move across it. Another had a map with the same blinking light. The third had an inset with a tighter view of the same map. This one also had what looked like a moving close-up of a hip bone as though the owner of the hip bone was sitting in a rocking chair—or, as Kate quickly realized, riding in the truck she was just in. All the sailors had on headphones with mics attached.

Dunc led Kate to the fourth computer and pulled a chair for her close to the one he sat in. Kate immediately recognized that it was Dunc's computer. She had spent a good many hours watching it while in Kilmartin. It had the moving hip bone on it.

"You're tracking the detector, aren't you?"

"Yep. I rigged it to track and send long-distant images and coordinates. I can also change it from x-ray to photograph. To make things even better, it now records sound. I figured they would put it in a sack or a pocket, and all we'd get was dark while they were traveling."

Kate was watching her brilliant friend with a smile. He was intently watching the screen. He clicked on several icons, and sound came up. The Somalis didn't talk often, but when they did, it was in their own tongue. However, there was a running scroll at the bottom of the screen, translating the audio into English. The sailor at the other computer that showed the x-ray was translating. He pushed a button, and a printer over his computer came to life. He handed the several papers that came out to Dunc.

"These are the translations up till now," Dunc said as he quickly scanned the sheets. "Nothing but idle chatter…except"—Dunc grinned—"Khalid can't figure out how I knew his name or why I warned him."

"Why did you warn him? And how did you know his name?" Kate asked.

"Because we have a little surprise waiting for the terrorists. And we found out everything there was to know about the terrorists and the Somalis."

"No, that's not what I meant. I figured there would be a surprise. I meant why not just let him get his with the terrorist?"

Dunc took a deep breath and thought a second. Warning Khalid had not been in the plan. He answered slowly as if figuring it out himself as he spoke.

"The Somalis used to be the world's best fishermen. It was the whole country's livelihood. Then all the big cargo ships and liners began dumping their waste in the Somali waters before they entered the Red Sea. This poisoned the waters and their fishing trade. So they turned to another trade, pirating. They have become every bit as good at being pirates as they were at being fishermen. It is very profitable. Even if you cleaned up the waters, I think they would continue with their new calling.

"They are not the Somali terrorists, El-Shabaab. They are businessmen. Often the terrorists use them to do exactly what they did with you." Duncan stopped and gathered his thoughts. Quietly he continued, "They use them because people have more faith that their loved ones will be returned if they comply with their terms. That's what gave us hope when they took you."

There was silence between Kate and Dunc as what he said sank in. Finally Kate rubbed his arm and said, "You're quite a man, Duncan McIntosh. I'm proud to be your friend."

He smiled and then thought of something. "Don't get me wrong, if they had hurt you, I would have led the charge to kill them all. However, what kept us going was that we knew they are good businessmen. Like many Muslims—now don't get mad—to them, women are just property. They knew if they damaged our...*property*, they wouldn't get paid." He stopped, half-expecting her to hit him.

The thought crossed her mind, but instead she started laughing. He let out the breath he was holding and smiled back.

There was suddenly an air of expectancy in the room. The dots had stopped moving, and the hip bone stood up and began walking. Those in the room could hear a loud knocking, a door squeaking open, and a voice giving a harsh greeting. They then heard the footsteps of five or so men walking on wooden floors. Once they reached what must have been their destination, the translator began audibly telling them what was being said.

Kate was deeply impressed, first by the incredible technology that allowed them to hear and see from deep beneath the ocean what was happening miles away, and second, that the translator continued to type word for word in English while telling them the gist of what he heard.

"The leader of the Somalis is telling the man who appears to be in charge that they have completed their task and to pay them. The man in charge says to show them everything and to wait until it is verified. The man in charge is making a phone call."

At this point, Kate and the men could hear the clatter of the shield. And for the first time, they could see that the detector was removed from the Somali's pocket.

The translator continued, "The man in charge is telling the voice on the phone that the artifacts have arrived."

"Can you hear the phone voice?" Dunc asked.

The translator nodded. "He is speaking with a non-Eastern accent. He is saying for the...the woman to verify the artifacts. The terrorists very harshly told someone else in the room to verify the items."

Kate could hear the shields being moved around.

One of the other sailors in the room turned to Dunc and Kate and said, "Headquarters says that the phone call was made to Scotland. See if you can identify him." The sailor pushed another button, and the voice from Scotland became audible.

Kate and Dunc looked at each other. *Another one among them.* Dunc felt there was something familiar about the man's voice on the phone, but he was speaking in Arabic with an attempted Eastern accent. Dunc couldn't pin it down.

"A woman's voice, also non-Eastern, says they are the real thing. The voice on the phone wants to know about the detector."

Kate and Dunc could see the detector being handed over to the woman. As she began examining it, her face came into full view. Kate threw her hands up to her mouth and gasped. "*My God!*"

Dunc's mouth dropped open in shock.

One of the sailors turned to them and said, "You recognize her. Who is she?"

Recovering a bit from the shock, Dunc said, "She's Sara Ross. She's a student at the College of Archeology. She worked with Henry Campbell, another brilliant budding archeologist." Then with deep sorrow in his voice, he said, "She *had* an impressive future in the field." He had emphasized the past tense.

Kate hadn't moved from the time she recognized Sara.

The Somali leader and the terrorist in charge began talking again, so the translator went back to talking. "The men are demanding she verify the detector...or verify it is a fake... She just said it is the real thing. The voice on the phone is talking. He is telling the woman that she has finally done something of use...that she has been more trouble than worth... The woman is pleading that she will do better... The phone voice interrupts her...is yelling obscenities to her and"—his voice dropped in sadness—"and has just ordered her execution."

Kate could hear Sara's screaming in fear, half in English and half in the foreign language. The detector fell from Sara's hand, and her screams became that of agony.

Dunc quickly shut the sound off and turned Kate toward him. "I'm so sorry you had to watch *and* hear that. I would never add to the trauma you have been through…"

Kate was staring at him with what he thought might be shock. But when she began to speak, her voice was very calm and even. "Duncan, there must be a third person involved with our project."

"What? Why do you—"

"The man on the phone that gave the commands wasn't there when the museum guard was shot. He would have stopped it. Sara was so tiny. She couldn't have gotten the guard into the bog by herself. Someone else had to either help her or did the killing. There is a third person involved."

Duncan was thinking this over. He was watching the scroll of translation at the bottom of the screen while he pondered what Kate had said. *Who could be the third?* The translation was a matter-of-fact financial conversation between the terrorists and the Somalis. The kidnappers were paid and appeared to have left since the terrorists were now talking between themselves about how to destroy the artifacts. By the sounds of it, they were placing them in something. There was nothing said, nor did there seem to be any concern about what had happened to Sara.

The translator suddenly gestured to Dunc to turn the sound up. He did so, and he and Kate again looked at the screen. The detector was on the floor, so they couldn't *see* what was going on. They could, however, hear the worry and fear in the terrorists' voices.

"What's that droning sound?" Kate asked.

"Exactly," Dunc said. "The droning sound is a drone. It's the surprise I was talking about."

There was then an explosion. The screen went white and then black. It slowly cleared, and the clatter of wood and bricks falling could be heard.

"Oh, Dunc, they've destroyed your detector."

Dunc was smiling, as were the other men in the room. Dunc looked at Kate and said, "Evidently not. My thingamajig is still recording—sight and sound."

The gray smoke and red flames began to clear, and a bright blue sky came into view.

Chapter 17

Within a few hours, the submarine reached the US aircraft carrier. Doc and the other sailors got Kate and Dunc on board and said their goodbyes. Kate could see the enormous admiration the sub crew held for Duncan. What she didn't realize was that they had the same feelings for her.

The two archeologists were separated and whisked to different cabins where they were interrogated by representatives from the different intelligence agencies from all over the world. Kate was very uncomfortable with all the strangers after her, harrowing experience. After all, it had ended only a few short hours before.

She was especially leery of the agent from MI6. They had labeled her a terrorist not that many years ago. To her surprise, Agent Smyth was very warm and showed her great deference and even admiration.

"Agent Smyth, I can't help but wonder about your attitude toward me. I'm not well liked in London because of my participation in the Scottish separatist movements."

The British agent laughed. "Ms. Wallace, I checked into those charges. I even interviewed Ms. Margaret Hogan, whom you were protecting, when the Bobbies pushed her down. I found the charges against you to be totally without merit, and in my opinion, your actions were brave and caring. If you ever need anyone to stand up for you, I'll be there, but I also suggest you call on Ms. Hogan. She'll march into Parliament for you. I wouldn't want that lady angry with me."

Some of the interviews were more intense than others, but in all, Kate was shown respect. Plus, there was a great deal of concern for what she had gone through. When Kate was feeling she couldn't say another word or recount her story one more time, she was reunited with Dunc, and they were hurried aboard a military helicopter. They would fly to Israel, where they would spend the night at the US embassy.

The agents warned them they were not to talk to *anyone* about anything that had happened, especially about Sara. There was an agreement that there must be a third person among the archeologists involved with the terrorists. They looked at each student as though through a magnifying glass. They were also working hard to find out who the leader in Scotland was. This person was very elusive.

As the helicopter lifted off, Kate could see that Dunc was holding on to his seat with white knuckles.

"Now, Duncan, it's my turn. You are to watch me, and if I'm calm and secure, you know you are to stay calm," Kate said as though she was talking to a four-year-old.

"Yeah, sure, how many times have you flown in a chopper?" he asked, a bit cynical.

Kate looked back and forth as though she was counting and finally said with a chuckle, "This is the first."

"So how are you going to know if something is wrong?" he asked with a lot more cynicism.

Kate raised her hands, palms up, as though admitting defeat. "Okay, that's true. So let's just talk. I do have questions for you."

"Yes, ma'am, what would they be?"

"First and most important, how's Mary?"

Dunc smiled and took Kate's hand in his. "She is just great. Jacob and Miriam took her to your parents and—"

"No, they didn't leave her? She hates being left with Mother."

"No, they didn't leave her. They have stayed with your folks and Mary this whole time."

"Jacob and my father? Were my folks rude to him? I don't think they like Jews." Kate was dumbfounded and worried.

"Well, according to Jacob, he and your father have become fast friends. And Jacob has managed to convince your father that your profession is a very respectable one, and in that field, you are a deeply respected archeologist. Mary is very happy because Miriam is there. Now don't get me wrong, Mary asks for you all day long, every day."

Kate couldn't hold back the tears that ran down her cheeks. She was just then realizing that she would see her daughter again.

Without thinking, Dunc reached up and brushed away a few tears. The gesture embarrassed them both. To cover his feelings, he asked, "You said you had several questions. What else did you want to know?"

Kate sniffed and got herself together. "I had no way of knowing how long I was unconscious or even how long I was held. Have I missed teaching my course?"

Again Duncan smiled. "You were taken on Thursday night, and this is Tuesday. No, you didn't miss the class. You still have two and a half weeks to go."

Feeling more fortunate than just lucky, Kate said, "Dunc, I prayed…well, sort of. I was terrified of the pitch-black dark, and I yelled, 'Oh God, oh God,' and suddenly there was a light. That's when the woman opened the slit in the door, pushed through water and bread, and I could see the cell. I know that she gave me the food when she heard me wake up, but still…" Kate stopped, a bit embarrassed.

"I prayed too, Kate. Believe me, I prayed too."

Kate smiled. She really didn't want to make a pronouncement of any sort of conversion. And Dunc, by what he said, had given her the freedom of saying more or leaving the subject alone.

A little over two and a half hours later, the chopper was cleared to land at Ben Gurion Airport in Tel Aviv. By the time they reached the US embassy, it was 10:15 p.m. The couple was fed while they met with the ambassador and another agent from the Mossad. Both had been briefed on the events of the day. Both realized the weariness of their guests and cut the meeting short.

An employee of the embassy led them to the upper level, where they would each have a suite of rooms for the night. The employee unlocked the first door and handed the key to Kate. "I think you will be comfortable here," he said with a heavy Israeli accent.

He and Dunc started to leave for Dunc's room until Dunc saw the stark terror in Kate's face. Realizing her horrific ordeal had begun with just this sort of thing, he turned to their host and said, "Give me my key and point out my room. I need to be sure Ms. Wallace feels safe."

The employee did just that and left. Duncan walked into Kate's room and smiled. Kate smiled back. They were feeling a bit awkward, but both were sensing an unspoken communication between them.

"I'll check the place out for boogeymen," he said and walked through the suite, opening every door and checking under the beds and sofas.

She watched him make his search, always keeping him in view.

"It looks safe to me," Dunc said. However, when he turned to look at her, he could see the anxiety in her face. "You don't want me to leave, do you?"

Kate shook her head vigorously. "No," she said with a quivering voice.

"I'll be right here as long as you need me. You go get ready, and I'll wait here. You have got to get some sleep."

Kate felt enormous relief with her dear friend's understanding. She nodded with a smile and hurried into the bathroom. There were amenities that let her wash up, but she quickly realized that she had nothing to sleep in. She almost resigned herself to sleeping in her clothes when she spied an embassy bathrobe hanging on the back of the door. Kate stripped to her panties and wrapped the robe around her.

Dunc was sitting in an overstuffed chair near her bed. As Kate climbed under the plush duvet, he smiled and said, "I'll just use the bathroom and be right back." He turned out the bedroom light and disappeared behind the bathroom door.

Even though she could hear water running in the bathroom and see the light under the door, Kate began to tremble uncontrollably. When Dunc came back in, fully dressed, he turned out that light and found his way back to the chair.

He had just settled back when Kate found the courage to speak. "Dunc, would you…would you come and…would you come and… lie with me?"

Duncan slowly stood and walked to her bed. With a voice as full of anxiety as hers, he said, "I…don't have any protection. I—"

"Duncan McIntosh, I'm not trying to seduce you," she said, still trembling but now with a bit of irritation. "I cannot stop shaking, and I just want you near me."

"Oh, dear gussy, you must think I'm the biggest dope around," he said, sitting down on top of the covers and pulling her into his arms.

This gesture gave her back a sense of security so she was even able to find humor in the situation.

"No, Duncan, I don't think you're a dope, but I do have a question. Why is making love to me so scary?"

Slowly Dunc explained himself, "Making love to you is not scary. As a matter of fact, I've thought about that quite often recently. It isn't *making* love to you…it's *falling* in love with you that terrifies me."

"Why would that be so awful?"

"It's not awful. I guess it's just because I've done that before, and it didn't end well."

"What happened?"

"She cheated on me. She cheated three times. Three times she asked me to take her back, and three times I did. Finally the fourth time, she got pregnant and was merciful enough not to ask me to take her and the baby back."

"Would you have done it if she had asked?"

"I don't know…probably."

"What a fool!"

"Oh, I've called myself far worse than just a fool."

"No, Duncan, no…I wasn't talking about you. She's the fool. How stupid and foolish to throw away a love like yours, a forgiving, steadfast love. No, Dunc, she's the fool. She'll never find that again."

Dunc thought this over. Other than his sister, Kate was the only person he had told about this painful time in his life. For an instant, he had wished he hadn't shared what a *dope* he had been. That is what his sister had called him. Kate's statement had made all the difference in the world. Kate made all the difference in the world. He stared at her for a few seconds and then bent his head and kissed her. And she kissed him back.

When they broke for air, Kate smiled up at him and whispered, "Did I scare you?"

He had to laugh. "You scared the living daylights out of me." And he kissed her again.

"It's a good thing there's a blanket between us," Dunc said after a while. "As I said, I wasn't prepared for what *will* happen if we don't quit this...for now, just for now. I feel guilty about taking advantage of the trauma you've been through."

Kate knew full well that no one was taking advantage of her, but she did realize that this was not the time and place. She smiled at Dunc and pressed her hand against his cheek. "I know. We need to rest...for now, just for now. But, Dunc, I cannot help but think what a very stupid person that woman was. I don't know her, but neither do I want to."

"Well, actually you do know her," Dunc said, a little amused.

"What? Don't tell me she's one of the students."

"No, you just met her. She's Jill Black, the doctor on the sub."

Kate just stared at him in shock. "Dr. Jill Black was the fool?"

"Yep, we met at school. I guess I just wasn't good enough for her."

"I'm quite sure it's the other way around," Kate said, touching his cheek.

Despite his knowing it was dangerous, he kissed her one more time.

"Good night, Ms. Wallace."

"Good night, Dr. McIntosh."

Kate woke early the next morning. The blanket was still between them. Dunc was lying beside her, and her head was on his shoulder with his arm around her. He was flexing that hand.

"Did I put your arm to sleep by lying against you?" she asked.

"No, it aches from the shields."

"You were holding the shields by your other hand."

"Yes, but I was slinging them with this one. The arm I held out over the water for so long is so sore it hurts to flex just that hand."

"Oh, Dunc, I think about losing those treasures because of me, and I want to cry."

"And I look at you," he said, raising her face to his, "and I have no regrets. How do you feel this morning?"

She rose up, grabbing the bathrobe close, and said, "I feel like I've been reborn."

"Oh no, now I'm going to have to teach you how to walk and talk and even potty-train you all over again," he said with a laugh.

She laughed as she climbed over him and said, "I don't think that'll be necessary. But now that you mention it, I do have to use the loo."

"Well, hurry up because so do I."

"Listen to us. We sound like an old married couple."

With that, Dunc's eyes flew open—an old *married couple*!

At breakfast, both the ambassador and his wife were there. She was a very beautiful woman with a gentle way about her that put Kate at ease. "I'm so sorry I couldn't join you for dinner last night. I've had this ongoing cough. I hope you had everything you needed in your rooms. I'm going to scold Charles if he forgot something," she said to Kate.

Kate smiled back. "Everything was just fine. I thank you for your concern."

Everyone in the room knew that the ambassador's wife was not there the evening before because the topic at dinner was top secret. After breakfast, she excused herself. Kate suspected there was a cue for her to do so because the minute she was gone, the ambassador turned to Dunc. "I have some good news for you, Dr. McIntosh, and you, Ms. Wallace. A special ops team swooped in right after the bombing of the terrorist hideout. They found your detector with absolutely no damage."

Both Dunc and Kate knew it had survived. Now they were more than grateful that there was no damage at all.

"You will probably be called in to help us get all the information it has on it."

Dunc nodded in agreement.

"I have more good news," the ambassador said. "Evidently, the site where the terrorists were was used for melting metal. They must have put the shields in an oven to destroy them. Because they didn't have time to turn the ovens on, the ovens did just the opposite and protected the shields from the bomb. They have been recovered, undamaged, and have been taken to an undisclosed location until we can deal with the whole nasty bunch of savages."

Kate couldn't keep the tears back. The artifacts were safe. With this news, Dunc was close to tears himself. He patted Kate's hand.

"Of course, this is just one more thing you must keep under wraps until told otherwise."

During the five-hour flight to Edinburgh, the couple didn't mention the night before. What they did discuss was where to take the search for the lost tribes from there. The idea, from the discussion with the students, that the tribes would have followed the coast of Scotland north made sense to all there. The consensus was that newcomers to a land would build with the sea to their backs to cut down on the area they had to defend.

"The problem is," Kate said, "all the castles on the coast and on the Scottish isles have been thoroughly studied. There was nothing there to indicate Hebrews populated the area."

"That's true, and most have been clearly identified as to their builders. Also none were as old as sixth or seventh century BCE," Duncan said, deep in thought.

"What about the brochs?" Kate offered.

"Well, your little round buildings, which nobody knows what they are, could be a possibility. They were definitely late Bronze, early Iron Age. Problem with that is they are scattered all over kingdom come. Jewish settlements don't tend to spread out like that." Duncan was beginning to feel they were on to something, however.

"Could the brochs have been inspired by the Hebrew buildings?" Kate said after some thought of her own.

"You mean some great round building that was all of those things we think the brochs were: a home or at least a shelter for the peasants during invasions, a stockade or fort, a castle or palace for the royalty…possibly a whole village?" He looked at Kate expectantly.

And she smiled back. "Possibly."

After their plane landed, because of who they were, they were escorted through back ways to a private lobby. Kate almost burst with joy. Waiting for the couple were Jacob, Mary, Miriam, and Kate's mother and father. Once again, Dunc had to brace Kate as Mary threw herself into her mother's arms.

"Mommy, go home. Mommy, go home. Me, Mommy, Miriam go home," the little girl absolutely demanded.

For the first time, Kate realized that she had made a home for herself and her child. Miriam had become a part of that home and that family, and this little girl wanted to go *home*.

"We will, sweetheart. We are going home," Kate whispered in the child's ear.

Kate also realized that without her mom's actions, she wouldn't have made the changes that gave this child a home. Kate looked at her mother, who was staring at her with a wavering smile. Kate smiled back, and the older woman approached her daughter and granddaughter and kissed Kate on the cheek. She stepped away very quickly without saying a word.

Kate's father was a tall, thin stooped-shouldered man who spoke with none of his wife's Scottish brogue. As he approached her, Kate realized she barely knew this man. He had always worked two jobs and was never home when she was a child. The only time they spent together was on the trip to and from church on Sunday morning. He seldom spoke, and when he did, it was to her mother. During these rides, Kate was always lost in fascination with the highlands and the lochs they passed in the car.

He walked over to her and hesitantly patted her on the back. "We are glad you are safe, Kathleen. We are glad they did not hurt you." He smiled and backed away.

"Thank you, Father." Kate was totally bewildered with her parents' affection, minimal though it was.

Jacob, with Miriam in tow, had given Dunc a bear hug and was standing close by, watching Kate's family greet her. Once Kate's father stepped away, Miriam rushed up and hugged her. Kate hugged her back and looked over at Jacob. Jacob smiled at her with such warmth she could not hold back the tears. She knew that if her parents had not been there, she too would have gotten a bear hug. Jacob would never make her father feel less than in the eyes of his daughter.

"My girl, my girl, you must never give us such a fright again," he said.

"Believe me, I'll do my best at that," she joked back.

Duncan was taking all this in. He could tell that Kate was shocked at the affection she was receiving from her parents. And everyone was feeling a bit awkward.

The strained silence was broken by Mr. Wallace's enthusiastic interjection. "We have found out that Jacob's family and your great-grandparents came from the same part of Illinois. They may have even gone to the same synagogue."

Chapter 18

There was dead silence in the room. Kate and Dunc stood with mouths open. Kate's mother lost what minimal smile she had. She stared at the floor with obvious disapproval. Jacob was trying hard to keep from chuckling.

"Synagogue?" Kate said when she found her voice.

"Yes," her father said matter-of-factly. "They were probably members of the same synagogue. There was only one synagogue in the whole county."

"My great-grandparents were Jewish?" Kate asked.

"Yes, of course, and so was your grandmother, and so am I."

"Why didn't I know this?" Kate asked.

"Well, I guess I just never told you. Your mother wanted us to raise you as a Christian."

Kate stared at her father and then her mother, who was still studying her shoes and pursing her lips. Kate then looked at Jacob. He looked away to hide the mirth in his eyes. Kate gave him a look of irritation, which made him have to cover his mouth to keep from laughing out loud.

"You are not upset that I am a Jew, are you?" her father asked.

"Absolutely not!" Kate said with force. "I would just like to have known my history, to have known that I'm Jewish."

"You're not Jewish. You're a Christian," Mrs. Wallace said with as much force as her daughter had used. She then realized that she might have insulted Jacob and Miriam. Despite herself, she had grown fond of both the Rubins. She just shrunk back next to her husband.

Kate was struggling with the idea that her mother was probably wrong on both parts…or was she? This whole religion thing was so confusing to her. So much had changed since her kidnapping and, for that matter, since knowing Jacob and Dunc. Neither of them judged her or tried to change her.

All this while, Dunc was feeling very awkward, so he threw in his two bits, "Well, isn't that an interesting piece of information?"

This allowed Jacob to finally let out the laugh that he had been stifling. Still chuckling, he said, "Well, let us get out of here. It is time all of us got home."

Somewhere in all this, Kate began to realize that her father's accent and use of English was closer to Jacob's than to that of her mother's.

Afterward, the Wallaces left for Edinburgh in their own car. They wanted to be sure Kate was all right. This meant a lot to Kate. Despite the fact that she was upset with them for not telling her of her heritage, she hugged them both as they left to go home. Once they left, Jacob took Kate in his arms, and with a wicked grin, he hugged her and said, "Welcome to the club, my dear. I hope you are not too upset by your newfound membership in Judaism. You know it is said that to be Jewish, you have to be related through your mother, so if you want to be excused from the club—"

Kate cut him off, "It's not that, Jacob. I don't understand why I was kept in the dark."

"Well, I think your father wanted to make your mother happy, and she wanted to raise you as a Christian," Jacob said very gently.

Kate laid her head against his shoulder and nodded. With this news, she felt a deep kinship with Jacob and his daughter. Then the thought struck her. "Jacob, do you think I could have some relationship to the lady of the bog?"

"Perhaps, my sweet Kate, perhaps."

Duncan interrupted with a desire to get back to the quiet of his room at the university staff residency. "Could we discuss this on the way back? I would love a beer and a night's sleep."

The group agreed wholeheartedly. Kate and Dunc would ride back to the university with Jacob, Miriam, and Mary.

Jacob let them know immediately that he had been briefed by MI6 as to what had gone on so they could talk relatively freely. They did have to keep to basics with Miriam and Mary in the car. Jacob knew Dunc's thingamajig and the shields were safe. He also knew about Sara and that the leader of the terrorists was someone they probably knew from Scotland and that there was probably a third actor in all this. He too was heartbroken that Sara was involved and that she was so brutally murdered. They couched their talk in far less violent terms both for Mary and for Miriam. Miriam had never fully recovered from her mother's murder by a suicide bomber.

"Have you talked to the students, and have you any suspicions as to who the two players might be?" Kate asked Jacob.

"I have said very little to them as I'm under an order of secrecy, as are you. I have thought about each one over and over, but I was blown away with Sara. She was on the very bottom of my list. So I have no confidence that I can figure out the other two," Jacob said, shaking his head with sorrow over a promising young woman gone so wrong.

"Sara's death will have to come out soon. I gathered it would, as soon as her family is notified," Kate said.

"Yes, I agree," Jacob said. "MI5 has agreed to notify me before it hits the news. I personally want to tell Henry."

Kate couldn't help but wonder if the news would really affect the awkward, brilliant loner.

No sooner had the group pulled into the parking area than Jacob's Blackberry rang.

"Yes?" he answered. As he listened, his brow knit together in what everyone could see was worry and even anger. "No, Director, I have spoken to no one, and I can assure you neither have Dr. McIntosh or Ms. Wallace. They are here now. I have just picked them up from the airport."

He listened for a while longer with the same angry expression. Everyone in the car was watching him breathlessly.

"Did it occur to you, sir, that it would be to the benefit of whoever is responsible for this tragedy to get this information out? From what you tell me, they still think they have an enormous victory. They do not know that the artifacts are safe and that their people are all dead. The death of Ms. Ross simply shows that they can recruit Europeans and that Europeans are unreliable."

Again Jacob listened, but now he was beginning to smile. "That is quite alright, Director. I continue to appreciate the delicacy of this operation. Before you put out the press release, I would appreciate it if you would allow me time to tell the students closest to Ms. Ross of her death… Thank you very much."

Everyone knew that even though he used the plural in students, it was Henry that he wanted to talk to.

"That was the director general of MI6. The press was informed that the terrorists had succeeded in destroying the pagan artifacts, that Sara was killed, and that we traded the shields for you, Kate. They also reported that you and Dunc were killed in an unfortunate explosion on the boat. He thought one of us talked out of turn. I simply had to remind him that which he already knew. The information was mostly false and must have been put out by the terrorists. He was rather apologetic once I did. Now I have to get to Henry before he hears about it from the press."

Kate was the first to react. "Number one, is he going to tell them that we, the detector, and the shields are safe? And number two, will they attempt to trace the call from the informant?"

"Yes to the first and no to the second. It went to Al Jazeera, and they're not likely to share their sources. Duncan, do you want to go with me to talk to Henry?"

Duncan was deep in thought. He looked up and thought for a minute. He really wanted to go home and take a hot bath. "Yeah, sure, anything I can do to help Henry."

They dropped the girls at Kate's apartment and drove to Henry's dorm. Finding out that he was there, they quickly took the stairs and knocked on his door.

"Hey," Henry said, surprised by the visit. He wasn't good at interpreting body language, but even he could tell that they weren't there to tell him he won the lottery.

"Henry, I'm not going to beat around the bush," Jacob said. "You know that Kate was kidnapped and held for ransom to trade the shields for her life."

"Yeah, we've all been glued to the TV. Is she all right?" Henry said, looking back and forth at Jacob and Dunc.

"Yes, she's fine," Jacob continued. "However, during the transaction, we were able to track the shields to the terrorists…" He stopped and took a deep breath. "When we did, we learned who the person was, who was working with the terrorists, the person who infiltrated our group. Henry, it was Sara Ross."

Henry stood very still. "She is a terrorist?"

"Yes, she was the one who shot the museum guard. She identified the shields and Dunc's detector for the terrorists. Henry, this is the hard part."

Henry couldn't imagine what could be worse than his friend being a terrorist.

"Henry," Jacob continued, "after she verified these things, whoever the leader of this group ordered her execution, and she was killed."

Henry stood stone-faced for a few minutes. He then sank to the floor and sat cross-legged with arms on his knees and his head bent down. Dunc immediately sat down beside him. He put his hand on Henry's back and asked quietly, "You okay, big guy?"

He didn't answer at first and then said, "She just pretended to like me."

Dunc sighed and said, "She pretended a lot of things, but I don't think liking you was a part of the pretense. She was a very talented archeologist. I think that part of her deeply admired you."

"I agree, Henry. I saw that admiration while she worked with you," Jacob said.

There was a long silence, and finally Henry said, "I'm not going to school this semester. I'm going to look for the Hebrew tribes with you."

Dunc started to protest, but Jacob stopped him. He had been sitting on Henry's bed. He stood up, walked over to the stricken young man, and patted him on his shoulder. "Then that is what you'll do. I will be more than pleased to have you by my side," he said.

When the news of what had happened hit the papers all over the world, the little group of archeologists were inundated by the press. Police Scotland was called in to help the campus security keep the peace and to protect Kate and Dunc, who had become immediate celebrities. The director general of MI6 made it very clear that they were to refer all questions to the MI6 office and that none of the archeologists were to be interviewed.

This was a great relief to Dunc, Kate, and to Jacob. The only problem was that they were almost prisoners on campus. They felt they would have to wear disguises to go look for future sites. This was a small price to pay for not being attacked by the press.

The day after Kate and Dunc returned to Scotland, Mamun Hakeem Al-Khaldi arrived to begin his collaboration with them. Were this known, it would have been a headline story in itself. Here were archeologists from Israel, Saudi Arabia, America, and Scotland all working together to research the possible travels of two of the lost tribes of Israel.

The days to follow were extremely busy for Kate. There were meetings with Jacob, Dunc, Mamun, and the students, some with security agencies—worldwide. There was also preparation for the course she was to teach and caring for a little girl who was terrified to let her mother out of her sight.

All the students who worked on the Moine Mhor site except Bartholomew Guthrie were going into their first semester of the last year of their doctorate programs. Bartholomew was in his final year in his master's program. Henry had put his last year on hold. For the rest, this semester would involve heavy classwork. After Christmas, they would start their internship. Each and every student had signed up to do that internship with Jacob, Dunc, Kate, and now Mamun in what was now being called the "sheaf, horn, and ox dig," or SHOD for short. This, of course, was after the symbols of Joseph and his sons.

Henry, Jacob, Dunc, and Mamun, with Kate and Bartholomew joining them on weekends, would use this semester to start combing the coast of Scotland in search of the lost tribes. The weekend before classes were to start, the six were gathered in Kate's apartment to finalize plans. Of course, Miriam and Mary were there. Will Elder was also a part of this. He agreed to lend Dunc a van from the Trust to carry the archeologists and some equipment in their search—*if* he could go along. And so it was agreed. Dunc knew Will was anxious to use part of what he found out in the book he was writing.

The brochs held the archeologists' interest because they were of the time period in question but probably more so because they were themselves a mystery. Jacob smiled to himself. *This group does love our mysteries.* The densest concentrations of brochs were, one, in peninsulas of the Isle of Skye, Duirinish, and Trotternish, and two, up north in Caithness, Sutherland. Their first destination the following weekend would be Caithness.

The first trip was on a weekend, so Kate and Bartholomew could be there. The archeologists in the back went over the route and the castles and brocks to be visited that day for the umpteenth time. They finally all quieted and just sat back to enjoy the scenery.

Kate and Dunc sat together just making small talk. Neither had mentioned the night in Israel to each other or, for that matter, to anyone else. They were, however, usually close to each other in thought and in proximity.

The group made plans a week in advance to stay in a motel in the middle of the known brochs, which were numerous. After settling Mary and Miriam in the lodge, the archeologists set out to first investigate the castles and those brochs closest to them. None of the castles were old enough to have belonged to the Hebrew tribes in the seventh or eighth century BCE.

The day before the planned trip, the CIA had returned Dunc's detector. It was perfect timing, and he, of course, brought it with him. He used it to check for belowground structures that might date earlier than the present structures. The few that had substructures had previously been thoroughly investigated. They found nothing that gave them even a hint that the tribes had been there.

The next thing was to cover the other brochs. Doing this was very labor-intensive and very time-consuming. They had to keep looking, but it was becoming evident that they were not finding anything more than the earlier archeologists had discovered years before. Also, there was nothing in the brochs that connected them to the castles or the tribes.

They barely made a dent in the number of brochs when it was time for Bartholomew, Kate, Miriam, and Mary to return to school. Duncan rented a car and drove them back. The group was obviously depressed over the lack of progress. Except for Mary chattering and asking questions, the group was rather quiet. Once at the school in Edinburgh, Bartholomew left for Glasgow. Duncan followed the girls into their apartment.

"Can I use your loo?" he asked with a bit of a grin. He was thinking about the morning after the night in Israel.

"Of course." Kate smiled back. She was reading his mind.

When he came back into the sitting room, Kate was on her computer.

"Dunc, I had a message from the school for you to call your sister. They said nothing is wrong. She just needs to talk to you."

Dunc sat at Kate's computer and connected with his sister on Skype. After a few minutes, he closed Skype and turned to Kate.

"My sister, Nan, is sort of my nonpaid secretary. We have a joint bank account back home, and she pays my bills for me and handles my mail. She said the archaeological department at the school in Cambridge is having some problems and that I need to contact them. I'll do that in the morning, or in Cambridge's morning," he said, thinking of the time difference. "She also got what looks like a personal letter from Lady MacKintosh and wanted to know what to do with it."

"Why would Lady MacKintosh be writing you?" Kate asked.

"She let Will Elder give me a tour of the MacKintosh Museum on their land at Loch Moy. She also gave him a book to give to me of the history she had written of the MacKintosh Clan. I wrote her a thank-you note, and she's probably responding to that. I told sis to send it on here."

"What a thoughtful thing for her to do. It's nice to know your history," Kate said. There was a bit of cynicism in her voice as she was thinking about the bit of her own history that had been kept from her until very recently.

Dunc put his arms around her and laughed, knowing exactly what she was thinking.

"Well, at least you know now."

He immediately got embarrassed, and though both were enjoying the closeness, he awkwardly let her go.

"Yes, I suppose you're right," she said and turned away.

"Well, I'll see you next weekend then," he said.

He was immediately blocked from leaving by Mary. "Please don't go," she begged.

"I've got to, sweetheart. But I promise to come back and get you guys next Friday," Dunc said, sweeping her up in his arms and giving her a hug.

"You promise?"

"I promise. Take care of Miriam and Mommy until I get back." He smiled at his girls and left.

Miriam smiled to herself. She had predicted this the moment she first saw Duncan and Kate together.

Chapter 19

Kate was pleased with her students' reaction to her on their first day in the classroom. She had practiced her presentation to be relaxed and self-confident. She pulled this off very well. It made little difference, however. Due to her fame over the recent terrorist incident, her students saw her as a celebrity. Kate really didn't care what affected their response to her, she was just grateful that, by whatever means, she was successful in getting her beloved archeology and her love of Scotland over to these young folks.

She was all but singing and skipping when she came home that evening. Both Miriam and Mary were excited for her. This changed to concern when the phone rang, and she recognized Duncan's name. He might be calling to find out how her first day went or to tell her of his day, but Kate felt a sense of dread as she answered the call.

"Hi, bad news."

"I had a feeling. What's wrong?"

"I called Boston this afternoon. My dean is very ill. They need me to come back and fill in for him…for the whole year. There are some other problems, mostly some dumb egos, so there is no one else to do it. The earliest flight I can get is out of Glasgow tomorrow morning. I'm leaving for Glasgow in a few minutes. We've worked it out that Bartholomew will come each weekend and pick up you three."

Kate was trying to catch her breath and absorb this news.

"Kate, are you there?"

"Oh, Dunc, the whole year? You're a major part of this project. How can we continue?" What she really meant was far more personal.

"I've given my detector to Jacob. He's now better at using it than I am. Anyway, he has you to help him."

"You'll stay in touch, right?"

"Of course," he said. "Oh, I'm sorry. I should have asked sooner. How did it go today?"

"Fine…until now."

"We'll talk. I'll call when I get home. I hate to have ruined what was a great day for you."

"It couldn't be helped. Goodbye, Duncan."

"Goodbye, Kate."

Jacob called later on to find out how she was. He heard the sadness in her voice and decided to come back to Edinburgh for the week. The others agreed and joined him. Kate was glad to have them close, and it gave the group a chance to reevaluate their strategy. It also gave Jacob a chance to let them know of another kink in their plans. In Kate's apartment that Tuesday evening, with everyone but Bartholomew, Jacob went on Skype to contact Dunc.

"We have a problem," Jacob said as soon as Dunc came online. "MI6 is concerned that we are again being watched by the terrorists. There have been untraceable contacts between Scotland and Yemen. The agency is going to cancel the project unless the agent they planted with us can be with us all the time." He smiled, knowing what he said was revealing who that plant was. "At this point, he can only be with us on weekends."

It took a moment, but suddenly dawning came. Everyone said at once, "Bartholomew?"

"Yes," Jacob said, "it is Bartholomew. He has been with MI6 for ten years, and though he chose to change vocations and study to be an archeologist, he was called back into action. Actually, it was a pretty lucky coincidence that he had knowledge in both areas. We do have to find out if he is willing to take more time off his studies. How about it, Bartholomew?"

Kate remembered the first night in Kilmartin. "Was he the man in your room at the travel lodge in Kilmartin?" she asked before Bartholomew could answer.

"Yes, he was. You were a bit pushy back then, weren't you, Bartholomew?" Jacob said into the computer. Those watching saw a grin and a slight nod of the head from the, until then, very emotionless student.

"As it was, he became very cooperative and has been quite an asset to the project," Jacob said, smiling at his protector. "The main thing is, all of you—and next semester, all the other students—will need to agree to continue, understanding we are still in danger. Well, Bartholomew?"

The MI6 operative/student-archeologist answered with just a nod of his head. Bartholomew was more than agreeable to be with the team full-time. He was not a very demonstrative person, but Jacob and Kate thought he almost became giddy when asked. *Well, at least he smiled*, they thought. MI6 had already spoken to him, and he was on board with the rest. He would stay with the archeologists all week long.

Jacob looked at those in the room and on the computer screen. He had to smile at the unity of support he had already known would be there. Nothing more needed to be said. They did have to bring Mamun up to date on all that went on in Kilmartin. Being there, of course, he knew what happened in Saudi Arabia.

Kate decided that with her newfound occupation, she could afford to buy a car and drive the three of her household to the site each Friday night. There had been some question as to whether Jacob or Kate wanted to have their daughters at the sites with this current threat. However, both felt that since the terrorists had already used kidnapping, they felt more secure with the girls with them, especially under Bartholomew's watch. They knew they were very secure on the campus during the week.

Duncan called Kate the next evening. "I wanted to know more about your class Monday. I have been thinking about it all week."

"There's not much to tell except the students were very receptive. I do think it had more to do with their interest in our adventure in Somalia. I got several questions about you. I think you have a budding fan club here. I wish I could tell you this in person."

"I know. I feel the same way." He completely ignored the fan-club statement because it embarrassed him.

"How are things at your school?"

"It's a big mess. I just hope the dean gets well fast."

Kate could hear the frustration and irritation in his voice. Dunc promised to call often and said good-night. Duncan was missed. He was in constant contact with Jacob, Kate, and the group as a whole. But his presence was missed. Kate stayed very busy to fill the void he left.

It took eight weeks in total for the group to investigate all the brochs in Northern Scotland. Jacob went over the inside and out of each structure with Duncan's detector. The group felt that there was nothing that led them to think that Hebrew tribes had been there. Jacob kept spirits up by reminding them that archeology was 90 percent looking, 9 percent wanting to give up, and 1 percent finding what they were looking for. An aspiring archeologist must accept this or find another occupation.

Kate and Duncan spoke to each other alone often. She told him of the students' frustration. "I hope they don't give up," she said.

"Oh, I wouldn't worry about that. They're made of tougher stuff than that."

"I know. I guess I'm just putting my feelings on them… I wish you were here."

"I do too, Kate. I do too."

There was a minute of uncomfortable silence.

"Oh, Duncan, I forgot. The school called and asked what to do with your mail. It's been piling up. I told them just to send it on to you. I gave them Lady MacKintosh's letter to send with the rest."

"I'm sorry, Kate. You're breaking up. I didn't get that."

"Can you hear me now?"

"I can't get what you're saying. We better hang up for now."

"Goodbye, Duncan." And the line went dead.

A repositioning meeting was held at the Edinburgh campus on a late October weekend. Several of the other doctoral students were also there. Matt Douglas and Hannah Sinclair had their reasons for wanting to join this part of the exploration. Kate imagined Matt didn't want much exploration to happen without his input. Since Duncan was away, Kate was sure the egotistical young man had visions of his stepping into a leadership role.

Hannah had been up front and clear that she had some ideas on excavating on the peninsulas of Skye. She knew the isle very well. Even though she spent most of her life in England, she was born on Skye and visited grandparents there her whole life. She found it intriguing. Anyway, she was chomping at the bit to get back to work with this group even if it was just on weekends.

Kate didn't know Matt's intent. She just hoped it wasn't to try and seduce her. She was uncomfortable around him from the very start. She thought that possibly Duncan being away might have inspired Matt.

Despite misgivings about Matt, Kate felt wonderful about the large group who filled the meeting room of the university. Jacob had set up a screen that projected Duncan, who joined the group by Skype. Kate smiled at the life-size Duncan McIntosh, knowing she was just one of a crowd on his small computer screen. She wondered if Jacob had enlarged his presence to impress on Matt that Dunc was still the leader.

"We're glad you could join us, Dr. McIntosh. Our group has expanded, as you can see," Jacob said.

Duncan smiled out at the group.

"There are some introductions in order for this meeting," Jacob said. He presented Mamun to Hannah and Matt. Kate thought Matt looked a little downcast at the addition of another renowned archeologist.

Mamun had an introduction of his own. While back in Saudi Arabia, he had met and married a young woman who recently joined his archeology team. Mamun arranged for her to join him in Scotland. Joodi was a slight young woman in her late twenties. She was soft-spoken and shy. She grew up in England, her father being an archeology professor in Edinburgh. He retired recently and moved the family back to their home just outside of Riyadh.

Kate immediately liked her. But she did wonder if this rather quick marriage was so Joodi could get away from the stringent restrictions on women in Saudi Arabia and back to the far more liberal British Isles. Joodi was welcomed by all, and Kate felt she fit in well despite her shyness.

Jacob then brought out a large map of the Isle of Skye. Most prominent were the two peninsulas of Trotternish and Duirinish. There were many black dots that located the brochs on those two areas. He then zeroed in on two prominent stone monuments and one castle.

"These structures have been of interest to both Kate and I," Jacob said. "The first one is on northeast Trotternish. It is the Kilt Rock. These basalt columns are the smooth cliff walls that drop to the sea. They remind all of the folds of the tartan kilts worn by Scottish noblemen of old. Although not man-made, they have inspired many legends through the centuries—and may have inspired the brochs. Or they may have inspired the structure the brochs were modeled after.

"There are no castle ruins on them and therefore no excavations. We have the capacity of excavating without turning over a spoonful of dirt. We have the DAM Detector. This is where we begin." Jacob smiled at a proud Duncan McIntosh.

He went on, "The next point of interest to us is Castle Duntulm near the hamlet of Duntulm. The building of the castle was begun in the thirteenth or fourteenth century. During the sixteenth century, it was the home of the chief of Clan MacDonald of Sleat. It was passed down to generations of clan chiefs with several renovations over the years. It was finally abandoned in 1732. However, the most important thing to us is its prehistoric past. There is thought that there was a broch or a fort here that goes back to the fifth century BCE. It was called Dhaibhidh. *Dhaibhidh* is Gaelic for—'David.'"

Jacob stood with a mischievous grin.

Most but Bartholomew stared at him with excitement and some shock.

The man that Kate now thought of primarily as an agent of MI6 stated emphatically, "If we are thinking that it was named for King David, he was of the tribe of Judah, which was not lost. It was in the kingdom of Judah, which was allied with the Assyrians."

This man seldom spoke, so his biblical knowledge was a surprise to all. Kate had a new respect for him. He really was a learned historian and archeologist.

"Ah yes, my young man, but David was the greatest of the Hebrew kings, and he reigned over an *undivided* kingdom," Jacob said, clapping Bartholomew on the back. "It is possible that a tribe of Beit Yosef took on the name and its symbols. Certainly, the Lion of Judah was far more impressive than an ox, a horn, or a sheaf of wheat."

"Then why didn't we start here first?" Bartholomew asked.

"I just found out about it two days ago. I started using Kate's Gaelic-to-English dictionary," Jacob said, full of contrition. Jacob went on, "The third area of interest is on the southern tip of the Duirinish peninsula. It is the stone structures called the MacLeod's Maidens, named after the ancient Chief MacLeod, whose wife and two daughters were lost at sea. There are ruins of a castle just south-west of there called Dunnasgual.

"I'll have to admit that Kate and I are presuming a lot here. There is nothing but a sense of intuition that a king, who left his lost queen in a bog farther south, may have found comfort in rock statues that reminded another leader centuries later of a lost wife and daughters. There is also the fact that much of the area is uninhabit-able because of the very boggy landscape."

This time, Matt objected, "Is this really enough to go on? Will we just be spinning our wheels like you did in North Scotland?"

Many were angered by his blunt questions, but not Jacob. "That's an important question, Matt. MacLeod's Maidens may be just that, and that is why we are going to the Kilt Rock first. I don't think North Scotland was just spinning our wheels though. Even if we find something here, we would have to follow all leads to where else the tribes might have settled."

Matt nodded his head in agreement but still showed doubt of Jacob's, and especially Kate's, reasoning. The rest marveled at Jacob's ability to keep even the most disagreeable among them involved.

"What does *Dunnasgual* mean?" Dunc asked from the screen.

"I'll let our Gaelic expert answer that," Jacob said, turning to Kate.

She stepped forward. "Normally, it would be three words. *Dun* is 'fort.' *Gual* is 'coal.' And *nas*—*nas*, however, is a little more difficult. It is part of a compound word for 'great' or 'greater than', *nas motha*. Many times, as Gaelic names were written by the English, words have been dropped, misspelled, or otherwise bastardized. I think what it was meant to be called was 'Fort Great Coal' because of the large degree of boggy land around here. Remember the peat from the bogs is dried and burned, providing much of the fuel for this area. Peat is often called Scotland's *coal*."

And so it was decided. The following weekend, a much larger crowd followed their instincts to the Isle of Skye. It was, therefore, in two separate vans: one for those there all week and one for the weekenders, the latter driven by Hannah. Kate was thankful not to have to spend so much on petrol.

Lodging had been secured, as well as areas for research and storage. They didn't have the permission for an actual dig but did have all the required paperwork to stake out areas to work on with Dunc's detector. This was in areas usually forbidden to the public.

The air in the buses was one of expectancy. Once the archeologists stepped out onto the plain atop Kilt Rock, they were all struck with awe at the vista before them: the endless sky above, the raging sea below, and the sheer cliffs of unimaginable heights. Their perfect rounded shape that reminded ancients of the folds of a kilt looked to modern folks that they must have been carved or built by modern machinery.

It took some time to come down from the exhilaration of this sight. When they did, they all eagerly began unloading equipment and setting up tents to begin their search.

Matt ran over to Kate the minute she stepped out of the van. He gave her a quick hug and said, "It sure will be good working with you again."

Kate smiled awkwardly and pulled away from him. She moved close to Jacob, who placed himself between them, seeming to understand her predicament.

Throughout Saturday, the group, starting near the cliffs, worked in an ever-widening arc with the detector, covering every foot of ground. Once again, the job was laborious and slow. And once again, they found nothing to suggest ancient Hebrews were there or, for that matter, anyone else. Three o'clock that afternoon, it was a unanimous decision to move on to the McDonald castle ruins. They packed up in record time and set out for the second site.

The minute Kate set foot near the castle ruins, she stopped dead still.

"I don't think we are there yet, but there is something here that will lead us to our goal," she whispered to Jacob.

He was nodding his head. "I feel it too. There is something about this whole area that intrigues me."

The group immediately went to work. They moved the detector over the ruins and then slowly outside toward the cliffs that dropped to the sea. By that Sunday afternoon, disappointment over yet another defeat was overtaking the group. Most of the weekenders were looking at packing up, ready to leave.

That was until Kate yelled, "Mark!"

Jacob, with tired, trembling hands and arms frozen in place, held the detector as still as possible. Everyone gathered around the computer. With Jacob following Kate's directions, the onlookers saw an emerging curved wall of stone beneath the surface. There was only about six feet of the wall. However, in calculating a circle from the curve of this wall, the detector found another length, slightly longer than the first, about four hundred feet away. If these two walls were joined in a continuous circle, the wall would encompass quite a large castle or a moderate-size walled city. The circle would include the ruins of Castle Duntulm.

The wall was only about three feet beneath the surface. Henry sank to his knees and started asking for different shape trowels. Taking the tools, and with the precision that always astonished the others, he cut down to the stone. He cut out a block of earth about four feet long and three feet wide. Henry lifted the entire block in one piece and laid it aside. This uncovered the top of the wall.

The wall was two rows of stones. Each of the large stones were one and a half feet wide by a little less than a yard long. The stones were staggered side by side to one another. With a small rotary saw, Henry cut out a thin layer of rock about three centimeters long. He replaced the plod of ground and repeated the entire process at the other length of wall. When Henry was finished, no one could tell the ground had been disturbed.

Kate gathered the pieces in bags and carefully labeled them. Going over them with the detector showed a surprising find. There was a slight difference in the makeup. They were both basalt, but a difference like this usually meant that they came from different quarries.

Jacob remembered there was a traveler's guide station down the rode a ways. It was also stone. He, Henry, and Kate drove down and spoke to the keeper. The elderly groundskeeper knew where the stones of the station had been quarried.

"There be three main quarries on the isle. They're all farther southeast. They dig for marble and slate. This old building is a low grade of marble," he said with such a heavy brogue that even Kate had trouble understanding him.

"If ye got that there basalt, then them builders dug it up close tae their buildings. And the holes they left have ere since been covered ore."

This would, to most, have seemed a discouraging end. To these professional and experienced archeologists, this was rather an exciting clue. The fact of two different ancient quarries spoke of a split in culture with this group having carried building blocks to a new land to begin a new and separate life. At some point, would the *sheaf* have again become the *ox* and the *horn*—or one of those and the *Lion of Judah*?

This was, without a doubt, an area for further exploration. Will Elder was contacted and immediately set out to acquire the necessary permits. The archeologists were again feeling that success was in sight. This was despite the fact that, except for the ancient name, nothing there pointed to Hebrew occupation. There was still determination to visit Dunnasgual. If there was a split in Beit Yosef, the other tribe was somewhere else.

This weekend trip had some disappointing moments for Kate. She noticed that Matt was quiet and didn't join the conversation with the others of "what might be." She was also aggravated over him pushing himself in beside her. She would counsel with Hannah as to a way to sit up with her on the next trip.

The archeological finds were reported to Duncan that afternoon. And all could see the excitement in the young man's face. Kate and Jacob saw something else. It was an attitude of determination. Determination to *what*?

Chapter 20

The weekenders left later than usual that Sunday evening. The whole trip back was full of speculation about what their find could mean. Kate had brought back the samples of rock. She wanted to use the high-powered microscopes at the school lab to determine if there was any organic material in the mortar that held the stones together. There was almost no chance that she could find enough to actually date the material. However, if she could identify even the slightest amount, they would look for more when the group got the permission to start the dig.

Trips to the lab meant little sleep for Kate. It would insist on an early-morning rise to get her and the girls ready for the day, a long day in class, an evening of preparing for the next day or grading papers, and only then a late night visit to the lab.

The walk to the lab was always dark and lonely. The halls were eerie and quiet. When she sat at the microscope in the darkened room, every creak of the old building, even the whisper of a breeze outside, rattled her nerves. It made it hard for her to concentrate.

This night, she thought she heard footsteps. They would have been on the stairs at the end of the hall. Kate stopped and listened but heard no more. She scolded herself for being paranoid and went back to work with the microscope. Then there was what sounded like a door creaking. Of all the usual creaks she heard all week long, this one was louder and closer.

She sat up, trying hard not panic and trying hard to breathe. Then she felt, rather than heard, the presence of the person behind her. She turned with paralyzing fear to see the outline of a man in the doorway. Was it Matt? Was it another abductor? She couldn't get out the scream that she desperately wanted to and didn't recognize him until he had grabbed her wrist and pulled her away from her seat at the microscope.

In the few seconds it took for Kate to react to his powerful embrace and kiss, Duncan McIntosh called himself every name in the book—*dope, imbecile, moron, fool*—for being so impetuous. Then Kate wrapped her arms around him and kissed him back.

When he finally let her breathe, she laughed and said, "Well, I'm glad to see you too, Duncan, despite the fact you scared the *bloody hell* out of me."

He stood back and said, "I'm sorry I scared you, but I had to…to tell you…I…love you. And yes, it scares me to death. I've missed you terribly. I can't be away from you for another four months or another day. I…I want you to marry me. Or you don't have to marry me. If you'll just date me…I mean…oh, geez! I'm so crummy at this. I—"

Kate laughed. Her heart was finally slowing its pounding. She placed a finger to his lips. "Duncan. I love you too. I've missed you terribly. And yes, I will date you. And yes, I will marry you. But you have to remember one thing."

"What's that?" he asked with apprehension.

"It's that I come, as you Americans say, as a package deal."

"A *what*?"

"A package deal. Duncan, I come with…Mary."

"Well, of course, you do. Should I ask her to be my daughter?"

"No." Kate laughed. "We'll *tell* her. Anyway, she's mad at you right now."

"What did I do?"

"It isn't what you did. It's what you didn't do. You didn't come back the next week, like you promised."

Duncan looked devastated. It hurt his heart that he hadn't kept his promise to this little one. "I'd never lie to her."

"I know, and I've told her so. It's just that she loves you almost as much as I do. It's a lot easier to be mad than to be heart sick. She may be angry at first, but then she'll be so glad to see you. And then to find out you're going to be her *da*. She'll be beyond joy."

She put her arms around him and reveled in the thought that they were finally speaking of their true feelings to each other. They gathered the stones and walked back to Kate's apartment, making plans all the time.

Kate suddenly remembered. "Duncan, what happened at your school? Did you just up and quit?"

"No, I convinced the dean that he was well. I told the professors, who probably made him sick to begin with, to shape up, or I would put them in charge. And then I convinced the powers that be that I would bring the school more attention, and probably more alumni funding, if I got back to work on this project." Dunc gave himself a quick nod of approval.

Kate gave him a broad smile of approval also. Touching his cheek with her hand, she said, "Well done, Professor, well done."

When they got to Kate's apartment, a three-year-old came running out to see her. She could never sleep when her mum was at the lab. Her being gone at night reminded Mary of when she was gone, and everybody was terribly worried. When she saw Duncan, she stopped still. She wanted to run into his arms, but she was still mad—or hurt—that he'd not kept his promise. So she stood and pouted.

Dunc stooped down to talk to the child face-to-face. "I know you're mad at me, and I don't blame you. I promised you I'd see you in a week, but I left. I hated that my boss made me go back to Cambridge. I felt so sorry for myself that I didn't think about others. I would never and will never intentionally lie to you. I'm sorry I left without explaining why, and I'm sorry for hurting you. It makes me hurt that I did that. Will you forgive me?"

It took a moment for all this to sink in. All Mary knew was that someone she loved was caring about her feelings. She burst into tears and ran into Dunc's arms. He and her mother smiled at each other over her reaction.

For the rest of the week, the new family spent as much time together as possible. It was time for finals, so it was a very busy time for Kate. Still, she and Dunc also found some time for themselves. This time, there was no blanket between them.

Later in the week, Jacob met with the two. The admiration these two men felt for each other was evident in their fond embrace.

"It's a good thing you're back, Duncan McIntosh. Kate and I are weary of your thingamajig. *You* can wave it back and forth for a while. My arms are tired," Jacob teased. He then got serious. "Kate, I told Duncan to stay out of sight when he got back. I didn't tell him why. MI5 is taking a very close look at each of the students. They felt their reaction might tell us something when he suddenly shows up. There will be one or two other agents there beside Bartholomew. They will be posing as experts in digs in the kind of landscape where we're going. The two of you, myself and Mamun, are the only ones to know this. To everyone else, they will be the experts we've called in."

"Am I still a suspect?" Kate asked very seriously.

"Absolutely not! First of all, I wouldn't be telling you this if you were. Second, your kidnapping proved your innocence, once and for all, to even the biggest skeptics," Jacob said, taking the moment to hug her tight.

Kate had to smile. Once again, she was feeling sorry for herself.

"We'll be headed for Dunnasgual this weekend. It will be just the three of us with Mamun. If we find anything, all of our students will join us after finals are over. Until then, Duncan, keep out of sight."

That weekend, Joodi stayed with Miriam and Mary. Mary was quite upset that she was being left behind. She was beginning to love being a family with Dunc and her mum. The women were given strict instructions to stay put until the others returned. Jacob and Kate made sure everything they might need over the weekend was in the apartment.

The group set out late Friday night and took turns driving to reach their destination on the southern tip of the Duirinish Peninsula, close to Idrigill Point. Though it was a favorite tourist hiking point, it was still eight miles from the nearest road and farther than that to a motel. Therefore, a coed tent was set up for lodging. A few sheets hung from posts was all the privacy Kate was afforded. Enough food for the weekend was stored in an ice chest in the back of the van.

As soon as the camp was set up, the small group set out to explore the area. Once again, the archeologists were on the coast. To the southeast, they could clearly see the three natural monoliths that formed the famous site of interest, McLeod's Maidens. The minute Kate saw them, she felt the deep pain that *two* chiefs felt for the loss of their loves. Yes, she knew there were two.

Farther north along the coast stood the ruins of Castle Dunnasgual. It stood back about three hundred feet from the sheer cliffs, on the side of a huge mound. On the opposite side of that mound from the castle nearly seven hundred feet from that castle was evidence of an ancient stone road that appeared to lead from behind the mound straight over the side of the cliff. They understood that land erosion was responsible for the road's abrupt end.

The group immediately hiked over the slope to the castle as if drawn by forces unknown. The men began investigating the castle. Mamun walked off measurements. Jacob and Dunc used the detector and the computer to go over the grounds inside and around the castle. Kate stood, as if in a trance, at the zenith of the mound. She turned around and around, drawn by the very regular curve of the side of the castle and the arc of the road. She walked down to the old road and followed it to the cliff. Looking down, she could see the corners of the stones that had obviously been honed by masons, cut to the same size as those in what could be seen of the road.

However, walking the cliff farther north, she found a surprise. There were, barely visible beneath the surf, a few other stones cut by man. Here and there, they led all the way to the area directly in front of the castle. Kate ran back to the road. There was something that disturbed her about it, and there was something very familiar about it.

Dawning hit.

"Jacob, Dunc, Mamun, come here!"

The men ran to her, aware of her frantic cries.

"What is it?" they all said in unison, watching her with concern.

Kate stood and calmed herself. "This isn't a road. In the first place, it's too narrow. Second, it's not a road. It's a wall. It's the size and configuration of the walls in Duntulm."

"Well, let's make sure. Let's see if there is more road on either side," Jacob said, although he was pretty sure that Kate was absolutely correct.

Kate dropped to her knees and reached her hand toward Mamun. "Hand me your sguab," she said.

"My what?" Mamun asked.

"Your sg—oh, I'm sorry. I've been pouring over too much Gaelic. I meant your hand broom."

Mamun looked at the brush he was using to clear some moss off the castle walls. He smiled and handed it over to Kate. She took it, bristles up, and started to use it to brush away dirt next to the stones. She stopped dead still and stared at the brush, still holding it with its bristles straight up.

"What is it?" the men kept asking her.

Kate's eyes widened in sudden realization. She brushed away some dirt and began writing in it. "What if instead of this…" She wrote in bold letters with her fingers "dun nas gual." Writing just beneath this, she said, "It's this? You move the letter *S* from nas, leaving na. Put the *S* with gual—sgual. Then what if the *L* is really a *B*?" The changes she wrote ended up as "dun na sguab."

The three men stared at the young woman, who was obviously very proud of herself and then at the words that meant nothing to them.

"So what does it change?" Dunc asked.

Kate pointed at each word and translated, "*Dun* means 'fort' or 'castle.' Rather than *nas*, which means 'great,' *na* is translated 'of the,' and *sguab* is 'broom' or 'hand broom' or"—she turned the brush, bristles up, once again—"or 'sheaf.'" She wrote boldly in the dirt and read, "Castle…of the…sheaf." She sat back with great satisfaction and said softly, "We've found Beit Yosef. We're home."

The men stared, at first, in disbelief and then laughter, and *whoops* of joy broke out. The men clapped one another on the back and hugged one another. Duncan looked down with pride at Kate, who was watching the revelry with amusement. He wanted to reached down, pick her up, and kiss her, but it would have embarrassed the heck out of him, and probably her. Jacob had no problem in grabbing her in his arms and planting a fatherly kiss on her cheek.

It was not lost on Jacob that Kate found the possible castle of Beit Yosef to be *home*.

This was not to be the only discovery of the day. Kate, at the computer, pointed out unusual markings while Dunc was sweeping the area over the mound with his detector. There were traces of the wall, or footprints of the wall, coiling inward all the way to the crest of the mound. All along the inner wall were darkened areas that Dunc assumed to be holes left by large wooden posts. These ranged as the wall coiled inward and uphill, from approximately ten to five or six feet beneath ground level.

In the center of the crest was the most exciting find. There appeared to be an empty space underground about forty feet beneath them. It was too irregular to be a man-made room. This apparent cave was very wide and approximately twenty feet high. The Isle of Skye was full of great and small caverns. Most, however, had entrances, a great many of them starting in the face of the sea cliffs. The detector did not pick up any passages leading to or from this cave.

Duncan and Mamun, after finding an accessible spot, slowly climbed down the cliff wall. They had to carefully pick their way over jagged rocks and slippery boulders. Standing knee-deep in the waves, they searched the face of the cliff for any sign of a blocked entrance. They found no traces of one. Even one closed over a thousand years ago would show some signs of an aperture. This was one mystery they would have to uncover later.

Within two weeks, with all the focus now on the Castle of the Sheaf, Will Elder had acquired all the permits necessary for the dig. Arrangements were made for student lodging at the closest elementary school. And a meeting was held with all the archeologists and students, this time at the Glasgow campus. Everyone but Duncan was there. This group now included two new faces of carefully disguised MI5 agents, Finley Ferguson and Anne Farley. They were presented as experts from the government on Skye and its topography who would also work alongside the others. Bonne and Clint were now there also.

Jacob introduced the new "experts" and Mamun and Joodi Al-Khaldi. It was also necessary to catch Bonnie and Clint up on their finds on the Isle of Skye. Mamun also brought out pictures of the mass slaughter of the Qedarites. He discussed the articles found there that led the group to believe the Hebrew tribes they were tracking had been with these people and may have even caused directly or indirectly this ancient tragedy.

"Tragedy or not, it did bring us the great luck of now working with Mamun and Joodi," Jacob said, smiling at the Al-Khaldis. His mood then became very somber. "With all the news in the media, I'm quite sure you are all aware of Kate's kidnapping and our successful rescue. You also know that despite the terrorists' best efforts, we have both Dunc's detector and the ancient shields safe. You have each been informed that there are still threats, and each has signed on despite this. I am very proud to work with such a courageous group.

"And last, I need to talk briefly about *our* great tragedy. Everyone here was informed that Sara Ross was a part of the terrorist group that sought to destroy the ancient artifacts we discovered. You also know that she paid for her decisions with her life."

Jacob looked out over the group. He saw disgust and anger in some, disinterest in others, and enormous sadness in Henry and Hannah. He noticed that the MI5 agents were carefully studying these reactions. At a later time, the different reactions would tell them a great deal.

It was then time to bring Duncan out of hiding. Once again, the agents were watching for reactions. What they observed told them nothing. The students that were there for the first time and Will were all surprised.

"I thought you were in America," Bonnie McGregor said.

"Just got back," Dunc said, finding an empty seat.

"I would hope," Jacob went on, ignoring Dunc's entrance, "that we could remember, at least, the part of Sara that was a gifted archeologist."

Jacob moved quickly away from this subject and flipped the chart to renderings of the entire dig site inside the wall, all the possible postholes, and the cavernous area Dunc's detector had found. He discussed the fact that there didn't seem to be an access to or from the area and that to get to it, they would simply have to dig into it. He started to go on when Hannah raised her hand. Jacob immediately recognized her to speak.

The large, sturdy woman stood. She felt very awkward speaking in front of a large group. She cleared her throat, tugged nervously on the pockets of her jeans, and said, "I have been looking on a way to build a boring machine, modeled after the EPB tunneling machines used to build some of the longest and deepest undergrounds in the world. I guess you call them *subways* in America," she said to Dunc.

"These have massive machinery to bore into any kind of rock and soil, conveying apparatus to dispose of the displaced soil, tunnel-wall-building tools and material, and areas for people to monitor the process and make repairs as needed. They also need machines to measure the outside pressure of the soil against the torque of the boring apparatus. To do all this, the machines need to be as large as the finished tunnels.

"Our machine would be far smaller. All we need is one that creates a tunnel that fits one person and a ladder through the opening. We would operate a machine that can bore into any material. It would have a solid face with raised steel blades. It needs a device to keep pressure on to move it forward. We could be that device ourselves by pushing it forward with pole that could go as far as we want, as long as we had long-enough poles or add-ons.

"It would need a hoovering system that carries the bored material out. And I can adapt a vacuum cleaner to do that. We would manually insert lining in pieces that fit together to form the passage walls. I would suggest a stiff rubber material or concrete. Local sewer-building companies would probably help with that if we used concrete.

"I have figured all this out except for one problem. If we are trying to get into an open space beneath the ground as we are in this case, I can't figure out a safe way to bore straight down, which would be the shortest route, disturbing the least area. Anything I came up with would endanger collapsing the ceiling of the room, cave, whatever it is. I think we could safely bore at a steep angle into the top of a wall." She sat down, without a further word, and stared at her hands twisting nervously in her lap.

At first, there was dead silence. When she looked up, there was a room full of very professional people staring at her with great admiration.

Jacob smiled and broke the silence, "And, my brilliant young friend, how long would it take to build this wonderful answer to our biggest problem, and what is the cost?"

"Oh, I'm almost finished. I showed it to some guys in the Engineering Department, and they helped me get right on it. All we're really trying to figure out now is the lining. Should it be rubber or concrete? It can be ready in a week. We adapted parts we already had. The main expense was the face with the steel blades that was about one hundred pounds. I'm not sure about the lining, but the school seems to think it's a good investment."

Jacob mused to himself. *As horrible as it was for Kate to be kidnapped, now that she is safe and sound, the publicity it garnered has certainly made funding a lot easier to come by.*

"Thank you, my brilliant and industrious young friend. You have solved our most pressing problem." He then turned to the rest of the team. "We will begin our work at the sight of Dun Na Sguab. We will move to Duntulm when we are finished there. I'm sending you out with homework," Jacob said. "We are not sure of the time periods we are working with. Because of this we need to have an abundance of knowledge in several different cultures. They are the indigenous Picts, the Romans, the Scots, the Norse, and of course, the German components of the Angles and Saxons. We have a short time to do this, but I have all the confidence in the world in you, my learned friends."

Chapter 21

Within three weeks, the group stepped off the bus onto the plains of the Duirinish peninsula. With them came the bright and shiny new boring machine. Hannah, in consultation with Henry, had decided that concrete for the lining would give the strongest support to the tunnel. It wouldn't need to be the thickness of most tunnel linings, thereby cutting down on the weight. Therefore, a flatbed truck carrying the machine, along with the pieces of lining, had accompanied the caravan of bus and cars.

There seemed to be an air of excitement, but there was also a feeling of apprehension along with it. Kate was particularly aware of this. Bonnie, who was so cooperative in Kilmartin, was back to her snobbish old self. She had intentionally made a statement about Kate being an atheist, which made Clint completely dismiss Kate and whatever she had to say.

What Kate didn't know was that Bonnie's thesis had been rejected because she had taken on too much, fallen behind, and failed to meet deadlines. Also she had frankly lied about some of her research and had been caught. There were other reasons as well. She now wanted to revive her ego by stepping into the lead in this project. Kate was the person she had to replace—or do away with.

Also Matt had stepped up his advances toward Kate. There would have to be a strong rebuke if this didn't stop. Kate hated conflict. She determined to stay close to Jacob and Dunc.

The other thing that worried Kate was the fact that it was decided that the safest place for Miriam and Mary was with Kate's parents. She knew this was right, but she also knew Mary hated being there. At least she would have Miriam with her. Joodi came with the group and stayed in the women's tent with Kate, Hannah, Bonnie, and Anne Farley.

Jacob, Kate, Mamun, and Duncan laid out the plan. With Hannah in charge, she, Bartholomew, and Henry would begin boring. The cavern area was carefully marked out with Duncan's detector. The rest of the area within the ancient walls of Dun Na Sguab was roped off into four quadrants following the inner curve of the buried wall. Kate, Duncan, Mamun, and Jacob each supervised one of the sections. The remaining students were divided up to begin sifting for chards and other artifacts in these areas. The two of the sections under Kate and Mamun had a MI5 agent. This grouping had been determined early on by Jacob and the MI5 agents.

The four with the boring machine each took up their long steel pole. They fit them into the slot in the back of the framework that held the face of the machine. The device already had the rotating machine and the hoovering machine with its long hose attached. With a deep breath and a quick prayer, Hannah turned the machine on. A great roar went up, and the three had to quickly adjust to the powerful torque. However, they did, and it worked; it really worked. The others stood, clapped, and cheered.

Within a half hour, the machine had dug down, at just the right angle, about six feet. The machine was cut off; and with great effort, the three, with the help of the others, lifted the first of the six-foot-long concrete rings. With great effort and careful precision, they slipped it into the hole. Gravity would hold it against the frame. After the next six feet, the next ring was shoved in the hole and twisted to lock into the back of the first ring. Twice they had to screw added lengths onto their poles

The group had locked in four concrete links before the weary archeologists felt the face of the machine break through the wall of the cave. The three were too busy to stop and accept the applause from the others. One more link had to be added. With a remote control, Hannah unlocked the face of the machine from the frame and pulled it out of the tunnel by the vacuum bag. They quickly brought out L-shaped planks of steel. The smaller part was bolted to the last concrete ring, and the longer part was staked into the ground. This was to prevent the concrete lining from falling into the cave.

Three ten-foot metal ladder links were hooked onto the concrete liner. There was a fairly long rope ladder attached to the last rung of the ladder. This length was estimated to reach the floor of the cave. The entire effort took seven and a half hours.

It was time for a break and a few refreshments. The three tunnel builders were mobbed by the others, congratulating them. Kate sat close to Jacob to avoid Matt's attentions. It was also to discuss the progress, or rather, the lack of progress of the others.

"We're down to where we should have found at least pieces of wooden structures, but we've found nothing," Kate said. "I checked with all the finds of the earlier digs. There were what you would normally find in trash piles of the fourteenth and fifteenth centuries. The items were consistent with the Scots that were known to live here at that time, nothing earlier. There was nothing found in areas surrounding the castle, and there were no digs done in the wider arc that we are looking at now."

Jacob was nodding his head in agreement. "It's as though all evidence of their existence was intentionally removed," he said deep in thought. "We've determined that the stones here are closer in makeup to the eastern wall we found in Duntulm, and they are the same makeup of basalt as the walls of the closest brochs in this area. It would appear that some stones from here were used to build the walls of Duntulm. And some probably shared with neighbors here."

Kate looked at Jacob. "Whoever was here intentionally removed all evidence of their life here."

Jacob nodded. "And similarly in Duntulm."

Just then, Duncan walked over to them. "I'm going down into the cave. I want to be sure it's safe. Then I'm coming back for you two and Mamun."

"Be careful," Kate said with more anxiety than she had intended.

Both men smiled at her.

Fitted with a minor's hat with a strong light attached, Duncan started down the tunnel. It was very close in there, and he knew Kate would have trouble with that. Hannah handed him a cable attached to a generator to bring more light into the cave. The metal ladder was easy enough to navigate, but he had some problem getting a footing in the rope ladder that hung down the wall. Plus, the rope had snagged on a rock just below the tunnel. Trying not to drop the cable and untangle the rope while holding on to the last metal rung was quite precarious.

Duncan breathed a sigh of relief when his foot finally touched the floor of the cave. Turning around, he slowly scanned the small cave. The walls, ceiling, and floor all looked very solid. There was one area in the wall to his right that, with the light shown directly on it, showed the very beginning of a staircase, the rest of a passage that had been blocked with mud and stones. This explained the entrance mystery.

"There is a man-made staircase. Or I should say the beginning of one. It seems to have been intentionally blocked," Duncan said, his voice almost breathless with excitement.

"My God," Jacob said, staring into Kate's excited face. All either one could think about was the underground stairs of the brocks at Orkney, especially the one at Gurness that led to their mysterious cellars.

The whole of the area was fairly cubed as it had shown on the detector. There was a stream that ran diagonally across the length of the cave. It fell at a slight angle and disappeared under the far wall to Duncan's left. He could hear a waterfall in that direction, which Duncan surmised took it out to the sea far below the waterline.

Here and there on both sides of the stream were piles of rocks. He reported this to Jacob, knowing full well that this would mean burials, particularly burials of Jews. Again scanning the far corner, he saw two very regular shapes. He reported what he saw through his Bluetooth and set out to investigate. The minute he started out, he slipped and went down with a crash.

"Are you okay?" Kate called into his earbud.

"Well, most of me is," he answered her, rubbing his bottom. "The floor down here is very slippery. Hopefully it won't be as bad on the other side of the stream. It looks higher over there."

Duncan inched his way to and across the stream in his bare feet. The floor on the other side was dry, so he put his shoes on and carefully made his way to the items of interest. First was the staircase that disappeared into the blockage. He described the approximate dimensions of the stairwell, including the height of each step.

Duncan then went to the two regular shapes. He knew immediately that these were stone caskets. They sat side by side in a carved-out alcove. The bottom of one seemed to have been carved out of single slab. The other was made of pieced-together stones exactly like the ones that composed the walls. Thick slabs lay atop each. Duncan felt he was standing on sacred ground.

There was no writing on the slabs that he could see, but when he ran his hand over the one, he felt the slightest rise of a carving. Duncan trained the light on his cap directly on the carving. Those listening above heard his sharp intake of breath.

"What's wrong? What is it, Duncan?" Jacob called.

"There are two stone caskets, and on each lid is carved a sheaf," Duncan said with near reverence in his voice. "Send Jacob down. I'll get him at this end."

Duncan guided a barefoot Jacob onto the rope ladder and then across the stream to the caskets. Jacob ran his hand over the carvings and then covered his mouth to hide the emotions. Mamun came down next. He was less emotional but very excited. Duncan had to lead Kate down with her eyes closed.

"I will see this. I will not be a bairn about this," she rambled all the way through the tunnel.

Kate had no problems letting the guys see her tears of joy.

The rest were brought down and helped navigate the slippery rocks and the steam.

They were asked to stand way back as Duncan and Henry worked to loosen the lids. The others stepped up to help lift it off. Beneath the carving of the sheaf was a mummified man in ancient velvet robes wearing a golden crown that, albeit larger, matched that of the lady of the bog.

"Remember, we Jews spent a long time in Egypt. We picked up a few secrets from them, including mummification," Jacob said, staring down at the mummy in awe.

Duncan ran his detector over the body, and Kate read off the elements from the computer. Along with human remains, it registered traces of the wine, spices, and salt used in mummification. The dating matched that of the lady of the bog, from 700 to 600 BCE.

Further search of the coffin revealed a scroll beside this king with the parchment entirely disintegrated. Duncan caught sight of a slab at the foot of the king. Not wanting to disturb the body, he trained his light on it. And with that, Jacob looked at the barely visible carving.

"Let me see it closer," Jacob said.

The closer inspection revealed a wonderful surprise.

"Duncan," Jacob said, "this is a tablet of Gilgamesh. Our king is the lowly scribe from Israel. *This is King Talmai!*" He explained his research into Hebrew literacy to those in the group who didn't know about it.

While others may have thought it, Matt and Bartholomew gave voice to the doubt that a coincidence like this could have happened. Jacob was hurt by this but had to admit that there was no proof of any of his theories. Kate and Duncan both quickly expressed the thought that there was also no proof against it and urged the group to stay open to possibilities.

The other casket was opened to find two skeletons. The smaller one, judged to be a female by her bone structure, appeared to be embracing the other larger male. There were also remnants of regal robes. There was no crown in this grave. However, there was a scroll. On the lip of the scroll were ancient Hebrew letters, which Jacob translated as "Torah." At the foot of the coffin were two other stones. On one, Kate authenticated Pictish carvings. On the other, the archeologists recognized Norse runes Jacob translated as "the tests of Oden."

"It would appear that we have a later king who also enjoyed pagan tales."

"Wait!" Duncan said with real shock in his voice. "Look there… under the rune. Is that…is that a *cross*?"

There was silence among the archeologists.

"It most certainly is," Jacob said.

"What could that mean? Do you think these Jews took on the Christian faith?" Dunc asked.

"In the first place, the cross was used in several ancient religions. I tend to think that since this tribe has shown a fascination with the religions and mythologies of other people, perhaps this is just part of their collection," Mamun said.

This made the most sense to all there. But this was still a question that intrigued most of the archeologists.

That evening after a hasty supper, a weary but exhilarated group wandered off to their tents. Bartholomew would take the first watch at the entrance to the tunnel. Just as Kate was about to follow Bonnie into the women's tent, a hand grabbed her wrist. She turned with the full intention of slapping Matt for such a move, only to see a rather bewildered Duncan.

"Oh my!" she said. "I thought it was someone else."

"Well, that's a relief," Dunc said. "I thought you were mad at me." He nodded toward the castle ruins. "If you're not too tired, can we steal a few minutes together?"

"I would love that," she answered.

Bonnie looked back at this with a snarl of resentment.

When the two were settled on a narrow wall of the old structure, Dunc pulled her close and kissed her temple. "May I ask who has been bothering you, so much that you almost hit me?"

"It's that Matt. He's gotten more and more brazen. He absolutely will not take no for an answer."

"Do you want me to talk to him?"

Kate had always had to fend for herself. The thought of someone else, especially someone she loved, standing up for her was too good to be true. She wanted to cry, but instead of that, she just nodded with gratitude and relief. She laid her head on Dunc's shoulder.

They went over the events of the day and could even laugh over Duncan's very sore, not to mention, bruised bum.

Dunc did approach Matt the next day.

"Matt, I'm going to ask you to let Kate alone. I realize we haven't made a big deal of this, but we're going to get married."

Matt looked a bit angry but knew he'd lost this one. "Oh, sorry, guy. I had no idea."

Duncan reported to Kate that he felt it went very well. Would time, however, prove him wrong?

The next few days were very busy. Will was called to the site and then dispatched to Edinburgh to bring back all the papers necessary to allow for an expansive dig to exhume the two graves. Machines were acquired to lift the heavy caskets without disturbing their occupants. Will returned with all good news.

The day before the dig to remove the caskets was to begin, the team had reached the level of the postholes. They still had found not a single artifact, not a chard of pottery nor even evidenced of burned parchment. There were only some scorched hearths.

Duncan, Jacob, and Henry were in the cave readying the precious cargo. The caskets had been closed immediately after the archeologists had all seen inside. They wanted to prevent contamination of the ancient corpses. Henry had come up with an adhesive that locked out the air and held the lids tight. He carefully applied it so as not to get any on the corpses.

The three had just replaced the second lid, and Jacob was headed toward the tunnel. He stooped down to take his shoes off when the commotion started above. At first, there was yelling. Then there were gunshots and screams. Dunc and Henry joined Jacob at the dry side of the stream. They stared helplessly up the tunnel.

The explosion was so powerful it shook the cavern floor. All the lights in the cave went out. Duncan was fumbling around for his phone. He was half in shock. He found it and turned the light on, hands shaking. Henry knelt over Jacob, who was facedown on the ground. There were chards of concrete around him. Henry had his fingers pressed against Jacob's neck.

"I can't feel a pulse," he said.

Chapter 22

The western isles of Caledonia
Hebrew year 4152 (392 CE)

The soldier rode on, clutching his chest. He would follow the orders of his king even though he knew the arrow in his back was killing him. He was almost to the castle when the enemy following him was close enough to shoot the fatal arrow. The man prayed that the vision of Dun Na Sguab was real and not a mirage brought about by his pain. *No, the massive circular castle was real.*

His bleary eyes barely saw the mighty gates of the Hebrew enclave.

The soldier gathered all his strength and shouted to the guards atop the great wall, "King Tobias has need of his cousin!"

With this, he fell to the ground. The gates were flung open after soldiers of the castle were dispensed to bring King Jebediah to the dying man. The king rushed to the man's side and lifted him up. "What is it, my son? Who did this to you?"

"Orcadians fell upon us in the night. King Tobias sent me to bring help. They had spies inside…all our people…gone. All is lost…" The soldier's head dropped on the king's breast, and he was dead.

King Jebediah gathered a large force of his men to follow him, leaving as large a force on high alert at the castle. He left orders to bury the poor retched soul and headed out to the tribe of Manasseh. Along the way, he alerted the great tribes of Brode Talorc. The Pict king had long warned Jebediah of the rising threat of the Orcadians.

He and his forces were ready in an instant. Jebediah was thankful that the fury of the horse beat would not let Talorc's sarcastic "I told you so" be heard.

As the dual force crested the hill, the two old warriors were shaken by the carnage that lay before them. The castle of Manasseh had been sacked. There was smoke rising from every corner of the castle. Bodies lay everywhere. A quick counting showed one fallen Orcadian for every fifteen or twenty Manasseh soldiers. A force of Orcadians carrying off large bundles of goods were streaming from the castle. Another group was even carrying away the blocks from the great wall that had failed to protect the people of Manasseh.

From within the ruins of the castle, a large man strode with the swagger of a victorious leader. By his uniform, he could only be the captain of the Orcadian forces. He was dragging behind him an old man in shackles. That man was stumbling, barely able to keep up with the captain.

With fury in his soul, King Jebediah grabbed his bow and let an arrow fly. It struck its mark, crashing through the skull of the captain. The Picts and Hebrews then rained down on the marauders from the northern isles of Caledonia. The cries of these attacking Picts were unearthly sounds never before heard by the Orcadians. They froze in terror and were quickly defeated.

Jebediah dismounted and rushed through the chaos to fine the old man the captain had thought was his prize captive. He found the man lying on the ground still shackled to the dead captain. With his sword, Jebediah cut the bonds and lifted the old man to him. King Tobias was babbling and totally disoriented. He kept talking about his treasure, safe in the dungeons.

"Are there survivors?" Jebediah kept insisting.

Tobias, in a moment of lucidity, stared his cousin in the eyes. "Only the old, the women, and the children…they have fled to the woods. They are all that are left. Not all, not all, no my treasure, my treasure. My treasure is safe deep in the dungeon." With this, the king went back to incoherent babbling.

The tribes of Ephraim and Manasseh had, at times through the ages, good relations. And the kings even spent time in each other's castles. However, it had been several generations since this was the case, despite the fact that these two kings called each other *cousins.* Jebediah had no idea where to find the dungeons. He would have to search, but before he did, he ordered King Tobias be cared for, the bodies of the Orcadians burned, and those of the Hebrews buried. He sent men to gather the women and children. Talorc set out to find all serviceable wagons and load them with all the goods of Manasseh. This was to include tearing down the walls and carrying the stones with them. Talorc knew his friend well enough to know they would leave nothing to tell future generations that the Hebrews had lived here.

After hours of searching the castle, Jebediah slapped his hand against his forehead. He had suddenly remembered the cave beneath the Temple of Neriah. This cave held the coffin of his great patriarch, King Talmai. He wandered the ruined streets of Manasseh till he found what might be a temple. After entering it, he searched the floor until he found the trapdoor beneath an ornamental carpet. He opened it to see a dim light. He then climbed down the stone stairs and followed the light. As he did, he began to hear shouting, angry shouting.

To Jebediah's shock, he came upon a cell with locked iron bars. Within the cell were twelve lamps. Four were still lit. There was smoke curling from two or three of the others. In the middle of the lamps sat a very angry young man. He was sitting crossed-legged with his ankles bound together. His hands where bound behind him, and his mouth was gagged. It didn't take much to realize what the young man would say if he could. Jebediah recognized this angry soul by his striking resemblance. He was Prince Caal, the son of King Tobias.

Jebediah shook the bars, but they were solidly locked. Caal nodded vigorously toward the wall behind the king. When Jebediah turned, he saw a ring of keys hanging on a hook. He quickly unlocked the cage and pulled the gag from the prince's mouth.

"You vile piece of excrement—you stinking, savage Orc! You let me free, and I will ring your murdering neck with my bare hands!" the prince yelled.

"It does not seem a very wise decision to set you free if I am to be immediately murdered, now does it?" King Jebediah said with a bit of mirth in his eyes. He leaned back against bars of the cell. Jebediah continued, "If I were the vile, stinking, murdering piece of excrement you spoke of, I would have killed you outright, ensuring the end of the reign of King Tobias's family."

"Then *who* the hell are you?" the young man screamed, sweat streaming down his bright-red face.

"I am King Jebediah of Beit Yosef and the tribe of Ephraim. I am here both in the city and in your cell at the behest of your father. Your father who, if I am any kind of a judge of human anatomy, may already be dead. He was alive when I left him. Now, if you wish to see him and receive his blessings before he dies, you must cool your extremely hot head and answer one question. Why are you in this cell trussed up like a lamb on its way to slaughter?"

The prince had cooled. Both the news of his father's impending death and finding this man to be a savior, a kinsman instead of an enemy, had taken his temper away.

"My father put me here to protect me. He would not let me fight the bastards." His voice was considerably softer, and his head hung low with sadness. He had wanted to prove to his father that he was a man worthy of battle, not a child to be hidden away from danger.

King Jebediah realized the young prince's humiliation and spoke softly as he loosened the bonds.

"The king was not treating you as a child. He was protecting his family's reign. With you alive, the tribe of Manasseh will continue on, regardless of however many others are killed."

Prince Caal stared at the man he was beginning to admire. "Would you have done the same with your son?"

King Jebediah laughed. "Yes, I suppose I would, if I had time to think. However, that could never happen."

"Why? Are you without enemies?"

"Heavens, no. I have many and have just made one more, one very dangerous one. No, the reason I will never hide a son to protect my lineage is because I have no son."

"Could you not make one?" The young man realized he was being very impertinent and started to apologize.

The king did not take it that way and answered very bluntly. "No, my wife cannot bear any more children."

"Our kings have often taken second wives to bear the needed heir."

"Yes, that is true. However, in our tribe, we no longer commit adultery for reasons of royal pride."

Prince Caal stared at this man, as regal as his father, as strong as his father, but there was something different—something more to this man. He then thought of something. "You said your wife cannot bear any *more* children. Did you have a son?"

"No, I never had a son. I *have* a daughter."

Chapter 23

Prince Caal blinked against the sunlight as he followed King Jebediah out of the dungeon. He staggered for an instant and held fast to the post beside him as he surveyed the enormity of the destruction before him. Jebediah stood still, allowing the young man to pull himself together. Caal nodded and went on. He began to realize that the men of Ephraim were the ones destroying his home.

"Why do you lay waste to the kingdom of Manasseh?" he raged, his anger again rising.

Jebediah turned and, with all the force of his station, said, "We cannot protect this kingdom so far from ours. Your army is dead. If we leave it, the Orcadians will come and ransack it as they were doing just before we arrived. All of your history will be mocked and destroyed or turned into the wealth of your enemy."

Prince Caal immediately understood the wisdom of this man. He also understood that if his father was dying, he must begin to act with the same wisdom and force of the man standing before him. And he *must* be taken to his father. Jebediah smiled at the transformation going on deep within the soul of this young man. He turned and led him to the pallet that bore King Tobias.

There was light in the old man's eyes when he saw his son. Caal was alive. He reached out a feeble hand to his son. Prince Caal went down on one knee and caught the wavering hand of his father.

"My son, you have come in time," Tobias said. "You have a great burden to bear. It is on your shoulders that Manasseh must rise again."

"I will not fail you, Father," the young prince said with a voice he was forcing to keep strong.

The old king smiled and said, "The women, the children, the old men—they have fled to the woods. Gather them and lead them on. There are young boys who will grow to be your soldiers. There are young girls who will grow to be the mothers of a nation. And now, my son"—Tobias pulled his hand from Caal's grasp and placed it upon his son's head—"through Abraham, Isaac, Jacob, Joseph, and Manasseh, I pass the reign of the kingdom of Manasseh to you. May the blessing of YHVH keep you strong and fit."

Tobias's hand slipped from Caal's head, and he gently patted the prince's cheek as a father might pet a small child. That hand fell to his breast, and he knew no more.

King Caal stood before King Jebediah. The older king nodded his head to the younger, a gesture that recognized him as of equal station. As he did so, Brode Talorc appeared carrying an object of gold.

"I suppose I am looking at the new king of Manasseh?" he said in Pictish.

Caal, hearing the foreign language, lunged forward. King Jebediah grabbed him with force. "You petulant child!" he said. "King Talorc is the greatest ally our people could have. This tribe of the Pictish lands has been our friends, our teachers, and our allies for nearly a thousand years. They go back to great King Viporg, who gave our King Talmai lands to settle both our tribes. If you wish to govern a people, you must be able to, in an instant, know your friends from your enemies." With this, Jebediah stood back and introduced Caal to Talorc.

Caal realized his childish outburst and apologized to Talorc. King Jebediah smiled. He realized that, along with wisdom, which Caal must quickly gain, he did have some of the humility also needed in a ruler.

Brode Talorc smiled, bowed in acceptance, and demanded the young man kneel. Caal looked shocked and turned to Jebediah. The king smiled and nodded to the prince to do as he was told. The brode stepped forward, revealing the golden object in his hands. It was the crown of the king of Manasseh. The Orcadians were in the process of taking away the crown, along with the rest of their plunder, when the Hebrew and Pict forces attacked.

Brode Talorc placed the crown on Caal's head and repeated the Pictish blessings of coronation in the Pictish language. The three kings stood and marveled at one another.

Many weeks passed before the job of annihilating all evidence of the kingdom of the horn, Manasseh, was complete. All of valued was packed and carried back to the Castle of the Sheaf. Everything that could be burned was. Everything that wasn't was carried to the sea. Only a few parts of the outer walls of the kingdom were left. Over the hundreds of years to come, those building blocks were carried off and used to build brochs, forts, and the roads of the people of the land.

King Caal gathered the remnants of his people. His heart broke at the sight of the frightened and anguished people. There were women of all ages but only males who were very young or very old. How, in the name of YHVH, could he build a kingdom from this? There was, however, a spirit within the two kings who stood beside him that led him to know, somehow, he would.

The tribe of Manasseh settled in a village not far from their distant cousins. A castle of modest proportions in relationship to that of Manasseh was built in the midst of the village. This was partly to give the young king a sense of decorum, as well as to allow his people to know they *were* a kingdom. Two of the Levite priests of Ephraim settled with the Manasseh people and built a tabernacle. The people of Ephraim shared their fields with Manasseh.

This all took several years, and the young king stayed very busy during this time. He was in and out of King Jebediah's palace many times, but only briefly, to get advice on building or on strategy for leadership. Though he realized with gratitude that his and his kingdom's very lives were owed to Jebediah and to Talorc, there was deep inside a resentment that he must live in a house of wood and reign over a village of elders, women, and children instead of the nation of his mighty neighbors. He felt it would be generations long after he was dead before his kingdom would regain its power and prestige.

He found comfort from these selfish thoughts with his priests. They spoke of his future in cloaked terms but with the hint of Caal leading his people to a far greater kingdom than even that of Ephraim. *Would he lead his people back to Israel?*

The time did come when King Caal could relax and begin to have control of his time. Much to the dismay of his priests, he had abandoned, like his forefathers, the many practices of the Hebrew faith. They simply had no meaning to him. His priests had speculated to themselves that this was more than likely the reason his people were attacked and decimated. *Mighty YHVH reaped vengeance for this betrayal of His commandments.* They knew their place and did not voice this to King Caal.

They did speak to their relatives in Ephraim. These priests, knowing the faith of King Jebediah, told their king.

"It does not escape us that the young king has inherited the wrath of YHVH that his father brought upon his people by the abandonment of the law," said Elisafat, chief priest of Ephraim.

King Jebediah sat as he always did when deep in thought—his chin resting in the palm of his hand and that finger rubbing back and forth across his lips. A light came in his eyes. He wanted to handle this gently. He knew the turmoil deep within Caal, and he did not want to scold him like a child. He did, however, know that what the priest was saying was probably very true. Being a literate man and one well versed in the Torah, he saw that his priest was right.

"Prepare for the first Seder of Passover. Also prepare a royal invitation to King Caal. Invite the elders and priests of his tribe."

On horseback, King Caal led a procession of thirty men—twenty-eight elders and his two Levites—into the gates of the Castle of the Sheaf. Caal was dressed in his finest robes, saved from the fire in his father's palace. The rest of the men were dressed as presentable as possible. The young king was announced by trumpeter. Jebediah personally escorted Caal to his seat of honor at the banquet table. Caal took his seat at the side of King Jebediah.

The young king did his best to show outward signs of strength and confidence. Inside, he feared embarrassment, well aware of his ignorance of the Hebrew festivals. Though they had studied them, as did all the young men of his tribe, the kings of Manasseh had long since stopped participating in them. They were seen as a nuisance, too much trouble. The Levites of Manasseh were grinning with delight that their king might actually begin to follow the laws of YHVH.

Once the introductions were made, King Jebediah nodded to a servant standing by a side door. The servant nodded back and announced two names, "Queen Naftali and Princess Maura." The door was opened, and the women walked in. The men all stood for the ladies.

"King Caal, may I present my wife, Naftali, and our daughter, Maura?"

Caal judged the queen to be about Jebediah's age. However, she was one of the most beautiful women he had ever seen. Her smile to him was gracious and touched him in a way no other had since his mother's death. He gave her a smile back and a semibow to show her honor.

The young king was well aware that Jebediah had left off the women's titles, as was the custom when women of any stature were presented to royalty. He knew this was done to honor him. He also knew that this had angered the princess. If her mother had shown caring, Maura was looking at him with the opposite—anger and disgust? Whatever it was, Caal nodded to her and smiled but was thinking to himself that he was thankful that he did not have to deal with this woman more than once or twice a year.

Caal was relieved that Jebediah presided over the feast, presenting the elements and relaying the story of the Hebrew exodus out of Egypt. He listened carefully. *I will return the honor next year and invite Jebediah and his family to the halls of Manasseh for Passover— well, at least the king and queen.* He could just see the princess sneering with satisfaction at his humble dwellings.

Being honored by Jebediah and his court had a positive effect on Caal. However, he kept the words of his priests close to his heart that someday he might lead his people back to Israel.

The Levites of Ephraim were far more concerned with their prophecies of the future for all of Beit Yosef. Though Jebediah was a man of great faith, he did not hold to fortune-telling. They had to approach him carefully. Chief Priest Elisafat begged audience with the king. He had found a way to approach the subject of his great concerns.

"Your Majesty, I have troubling news from the priests of Manasseh. I felt I must let you know, whether or not it is true. They have traveled farther south to the great mainland and have spoken to some of the Caledonians who have mixed blood with the Romans. They speak of people from far off who are seeking their fortune in our land."

The king raised his hand to stop his priest. Jebediah was beginning to see through this farce. "Elisafat, Caal has never told me of traveling Levites, much less of news of invaders. You obviously want to tell me of what you have been warned in a dream or a trance or some sort of talking bush."

The old priest hung his head. "It was in a dream, but it was a dream seven of your Levites had," he said, looking much like a child trying to convince his mother of his deep regret at his wrongdoing. He did steal a look to see if his penitent posture and sorrowful voice had worked to fool the king.

Jebediah laughed. He did love this old fool. More than that, he did know that YHVH loved this man also and often spoke to him.

"All right, my dear friend, tell me of your collective dreams. After all, it is my great patriarch, Joseph, who saved Egypt and Canaan from a seven-year famine by his dreams. Tell me of the invaders you see coming."

With relief, the priest smiled and then showed solemnity as he began to talk. "We see men from far distant lands coming in waves. They come from the northeast. They come from the south. They are so deadly that they may even take away the mighty Picts. They are those who come from the western Isle of Hibernia."

The king was no longer smiling. The words of Elisafat hung heavy in the air. Jebediah knew he was telling his king the truth. This land that had become as blessed to Beit Yosef as Israel itself would soon disappear. Once again, YHVH would lead His people out into the wilderness. The king stared at the ground for a long time. Elisafat could see the anxiety and sadness in his monarch's face.

"Tell me who these people are," he asked without looking up.

"We believe the ones from the south are the first wave. They represent invasions of the Romans. We were vital in helping the Picts frustrate the Romans into building their wall and leaving all of us be. The third wave will come long after Beit Yosef have left this land, and they come from the northeast. These invaders come riding atop great sea-bound dragons. They are the Norse."

The king looked up. "Elisafat, you tell me that our friend Bjorn, who sails here from Norseland to show off his funny-looking boats, is our enemy?"

"No, not at all, my king. He is a friend and will be a savior of our people. However, it is his funny-looking boats that will give future Norseman the power to control all of Pictavia. After their invasion, people of the earth will never hear of the Picts again."

The king weighed what he had just been told. "From what you have just told me, the Romans have already been pushed back and will no longer cause us danger. And it will be in future generations that the Norse will bring danger, but not to us. Who is it, Elisafat, who gives us concern now? Where do they come from?"

"They come from Hibernia," the priest continued. "They are the Scots."

"But, Elisafat, the Scots have already come to Pictland. They are, at times, a nuisance, but not a major threat. They have remained on the mainland, and they even joined the Picts to force the Romans to retreat from our lands."

"Those Scots who would wipe us off the earth, those who hate us the most, are not a great power or a mighty army. Their invasion will be slow and will not bring much warfare. Their power comes from their new religion and the belief that their god demands that all believe as they do. Their hatred for us comes from their belief that *we* killed their god."

"Who is this god? Is it one of the Roman or Greek gods? Zeus, Jupiter?"

"No, Your Majesty, this is where our dreams stop, and they make no sense to us. Their god...is YHVH."

Chapter 24

King Caal rode his horse out among his fields. The men at work there would stop and bow to their king. He smiled and gestured to them to continue what they were doing. The honor paid him was uplifting so he could respond with humble acknowledgement. What was also helpful was that these men, though some still children, were mostly strong young men, quite able to drive a plow or pick up a bow or sword in defense of their people.

What was even more encouraging to Caal was seeing young girls also working in the fields and some carrying water to their men. Those, quite often, were pregnant. This filled him with hope.

As he rode along, he saw a man lying on the ground and clutching a bloody leg. A woman crying in fear was holding on to the man, who was obviously in great pain. Caal dropped from his horse and ran to the couple. By then, onlookers were gathering.

The woman sobbed, "He swung the thrasher too close to himself and tore his leg nearly off."

Caal could see that blood was gushing from the wound. However, his leg was still quite well attached. The king took off his cloak and tore it into strips. He bound the wound tight and called for others to bring the suffering man some wine.

As he rose, he saw for the first time that the woman was in labor and due any minute to bear a child. He ordered the women standing watching the accident to find the woman's mother and carry her and her mother to the birthing hut.

With voices of gratitude from all there, the king turned to go back to his horse. He realized clearly that he needed to wash the blood that covered his hands and clothes. He was concentrating on this, so he was shaken to realize that six men on horseback were sitting behind him. With his shock of having this many people ride up behind him without his hearing, he instinctively went for the knife on his belt.

In an instant, five of the men were off their horses with swords drawn. They immediately threw him to the ground and disarmed him. They then turned to fend off any men from the fields that might try and attack.

A forceful voice from behind startled all. "I will not stand for any violence. You, there on the ground, stand up and tell me where I may find your king. I will tell him what slothful men he has who allow strangers to come up upon them without the notice of a single one of you."

Caal heard the voice of Jebediah, long ago, telling him he must instantly be able to tell friend from enemy. He had, for a second time, failed that test. And now he stood with turmoil in his gut and bile in his throat. He was totally defeated and humiliated in front of his people. The sixth person on horseback was none other than Princess Maura of Ephraim.

Caal, shaking with hurt and embarrassment, started to speak. "You are looking at—"

"You will address me as *Your Majesty*, Princess Maura, daughter of King Jebediah!" she demanded.

Her silly pomp had changed the king's humiliation to anger, tinged with a bit of humor. "Your Majesty, Princess Maura, daughter of my dearest friend King Jebediah, whom I have a meeting with this afternoon. I am *King Caal of Manasseh, son of King Tobias.* No, I did not hear your approach. I was attending to a severely injured man and to his wife, who was in labor. Your father is well aware of my great need to grow my people and keep them healthy. He would certainly understand my preoccupation in doing so. And further-more, none of your men are in military uniform, and you, dressed in riding apparel, look like no more than a young boy. Nothing about you should have made any of us fearful of an attacking enemy. Now, if you have something to say, say it now. I must both wash and dress for your father's and my meeting this noon."

The king, now feeling much more in command and much less humiliated, with mirth in his eyes, stood waiting on the befuddled princess to answer him.

"I…I did not…I…"

"Princess Maura, you will address me as Your Majesty, King Caal."

"I…I…" The princess stopped, stuck out her chin, and yelled, "No!" She immediately whipped her horse around and rode off. Her men were quite bewildered by the entire scene. They too scrambled to their horses and followed their princess. The men and women of Manasseh were happy that their king had thoroughly put the princess in her place.

Later that afternoon, the princess was called to the great hall where the two kings sat in congenial conversation. Maura stared at Caal with pure hatred.

"My dear," her father said, "I have called you here to tell you how honored King Caal was to have you pay him a visit this morning. That was most gracious of you."

The flabbergasted young woman stared at her father and then at the younger king. He was staring back at her with a smile—a smile that held far more humor in it than kindness. The princess stood and thought carefully as to what she should say. She quickly decided upon her response.

"Father, King Caal is being very kind. Not recognizing him, I was quite rude to him. He was helping a man in his fields who had been severely injured. King Caal was covered with blood and dirt. Instead of appreciating his concern for his people, I lashed out at him for not being aware of strangers riding up upon him."

The young woman looked down with what Caal thought was a bit too dramatic a look of shame.

"My, my," Jebediah said. "This is a different story."

"Actually, it is not, Your Majesty. We were both correct. She did honor me by her visit, and I was very stupid, in this time of great danger, to allow people I did not know to come up behind me like that. Had they been Orcadians, my people and I would be dead."

King Jebediah looked back and forth at these two young peo-ple. The two were looking at each other with wary respect. Jebediah wondered. *Respect and possibly even the beginning of fondness?* Then he began to laugh. He rocked back and forth, slapping his knee. The two young people stared bewildered at him and then at each other.

"My darling daughter, will you join us?"

"I think not, Father. I have things to attend to," Maura said very slowly. "I do hope you will both permit my leave."

King Jebediah smiled and nodded.

As the princess turned to leave, King Caal called to her, "Your Majesty, please come back and visit."

The princess turned to see if he was being snide. He was not. "Yes, I will. I, however, promise to let you know ahead of time—and I won't dress like a *boy*."

King Jebediah smiled. *There was hope for Beit Yosef yet. There was hope.*

Later in the week, Queen Naftali, Princess Maura, and King Jebediah sat in their personal sitting room, as they did most days at this time. The ladies were doing their usual needlework, and the king sat with his full attention on the reader Ehud. The young man was the king's nephew, son of Jebediah's youngest brother, Ovadyah. Ehud was Ovadyah's youngest child and only son. The kingdom had rejoiced when, at a very early age, the child began writing and found great satisfaction in copying and writing down both the Torah and the history of Beit Yosef from the time of great King Talmai.

YHVH had blessed the royal families from the time of Talmai with sons who were gifted with one of four different and very valu-able talents: one was a scribe, one was an innate translator, and one was both fascinated by and respecting of the mythology of the peo-ple whose lands through which the Hebrews traveled. These talents led to great communication with these indigenous people. Along with Ehud the scribe were Reuven the translator and Shemu'el the mythologist, both sons of Jebediah's other brother, Uri.

With this generation, however, the fourth talent had gone to one who caused quite a stir in the kingdom. Much to the king and queen's concern and to the disbelief of the people of Ephraim, that talent of strong leadership had not fallen to one of Jebediah's nephews but to *his daughter*. It was Princess Maura who would lead Beit Yosef into the next generation.

The priests of Levi had been adamant that YHVH had ordained the princess would carry this mantle. "You would have been given a son if that was YHVH's wish. What we see now as arrogance and stubbornness will become strength and determination under your guidance, Your Majesty," said the priest Elisafat. "The examples both you and the queen offer this young woman will guide her to be as benevolent and as wise as you are."

Jebediah was thinking of this as he listened to Ehud. There had been queens in Hebrew history. Many were brave and wise, but none *ruled* over their people. Both King David and King Solomon had whole harems full of wives. Some were brave, and some were wicked. None of them ruled.

Ehud was reading about one such woman. This was the only one Jebediah thought of who might be an example for Maura. It was David's first wife, Abigail. She was married to an enemy of David's. She stopped David from killing her wicked husband and their people by bringing David food before he got to their land. The wicked husband died of embarrassment when he found out his wife had saved him and his people. David was smitten and married her—along with a whole bevy of other women.

Jebediah looked over at Princess Maura. He then closed his eyes and shook his head. Maura had the intelligence and ingenuity to handle such situations. But who would marry her and put up with her insolence? His mind went to the interaction between Maura and Caal. Yes, he saw signs that they might grow to care for each other. But which of these two petulant young people could ever give up the right to rule and merely become the other's consort? The king found himself glad that at least he would be dead when this decision had to be made.

Jebediah's attention went back to Ehud and his story about Abigail. Once again, he compared his daughter to David's wife. He had to chuckle to himself. He could just imagine Maura being told that she had to share her spouse with even one other woman, much less a harem. *Someone would definitely get seriously injured. Besides that, she could not cook an egg, if her life and those of all Beit Yosef depended upon it.*

This, of course, was not all of his concerns. What about this threat his Levites spoke of? A people who believe the Hebrews killed YHVH. And what of Bjorn, his tall blonde friend from Norseland being a savior to the Hebrews?

Jebediah's mind left Ehud and his women. It went back almost ten years earlier when the guards atop the mighty walls of the Castle of the Sheaf yelled warnings of approaching ships. It turned out to be only one ship. It was, however, the shape of the bow that had frightened and confused the guards. It was that of a dog, or a horse, or was it a lizard? It was very crudely carved, and one could not discern exactly what it was.

The king ordered his men to take to his own fleet and surround the strange vessel. The men were on their ships and headed toward the new ship when Jebediah could hear a horse thundering from the north. He immediately recognized Brode Talorc. The Pict king was waving at Jebediah.

"Call your men back. This is no enemy. This is merely a lone shipbuilder from Norseland. I have known him for years. He simply sails off course quite often and ends up where he should not."

The Norseman was brought ashore and introduced to King Jebediah. His appearance was a complete anomaly from all the people the Hebrews had seen. They themselves were a swarthy race, with dark eyes and hair. They much resembled all the Semitic people that were their neighbors in Israel. Even the Picts were brown-skinned beneath their tattoos. This man was tall, yellow-haired, fair-skinned, and blue-eyed.

Talorc put his arm around the young man and walked him up to Jebediah. "May I present the great shipbuilder of the Norse people, Bjorn," Talorc said with a bit of a flourish. Jebediah knew there was some mocking in Talorc's introduction. However, there was also respect for the man and his work.

Jebediah immediately sent for his nephew Reuven the translator and Shemu'el the mythologist. Together with these two young men and Talorc, King Jebediah soon found that Bjorn was a skilled craftsman. He worked in the service of the warlike king of the Norse, Alaric. Bjorn would pretend symptoms of terribly contagious diseases and rush off for weeks at a time to work on his own vessel. His ship was hidden in a cove miles from his town. He would travel the distance at night to again work on his project, his beloved ship. He hoped one day to build a ship to take his family far away from the brutal ruler who sacrificed innocents in the bogs of Norseland.

Shemu'el immediately pressed the foreign-looking man about his faith and beliefs. There was a wealth of knowledge that Bjorn could only touch on. But it was enough to intrigue the mythologist. Bjorn promised to bring back samples of such things as magical runes, but could not say more. He must return looking weak from his last bout of illness. His family would be murdered in a most awful way if the king even suspected he was faking. Fortunately, he was one of thousands pressed into near slavery by this regent.

Bjorn had to return after talking to Jebediah's nephews. But now and then over the next ten years to once more intrigue Shemu'el, Jebediah, and Reuven.

All of Jebediah's musings about ten years previous were interrupted by, miraculously enough, Bjorn himself. A servant entered the room. "Majesty, the man with the dragon-looking boat is here and wishes an audience with you—"

Before he could finish, Bjorn bounded into the room. His face was full of excitement, and he was tripping over his words with what he wanted to say.

The women and Ehud were startled. The young servant was lost as to what to do. Had he committed an egregious sin by allowing this man to get past him before the king gave permission? The king saw his servant's distress and let him know it was permitted this time.

Bjorn the shipbuilder was very eager to share his new creation with his friend. After the warnings of the Levites of impending doom and their assurance that this man would save his people, Jebediah was more than glad to see Bjorn.

"Majesty, Majesty, come see my gleaming new ship. It sailed from the Norseland here in record time and without a single leak. I was in a race with my cousin Dagfinn. He raced off to the ends of the earth, the fool. But I first came to show my friend my new ship."

The king made excuses to Ehud and to the women and followed the Norseman out to the cliffs overlooking the sea. A much larger ship than Bjorn's first attempts was anchored just off the coast. There was a far more realistic dragon head adorning the ship's bow. Jebediah was also impressed by the two great sails billowing in the wind.

"Bjorn, this is a beautiful vessel. How long did it take you to build it?" The king was beginning to form a plan.

"It took me about two years, why?"

Ignoring Bjorn's question, he asked another, "How many passengers does it carry?"

Bjorn was studying the king. "About fifty, if everybody sits close together."

"How many if they must lie down to sleep?"

"Possibly half, twenty-five. Your Majesty, do I detect a need for transporting a large group of people?"

"It is possible," the king said, rubbing his lips with his finger and adding in his mind what the number of that need might be. "It occurs to me that you also build ships for your king. If you were to spend all your time building ships that could hold two hundred people who could lie down, how long would it take you to build fifteen ships?"

"By myself?" the shipbuilder asked incredulously.

"Certainly not, you would have all the help you needed, along with all the material you would need."

A thousand things rushed through Bjorn's mind. Leaving his country; working for this man whom he much preferred over his own militant and brutal king, taking all his family to a new land because they would be killed if he was found out. *It took me two years to build one ship a quarter as small as those in question. However, I could do it full-time with all the help I would need.*

"Bjorn?" the king asked, bringing him back to the present.

"Ten years," the Norseman answered with conviction. "I would need to get my family out first."

King Jebediah smiled and nodded. "Of course, you would."

The king suddenly felt a hand upon his arm.

"Father, fifteen ships to carry three thousand, both Ephraim and Manasseh…where?"

"To the ends of the earth, my dear daughter, to the ends of the earth."

Chapter 25

Of course, all would have to wait on Bjorn's cousin Dagfinn returning from the *ends of the earth*. And that depended on his being *able* to return. The legends state that if you approach this mysterious place, you fall off into oblivion. Jebediah did not believe that, but still the other side of the mighty sea was an enigma, a great unknown to all people.

During this time of waiting, Jebediah brought Princess Maura and King Caal into conference. He also included his chief priest, Elisafat. The younger royals were very skeptical about dreams and, for that matter, about the Levite's ability to speak with YHVH. Caal didn't totally dismiss the idea. Secretly, he kept in mind the Levites' prophecy that he was to lead his people back to Israel. But after all, Israel lay across land to the east, not across unknown waters to the west.

Also, it felt to Maura and, in small part, to Caal that if anyone held audience with the ruler of the universe, it would be those of royal blood. Jebediah had to exert all the parental force he knew how to bring these young upstarts into the real world. "YHVH allows us to call ourselves kings and queens. He may approve some over others. However, from the time of Moses and Aaron, He has *ordained* the Levites to be priests. They have guided us for lo these many years by the word of YHVH."

Maura and Caal were not totally convinced, but they were penitent as to their exalting themselves above the priests of YHVH.

It had been twenty-three months since Dagfinn left for his trip into the great unknown. The king had almost immediately moved

Dagfinn's family as well as Bjorn and his whole family to the safety inside the walls of the Castle of the Sheaf. Caal and Maura felt it was over, and this whole thing was but silly histrionics begun by Elisafat. King Jebediah, trusting in Elisafat, was concerned that Bjorn's ships may not be the answer to what he believed to be a real threat.

The concerns and doubts of the royals of Beit Yosef had reached a peak when the guards atop the great walls of the castle shouted for all the people to hear. "Ship ahoy! The dragon comes from the west!"

The people of Manasseh and Ephraim left their villages and fields and ran to the cliff overlooking the sea. Brode Talorc and his people joined them. However, those who ran the fastest, those who were the most excited, pushing through the throng to meet the dragon, were Bjorn and his and his cousin's families.

Dagfinn was at the helm and recognized his cousin waving. He saw his wife and children cheering. He heard the cheering and shouts of joy of all watching him. The Norseman, exhausted, near starvation, and battered by the elements, suddenly felt like a conquering hero. His crew, which were his six oldest sons, began to wave and cheer also. Dagfinn dropped anchor and ran to his cabin to gather his records of his long and danger-fraught trip. Small crafts were in the water and headed toward the ship as soon as it dropped anchor. They brought the heroic seamen ashore.

King Jebediah allowed Dagfinn's wife and younger children to greet him first. Then Bjorn grabbed him and hugged his cousin with joyful exuberance. Jebediah and Caal stepped up and greeted the new hero of all who watched.

"Captain Dagfinn," King Jebediah said, "you obviously are in need of food, water, and sleep. I will ensure that you get all your needs met, but answer me this one question first. What is at the end of the earth?"

Dagfinn thought for a moment and, with a smile, answered, "It is land, a beautiful land. It is a land of high mountains and clear running streams. It has lush forests and fine-ground sandy shores. It is a land with a great inland sea as wide as the islands we live on. Great rivers flow from this mighty bay. It is a land of people, people who are red in color. They hunt the animals of the great forests and eat the leaves and roots of the forest trees. They fed us and gave us warm clothes."

He looked into the eager eyes of the two kings. "I would say it is a land of great promise."

Jebediah gave the seamen to their family to attend to their needs. He would learn more of their adventure later. However, he had heard the most important thing, and so did King Caal.

Jebediah said with a knowing smile, "It is a land of *great promise*."

"Yes…," Caal responded, "*a promised land.*"

Later on, after the weary Norsemen had been fed and rested, they sat with the two Hebrew kings and gave them a complete story of their travels. Bjorn joined them. Jebediah's nephews—Ehud the scribe, Reuven the translator, and Shemu'el the mythologist—were also there. They would be vital in all phases of moving the Hebrews to their new land.

Dagfinn and his sons spoke of passing lands to the north, some with great raging volcanos spewing ash and lava from their bowels. Some lands were covered with ice thicker than the longest of the harpoons they had aboard ship. They also spoke of a great river that flowed within the sea. The listeners showed signs of disbelief at this.

"No, 'tis very true," Dagfinn said. His sons were all nodding in agreement. "It is a different color than the sea, and it has a powerful flow to the east. As we neared the western lands, this strange river was coming from the south. We could not sail against its powerful tide, so we had to stay far north of it on our journey west. We, however, sought its strength on the return trip, which, because of the forceful tide, took us half the time. The people of the new land call it the *Gulf Stream*. This gulf refers to some sort of sea on the other side of the land."

This was incredible news to the listeners. *Did this earth YHVH made for us go on with land after sea after land forever?* All doubt was gone, and the people of western Caledonian isles began in earnest to prepare for their trip to the new land, the land now called *the promise of YHVH.*

The people of the Sheaf began to build the ships. The young men of both Manasseh and Ephraim were more than thrilled to learn the new skills needed for this task. The kings had to ration their time. They had left their regular vocations to build the ships.

"You can, each one of you, build our ships, but you must spend at least half you time in your shops or in your fields. Otherwise, all our people will starve to death before the first ship is completed," said King Jebediah.

Begrudgingly, the young men realized the truth of this and obeyed their king.

It was very necessary to bring Brode Talorc in on the plans of the Hebrews. This included telling him of the Levites' prophesies. The brode sat in quiet contemplation.

"We have been in search of an answer to the fears and prophesies of our 'wise men,'" he said. "We have been consulting our ancient stones. They hold our history as well as our future."

Jebediah had to smile to himself that his Norse friend Bjorn said his fortune-tellers had been consulting with their magical runes because of their visions of similar groups of invaders. *Does YHVH speak to all people besides the Hebrews?*

Talorc continued, "Our sages also have premonitions of a wave of enemy forces who will destroy our way of life. They will be even stronger than the Romans. Our sages also see many conquerors coming to us for over a thousand years. This is true of all the Picts all over Caledonia. Even the Orcadians seem to know something will eventually come their way.

"We know of the land your seaman has discovered. Hundreds of years ago, we were a seafaring people. We also found a land with its glorious mountains much like those of our own highlands. Tales of the beautiful land have become the stuff of legends. I'm not sure I believed them anymore…not until what you just told me."

Jebediah watched his friend. He saw the same pain in his eyes that the king felt. They were thinking of leaving this land that for centuries was their home, nurtured them, and allowed them to grow into strong nation, both Picts and Hebrews.

"Then will you go with us?" Jebediah asked.

Talorc thought for a long time and then slowly began to nod. "I think all of Pictland will be forced to go with you or bend to the will of their conquerors."

Talorc and Jebediah, along with Caal and Princess Maura, spent many hours talking strategy. They would sail in groups as sufficient ships were completed. Who would go and who would remain to govern their people before the next wave? The next problem would be that of obtaining enough lumber for all the ships without denuding their forests. Where would they go to obtain more lumber without raising suspicion and perhaps causing a great panic?

It was decided that Bjorn would also instruct Talorc and his men to build ships. They were a far smaller tribe than Ephraim, though much larger than Manasseh. When the first five ships were ready, Caal would lead the first wave with Manasseh, and Talorc and his tribe would follow him with their ships. Dagfinn would captain the lead ship and his sons the other four. Jebediah's nephews—Reuven the translator and Ehud the scribe—would go with this first wave.

Once they were settled, Dagfinn would return with at least one of his ships and lead Princess Maura and part of Ephraim with some of the Pict tribes that Talorc trusted to join them, along with Bjorn and his family. Shemu'el the mythologist would accompany Princess Maura.

Once the princess set sail, King Jebediah and his remaining people would dismantle all vestiges of the Hebrew settlement, both the Castle of the Sheaf and the village of Manasseh. He would follow with the remainder of his tribe.

The problem of the lumber was solved by Brode Talorc. His tribe had a vigorous trade with other Pict tribes. He used the goods that he saw his Hebrew friends creating. Once his Hebrew friends taught his people to produce and trade them, all the products of both Hebrew and Talorc's tribe would go toward trading for lumber with tribes on the mainland. The trade partners would be told the lumber was for building larger walls and inner structures to guard against the invasions all feared.

Princess Maura felt the hot tears in her eyes. All of their life in this beloved land would be *lost*. She, however, would not fail her father. She would be strong, and she would lead her people to their new promised land.

Maura walked out into her small garden, which she and her mother loved so much. The roses were in full bloom. They scented the air with their heavy perfume. She sat on the stone bench and allowed the tears to fall. She knew this would take quite a few years. However, she once thought that she would rule her tribe, in this beloved place until she died. The thought of leaving it and traveling across the angry sea was almost too much to bear.

"My heart is heavy also," came the voice behind her.

Maura was startled, having thought she was alone. She tried to wipe her tears away, but King Caal took her hand and held it. With his other hand, he wiped her tears as he knelt on one knee beside her. Maura was trying so hard to be strong and not show any weakness, especially to this king.

"My princess, do not fear showing how much you care for your land and your people. Our road ahead is very long and treacherous. Your tears are quite appropriate. Besides, I have wept bitterly over the losses my people have suffered. I have also seen my father weep both with sorrow and loss, as well as with joy."

The princess allowed a slight smile. She was beginning to realize some deep feelings for this man who had started out as her adversary. This scared her as she had no intentions of allowing herself to become a mere chattel to a man, regardless whether he was a king or a peasant. At the same time, she had to smile at Caal's kindness, as well as the fact that he held her hand so tightly. She somehow knew that their lives would be intertwined for the rest of their time on earth. As she looked into his brilliant dark eyes, she also knew she wanted to kiss him right then, regardless of the consequences. Gathering her bravado, she did just that.

Caal had been deciding whether or not to venture a kiss with her, something he had wanted to do for a while. He gloried in the tenderness of her lips and gathered her close to his chest as he returned the kiss. It was a while before they broke.

Maura looked down with a bit of mischief in her eyes. "Do you have a problem being married to a wife who is herself a regent over a large nation?" *Great YHVH, where did that come from?*

"Your Majesty, are you proposing to me?"

She stopped and put her thoughts together. Everything had changed. She smiled and, with even more mischief, said, "I suppose I am. Can you handle such a forceful, forward wife?"

"I most certainly can. Do you think you can allow yourself to be…shall we say, *handled?*"

"If you do it right," she whispered in his ear, once more wrapping her arms around his neck.

From the castle window above the garden, the princess's mother and father looked down upon the loving couple.

"I suppose we must prepare for a marriage," Jebediah said while smiling down on the scene he had long hoped for.

"Yes, so much to do, so much to do," Queen Naftali said. She, however, did not tell her husband what she was thinking. *My headstrong, often stubborn, and lacking-in-common-sense, beautiful daughter will now be safe in the arms of this strong, sensible young man.*

That sensibility in the queen's mind was probably far more in contrast to Maura's brashness rather than in actuality.

Later that day, Princess Maura begged audience with her father. King Jebediah sat upon his thrown. Queen Naftali sat beside him. The king wore his crown in recognition of the importance of this occasion.

Maura was also dressed in regal robes, as was King Caal.

"Your Majesty," the princess said with all formality, "I have chosen my husband. If my choice pleases you, I wish for you and him to enter into contract."

The kings smiled at each other. Jebediah was a bit taken back that his modern daughter was so well aware of and willing to participate in the ancient ketubah, the contract of marriage.

"And you, my young man, what say you of this marriage?" Jebediah asked of his soon-to-be son-in-law.

"I am willing to offer you my life and my possessions for the love of this woman."

Both kings were well aware that Caal would not offer his people, his kingdom. Both deeply respected this decision.

King Jebediah smiled, but then his expression became deadly serious. "I have only one provision that I require for this contract. I ask that the marriage not be consummated until both you and my daughter are established in the new land." The king stopped for a moment, noticing the shock in both the future bride and groom, and for that matter, in his wife.

He then continued with his explanation, "There is much danger in this move. A child born at this time would keep the princess from performing to her ability as a leader during this dangerous trip. And the worry to you, King Caal, for both the lives of your wife and your child would make it difficult to carry out your strenuous duties of establishing a new kingdom for both our tribes."

The young couple looked at each other. This was the last requirement they had expected. Both knew, however, this was exactly what must be done. They nodded to each other with enormous disappointment. Caal then stepped forward and shook Jebediah's hand. This simple act completed the marriage, though not the contract.

"I feel sure that judging from Dagfinn's journey, it should be, at the most, a year and a half to the new land and a half year back. It is not taking our men five years to finish the ships needed for the first voyage," Jebediah said, trying to lighten the young people's spirits. "We should have the first five ships ready within the next year. My calculations make that to be three or four years before you would be together."

That was better but still an "eternity" to wait for both Maura and Caal.

"There is one good thing about all this. We have, for centuries now, done away with the chuppah, the proof-of-virginity cloth. We now leave it as a matter between the husband and wife. We do strongly encourage the groom to go on the word of his wife that she has remained a virgin until consummation." King Jebediah smiled, knowing full well that these two would not find much comfort in this.

Chapter 26

It was not taking even as long as Jebediah had speculated. The five great ships stood side by side, completely ready to sail within seven months of the king and princess's marriage. The Picts had completed two of theirs. The powerful vessels were anchored side by side in the hidden harbor. Each of Bjorn's ships had an individually carved dragon's head at the bow. The ships were far greater and far more imposing than anything anyone of the Hebrews, the Picts, or the Norsemen had ever seen or dreamed of. The next five ships were also further along in their completion than expected.

Bjorn and his family, along with the people of the three nations, were gathered at the water's edge to celebrate the completion. There was great joy and merriment in the job well done. Most had little thought that with the readying of the ships came the first wave that would leave the home all there loved so dearly. Maura could think of nothing else.

She and Caal had held to the contract but had found time to be in each other's arms to share their dreams of forming a new nation and of starting a family. The thought of a three-year separation now seemed unbearable. There would be much for Caal to do once the celebration was over. But for now, the two held tight to each other.

"You will come to me, my queen. It will not be long. Each of us will have so much to do it will pass quickly," he said, trying to convince himself as well as her.

"I am not the queen, for my father still lives."

"You will be once you leave these shores by virtue of ruling over those entrusted to your care and when you land by virtue of being my wife."

She nestled close, knowing he would leave her for the night, and tomorrow he would sail away.

And the morrow arrived. The people of both Talorc's tribe and those of Manasseh carried the last of their belongings aboard. The belly of each ship was a massive storage area to even include stalls and pens. Jebediah had likened these ships to the Ark of Noah. The Hebrews had taken their belongings, their tools, their animals, and all the food they could carry. They placed them in those storage areas.

Along with these things, they carried all the vestiges of their faith such as scrolls of the Torah, the doorpost mezuzahs, and even their tallits. Manasseh had fallen away from YHVH's mitzvahs in the past. However, under King Caal's rule and their Levites' instruction, they had come to follow their Ephraimite cousins in their adherence to these laws.

It was now time to place themselves aboard the ships. There was excitement, along with great fear. At least they were with their families. As the Levites of Manasseh boarded their ships, Caal and Maura stood looking into each other's eyes.

Maura was changing into a woman both her husband and her father knew could rule a nation with strength and good judgement.

"You *will* come to me, my princess, my queen," Caal said. "I cannot rule without you."

"Tell Dagfinn to hurry back. We will be ready, and then nothing will ever part us again."

Caal smiled at her and kissed her gently. He then turned to Jebediah and Naphtali. He bowed his head in respect to these people who had saved his life and taught him how to rule despite all his arrogance and foolishness. The queen rushed to him and kissed his cheek. Jebediah took him in his arms and gave him a powerful hug. Caal smiled at his mother-in-law and father-in-law as well as his beautiful wife and boarded the craft that would take him to his ship.

Brode Talorc stood before his friend with a broad smile. "My dear friend, hurry to us." As he said this, his eyes saddened. In his heart, there was a strong foreboding of things to come. He saw the same look in Jebediah's eyes. The men parted with sadness.

Maura and her mother and father stood watching until the ships slipped below the horizon. Then Maura fell into her mother's arms and wept bitterly.

The next three years were extremely busy. The Picts that had filled the lands that Talorc's tribe had left were much a more savage and aggressive group. They represented nearly two-thirds of the Pict population, tribes from all over Caledonia. This was far more than the few tribes that Talorc had brought in on the plan of evacuation. Despite efforts to the contrary, the word had spread far and wide of a pending invasion, as well as the building of great ships to carry their passengers to safety.

The Picts labored well in completing their ships, but they would not bow to the commands of King Jebediah and literally scoffed at being under the rule of a woman. Jebediah worried about sending his daughter out with these men in tow.

This problem was solved in a most egregious way when in the dead of night, the Picts boarded the ships they completed and stole three of Bjorn's ships. Thousands of men, women, and children jammed into the ships and left before dawn. In a way, Jebediah was thankful that Maura would not have to contend with them. However, this would mean they must build three new ships before Dagfinn's return.

It was earlier decided that with each wave of emigrants, Dagfinn would be sent back with only one ship to add to the five new ones. This was so the settlers would have their own fleet in the new world. Also they might possibly need the lumber to build their new towns.

By this time, the tribe of Ephraim had grown in population, and so had that of the Norsemen. They had to have the three more ships. The group went to work building. They had no time to grieve or be bitter over their loss. Maura felt the loss, deeply knowing it would definitely lengthen the time before she could be with Caal.

It was only ten months later that the weary folk of the western isles of Caledonia were awaken with the cry, "Ships ahoy!"

"Did I hear *ships*, not *ship*?" Naphtali asked her husband as they hurried to dress.

"That's what I heard," her husband said.

As the people rushed to the cliffs to greet Dagfinn, there was a murmur of excitement that grew into cheers as not one, not two, but four dragon heads appeared over the horizon.

The king grabbed Captain Dagfinn with great affection the minute he stepped ashore. "How did you manage to defeat that throng of Picts?"

"There was no one to defeat," Dagfinn said. "On our return from the new land, we had to sail far north of the Gulf Stream to avoid a vicious massive storm. As we approached the land of volcanoes, we began to see boards floating in the water. When we drew nearer to land, we saw our three ships and one of the Pict ships. We also saw that the volcanoes were spewing billows of hot gasses and bright-red lava that covered the land. It flowed into the sea, causing a wall of steam. We saw no people on the land or in the ships. Some of our crew led by three of my sons boarded our ships, and here we are."

The king was stunned. "All those people gone? Was it the storm or the eruption?"

"There' no way of knowing, Majesty. Probably both."

Elisafat the Levite stood nearby. "It is the wrath of YHVH," he pronounced.

The king and the captain stared at the priest. Neither could deny what he had said. However, the destruction of nearly an entire race of people seemed way too harsh, no matter how irksome they were. Both would have rather seen it in terms of bad luck or careless workmanship with their vessels.

It was Jebediah's two brothers, Ovadyah and Uri, the fathers of Reuven and Ehud, who asked the question all really wanted to know, "What of our sons? What of the first to the new lands?"

"I can't be sure," said Dagfinn. He had turned very pensive. "We, of course, were a far greater throng of people, in many more ships than when just my sons and I arrived in only one much smaller ship. So we were met with a very large group of natives. These natives were well armed."

Maura felt a chill run through her. She had to steady herself against her mother, who had also turned quite pale.

"Reuven stepped up very bravely—as did I, of course." Dagfinn puffed up his chest. "I believe Reuven made himself understood that we were not there to take from these natives. They were presented with the gifts that we took for that very reason. King Caal made it known through Reuven that we needed land but would not take that of the natives. He asked for only the most useless land that they knew of. We all knew that you Hebrews could make solid rock bloom with all the grain and fruits needed to survive.

"King Caal told me to quickly take my sons and return to our land. As we left, the king seemed to be winning the natives over. I, of course, have no way of knowing this for sure."

Jebediah stood in silence. His two brothers did the same. The children of the three men were all they could think of.

Elisafat walked to the king and placed his hand on the king's shoulder. "My king, the word of YHVH states in the Torah that He will move the tens of thousands of Ephraim and the thousands of Manasseh to the ends of the earth. You must have faith in His word."

The king looked at his priest and slowly began to nod his head. He then turned to his daughter. "Prepare to leave as soon as Captain Dagfinn has rested from this trip."

Maura was smiling with the thrill of adventure and the certain knowledge that she would soon be in the arms of King Caal. Her mother, however, held on to her daughter with all the force of her maternal strength. The queen knew in her heart that she could not keep her headstrong daughter from either her mission or King Caal.

Jebediah, seeing the agony in Naphtali's eyes, spoke, "My beloved wife, I intend to send you with your daughter. She will need your wonderful counsel as she takes on the mighty task of ruling her people."

This was of little comfort to the queen. She had no more desire to leave her husband than to see her daughter sail away. She knew that this was, however, what had to be. She nodded in solemn agreement. At least there was no longer the fear of danger from the unruly Picts.

Those of Ephraim who would sail in this wave had been ready for months to dismantle their homes and shops. Their belongings and religious articles were packed, leaving out only that necessary for their daily tasks. They immediately began bringing their animals, food, and belonging on board the ships.

The princess, likewise, had been prepared. Her servants were already moving her things aboard the lead ship. She went with her parents to help Queen Naphtali prepare for the voyage. The king followed his two most cherished people in all the world. The queen was so upset she could not determine what she had to do. She just stood in bewilderment. The princess was doing what needed to be done for her.

Jebediah took his wife in his arms. "My beloved, we will be together very soon. If our young lovers have managed to hold on to their hope of reuniting, you know that we will manage to do the same."

Naphtali laid her head upon Jebediah's chest. Her strength was returning. She smiled and said, "Yes, my dear, I feel it also. We will be joined again soon. It is just that, before either of us was twenty, we were contracted into marriage. And before that, as children, we played together at being king and queen. At your father's death, we took on the parts rather well, having practiced so long. I do not think I can remember not being your queen, not knowing you, not loving you."

Jebediah smiled in agreement. It was time for the ships to set sail.

King Jebediah, the priest Elisafat, the king's brothers, and the young men picked to carry out the task of finishing the dismantling of the home of Ephraim stood atop the cliffs and watched the ships with their families disappear over the horizon. Jebediah realized that he must change the sorrowful mood of all there. There was too much to do.

"Now we must celebrate our families heading to the YHVH's promise." He called to his brewer, "Jonas, bring out the shekar. Fill all the bottles you have and bring them to the celebration field."

And so the saddened group began to sing and drink. It was not long before they were *very* happy. Jebediah and Elisafat were far more measured in their imbibing. They sat together watching the merriment before them.

"You realize that these men will not be worth much tomorrow in the tasks that lie before us," Elisafat said to his king.

"Yes, I do, but there will always be the day after and the day after and so on. The knowledge that once a week they can celebrate will get them through this difficult time."

And so the final destruction was underway. The reason for this destruction was to keep the invaders from knowing that people of YHVH had lived there. They were concerned that the invaders would try to trace them to the new land. Hebrew history was full of invaders who carried them into bondage.

The Picts had passed on to King Jebediah what they were told by the Romans. This had to do with those Hebrews still in Israel. These Romans were in Israel and had seen the final destruction of the Hebrew home. Romans ruled over Israel with an iron hand. The Hebrews were allowed to worship YHVH only as long as there were no problems. Evidently, there were problems, which was no surprise to Jebediah because they had once again been driven from their land.

The outer walls of the Castle of the Sheaf would be dismantled. A huge pile of rubble would be as much an evidence of their having been there as the great walls themselves. The men were charged with carrying loads and loads of the great blocks to a long distance. They would then build many brocks as the Picts had built. The Picts built these smaller versions of the great Castle of the Sheaf when the Hebrews of long ago first arrived in the land of the Picts. The Hebrew masons showed them how to build strong stone homes and forts.

This had been a great fortune for the Picts as there were often wars between the Pict tribes. Now the Picts in Caledonia were all but depleted. With the vast majority that disappeared at the site of the volcanic eruption, along with massive group that sailed with King Caal, there was but a tiny remnant left. None to tell which brocks were ancient and which were the Hebrew replicas.

The palace would remain until the last. The men would live in its spacious, plush rooms turned into dorms. The temple would be next to the last so Jebediah's people could worship right up until their ship returned.

King Jebediah's task was to go through all that had accumulated in the palace over the centuries. Several ships would have to return for all to fit. Since there were so few people left, the king had ordered that only one ship return. There would be no more building of ships as Bjorn and his family left with the princess's ships. So the king must decide what could be saved and what must be destroyed. The priest Elisafat would do the same in the temple.

The king gathered all that was religious. All would go. He went into the library and gathered all the scrolls. These were copies of the Torah as well as the those scrolls that held the history of his people, starting with the yellowed and fragile ones the great King Talmai wrote so many years ago. Only one scroll of the Torah and one copy of a scroll with history of Talmai's flight from Israel were left in the great king's tomb. The history had been unbroken, right up to those words that were put down by Ehud. These scrolls would go even if the king had to swim behind the ship.

The king walked the halls of the great palace. He took note of the portraits hanging there. Once in a while through the years, a king would command his portrait be painted. Jebediah folded his arms and leaned back against the wall. *This would tell us what some of our ancestors looked like.* He thought for a while then smiled. "However," he said out loud, "they are only the pompous egotists of our line. Burn them!"

There were many knickknacks that he would melt down for their gold and silver. All the precious metal would go. The other art and tapestries would be burned. The furnishing would also be destroyed. The king wondered if he would ever again sleep in a bed so soft and warm. The task was long and tedious. However, Jebediah was ruthless in what he sent to the ovens.

Finally, in a nook in the room of his nephew Shemu'el, he found a stone carved with the runes of the Norsemen. It was a gift from one who lived among them building the ships that were taking them to the promised land. There was also a small Pict stone. It was given to Shemu'el by Brode Talorc to satisfy the young lad's fascination with the Pict customs. The stone had marked a small portion of land that held only a few families. It was led by a false brode until he was found out and done away with. The story had fascinated Shemu'el.

Jebediah started to send them to the ovens. After all, Ehud had not seen them as valuable enough to take them on the ship. Then he remembered an incident of long ago when he was fifteen.

* * * * *

He and Naphtali snuck into the cave that was the sacred burial ground of King Talmai. If this was forbidden, what they did next was almost worthy of a death sentence.

They approached the sarcophagus of the late king. Curiosity took over, and they decided to look in. The lid was not sealed, but it was still too heavy to lift. What they could do was swivel the lid so they could look in. Naphtali screamed at the perfectly preserved king who lay beneath the lid. Jebediah clapped his hands over her mouth.

"The whole temple will hear you," he warned.

His eyes went to the foot of the dead king. There in the corner lay the tablet of Gilgamesh. Jebediah was, as he had always been, fascinated by the pagans of this world and their customs. He knew from his studies in Hebrew school what this was. He ventured to touch it with his figure.

Naphtali grabbed his hand. "We are already committing a terrible sin. YHVH will punish us terribly."

Jebediah quickly pulled his hand away. He knew by his father's faith that what she was saying could be true. The two began replacing the lid. Naphtali's hands were shaking and wet with perspiration. The lid slipped once and clattered down. She began to cry. The young boy put his arm around her and led her away from the great king's tomb. He slowly and carefully pushed the lid from one side to the other until it was perfectly lined up and was securely closed.

Jebediah gathered Naphtali to him and turned to leave. Standing on the bottom step leading out of the cave was Jebediah's father. The king stood with his arms crossed and a stern look on his face. Both young people stood in shock. Dead silence flowed through the cave.

Then Jebediah, realizing that Naphtali was shaking so hard she might faint, stepped forward and bowed to his father. "Father, I am the one who has sinned. I made Naphtali come with me. I am the one to be punished, not her."

Naphtali shook her head no, not wanting Jebediah to be punished so severely.

Her future father-in-law did not change his severe demeanor. Finally, he broke the silence, saying very calmly, "Naphtali, you are to return home. There is no need for you to mention any of this to anyone."

The girl stood for an instant, looking back and forth at both. Jebediah nodded to her to obey the king. She turned, bowed to the king, and passed by him with great fear in her heart. The next day when she saw him, she just looked him over to see if there were any visible wounds.

He smiled and said, "I got a lecture and then was told that, apparently, I am in a long line of future kings who have taken a peak at our patriarch. Then my father said, and I quote, 'It would probably be wise not to take a girl, given to screams, on any further nefarious operations.'"

* * * * *

Jebediah smiled at the memory. He then decided exactly what he would do with Ehud's treasures. He gathered them and went into the temple. He opened the door to the great staircase and traveled down the darkened way. Torches were kept lit by the Levites in the cave itself so the king could see clearly where the sarcophagus was.

He knew the final act after the temple was demolished. The door to the stairway would be removed and burned. The staircase would be filled with the great stones of the temple and sealed. *King Talmai's resting place and all these treasures would be protected forever.*

Jebediah placed the treasures beside the bottom of the sarcophagus and bowed to Talmai. *An appropriate place to be watched over by our great king.*

Chapter 27

King Jebediah was grateful that he had finally winnowed all down to that which would fit in the ship. But his heart hurt at the thought that his palace would soon be demolished. This was his home, his family's home, and the home of his forefathers for nearly a thousand years. He quickly shook his head. This train of thought was not helpful with all still left to do. Still he could not help but sit upon his throne and think back of his family and the joy they had experienced here: his marriage to Naphtali and the birth of his rambunctious child, Maura. Then there were all the times before, in between, and after.

His thoughts were interrupted by a scuffle and loud yelling outside the door. He stood with concern. Several of his men burst through the door to the throne room, dragging three men who clearly did not want to be dragged.

"Your Majesty, we found these three lurking in the bushes. They must be spies of the Orcadians."

The men were dressed in plain brown sacks with ropes around their waist and sandals on their feet. They looked nothing like the dangerous Orcadians. Two of them were protesting loudly in what sounded to the king like the Gaelic of the few Scots he had come in contact with from Hibernia. *Oh, if only my nephews were here to help us communicate!*

One man was not protesting, nor was he struggling. He appeared to be trying desperately to listen to his captors. He said something in Gaelic to his companions, and they too stopped struggling. He, seeing the crown of Jebediah, bowed and motioned to the other two to do the same.

"Let them stand, but stay close," Jebediah said.

The one man's eyes lit up with pure delight. He said in perfect Hebrew, "You are a Yehudi!"

The king was taken back at first but calmly responded, "No, we are not Yehudi. Judah betrayed us to the Assyrians. Our tribes left before they could destroy us, as they did those tribes east of Jordan. We will always be Israelites, the true Hebrews of YHVH."

The king didn't realize how passionately he spoke. The other two, who were not conversant in Hebrew, were cowering in front of him. He smiled to relieve their fears.

The one who understood the king looked as though he might explode with joy. "You are one of the lost tribes of Israel. Dear God in heaven, which tribe are you?"

"We are Beit Yosef. I am king of the tribe of Ephraim, and—" The king suddenly realized he had said too much.

"And your brother tribe, Manasseh, where are they? Are they here also?"

To avoid this question, the king changed the subject and asked, "And what of you, my new friends? Are you Yehudi or another Hebrew tribe? You speak Hebrew fluently."

"I…I studied Hebrew in seminary. And no…we are Christians, Christian Scots from Hibernia."

King Jebediah stood in solemn realization that he was speaking to the first of those who would destroy his people, all they were, and all they had. "Our priests have warned us of you. You have come to destroy us and our way of life."

"No, no!" the Christian said, horrified that anyone could think this. "No, Your Majesty, we are missionaries, come to bring you the knowledge of our Lord, Jesus the Christ. He is the Prince of Peace."

"Who is this peace prince, this Jesus? And for that matter, what is your name?"

The man was doing all he knew how to remember words from his holy book that he carried on his backpack. The guards had taken these packs from them. "First of all, I am Amos. This is Thomas, and this is Stephen. Second, our holy book says, 'In the beginning was the Word, and the Word was with God, and the Word *was* God.

And the Word became flesh and dwelt among us.' I cut out a lot, but basically that is who this Jesus the Christ is. He is God come to earth. Your famous prophet Isaiah spoke of the coming of the Messiah." He did not know what else to say.

"Which god is this 'word' become man?" Jebediah asked, knowing full well what the answer would be.

"He is the one God, both yours and ours. It is Yahweh."

The king flinched at the spoken name of his creator. Ignoring this, he asked "Who sent you here, Amos?"

Amos smiled and said, "Well, first we believe God ultimately sent us. But it was our leaders in Hibernia who sent us to convert the sav-sav-savages." His voice dropped as he realized not only were these people not savages, but they were the chosen people of God, the people of his own holy book. Also they disappeared long before the birth of Jesus and could not have been a part of His crucifixion.

The king stared at Amos for some time, then, "You were sent to soften us up so your leaders could come and wipe us out."

Amos started to object but then bowed his head and nodded. "Yes, I suppose you are right. I never thought of it this way." He was almost in tears.

Thomas and Stephen began questioning him. He spoke to them in their tongue. At first, they protested against their captor. "These are the murderers of Jesus," they said.

Amos was quick to stop them and explain what he had just realized about who these people were. Stephen and Thomas stared at the king in wonderment, realizing they were standing in the presence of people of the long-lost tribes of Israel.

Elisafat came in the room as the men were being dragged in. He heard the entire conversation. He stepped forward and whispered to his king, "These men must not return to Hibernia. We have much to do before we leave, and the ship is not due for at least a year."

Jebediah realized the truth in this. He had become fond of these honest and kind men, especially Amos. He still could not make heads or tails of their beliefs, but he did not want to jail them. At the same time, they knew too much to return.

"Are there others of your faith sent out to convert the, uh, savages?" Jebediah asked Amos with mischief in his smile.

Amos was embarrassed that he had used the term, but he nodded and said, "Yes, there are many of us sent out."

Elisafat turned his back on the Christians and said to the king, "We cannot even let them leave us. They may meet up with others, and word will get back to the Scots."

The king thought for a while. The Hebrew guards standing around were anxious to get back to work. The priest knew his king would make a wise and just decision, but he was anxious. However, the Christians were concerned about the king's decision, knowing their lives and safety depended on his decision.

Finally the king looked up. With a smile, he said, "My brothers, you have been honest with me, so I will be honest with you. Our Levites have been told in dreams that the Scots will come and destroy us. We are leaving this land forever. We are also taking with us or destroying all vestiges of our presence here."

The king's expression became very serious. "We cannot allow you to return to Hibernia—or to have contact with the others sent to spread your faith."

There was dead silence in the room as Amos thought about the king's words. The Christian finally spoke, "Are we to be martyred?"

The king was impressed by Amos's courage. He smiled and said, "I give you a choice. You will give us your word, as a follower of this messiah of yours, that you will stay with us all the way to the land of YHVH's promise—or you will become martyrs for your country."

Amos was overwhelmed with thoughts. Somehow giving his word on their Messiah was too much like swearing and taking Jesus's name in vain. And both were sins. Also, if he was to be martyred, it must be for Christ, not Hibernia. However, the thing greatest on his mind was the thought of being taken to the "land of YHVH's promise." This was more exciting to him than his mind could fathom.

Stephen and Thomas were frantic with worry, not understanding a word that had been spoken.

"I must give my brothers your options."

He turned to the other missionaries and told them what the king said and, most important, why this king was giving them this choice. At first, they were terrified. Then Amos emphasized the Levites and their dreams and the opportunity to see the new promised land.

"Can we trust this king? Will he just kill us whatever we decide?" Stephen asked.

Somehow Amos knew that, without question, this king would not lie. He answered Stephen's spoken question and Thomas's unspoken one, "We can trust him."

Each one had to make up his own mind.

Amos said to Jebediah, "I will not swear on my Savior's name. It is a sin for me as it is for you. But I will give you my word as a Christian that I will remain with you all the way to this promised land."

The other two discussed the options. Either way, they believed they would see heaven. But if they went with these people, they would also see this land of promise. They began nodding to each other. Stephen told Amos that they agreed to stay with the Hebrews. Amos relayed their decisions to the king.

The king smiled and said, "That is what I hoped for. Now let us discuss your position with us. The three of you will be both students and teachers. I ask you three to sit with our Levites and give them understanding of what has gone on with our fellow Israelites and the Yehudi of Judah. I will instruct Elisafat, our head priest, to write it down. I will also instruct all our priests to answer all your questions."

Jebediah smiled at himself. He had come up with a solution that benefited all there. Both the Hebrews and the missionaries would learn from one another. And the missionaries would stay under the vigilance of the priests. Though he felt certain he could trust Amos, Stephen and Thomas had not quite earned his trust.

In the weeks and months to come, much was accomplished. Most of the structures had been torn down. Many of the stones were transported to distant areas or dropped into the sea. The Hebrews had fashioned tents and were living along the cliffs. They worshiped in the cave that held their great king Talmai and the graves of many other kings and Levites. All worked and worshiped diligently to prepare their necessary and precious possessions for travel. This was to include the Christians. The final task would be to fill the entrance of the cave with the remaining stones from the castle, along with mud and sand from the area.

As days passed and the work was nearing an end, there was more time for the Christians and the Hebrews to compare their religion. Jebediah could see that the base for both was very solid in the Torah. What he could not accept was that Great YWHW would find it necessary to come to His creation in human form and then allow Himself to be humiliated and destroyed by the very same people. Albeit, the lessons this carpenter from Nazareth taught were strong, moral, and some quite beautiful.

At the same time, the Christians were deeply regretting the growing hatred toward the present-day Yehudi. Amos, Thomas, and Stephen had seen the iron rule of Rome. They recognized the necessity of those beneath that rule to keep the peace or be annihilated. *Look at what happened to the zealots at Masada in 66. In handing Jesus over to the Romans, were not the Pharisees just trying to 'keep the peace'?* All three recognized that their Savior was anything but shy and peaceful despite being called the Prince of Peace.

What was happening was a deep growing respect for one another and for their individual faith. As they labored and learned together, the great journey ahead was giving each one a sense of excitement. Then it happened. Those guards on duty yelled, "Attackers armed and advancing from the northeast!"

All the Hebrews, including the Levites, armed themselves immediately and advanced toward the enemy. King Jebediah led them, shouting orders. The Christians, having no experience in battle, stayed behind, feverishly praying for the Hebrews. Though to the Christians the battle lasted for hours, in reality it was less than one-half hour. The Hebrews were victorious. All the Orcadians were dead or dying. But the victory came at great cost. Six of the Levites and fifteen of the Hebrews were dead.

Once the fighting ceased, the Christians rushed to the bodies of all and prayed over them. They started over to Elisafat, who held a man in his arms. To the shock of the Christians and all who saw, the man in the priest's arms was King Jebediah. All knelt in honor of their wounded leader.

The king raised his hand to Elisafat's shoulder. In a soft voice, he said, "You are now the leader who must take these people to their land of promise. You must rule them with strength and…with kindness. I feel these Christians have a way about them that we can learn from. Find my wife and my daughter and give them counsel in their grief. I have great faith in you, my dear friend."

The king lifted his crown off his head and handed it to the priest. "You are to give this to Queen Maura. You are to tell her that I send it to her with love and great confidence that she will wear this with the strength, good judgement, and humility that I send with it." With these words, the king died. Every man there was stunned beyond words at this great loss. Elisafat looked to the heavens at the noonday sun and prayed.

At Elisafat's orders, the Hebrew men, though weary from battle, took great stones from the castle walls into the cave. They fashioned a sarcophagus like that of the one holding King Talmai. They carved from the stones near the fallen castle walls a slab to fit on top. Elisafat and the Christians carried the body of the king into the cave and laid him in the tomb.

Elisafat recognized the pagan articles Jebediah had brought and laid at the foot of King Talmai's tomb. The priest wrestled with what to do with them but thought of his king's last words. He picked up the stones that held the pagan writings of both the Norse and the Picts and placed them at Jebediah's feet.

Amos stepped forward and asked humbly, "May I add my cross to what you have laid here?"

The priest had seen the terrible agony of the victims condemned to death on these horrible Roman instruments of torture. But he also saw that these men, these Christians, had changed this symbol into something for good. Again, over Elisafat's strong fundamental senses, he followed what he knew his king would say and nodded in agreement. Amos took the cross from around his neck, prayed over it, and placed it among the other articles at

Jebediah's feet. The Hebrew men lifted the heavy lid and laid it over their king.

All the Hebrews and the Christians stood and stared. The Hebrew men, all powerful warriors; the Levites, unbending in their faith and traditions; and the Christians, undeterred in their solitary mission—all there, strong and determined men, bowed their heads and wept.

Queen Naftali had firmly insisted that she would return with Dagfinn, who would bring the king and the remaining Hebrews back to the new land. She had much to tell her husband and could not be parted from him any longer. On deck that day, she stood stoic, with the wind in her face. Her face was toward the land that held her beloved Jebediah.

Dagfinn stood beside her. "My queen, I fear you will become ill from the chilly wind."

"No, Captain, I will be fine. I must tell my husband of all that has happened. He must hear it from me."

As soon as she said this, she began breathing heavily. She grasped her chest and gasped. Dagfinn, very alarmed, put his arms around her to support her. She sank against him and died. Dagfinn looked to the sun, directly overhead, and wept. Once he came ashore in Caledonia, Dagfinn and Elisafat would discover through their deep sorrow that the king and queen died the same day, the same hour, and as nearly as both could discover, the same moment. The queen's body was brought ashore and placed in the sarcophagus beside her beloved husband. They were indeed together again.

Chapter 28

A year and seven days before he returned to the Caledonian Isle, Dagfinn landed the five ships carrying Maura, her mother, and the people of Ephraim. They entered the great river Dagfinn had described from his first voyage to the new land. They finally reached the land they hoped to now call home. That was, of course, if the people he left on the first trip over were still alive and not slaughtered by the strange-looking people of this new world.

"Stay aboard, my lady, until we can determine what is going on." Both Dagfinn and Brode Talorc lowered small boats from their ships and rowed ashore. Both Maura and her mother peered into the lush forest just beyond the white beach. They were both struck by the unnatural silence that hung over all. The only thing that could be heard was the creaking of the great ships as they settled in the waters. The leaves in the canopy of the forest were perfectly still. It seemed this whole new world was holding its breath.

Suddenly the forest on both sides of the river came alive with hundreds and hundreds of men stretching as far as could be seen up and down the river. They had dark-reddish skin and straight black hair that hung down their backs. They wore animal-skin breechcloths and leggings. More soft animal skin covered their feet. Around their foreheads were beaded leather bands with bright feathers attached to them. Each was bare-chested, with garish paint marks on their face. Each held an ornate spear at his side.

The two queens grabbed each other in shock and fear. The people in the ships grabbed their weapons and held them out of sight, not wanting to cause their captain and their brode to be killed. Dagfinn felt terror. He had not been met with such a fearsome force on his previous landings. Talorc, on the other hand, had an immediate sense of kinship with these painted folk.

From behind the men came the sound of drums. They seemed to be beating out a message repeated up the river and then again and again farther west. There were also large puffs of smoke, again answered by others in the same direction. This seemed to go on for hours. During it all, the red men stood perfectly still, neither threatening nor retreating.

Suddenly Maura pointed down the southern shore of the great river. "Mother, I hear horses." The women watched as tiny figures nearly at the horizon drew closer and closer.

"Mother, it is Caal. Mother, he is coming for us. Quickly, we must go ashore to meet him," Maura yelled in delight.

"No, my dear child, you must go ashore to meet your beloved. It is obvious that these people honor you and your king, both in their number and in their finest dress. I must stay here. Tell Dagfinn that he is to get these people and all their goods ashore very quickly. Then he must get me back to your father so I can be the one to tell him of the beautiful land and people that you are to reign over."

"Mother, I will wait for you. You must need rest. It has been a long, difficult trip. I have seen the toll it has taken on you."

"Child, go meet your husband. I will rest while the captain unloads, and then I will go back and tell your father the wonderful news of our new land."

Maura hesitated but saw the determination in her mother's demeanor.

"Go, now meet your husband!"

"Mother, I—"

"Go!"

Maura threw her arms around the queen and hugged her hard. Naphtali smiled at her daughter and brushed her hair from her eyes as she had done a million times since Maura was a baby. The young queen hugged her mother once more and ran to board her boat. She kept looking at her mother standing at the railing of the great ship. Then Naphtali smiled with great satisfaction as she watched her son-in-law jump from his horse before it came to a halt, run into the water, and grab his wife into his arms. When Maura looked back to her mother, she was gone.

* * * * *

More than a year later, the last dragon appeared inside the great bay at the mouth of the wide river. This time, the natives of the new land had time to alert the Hebrews, the Picts, and the Norsemen of the arrival. A great crowd was gathered on the shore. Ahead of all were Brode Talorc, King Caal, and Queen Maura in her latter months of pregnancy with twins. Great cheers went up from the crowd. Only Maura was not cheering, not even smiling. The ship, riding low in the water, came in slowly. No one aboard stood cheering at the rails.

"It is a ghost ship," the queen whispered.

"No, no," Caal said, "they are all weary from travel." He knew in his heart that no matter how weary the passengers were, they would cheering for joy at seeing their new lands.

When only Priest Elisafat and Captain Dagfinn stepped into the boat to be rowed ashore, Maura turned her head into Caal's shoulder and wept bitterly. The king could only stand stone-faced with tears running down his cheeks.

"Your Majesties," Elisafat said in somber tones, "I bring sorrowful news that King Jebediah and Queen Naphtali are dead. Though thousands of leagues apart, the captain and I have determined that both died the same day and hour. Her heart gave out, and he was killed in an attack from the Orcadians."

Caal felt his wife strengthen. He knew with Elisafat's words, she had taken on the mantle of ruler. "Board your ship, Captain," the king said. "We will lead all to our new land. You will follow us farther down the river in your ship. We do not have far to go."

When all was ready, the royal heads of tribes boarded their own ships and led the massive regalia farther on the wide river that flowed southwest. The ships passed into an immense lake.

This part of the trip was long and somber. Many felt their lives aboard ships would never end. Only the Christians seemed to feel great joy as they took in the beauty of the new land, the new holy land, their promised land. The throng of people finally reached the shore where they would lay anchor. Cliffs over a hundred feet high lined the beaches.

The order to disembark was given. Bringing all ashore took some time, but the queen stood tall overseeing every last soul land on the shores of their new home. King Caal worried about her standing so long after hearing such devastating news.

Elisafat introduced the brode, the king, and the queen to the three Christians. These men told the queen of her father's courage and that her parents lay together in the same sarcophagus. It would take some time for the three rulers to grasp who these men were and why they were there. The queen found some comfort in their caring for her parents.

The priest took this moment to crown Maura with her father's crown. He repeated the words of the late king exactly, and the rule of Ephraim was passed.

The people began finding their way up the treacherous pathway to the top of the cliffs. Their hearts began to beat with gladness. When they reached the zenith, realization set in. They were overlooking their new home. Towns and villages were already built or very close to being so. There were no stones and masonry but wood structures with thatched roofs. There were fields with plants nearly ready for harvest. Pasture lands were roamed by grazing livestock. Lush forests in the distance surrounded the new settlements.

The late arrivals knew that some of the villages belonged to the Picts and some to the Norse. However, directly in front of them, the new arrivals recognized that the Hebrew tribes had settled close to the cliffs overlooking the great lake. A large circular stockade in the midst of the homes was built entirely of wood. It stood guard over the settlements while overlooking the steep cliffs. Though far smaller, it was built to resemble the castle these people had dismantled in Caledonia but still carried in their hearts. It was the Hebrew castle planned so many centuries before by great King Talmai.

There was one important difference. The gates to this castle, also wooden, stood fifteen feet high. The two doors of the gate swung outward to open. They were, however, closed at this time. This allowed all to see the carvings, identical on both left and right doors. The top carving was the head of an ox head. Beneath it was a downward slash. Beneath the slash was a unicorn. Once viewed, the mighty gate swung open to welcome the new arrivals. Never again would these kingdoms bind together beneath the symbol of the sheaf.

PART III

His glory is like the firstling of his bullock, and his horns are like the horns of unicorn; with them he shall push the people together to the ends of the earth; and they are the ten thousands of Ephraim, and they are the thousands of Manasseh.

—Deuteronomy 33:17 (King James Version)

Chapter 29

The Isle of Skye, Scotland,
Hebrew year 5775 (2015 CE)

I
t took all of Duncan's effort to calm himself, to will himself steady. He walked over to Jacob, knelt, and reached his hand toward Jacob's neck.

"Henry, let me feel his throat. Your hands are trembling." The lingering odor of the C-4 plastic explosion stung Duncan's nose and eyes. He couldn't remember why he knew the smell. *It must have had something to do with the forensic archeology course I took. That was so many years ago. Or did I teach it?* Again he realized his state of shock and confusion and willed himself back into control with a shake of his head.

He pressed his fingertips against Jacob's neck. To his relief, he felt a light pulse—but nevertheless a pulse. The light on his phone also showed him Jacob beginning to regain consciousness. Jacob moved his hands and then tried to raise his head.

"Can you hear me? How do you feel?" Dunc said. He could hear the anxiety in his own voice.

Jacob didn't answer him but began trying to rise to a kneeling position.

"Hold on there, buddy. Take it easy. There's quite a lump on your forehead. At least I don't see much blood," Dunc said.

"The terrorist, the damn terrorist! Why couldn't they stop them? Did it damage our kings? Henry, where's Henry? Is he hurt?"

"I'm right here, Jacob. I'm here. I…I'm okay. No, it didn't damage the sarcophaguses."

At this point, there were voices outside the tunnel entrance. A male voice yelled down, "Is everybody okay down there?"

Henry started to respond, "We—"

Dunc grabbed his arm. "Don't say anything," he whispered. "We don't know who's on our side."

Jacob closed his eyes and shook his aching head. *What have I gotten these young people into?*

Dunc's phone began to ring. He looked at it and saw Will's name come up. He automatically started to answer but hesitated.

"It's Will. But what if he's being forced by the terrorists to call us?" he said to Jacob, again in a whisper.

Jacob watched him for a second before saying, "Answer it. If he's being forced, then we're dead whether you do or don't. If he's not, he needs to know we're safe."

Dunc nodded at this logic and clicked the phone on. "Will?"

"My god, laddie, you had us terrified. How are you, and how are Jacob and Henry?"

"We're okay. Jacob was hit by some concrete, but he seems to be coming around now. What in hell happened?"

"We now know who the terrorist was. She tried to get down to you and the crypts and blow both up. The MI5 agent got her just as she got to the tunnel."

"She?" The terror of who it might be was loud and clear in Dunc's voice. Had the first suspect, the woman he loved, been the terrorist all along?

"Yes, *she*. Mamun's wife, Joodi, is…was a suicide bomber. She was shot just before she detonated the bomb."

Dunc's phone was on speaker. He and Jacob blew out sighs in relief, then hunched their shoulders in guilt. Both reacting to the same relief and now the same shame—lack of trust in Kate. Then the realization of what Will said set in. Joodi, *Mamun's wife*, was a part of this miserable terrorist group!

"Is anybody else hurt, and is Mamun a terrorist also?" Henry was the first to react with logical questions.

"Matt was slightly injured, and the MI5 agent Anne Farley, who shot Joodi, was badly injured in the blast," Will responded. "Mamun's wife waited till the rest of us were all away from the tunnel entrance. I suppose so we wouldn't get in her way. And I'm not sure about Mamun. He, of course, is being detained. But judging from his sobs, I don't think he had any idea what she was up to—unless it's an act to throw us off."

Jacob, Henry, and Dunc all looked back and forth at one another, trying to digest what Will just said.

"There seems to be less damage to the tunnel than we first thought," Will went on. "The agents are clearing out some blockage, and then we'll come get you."

Duncan was struck first by the mayhem that just happened and then how calmly Will conveyed it. *Nothing ever fazed that guy.* Dunc was remembering how he and Will drove up on a gruesome accident at school. Will was in the midst giving CPR while Dunc had to go find a spot to barf.

Duncan began to see unfamiliar uniformed people coming through the tunnel. He was surprised that paramedics could arrive on the peninsula so quickly. They carried large lanterns and what looked like a duffle bag attached to a rope that went up the tunnel, which they explained was a pliable stretcher, intended to be used to strap Jacob in so he could be hauled up the tunnel. Jacob would have nothing to do with it. With helpers on all sides while being very unsteady, he stood and moved with determination toward the creek.

One very familiar figure followed the rescuers down. Kate struggled as quickly as she could over the slippery stones and through the creek. She threw herself into Duncan's outstretched arms. He grabbed her up and kissed her cheek, holding her tight to his chest.

"Duncan, it was Joodi!"

"I know. I know."

"I trusted her. I left Mary with her. What kind of a mother am I that I would leave my bairn with a madwoman?"

"You're a wonderful mother. No one could have possibly known she was this." He then smiled at her and said, "You made it through the tunnel by yourself."

"I did? Oh, I didn't even think about it."

Jacob laid a hand on Kate's shoulder. She turned into his arms. "Tell me you're going to be all right."

"With you and Dunc to look after me, I can't help but be better than new."

With a paramedic in the lead, Jacob holding straps attached to that medic, Duncan right behind Jacob, Kate right behind Dunc, and the rest following, the group made their way up the rope ladder, through the damaged tunnel, and into the late-afternoon sunshine.

Agent Farley and Jacob were airlifted to the nearest hospital in Dunvegan, but not before Jacob and Mamun looked hard into each other's eyes. There was something very wrong. Something didn't fit. Jacob needed his mind to clear. All he could do at that time was lay his head back and rest. Oh, how he hated hospitals. The authorities took Mamun to Edinburgh for interrogation.

Duncan wanted to go with Jacob. He also wanted to see to Mamun. This man, his dear friend, could not be a part of this terror. He just couldn't be. But Dunc had no choice. He had to take charge. There was a great deal to do.

What wasn't necessary, at that time, was for further excavation aboveground over the cave. Twenty-four-hour guards were placed around the cave by MI5, and immediate clearing of the blocked staircase would begin. Then the two sarcophaguses would be exhumed and taken to a secure location. *King Talmai and his lady of the bog would be reunited, a mere 2,700 plus years later*, Duncan thought.

Dunc gathered the students together and assured them that they were to be a part of all the studies and presentations of their work. He would also be certain that, whatever medical or emotional problems brought on by these terrorist attacks, would be taken care of by the project's funding sources. He relieved a great deal of stress for them by insisting on ongoing meetings to put together a joint report on their findings.

This encouraged the students as they were now a team, a first-class team, truly fond of one another. Even though a couple had problems with Kate, they realized how important she was in all this. Their admiration for Duncan and Jacob was without question.

Beyond this, they also speculated to themselves and to one another that this quest might not be over. *Where had the two lost tribes gone from Scotland?*

Kate was as involved as Duncan in wrapping up the site on Skye. This gave them time with each other to try and piece together the events over the past months and what they thought might happen next.

"I don't think we've seen the end of this mess," Dunc said as he paced in front of Kate.

"No, I don't think so either," she said, shaking her head. "Duncan, do you believe Mamun is heavy in all this?"

Dunc immediately shook his head no. "I just can't believe it. I have known him for so long. He is and was totally dedicated to his work in archeology."

"That's what we thought about Sara."

All Dunc could do was stare at her. She was exactly right.

Jacob was released from the hospital with a good prognosis. Agent Farley was recovering but with severe injuries that would take some time to heal. Kate and Dunc visited her and then picked up Jacob, he not being allowed to drive. No one spoke in the car on the way back to Edinburgh. All anyone could think of was the violent and useless act against the archaeologists and their artifacts. *Would it continue? What would be next...who would be next?*

Dunc broke the silence with, "I want to visit Mamun. Do either of you want to go with me?"

"Yes, I want to see him. There is something that has been bothering me since I looked at him at the site. I don't know what it is. I'm still a bit muddled after having my noggin bumped," Jacob said. Serious concern hung heavy in his voice despite his attempt to be lighthearted.

"I don't," Kate said quietly. "I feel betrayed." Her voice sounded dry and emotionless. "Perhaps Mamun had nothing to do with this. But he may have everything to do with it, and I won't be responsible for my actions if I see *that* in his eyes." She turned her head and looked out the car window.

Both men glanced at her, smiled with concern for her, but said nothing. Each felt the fear and hurt in her statement.

The group arrived at Kate's apartment midday. Dunc helped her get her things inside, hugged Mary, and let Miriam rush out to check on her father. She held on to him fiercely.

"I'm fine, my little one. I'm too old and crusty to let a little thing like a bomb upset my day."

His attempts at humor did little to calm his sobbing daughter. With the promise of them all being together for dinner, she finally let him go. Miriam told Kate later she couldn't bear the thought of being an orphan, of once again losing a beloved parent.

Duncan and Jacob arranged to see Mamun at the MI5 holding center. He was brought into the room after the two were seated. The guard stood behind Mamun, who sat across from his fellow archaeologists. He would not look them in the eyes.

"Mamun, what happened?" Dunc asked. He had no idea what else to say. In his heart, he could not believe that his friend was a part of this terrible act.

Still not looking up and with a monotone voice, Mamun said, "If I had known what she was up to, I would have killed her. I'm leaving for Saudi Arabia as soon as they are through with me here."

Dunc wanted to hush him so he wouldn't incriminate himself with the guard there. He thought better of it, however.

Jacob just watched, trying to bring out of his subconscious what so desperately bothered him. Nothing else was said except for Mamun rising and telling the guard he wanted to leave. The guard nodded, and they left.

That evening at dinner, two daughters hung on to their parents. Neither wanted to eat very much. But then again, neither did the parents. Dunc tried half-heartedly to carry on a conversation, but to no avail. Too much loss and sadness hung over the little group. It would take time to repair all this hurt.

For the next several months, the group of archeologists and students worked on the final report. This would go to the three universities who were the funding sources. Each student, Jacob, and Duncan would put down in detail their contributions and findings. Jacob then assigned Kate to produce the final report. He told her how impressed he was in reading many of her other reports. "Kate, you have the ability to give credit to others and then to bring out the big picture," he said. "Also, your love of Scotland and all its natural and historic features shone through in your writing." This is what he told her, but a hidden motive would in time be evident.

The three universities located in Israel, Scotland, and the US cooperated to develop museums in each university to show the travels of the Hebrew tribes. Though no absolutes as to who these people were existed, there was enough DNA evidence to determine Semitic origin and date the bodies to the time of the Israel expulsion. The scenes of the archaeological finds in Kilmartin and on the Isle of Skye would be preserved as national historic sites, as would the site of the Bedouin massacre in Saudi Arabia. This site had been preserved and the entire site covered over with a glass. It would be a part of the worldwide story.

The remains of the two kings and two queens would remain in Scotland. However, they, the two Scottish sites and the one in Saudi Arabia, would be reproduced in photographs and holograms at the other museums. The Assyrian shields would travel, on a yearly schedule, to each of the museums.

The one thing Jacob was most proud of was the cooperation of the four countries involved. The one thing that most saddened him was that this marvelous adventure had come to an end. That which worried him the most was something he could not define.

What did I see in Mamun's eyes that…that…worries me? Or does it frighten me? What is it?

As the school year in Scotland came to a close, many of the students from the project prepared to graduate or move up to their next level. The two who knew they would do neither were Kate and Bonnie. Both felt this deeply.

The school in Edinburgh celebrated this, the greatest archaeological achievement of the young century. The heads of faculty asked

Jacob to speak at commencement. He brought a better idea to them. They agreed and asked Kate to speak using her final report.

She first responded to Jacob that she could no more stand before all those superiors in academia than she could fly, without rocket ship, to Mars. Jacob, in his own inimitable way, convinced her that she alone could convey the great gain all their work was to Scotland. Kate closed her eyes, swallowed hard, and nodded yes.

The university chancellor greeted the crowd, which included all the surviving students who worked on the project. Bonnie sat close to the front, right behind the graduating class. Her eyes could not have shown more hatred for her nemesis Kate, who sat on the platform behind the podium. Kate cared little about Bonnie's glare. She felt sweat trickle down her back and had to hold her notes tight against her legs to keep her hands from trembling. Jacob and Dunc sat on either side of her. They, like the faculty that filled out the row behind the podium, wore robes, bonnets, and stoles that bore the doctoral stripes and emblems of their school and degree. Kate wore her plain undergraduate robe and her master's cap.

Jacob nudged her and nodded to a row of seats to her far right. About five or six rows back sat her mother, father, and in between them—Mary. Kate smiled at her child and then at Jacob, whom she knew arranged this for her. He smiled back.

The chancellor went on for quite some time before Kate heard her name mentioned. At some point, he turned toward her and said, "And now please greet our honored guest, Dr. Kathleen Wallace."

Kate reddened with embarrassment. *Doesn't this fool know I'm not a PhD? Can't he tell I'm nobody?* Kate glanced over at her daughter, and it calmed her. She gained back her composure. She would make her daughter proud of her. Kate then began to speak of her beloved Scotland and all its hidden treasures. She spoke of an incredible team of students who withstood long hours, backbreaking work, and unspeakable attacks of terrorism. She spoke of Jacob's and Duncan's brilliance and leadership. She then spoke in detail of the work and immeasurable finds this group had uncovered. Her speech was kind and sparkled with well-placed humor.

The end of her speech was greeted with a standing ovation. Kate glanced at her daughter, only to find her also clapping with pride. To Kate's amazement, her parents were doing the same thing.

Kate was reveling in all this when she felt the chancellor's hand on her back.

"And now," he said, "before we present our certificates of graduation, we have a special presentation." He turned and nodded to someone or ones behind Kate. Jacob and Duncan stepped beside her.

"Dr. Rubin, will you do us the honor?" the chancellor asked.

Jacob nodded and stepped to the podium. What he said was short and to the point, but Kate knew it would remain, word for word, with her for the rest of her life.

"Over the last three semesters, Ms. Wallace has taught courses here at the university. Unbeknownst to her, this has earned her many credits. Also, unbeknownst to her, her report on our project was submitted as her doctoral thesis. It was accepted." Turning to Kate with a smile reaching from ear to ear, he continued, "Kathleen Mairi Wallace, I present to you this parchment stating that you have, on this day, earned the degree of doctor of archeological science. Congratulations, Dr. Wallace."

Chapter 30

From that day on, Kate felt herself a different person. She walked straighter, smiled and laughed more often. And she mingled with folks from all levels of wealth and education with a greater attitude of respect, both for them and for herself. Most important to her, she became a strong, assured mother. That mother wanted nothing less for her daughter.

Kate walked between the two men, whom she now appreciated not only for what they taught her and what they did for her but with an enormous degree of love and the knowledge she had much to offer them in return. She spoke to Jacob and Duncan about her own feelings of sadness at the end of their great adventure. They agreed but, each in their own way, expressed a sense of expectation that this whole thing was not quite over.

"Maybe it is just wishful thinking," Kate told them.

There was no answer to that by the end of the semester, when Dunc, Kate, and Mary stood in Kate's apartment, saying goodbye to Jacob and Miriam as they were about to leave for the airport to return to Israel.

Dunc smiled at Jacob with all the fondness he felt for his idol and colleague. "I don't think I can sleep at night not having to plan for a meeting the next morning with the eminent Dr. Rubin."

"Yes, you will, because you will still have to plan for a meeting with the eminent Dr. Wallace—not to mention the lovely Miss Wallace. He smiled at the mother and daughter. "Besides, you know the invitation to visit us in Israel is always open. We *will* get together

276

during semester breaks. And I will always be looking for another challenge fit for this group."

With that, Jacob hugged Kate and kissed her on the cheek. He stepped over to Dunc, brushed away Dunc's outstretched hand, and gave him a bear hug. "Thank you and your wonderful thingamajig for our grand adventure."

Miriam had been holding Mary in her arms. The child was holding fast to her friend, knowing they were about to part. Miriam stepped over to Kate and, with her free arm, hugged this woman who had pronounced her an archeologist. She then moved shyly to Duncan. Her hesitancy to approach him was brought on by the huge crush she had on him. She overcame it long enough to stand on tip-toe and give him a kiss on his cheek. He lovingly hugged her back. She then placed the child she held into his arms and kissed her on the cheek.

Miriam moved quickly out the apartment door, but not quick enough to keep all there from seeing her tears. Jacob followed with the same sadness, just short of tears. Duncan pulled Kate close to him. She and Mary waved. Both of Dunc's hands were busy holding tight to his two best girls. This he felt was far more like putting thousands of miles between family than professional colleagues, or even dear friends.

Kate, though now a full professor at Edinburgh, was not looking forward to starting classes. She, Duncan, and Mary would visit often, but both professors had duties at their base schools, so they would be apart for long periods. This hurt Kate as much as the Rubins' leaving. Mary lost much of the joy and playfulness she had gained being with Miriam, away from her stern grandparents. She would now spend her days in the university grade school for children of faculty.

In the months to come, Kate often found herself staring out her apartment window. *Can I wait for six months when we'll be together in America? Isn't part of this also missing Jacob and Miriam? When will I stop wondering about…about what? What am I waiting for?*

The answer came just one day before the end of the interminably long semester.

"Kate, my dear, pack your bags," came Jacob's booming voice over the phone. "I have spoken to Duncan, Henry, and to all three of our schools. We are going to America. I was contacted by a wonderful young lady there named Moira Joseph. Possibly, just possibly, we have found Beit Yosef. Miriam and I will meet you in St. Louis a week from Monday."

Kate felt like the lights had been turned back on in her heart. She kept in contact with the students and even Will Elder throughout the semester, all except Bonnie, who had left the group after what Kate thought she must perceive as her humiliation at the graduation ceremony. She hadn't been missed. Those Kate talked to were all excited over the news, and some even tried to figure out ways of being a part of this new phase. Henry was the only one who could manage the funds himself since the funding sources had not yet committed to this.

Will was also tied up but asked to be kept informed of their findings. "Remind Duncan that the laddie still owes me a story about this whole project for my book," he said.

The meeting at St. Louis Lambert International Airport was as joyful as the separation in Scotland was painful. This time, arriving just a few hours before, Duncan, Jacob, and Miriam met Henry and the Wallaces. Once again, this was more like that of a family reunion. Mary couldn't decide whether she wanted to be in Miriam's or Duncan's arms, so she ran back and forth to both. Kate knew full well in whose arms she wanted to be. She constantly found herself slipping her hand into Dunc's.

"Dr. Wallace, I've had enough of being without you and *our* child. I insist on marrying you. Is that okay?"

Kate laughed. "Silly, of course, it's okay. Yes, *we* will marry you." She kissed him.

The group broke into cheers and applause.

"What's going on?" Mary asked

"You're about to get a new papa," Miriam said. "Duncan just asked your mom to marry him."

No one believed the small child could have that large a smile.

Jacob led the group to a massive black limousine. A dour-looking man in a chauffeur's uniform got out and opened the rear door.

"Ladies and gentlemen, this is James. Mrs. Joseph has been kind enough to send her car for us," Jacob said. "She is also providing us lodging while we're here."

The group climbed into the spacious well-appointed automobile.

"Are we meeting royalty?" Henry asked as he eyed the black-and-gold trimmed amenities.

"I think we just might, Henry, my boy. We just might," Jacob said.

James drove the group southeast across the Mississippi River into Illinois. They continued south through the town of Collinsville. They passed close by the largest and most famous Cahokia Indian mound, Monks Mound. They also saw the winding circular mound that had just been discovered to be an ancient celestial calendar. All the archeologists had the expectation that these great archeological sites had something to do with their reason for being there.

"I cannot believe that those in charge of building your nation's highways would be so thoughtless of history and archeology to try and level these wonders just to build a road," Kate said with a tinge of anger.

"Yeah, I know," Dunc responded. "I know most of the group of archeologists that put a stop to that insanity. They really save all this for the rest of us."

With the great Mississippi River not far on their right, the area quickly became thick tangled forests intermingled with rolling farmland. The limousine eventually was following an iron fence with posts about seven feet high attached to one another by grillwork. James turned in at a gate attached to two stone pillars. Two words were carved into the stone archway over the gates, "Mission Hospital." The gates opened automatically, and James then followed a winding stone driveway through a heavily forested area. The stones reminded Kate in length and breadth of those on the Isle of Skye, once thought to be a road, now known to be the remnants of a great wall.

The road eventually broke into a clearing. There stood a massive, four-storied medieval building. There were over fifty cars parked to the side of the building. Wings jutted out from either side of the main building. Together, they surrounded three sides of a courtyard. Encircling the entire courtyard was a paved walkway, covered by an overhang supported by gothic columns. In the midst of the courtyard was a large statue of Jesus Christ holding a lamb.

The three archeologists stared with furrowed brows. *What could this very Christian structure have to do with the Hebrew tribes?*

James continued on as the stone road curved around the hospital and into an area of manicured lawn and formal circular gardens. The circles that the road followed were not concentric but one long winding line of beautiful roses and green hedges that wound up a gentle slope. The coil narrowed until it encircled a large, two-story manor house made of the same stones as the road. The Isle of Skye now came to everyone's mind. Because of this connection with the Skye castle, Dunc also remembered the manor house at Loch Moy with its building blocks having been formally used for its ancient castle.

As the limousine drew close to the front steps of the house, a woman of between five and a half and six feet walked out under the portico. She had brilliant white hair neatly pinned into a braided bun. Though resting her left hand on a brass cane, she stood tall and erect. She wore a floor-length long-sleeve black dress, reminiscent of the early twentieth century.

James got out and opened the door for his passengers. As the group climbed out, they were stuck by the broad front doors that were of aged wood and at least fifteen feet tall. On each door was carved the heads of an ox above a downward slash. Beneath the slash, facing in the opposite direction, was the head of a unicorn.

Jacob shook his head, and with moist eyes, he whispered, "We have found them."

Led by Jacob, they all began to climb the stone stairs. Only Kate, a little slower because of guiding Mary, noticed that James was smiling what she felt was a slightly wicked smile. Jacob reached their hostess first with an outstretched hand. He straightened his stoop shoulders a bit upon realizing her height. She took his hand in hers.

"Mrs. Joseph, you are so gracious to offer your home and your knowledge to us," Jacob said, feeling he had never seen such a warm and lovely smile.

"No, it is I who am so grateful for your responding to my inquiry," she said.

"We thank you for putting this crowd up for our stay and for sending your chauffer, James, to pick us up."

Mrs. Joseph gave him, at first, a quizzical look and then one that spoke of mild irritation. She raised one eyebrow and turned her attention to her supposed chauffer. "This, Dr. Rubin, is not my chauffer. His name is not James. It is Joshua Longfeather Joseph, and he is my nephew. As the oldest male descendant of this family, he is also *master* of our household. Why he is wearing this silly outfit, I do not know. We don't make folks around here wear uniforms."

Joshua took his hat off, and long straight black hair cascaded down his back. Climbing the stairs with an outstretched hand, he laughed and said, "Dr. Rubin, forgive my little prank. It was not meant to deceive as much as to see my aunt's reaction. It gives me great pleasure to tease her. I do, however, learn a great deal by anonymity. As you will find out, it is necessary to protect this lady with every bit of imagination I can muster."

He shook the outstretched hand of Jacob, who was quietly chuckling. Joshua put his arm around his aunt's shoulder and kissed her forehead. The warmth between aunt and nephew was evident to all.

Introductions were made all around. Lastly, Mrs. Joseph leaned over and reached her hand out to Mary. "And who is this lovely young lady?"

With a gentle prompt from her mother, the child stepped forward, took the outstretched hand, and said, "I'm Mary, and that's my mommy," pointing to Kate. "And that's going to be my daddy." She pointed to Dunc with a broad smile. Mrs. Joseph glanced up at the father-to-be and immediately knew she had made the right decision by contacting these people.

The guests were shown to their rooms, given time to relax and unpack, and then fed lunch. The women and children who served lunch for Mrs. Joseph spoke to her and she to them in familial terms. The guests found out later that this was because they all *were* family. The conversation remained light, and all who now knew Jacob Rubin could see how anxious he was to hear the history Mrs. Joseph could tell him. They recognized his impatience by the drumming of his fingers against his knee.

Mrs. Joseph must have also recognized this as she quickly suggested after the last course that the others spend some free time with her family as she and Jacob spoke. Some of the younger family members asked Henry and Miriam if they wanted to throw around some frisbees.

"I've always wanted to," said Miriam. Her ear-to-ear smile expressed her excitement at the prospect of this new experience.

"I guess so. I'm probably not good at it," Henry said, nervously pushing his glasses up his nose.

As the young people left, Kate took Mary up for a "wee nap." Joshua invited Dunc to join him for a tour of the grounds. The invitation was enthusiastically accepted.

Jacob and Moira retired to a sitting room, which displayed several Jewish antiques and artifacts. Moira walked Jacob around the room, explaining what each item was and from where it came. She showed him objects of worship as well as articles of Jewish home decor, which were from all over the world, some originating as far back as the second and third century BCE. Jacob was mesmerized, knowing from his own studies and experience that these beautiful and rare items were thoroughly authentic.

"Oh my," he said.

"I wasn't trying to impress you. I was thrilled to have someone of your great knowledge to come and see these things. It honors me that you did," she said.

He smiled at her, still overwhelmed at the priceless and rare items he saw.

"Now, down to business," she went on. "I asked you here for several reasons. First, to discuss your work in Saudi Arabia, Egypt, and Scotland. Second, to, shall we say, give you the *rest of the story.*

And third, to give *you* a surprise." She was grinning in a way not unlike her mischievous nephew.

"You have me totally intrigued, my lady."

Moira took on a very somber appearance. "However," she said quietly, "I must have your word of honor that nothing I tell you will go any further than our conversation, unless I agree."

Jacob was taken back but recognized what was close to fear in her eyes. He thought through what she was saying and then gently began nodding his head in agreement.

She smiled with relief, then added, "Jacob, can I be assured of the same response from Dr. Wallace and Dr. McIntosh? I'm also wondering if young Henry, who was so important in your work in Scotland, is to be included."

"Your second question first—Henry has become a permanent fourth member of our team and should be included. As to your first question, I believe all three will agree to your conditions, but we will have to ask them."

Chapter 31

As the conversation in the manor house was going on, Joshua and Duncan were getting to know each other as they traversed the vast grounds between the hospital, the house, and the area beyond the house. Dunc quickly realized that they were not standing on a hill but an ancient mound he assumed was built by Native Americans.

"Is the manor house built on a Cahokia mound?" Duncan asked with an uneasy feeling that this might be a sacrilege to the native tribe.

"No, this was built by Hebrews when they settled here. It was more or less to…fit into the neighborhood. And for other practical reasons."

From this vantage point, Dunc could see for miles in all directions. To the west, he could see the shimmering waters of the Mississippi River. There were other mounds to the north scattered here and there. He could even see the top of Monks Mound.

Duncan could also see with his trained archeologist's eyes that there were patches of what were, at one time, fairly large villages interspersed with farmland. Among the traces of what he felt must be older dwellings, there were more modern houses, most under construction or, possibly, deconstruction.

"This must have been quite a thriving community. Is all this a part of your land and/or the hospital's?"

"In a way, yes to all the above. Actually, this area was settled by five distinct groups. Four of them arrived about fifteen hundred years ago. The fifth, an Indian tribe, has been here since prehistoric times." Joshua was watching his guest very intently.

"Who were the four?"

Joshua smiled, looking down at his shoes. "My dear aunt would like to explain that to you—after we have come to an agreement."

"And that agreement is?"

"She will explain that also."

Once they returned, Kate and Mary had come downstairs, and Moira was busy finding a snack for the child. The kids came in also in need of refreshment. Henry was grinning broadly, having mastered the sport of frisbee.

"I never was good at that sort of thing before," he proudly told Jacob.

"Well, you were bound to find your place in the sport's world, my boy. You are talented in every other area you have entered," Jacob said.

"Well, I'm good at it too," said Miriam. "And I have never played before either." There was a touch of smugness in her voice. Henry rolled his eyes, and Jacob chuckled at the competitive youngsters.

Miriam swept Mary up in her arms. "I'm going to teach Mary, and she'll be as good as you by this evening."

Having finished their refreshments, the young people decided to go back outside.

"That's the most social I've ever seen Henry," Jacob said aside to Kate.

"You're right, and it would appear it's with your daughter that his social ability is burgeoning," Kate said, smiling at Jacob.

The whole group of young people left, laughing and teasing one another. Henry started to follow in his usual awkward manner.

Moira took his arm and, leading him toward the sitting room, said, "Henry, I want to include you in our talk."

Henry was surprised but thrilled to be included. She led the archeologists and Joshua back into the sitting room for the *agreement*. She settled in her chair before her expectant crowd. Jacob, Kate, Henry, and Dunc watched her with rapt attention. Joshua watched, his brow furrowed with concern.

Moira cleared her throat and began to speak, "I have asked the four of you here, and only you, after reading every word of your report, Dr. Wallace. I read the devotion to the truth all of you put into this work. I read the admiration and respect for the people you felt but were not totally sure you were following through the centuries. I also read of the terror you experienced from those who would destroy that history you uncovered." She paused and was quiet for some time, staring into her lap.

Joshua reached over and patted her hand, and she smiled at him.

"The history you have uncovered—mine and my family's history—has been blessed, but also at times, cursed. Cursed by the same factions that would destroy your work in Scotland. That is why I ask of you to not speak or write of what you find here." She looked at each of their faces. "You see, I truly want you to know how right you were in your conclusions. At the same time, I cannot allow that history of our lost tribes, lost over two thousand and seven hundred years ago, I cannot allow that history to be destroyed by those factions. We can only be safe if they don't know about us."

Kate was the first to speak. "I agree," she said without hesitation.

Practical Duncan McIntosh was thinking of the cost of an unpaid-for archeological project. But he knew he could not say no to this lovely lady and what she was offering. "I also agree," he finally said.

"Me too," Henry agreed, still a bit awed by being included.

"You have our word, my lady," Jacob said with a smile.

And as if she read their minds regarding the lack of funding, Moira said, "Don't worry about the financing for this project. That is our least concern."

She then began. She led them through the forty years journey from Israel to Scotland. Moira fleshed out the timid scribe who became mighty King Talmai. She presented them a living portrait of Miriam, their lady of the bog. Other characters of the journey were brought to life, such as the Manasseh leader and Queen Miriam's father, Peleg, and the Levite prophet, Neriah.

Filling in the gaps, she explained the travels with the Bedouins that ended in their slaughter and the curse of the desert; the years in Tartessus; and finally, the tribes finding their new *promises land*. She ended this part of the story with Queen Miriam's death, the building of the nautilus palace, and finally Neriah and King Talmai's deaths.

When Moira stopped and looked at the mantle clock, the archeologists resisted. They had barely moved or taken a breath as they placed their bits of information into the magnificent story being told: the remains of the massacre in Saudi Arabia, the Assyrian/ Hebrew shields in Africa and Scotland, their lady of the bog, and then the sarcophaguses on the Isle of Skye.

"Do we have to stop?" Henry asked.

"I think it is most important to do so," Moira said. "It is dinner-time. It is time to digest all this information, and it is time to refresh ourselves with rest. We will continue on tomorrow. I have centuries more to tell about. But that will be for tomorrow. We have been at this for over three hours." No one could believe this. They were so caught up in Mrs. Joseph's enthralling tale.

After a lovely and filling dinner, the group was told to relax, read, or enjoy the grounds. Kate put an already sleeping Mary to bed. To the mother's delight, many of the Joseph young people brought games and quietly played with Miriam and Henry in the sitting room of Kate and Mary's suite. This allowed Kate and Dunc to wander outside for a while.

Slipping his arm around her waist, Duncan asked, "What's going through your head?"

"So much, Dunc. Do you realize what we have learned today?"

He nodded slowly, his eyes wide, realizing exactly what she was talking about.

"Dunc, did you hear the history that we are being told and can never tell anyone else? There is so much false stuff out there. We have the real thing and can't tell a soul."

Dunc stared at the ground, pulling Kate a little closer. "I know that, but somehow, someway, when it's time the truth does come out." He pulled her into his arms and kissed her. "We just have to have faith that it will, even though it won't come from us."

She smiled up at him and kissed him again. "There you go again with that *faith* thing."

The next morning, Moira allowed Henry some time for exercise playing frisbee with the other young people. When he came in, so anxious to learn more, the group again gathered in the sitting room.

"I wanted to explain several things to you. I included Joshua in our discussions yesterday to let him judge for himself regarding your honor and integrity. You will notice he is not here today because he agrees with me that we have chosen well in bringing you into our confidence. He is a very busy man running our affairs and has heard this story many times over his entire life. You know how we Hebrews teach our children." This last statement was directed at Jacob, who smiled and nodded. "He will join us in about an hour."

She continued, "As you have written, Dr. Rubin, we Hebrews have been literate for eons. We are also storytellers. The Dead Sea Scrolls provide evidence that our stories have remained the same over the eons, as first told by our ancients."

"I know that, my dear lady," Jacob said. "That is why you have our *complete* confidence and attention."

The next part of the story began where the last left off. The tale wove itself through the deep friendship between the generations of Hebrews and the Picts, especially between the royal families of each. It spoke of the alliance between them when the Roman troops advanced north into Pictland. Moira explained how the strategy, laid out by the Hebrews, helped the Picts frustrate the Romans into building Hadrian's Wall and retreating south.

She brought the story down to Prince Arieh taking the throne after King Talmai, his father, died. She moved on into later centuries in which she spoke of the treachery of the Orcadian Picts that nearly destroyed the Manasseh tribe, the arrival of the Norsemen shipbuilders, and finally of the prophecy of those who would destroy all the Hebrews. Moira explained the decision to leave their home of many centuries in search of the new promised land. She gave insight into the occupants of the second sarcophagus in the cave on Skye: King Jebediah and Queen Naphtali of the Ephraim tribe. And to the love story between their daughter and Caal, at that point, the king of Manasseh. It was here that she introduced them to the fourth group to sail to the new promised land.

She explained that though this group was the first wave of those "who hated Hebrews for killing YHVH," they became dear and valuable friends—gentle and caring souls who gave them knowledge of the outside world and of the Hebrews who were left in Judah.

"We, to this day, don't quite understood a man who was YHVH and yet His Son. However, we have grown to love these Christians, who had—those many years ago and still today—a loving, giving spirit and quite an infectious sense of humor," Moira said with a laugh.

Mrs. Joseph explained how Jebediah and Naphtali never set foot on the new land. "They were buried together where you found them in Scotland. It was their daughter, the then *Queen* Maura of Ephraim and her husband, King Caal of Manasseh, who led the remnants of the Manasseh tribe, the Ephraim tribe, the loyal Pict tribe, and the Christians, along with the Norse in their dragon-headed ships, to this new land of promise. They landed on the southeastern shore of Lake Ontario in the early fifth century.

"Our folks sailed from Scotland above the Gulf Stream and found their way through the Saint Lawrence River to the great lake. Once our diverse people landed, they were met by the indigenous people, also a diverse group, known now as being from the Mississippian culture."

The lady of the house then turned to her nephew, who had just joined them. Joshua, as if on cue, took up the tale. "What do you know of the Hopewell tradition?" he asked.

"I have studied it, knowing we were coming to this area," said Kate. "To my understanding, it was a flourishing trade culture made up of many connected, but not related, Native American tribes. They primarily traded along the rivers that ran from the northeastern to the midwestern US and Canada. This was from approximately 200 BCE to 500 CE. Their primary trading goods were elaborate burial articles, some of the finest craftwork and artwork in the Americas."

"Very well and succinctly put," Joshua smiled at Kate with honest admiration. "After about two years on the shores of Ontario, the council of tribes—Picts, Hebrews, Norse, and Christians—met. This also included the Levite prophets. It was decided to once again become travelers, to pick up family, herds, and belongings and join the Hopewell culture. There was a great deal of Native American warfare going on in and near their location. At the same time, our people knew themselves to be expert traders.

"The one dissenting vote was from the Norse captains and their immediate families. They explained that they were seamen and not nomads. Many of the Norse had been converted to Christianity. Three of the Norse women had married the three missionaries, and they each had growing families. So just the two captains and their immediate families left their friends and relatives with deep sadness and a good deal of fear of what they would expect to find when they returned to Norseland."

"What did they find?" Henry asked.

"We do not know," Joshua responded. "There is no trace, which we know of, that was ever found of them."

A mood of melancholy fell over the room as everyone there had become attached to all the groups discussed these last two days.

The group then took a short refreshment break, just long enough to find out Mary loved her newfound game of frisbee. After a bite to eat and a good stretch of weary limbs, they regrouped in the sitting room, and Joshua continued.

"After five years of traveling and the group having done quite well with their trading, they arrived in this very area. It was apparent to all that this was where they must stop. The natives here welcomed them with open arms. They are the ones who gave them the land for their new home on this very spot.

"Now let me explain about what this gift of land meant," Joshua said. "The land given was expansive, beautiful, and lush. The indigenous folk, whose real name has been lost to history, known now as the Cahokia, treated the people from across the sea like royalty. They even helped build the castle for the Hebrew king and queen to these royals' specifications, which were the same as those King Talmai laid out. Our front doors are the ones that graced the gates of this magnificent castle."

Once again, the archeologists were thrilled to have studied, walked through, and even touched these physical pieces of ancient times. Even Henry, who seldom showed emotions, was visibly awed by this discovery.

Duncan interrupted, "Was the name of these people lost to you?"

"No, we do know their name and where they are. However, out of deep respect for their anonymity and, with it, their safety, we will keep their secrets."

"It sounds as though you are still in touch with them," Duncan ventured.

Joshua only smiled, and Duncan knew this was to be the end of this inquiry even though he was fascinated by the thought of learning even more lost pieces of history. How deeply he admired these people's respect for and protection of one another.

"Only one group was leery of all this generosity." Joshua continued. "The Picts, whose lifestyle and ideologies closely resembled these natives, had great reservations as to their underlying intentions."

Chapter 32

Southeastern shore of Lake Michigan
Hebrew year 4173 (413 CE)

King Caal walked into the family quarters of the palace. He had to laugh at his five-year-old twin sons playing with their mother. She was sitting on the floor. They would run to her and kiss her cheek and then run across the room and kiss their dogs. The dogs seemed annoyed but resigned. The mother was overjoyed.

The king's laughter was for the rambunctious boys and also for his lady sitting with legs spread wide apart. She could not cross them because of her huge belly, which held his third child, due to be born any day now. Caal could not figure out how she even got down on the floor. His joy was also in her laughter. It had taken these two energetic rascals to bring her out of her deep depression. Her sorrow coming from the realization that her mother and father were not aboard the last Norse ship carrying the rest of her family to this *new* promised land. They had both died and were buried in their former homeland before the last ship left.

"Am I going to have to bring some horses in to get you up? We have guests who wish to see us both," the king asked with a playful grin.

"You do not have to be rude, my lord. I can manage myself."

It became quickly evident that she could not. So with both of them laughing, Caal lifted Maura up with little effort, though he made grunting sounds to appear it was quite a strain. She laughed and slapped him on the shoulder.

The very large nursemaid who was standing in the corner, also laughing at her king and queen's antics, rushed over. She grabbed both boys by their wrists. "I will feed these monsters and put them down for a nap while you go greet your guests." The boys struggled against the idea of a nap. However, both knew that even together, they were no match for their portly caretaker. So they gave in.

"And who are these guests?" Queen Maura asked.

"Brode Talorc, Elisafat the priest, and the Hibernian Amos. We have found out some important information that we need to act on." The king's appearance became very serious. "Talorc has brought two of the natives. He feels we need to hear them out. I have never seen our native benefactors look as frightened and dour as this man and woman."

"What do you think is wrong?"

"I have no idea, but Talorc feels it is serious enough to have a royal counsel."

When the couple entered the room, both kings greeted each other with their mutual respect. The brode kissed the queen's hand. He then introduced them to the native man and woman. These two bowed in respect, but also a great amount of fear. They were dressed in very plain and shabby attire, nothing like the fine clothing of everyone the royal couple had seen before.

"These folks are from the village. They are farmers. They came to us for help," Talorc explained. "Some of my tribe whom they spoke with brought them to me. None of the native farmers and common villagers have been allowed to interact with us. They have taken their lives in their hands by doing so, but I believe for good reason."

King Caal ushered them to the great table and gestured for them to sit down. The couple looked unbelieving and a bit terrified. Brode Talorc spoke to them in their language. He picked it up very quickly after their arrival and was helping the Hebrews through Reuven to do the same.

Talorc turned to Caal and Maura with deep sadness in his eyes and said, "I have learned from these folks quite a bit about the reason for their rulers' gracious treatment toward us. You see, these people have been a mighty nation for centuries. This is evidenced by the great temple and burial mounds, and especially the celestial calendar mound that reminds you so much of Jebediah's nautilus castle. But during the rule of the last three chiefs, these chiefs and their families have been plagued with an illness that has grown worse and killed many of them. These chiefs are and were very tyrannical, making the commoners of the tribe more slaves than citizens. They have prayed and made sacrifices to their gods to save them."

He stopped and sighed. Continuing, he said, "When we arrived with our dragon head from the Norse ship, they believed we were those gods come to heal them. This is the reason for our magnanimous welcome. They have worked to build us palaces, and they have continued their prayers...and their sacrifices to incur our favor. These people came to me to beg our help. You see, their sacrifices are young virgin girls. This couple's daughter is to die tomorrow night."

There was dead silence in the room.

"We must stop this," the queen said, barely able to speak above a whisper. Her hands were trembling.

Caal began to nod, but his expression was one of concern. With furrowed brow, he looked at Talorc and said, "We cannot tell them we are not gods come to save them. That will not help us or these people." He gestured toward the peasant couple cowering together.

"No, we remain gods," Talorc said, his eyes wandering back and forth feverously as he thought. "First, we stop the killing. Perhaps we say this no longer pleases us. Next, we address the illness. When we first came in contact with the Romans, we caught some of their diseases, and they were deadly."

"Yes," Caal said. He was picking up Talorc's train of thought. "Yes, but these people were isolated or only in contact with other natives they were close to for millennia. This illness came to them long before we arrived. It must be something else."

"Is it something different they are eating?" Maura asked.

"Aha, spoken like a true mother," Talorc said. He turned to the natives, realizing that they were all strong and healthy, unlike their leaders. He asked in their language what sort of food their rulers eat that they do not. The couple thought for a while and mentioned several things different in their meager diet and the exotic foods of their leaders. The look on their faces showed confusion at the questions and irritation at the discussion of food when their daughter's life hung in the balance. *Are these people—gods—no more concerned for the life of our people than our own rulers?*

Talorc turned to Caal with a broad smile. "Our people have watched your people for centuries now. We have seen your strength, your height, and...your fertility." He bowed toward the queen. "We have sought your secrets and have long followed your strict dietary rules. It would appear that the peasants, the farmers, eat what they harvest and occasionally fowl. The rulers, however, are quite fond of wild boar and bear meat...*raw.*"

The king and queen both nearly gagged at this revelation. Caal looked at Talorc. "Lockjaw!" Talorc nodded in agreement. Caal called for the guard outside the door. "See these people safely home." He turned to the natives and said, "Your daughter will be home *alive* tomorrow."

The brode translated.

The leaders met and talked way into the night. "If we are gods, we must not lose the edge that gives us! How do we cure this illness? How do we stop the killing? How do gods act?"

Slowly they answered their questions, and then the beginning of a plan emerged. A few minutes before dawn, Caal and Talorc, each confident in his role, marched shoulder to shoulder into the center of the native city and climbed up the slope of the great temple mound. Word spread at lightning speed throughout the city that the gods were atop the sacred mound. The crowd gathered, with great anticipation, at the base of the mound. The rulers and their families came to the front of the crowds.

The instant the sun crested the eastern mountains, King Caal stepped forward and raised his hands. Brode Talorc stepped to his side. Caal began to speak in Hebrew. As he did, the brode translated into the native language. Caal's script had not been written the previous night. It had been written thousands of years earlier in Canaan, on Mount Sinai, and in the deserts of Egypt. They took sentences straight from the Torah.

They did, however, add and subtract a few words and phrases to make it specific to these people. King Caal said quick prayers to YHVH over the deviations. Amos said a long agonizing prayer the night before, begging forgiveness for perverting the sacred Word of God. Brode Talorc gave it little thought since this was not a part of their religion.

"And I will make of thee a *great* nation and bless thee!" Caal shouted with all the authority he could muster. He was quoting from the book of Genesis. It was a conversation between YHVH and his patriarch, Abraham. He had emphasized the word *great*.

He went on drawing, where applicable, from the book of Deuteronomy, having to insert the animals local to this land and eliminating those that were not.

"Do not eat any detestable thing. These are the animals you may eat—the deer, the gazelle. The pig is unclean. You are not to eat their meat or touch their carcasses." The king then added the bear and spoke of never eating any animal raw. Deviating from the scripture, he explained they could not be *great* in number if they were sick from eating that which was unclean.

The night before, there had been a discussion on quoting all the Ten Commandments. It was agreed that it should be limited to the one most pertinent—the sixth commandment.

"*Thou shalt not kill,*" Caal said in very demonstrative tones. He explained that young women were not acceptable sacrifices. They were given to the tribe to bear many children, thus making the tribe grow into a *great* nation. "If you wish to show your devotion, the first of your harvest or the firstborn of your herds are accepted. Now bring me the virgin you were to sacrifice this day."

The frightened young girl was brought to Caal, who blessed her and had her returned to her parents.

Chapter 33

Illinois, United States
Hebrew year 5776 (2016 CE0

M oira explained that the rulers never really recovered from their illnesses. She said the leadership became far more democratic, and the tribe began to flourish.

At this point, Moira stood and went to the phone. She greeted the person on the other end with great warmth. She said, "As I'm sure you know, our guests have arrived. Please join us for lunch on the veranda."

The group went outside and sat down at the long wooden table and benches already set for lunch. They could see the back of the hospital from the veranda. The archeologists had high hopes that they would find the meaning of this very Christian building in this very Jewish enclave, though they had some inkling that they had something to do with the Hibernian Christians they just learned about. They were excited to see a man and woman emerge from the hospital's rear entrance and approach the veranda.

Joshua went to greet the couple. They were dressed in casual attire, nothing that spoke of religious apparel except for the small cross the woman wore around her neck. It was noted by the archeologists that as the couple approached, they were just that: a couple. They were holding hands. Joshua stepped forward and shook hands with the new arrivals. "Rev. Dr. Paul Bruce and Dr. Leah Bruce, may I present our guests?" He proceeded to introduce those gathered around the table to one another. Moira then invited all to sit and have lunch.

Though some of the young Josephs served them, most of the youth along with Miriam and Mary ate inside. The conversation was polite as it was intended to be. How the Christians would contribute to the unfolding story would wait for the afternoon session. It was the Christians' turn to ask question now. They had also read Kate's thesis and were anxious to find out what of their history on Skye was found. They were a bit disappointed to find out that the cross in Jebediah's sarcophagus was all that was found. The Bruces were well educated in the spread of Christianity across the British Isles from the Scots of Ireland. They had hoped for more personal history.

Back in the sitting room, Moira let the Christians explain about their three missionaries being captured by the Hebrews in Scotland and how they came to join them to the new land. They talked of being allowed to worship here as they pleased after having met so much opposition in their motherland. They spoke of being taught by Hebrews how to build strong houses and to read and write, albeit in Hebrew. They told of converting many of the Norse to Christianity and continuing their linage by marrying many of them.

"The Picts kept to their own beliefs, though they did inter-marry now and then with First Nations. We also married some of the First Nations who became Christians, as did our Hebrew brothers and sisters with those who wanted to follow the Jewish faith," Leah Bruce explained.

"First Nations?" asked Kate. She had not heard the term before.

"Yes," Paul said. "The tribes of people who live in Alaska and parts of Canada choose this far more dignified and exclusive name rather than *Native American*. Of course, the term *Indian* became politically incorrect. *Indian* was nationally incorrect to begin with. We choose to use *First Nations* also because it honors these people we have come to love as being the original nations of this great land.

"*Native American* is to us also incorrect, seeing as how everyone who is born in any of the American continents can claim the title to include ourselves, our children, and all of us going back to the children of the royal couple who brought all of us to this land, King Caal and Queen Maura."

"Did the two tribes remain as one under the symbol of the sheaf?" Kate asked. She was thinking of the great doors with the ox and the unicorn carved in them.

"No," Joshua continued. "Twin sons were born to the King and Queen two and a half years after the king's arrival. The firstborn was named Manasseh, and the second Ephraim. The king and queen, he being of the Manasseh tribe and she being from Ephraim, corrected a mistake, or what seemed so to the Manasseh tribe, made by the ancient Hebrew patriarch Jacob when he blessed Joseph's second-born, Ephraim, as the firstborn. They both ascended the individual thrones of the tribes they were named for after *both* their parents died."

Jacob had to break in and ask the question, "The two tribes often warred and were contentious with each other. Did this continue here?"

"Not as much here," Moira said. "For one thing, I think they had grown up a bit over the centuries, and for another, they depended heavily on each other here. Though they kept their individual identities, they remained first and foremost as Hebrews."

"The chosen people of God," Leah Bruce said.

The archeologist clearly heard the respect these Christians held for the Hebrews and that it was mutually returned.

"What denomination of Christianity do you follow, Catholic, Reform Protestant, Baptist?" Duncan asked.

"We are Christians, my friend. We are well-versed in all the divisions our faith has gone through over the two plus millennia since Christ. We chose to simply be Christians," Paul Bruce said. "Each of us as ministers has attended a seminary of his or her choice, come back, compared notes, and then continued to minister to our people here. There has been no division in our ministry as we all respect one another's personal call from our Savior.

"You see, we found great need among our diverse groups for medical education. As far back as 1765, our missionaries attended the College of Philadelphia's anatomical lectures and studied its theory of physik. This was the first medical school in the US. It was all that served the original colonies. We became doctors and healed our people as best we could. We had already built our hospital in the fifteen hundreds for reasons we will explain later. We have continued our medical mission throughout the years."

The missionaries needed to return but promised to join the group the next day when the Josephs would explain what occurred among the First Nations, the Hebrews, and the Picts.

Later that evening, Kate and Dunc walked hand in hand out on the crest of the hill that overlooked the hospital.

Kate said, "I wish there was far more caring like we see here between Jew—or Hebrews, as they prefer—and Christian. And even Christian denominations all over the world. We wouldn't have seen such horrors as the Nazis, white supremacists, and the Crusades."

"Kate," Duncan said.

She turned to see him staring at her with love and a touch of concern. "I want you to marry me here and now. Well, at least in the immediate future. I want one of these men and women of faith to marry us. I feel we are in a sacred place, a place sacred perhaps even to an…an atheist?"

Kate smiled. "I no longer feel I can call myself an atheist. After seeing the faith of the two dearest men in my life, I'm keeping an open mind. Yes, we are in a sacred place, and yes, Dr. McIntosh, I will marry you here."

Chapter 34

The next day at breakfast, Kate made the announcement of their pending marriage and that they wanted it here. This was met with cheers and whoops of joy from everyone. The Josephs agreed. Duncan told them that Kate did not wish to invite her parents, but he did want his sister there—only if it was acceptable to Joshua and Moira. Joshua stood and walked over to Duncan. He reached out and took Dunc's hand in his. "She is as welcome as you are," he said.

The Bruces arrived shortly after breakfast. All agreed to the marriage and that they would be thrilled to officiate. This morning, they were accompanied by five more of the Christians. "We wanted you to meet more of our folk. You see, we are not all doctors. Some are preachers, some teachers, and some actually work for a living." Paul had to stop here and chuckle to himself, as did everyone else in the room.

The archeologists could not help but admire people of such great service who could laugh at themselves with so much humility. They were becoming very fond of all their new friends. Introductions were made all around.

Moira again led the group into the sitting room but stopped them from sitting down. She cleared her throat and smiled. "I have some very important things to show you, but first I promised you, Jacob, that I had a surprise for you. Kate, my dear, this is also for you. I understand that you have discovered that your parents, Jacob, and your grandparents, Kate, were originally from the same temple in Chicago before immigrating to Israel and Scotland."

Both nodded, not having any idea what she was getting at.

"Well, now, *our* ancestors started that temple a century or so ago. Now, many Jews from many different places have come and gone from there, so there is no way of telling, but it is possible that we are kinfolk."

There actually was a way of telling which everyone in the room immediately thought of—but just as instantly dismissed. DNA testing could tell a relationship, but none there would put that DNA out where it could possibly be discovered by the terrorists.

Jacob and Kate stared at each other and, smiling, fell into each other's arms. This told both that the love and respect each felt for the other was not just by chance. Kate knew she felt a relationship with the lady of the bog when she first saw her. And now she knew in her heart that same relationship was there with Jacob and Miriam.

Kate looked at Moira and ventured a question on her mind for some time. "I have noted the prominent women of your stories, yourself, Miriam Rubin, myself, and my daughter all have names which are versions of the name *Mary*. I have felt a connection with each one. Of course, with mine and Jacob's daughter but also with you and, most surprisingly, with Queen Miriam. You just told us of the possibility of Jacob and I being descended from the house of Joseph, having both come from families attending that temple in Chicago. Is it possible we are descended from these women I just spoke of?"

"Is it possible?" Moira said with a smile and raised eyebrows. "No, it's very probable. I am descended from these royal women. And like you, I feel the same connections you do. That is the other reason we asked you here." She smiled a loving smile at Kate.

"I hate to break up this reunion of sorts, but there are things you now need to see," Joshua said. "Please follow me."

The sitting room was an inside room with several open archways and doors leading off all four walls. Several of the archways led to hallways, several to staircases. All were quite dark with only the slightest outline of walls or stairs and railings visible. To everyone's surprise, Joshua walked not to an archway or a door but to a bookcase. His hand touched something hidden inside, and the entire bookcase slid silently to the right, revealing a pathway that sloped downhill. A string of electric lights lit the downward path.

The archeologist stared in shock. This felt to the newcomers to be something out of an old movie. The residence of the area took it in stride as an everyday occurrence.

As the group approached the opening, they could see it was an underground tunnel. Joshua turned to his guests and with laughter in his voice said, "Now, my dear friends, we descend into the bowels of the earth." He gave a ghostly laugh and led the way.

Moira and the Christians shook their heads at his dramatics. The group moved slowly but intently down the long, long winding passageway. Duncan did his best to calculate their decent to the rise of the mound on which Mrs. Joseph's manor house stood. He figured it could easily be the height of a four-story building.

At the bottom, they came to doors that hung from a great iron pole that stretched at least twenty feet across. Joshua and Paul slid the great door to one side, revealing what, at first sight, looked to the visitors like a massive well-lit room in one of the major museums of England or New York. Display cases lined three of the four walls of what was easily a one-hundred-by-one-hundred-foot room. Duncan realized his calculations were very nearly correct in that the ceiling was probably at least four stories above them.

Toward the middle of the room were displays of each of the cultures the archeologists now knew were a part of this great migrations. There were Hebrew articles of worship and clothing, along with everyday items of use over the ages. There were stones with Norse runes carved in them. There were Pictish stones along with partial-rebuilt dwellings. In one area, Paul explained that the crude structure there was the first pulpit that the Hibernians built in America. On it rested a cross of wood held together with reeds exactly like the cross found in Jebediah's sarcophagus. There were also earthenware cups and plates for the "Lord's Supper."

The most spectacular display was in the very center of the room. It was the bow of a great ship. It reached to the top of the room. One could walk around it and see a section of the bow's three inside decks. Attached to the bow was the huge carved neck and face of a fierce dragon with flaring nostrils and eyes blazing from the red stones that were set in the sockets.

"No wonder the First Nations thought these folks were gods if they carried this with them," Kate said.

"We came over in several of our dragon ships built by the Norse," Joshua said. "Many were broken down and the wood used to build homes and stores. Others the Norse captains sailed back across the sea. We have read of the Viking dragon ships and feel sure they are related to our dear friends. We used a couple as we sailed the rivers during our Hopewell experience. We have always been surprised that little has been told in history or legend of our dragon ships. Perhaps it had to do with the fear people of that time had for us, thinking we were gods. This is what is left of them, and only the bow at that."

Jacob and Duncan were making their way around the display cases. These held the writings of all the scribes of the Hebrews starting with those of the great King Talmai. These told the story of their journey. Later writings were journals in books, opened to one page. The last of the journals were closed books. Jacob knew in his heart that there was more to know that they would not be privy to.

Over the display cases, all around the room were pictures drawn to show the people over the two and a half thousand plus years of their travel. There were tattooed Picts, the different clothing of each of the cultures during the different eras of their travels. There were pictures of the Greek attire of the folk of Tartessus. There was a drawing of the tablet of Gilgamesh, one of the great Norse fleet, one of the First Nations as they looked when the travelers first arrived in the new land. There were drawings of many of the mythological treasures that had to be left behind.

What took the breath away of the three archeologists were the two Assyrian shields hanging side by side with the symbol of Beit Yosef carved into the center of each and inlaid in gold.

Jacob felt lightheaded at the sight of all this. There was great joy at having seen all this history; there was also great sadness that he would never see it again. It was very hard leaving these treasures, but Joshua was adamant that there was more of a story to be told. Jacob felt great resistance at leaving but was ready to hear the next chapter of the story.

Back in the sitting room, the visitors realized it was way past noon. Time had flown. All there were given snacks to hold them over until dinner.

As they ate, something occurred to Dunc. "So far, we have met our Hebrew descendants. We have met those of the Christian missionaries, and those of the Norse who married them. We know that the Indi—please forgive me, the First Nations have relocated. What about the Picts? Have we met any of them, and if so, who are they?" He was almost giddy with curiosity.

"Again, my good friend," Moira said, "they are no longer here. They have moved on. It has nothing to do with a lack of trust in you. It has to do with their wishes. We honor their desire for us to keep their confidence as to where they've gone."

Dunc smiled and nodded, but all there saw the deep disappointment in Dunc's eyes. All the archeologists had the same look. They could not know what was knowable about one of the greatest mysteries of all times.

"Well, at least we have more understanding now of our mysterious Picts than we ever did before," Jacob said with his glass-half-full philosophy.

Moira settled back in her chair. She allowed time for Dunc and the others to accept this disappointment. She then continued, "Once again, we were confronted with the realization of antisemitism." Her face was drawn with the dark shadows of sadness. "Has anyone heard of Joachim Gans?"

Each archeologist nodded and began speaking.

"First Jew to set foot in America."

"Brought over by Sir Walter Raleigh to the colony on Roanoke Island because of some talent."

"Knew how to make copper."

"Yes, yes," Moira said. "I see that you do. Well, he played only a supporting role in the *rest of the story*."

Chapter 35

The Atlantic Ocean
Hebrew year 5344 (1584 CE)

Dougham Gans stood at the railing of the ship. He vomited overboard for the—he had lost count of how many times he stood here and retched. The other seamen steered clear of that section of the bow. Only his brother, Joachim Gans, ever approached him.

"Dougham, I do not know why I brought you. I still have a problem with this supposed mission of yours. I have always known how bad you suffer from seasickness, and—"

His brother interrupted in between retches, "It is not Dougham! It is *Douglas*! It is not Gans! It is *Smith*! Ooohhh."

"All right, all right, I am sorry. It is hard for me to think of you as not being a Jew, even if it is to save these mythical Jews you say have been living in America for ten centuries."

"They are not mythical. G-d told me. I must get to them and warn—ooohhh."

"Yes, yes, Dough—Douglas. Have you kept anything down this whole voyage?"

"Some, I must have. I am still alive. I think—ooohhh."

"Thank G-d, we only have a day or two to go."

The ship did reach the port at daybreak the following day. Master Joachim Gans and his supposed assistant, Douglas Smith, were with the captain in the first launch to go ashore. This was due to Master Gans's great value to the new colony because of the more efficient and faster method of smelting copper that he developed.

"I was informed that the colonists have built you a workshop to your exact specifications," the captain told Joachim as the master coppersmith helped his wobbly brother out of the launch.

"I am very grateful, Captain, and very anxious to get to work."

"You suppose your assistant will be able to *be* an assistant anytime soon?"

"Yes, yes. Everything will be fine."

The workshop was built with no way of viewing the interior from the outside. This was for two reasons: Frankly, Gans did not want his method to be seen and copied. Second, Joachim had known, when his brother first told him of his intended mission and insisted on accompanying him to the colonies, that people of the colony must not be able to see that he, Joachim, did not have or need an assistant.

While on board and in between trips to the railing, Douglas put together a travel satchel which he filled with bare necessities. Once ashore, the two brothers were brought meals by women of the colony. Both ate a bare minimum of the food for five days and packed what would keep in the satchel. On the sixth day, Douglas took two knives and a gun, which he strapped to his body. His brother handed him another smaller satchel, this one full of copper bullets. At midnight, under heavy cloud cover, the two brothers bade each other farewell, hugged, and Douglas disappeared into the forest.

Now being free to be himself, Dougham Gans set out on his mission. He was warned of the natives that were called Indians. These people were feeling the intrusion into their lands by these white interlopers. They were warring folk, as it was. This seemed to be because they were pushed into one another's different tribal territories by the same interlopers.

This was the reason for all Dougham's artillery and for the strong warning by his brother to only travel by night and avoid the natives at all cost. He felt a dread in his heart, knowing that part of the dream/prophecy he had a year earlier told him he must return within two years if he wished to return to Prague. Hiding out and only a short time for travel each night was daunting, considering this deadline. It was over eight hundred miles to his destination. The only landmarks he had to follow were rivers.

His father, David Gans, a famous Prague, Bohemia, mathematician and geographer had helped him figure all this out. He had made a map for his son to follow. Dougham's father, like himself, was a man of deep faith and believed his son's mission to be valid. Joachim was of more modern thought. He put little store in the visions, prophecies, and miracles of the Torah. He had agreed to take his brother with him to the colonies only after heavy prodding from their father.

When the morning light began to erase the shadows in which Dougham had traveled for four hours, he began to search for underbrush. He found a hiding place and moved himself around until he was sure he was hidden. His heart was pounding in his throat when he heard voices in a foreign tongue, closer than he could believe they could have gotten without his knowing much sooner. From where he lay, he could just see their moccasins pass by, evidently completely unaware of his presence.

It took nearly an hour before he found the courage to reach inside his satchel and pull out a piece of jerk meat to chew on. The food, along with the understanding that he was no longer going to spend his days retching over the side of a ship, both strengthened and emboldened him. He pulled out the map his father had made for him and thought through the course he would take on the next stretch of his journey. He had gone over and over this many times. He would stay to the north or west of the rivers he followed.

Each morning, he found a spot similar to the first morning and lay hidden during daylight. It was only a few days of this for his body to begin to burn with the itching rash of bugs or poison leaves or both. He found sticks and raked them over the red-skin misery. Several nights, if certain he was not close to population, Dougham would lower himself into the cold, cold waters of the river he followed. This brought some relief, but only for a short time, and it also brought on a cough, fever, and a constantly dripping nose. Despite this misery, Dougham prayed and pressed on.

Food very quickly became an issue. Hunger emboldened him to approach the dreaded Indian villages in the dark of night. At first, he found food storage and stole some. He finally realized he needed to hunt his own, so the next visit to a village, he stole a bow and arrows. He knew he would be heard if he shot his gun. He felt he would have more luck hitting his targets with an arrow rather than a thrown knife. Dougham caught squirrels and rabbit. Going against all kosher rules, he ate the meat raw, not daring to light a fire.

It had been approximately four months with his body raw or scabbed over and his insides weak from fever and cough. He realized he was, by his and his father's calculations, over two-thirds closer to his destination. Once again, he was encouraged and began to be aware of subtle things around him. He saw traps in the darkness. Dougham realized they must be set for humans as they were in traveled areas.

The Indians know about me! I must go deeper into the forest.

He was in a more mountainous area now. He climbed higher to get farther away from his pursuers. The underbrush was thicker, though the trees were thinner and smaller. He ran hunched over, looking from side to side—not down. His foot sank with a crunch into a foxhole. He felt the bone in his ankle snap. He could barely pull his foot out and almost passed out from the pain when he did.

Mighty G-d, have You tricked me? Was all this a mere joke? Are there even Jews that need my warning?

Dougham was always shaken to the core after hearing the voice of the Almighty. He stopped himself as he was about to question even that. What he did question was his sanity and his ability to overcome this broken leg. He began looking around as he painfully raised himself to a sitting position.

He quickly spotted two sprouts of oak, close enough for him to reach. They were each about five feet high. As he reached for them, he found their circumference to be a little more than he could wrap his hand around. Dougham pulled out a knife and spent the next few hours sawing the bottom of his soon-to-be canes.

With canes in hand, he rolled painfully to a kneeling position and lifted himself to stand on his good leg by balancing on his canes. Even with the knee of the broken leg bent, every move was agonizing, but he kept going. He knew the canes were a gift.

Dougham also knew he had to get off the mountain; it was impossible to negotiate the slope with one leg, with or without the canes. It took hours to move down the uneven terrain. It was daylight now, and there could be no more hiding. When he reached the pathway alongside the river, he just kept moving. This was the last river, and staying next to it would lead him to the people he was to warn. He moved on despite the pain and despite the increasing illness.

It was past noonday when Dougham began to notice the quiet, the unusual lack of nature's sounds—birds, insects, movement in the woods. He looked around not knowing what to expect. Suddenly what appeared to be trees and shrubs came alive as Indians, armed with bows and arrows, pointed at him. Some had knives. They surrounded him and slowly closed the circle around him. Dougham fumbled for his gun. The first native to reach him shoved him to the ground. His broken ankle was caught beneath him, and he screamed in pain. The natives came at him with knives raised.

The last thing he heard as darkness closed in was a male voice yelling one word.

"Stop!"

Dougham understood the word. It was not spoken in the language of the Indians, nor was it Bohemian or even English. It was yelled in haste and with authority—in Hebrew.

Chapter 36

Dougham opened his eyes with the same dread he had when he closed them. This quickly changed to surprise. He was in a bed in a completely white room. Every inch he could see looked clean. The room smelled as clean as it looked. He became aware of all his senses. He felt warm under an all-white blanket. At the same time, there was a cool wet rag on his forehead. His skin felt soothed from the constant burning, itching misery he felt for so many months.

He then saw his broken leg wrapped in a hard shell of what appeared to be plaster. It was raised in a sling hanging from a large hook jutting out from a bedpost. He felt a mild ache in his ankle, but none of the agony he had felt just before he fainted.

He then remembered the voice speaking in Hebrew. Excitement filled him with the thought he had found his Jews. He struggled to get up but found himself to be very weak. Lifting his hand was difficult. He could never remove his leg from the sling. So he called out, using Hebrew, with a very raspy voice.

A young woman entered the room dressed in a long white dress with an apron the length of the dress covering it. A few coils of blonde hair peeked out from under a white bonnet. Her smile added to the kindness glowing from her soft blue eyes.

Speaking in Hebrew, she said, "Welcome to the land of the living. We felt it was about time for your resurrection. How do you feel?"

Ignoring her question, he asked, "Are you a Jew?"

"No, I am a Christian. The Hebrews are waiting to meet you. They will be thrilled that you are awake. Are you a Jew?" She was confused by his look of concern.

Dougham was frightened by the thought that this might be a trap for him as a Jew. *Why did she call them Hebrews?* He decided to just keep quiet.

"I have upset you, and I am sorry. I think it best to call in the Ben Yosefs, our leaders." She left and returned with the couple.

The man was at least six feet tall and around the age of fifty. The woman was quite petite and, to Dougham, very lovely. Both had deep-brown eyes and dark features. They were both dressed in robes, and their hair was dark and curly. His smile was broad and warm. He reached his hand out to Dougham and said, "I am Yaakov Ben Yosef, and this is my wife Maria. We have been aware of a person from across the sea who was headed in this direction for some time now."

Maria stepped over and took his other hand in hers. "You have been through so much. We are thankful to see your eyes wide open and to know you are safe now. How do you feel?"

"Much better than I have felt for almost a year now."

"We are excited about what you can tell us of the world that our people left so long ago. Nurse Hannah said you spoke Hebrew. Do you follow the Torah as we do?" Yaakov asked.

This one statement set Dougham at complete ease. All his brother's doubts and, of course, his of late were put to rest. "Yes, yes, I am Dougham Gans. G-d has sent me to find you and warn you of the people who would do you harm. People who hate you... and me, because we killed their G-d. I mean, they think we did." He then remembered the nurse. "They are Christians, like...well, like the nurse." His voice got quieter, and the fear returned.

"Mr. Gans, we find you to have amazing courage. The danger you put yourself in to warn us is very real." Yaakov began shaking his head. "As we think about what you have just told us, we remember that we have heard this before."

"Do you mean you have already been warned?"

"No, I mean our people have heard this same threat almost a thousand years ago. As a matter of fact, Nurse Hannah is directly descended from the three Christian missionaries who were a part of the first to arrive in what is now Scotland, where we lived after leaving Israel. They were sent to convert all to Christianity. These missionaries were pleased to find we believed in what they call the Old Testament but a bit dismayed that we did not hold to their New Testament. However, as I said before, the three Christian missionaries were only the first wave of these people, and so with ships built by our allies the Norse, we fled our homes and traveled to this new land. The three Christians were brought with us. At first, as enemy hostages. However, as YHVH often does, he has made us allies and dear friends over the centuries."

Dougham started to ask more questions, but Maria stepped forward. "Now, now, we have met you and learned of your warning. But for now we must let you gain your strength. The doctors want you to eat something and try a little walking. There will be plenty of time for more talking later."

The couple left, and Dougham was brought the best food he thought he had ever eaten. Of course, he realized almost anything would be wonderful after the diet of raw squirrels and rabbits he ate for almost a year.

He rested a while longer, and then the doctor, Dr. Abel, himself a Hebrew, came in with Nurse Hannah. The doctor explained the severity of Dougham's injury, along with the very good prognosis. "You will probably always have a limp, but you will keep your leg."

The doctor and nurse then helped Dougham stand and begin to walk using the newfangled crutches they gave him. He was surprised how little pain he felt walking with the plaster cast on. This patient could not help but noticed the respect both doctor and nurse, both Hebrew and Christian, showed each other. After this, he rested again, ate a little more, and was finally helped into a sitting room.

There he again met Maria and Yaakov Ben Yosef. Yaakov introduced the others there, "This is Brode Oengus of an ancient tribe of Scotland, Chief Chicogou of a tribe native to this land, and this is Kohen Levi and his wife, Eve, of the Levite tribe. You have already met Mrs. Hannah Eriksen, and this is her husband, Dr. John Eriksen, both Christians and both of Norse and Gaelic descent. This is Dr. Abel, himself a Hebrew."

Dougham was overwhelmed at the combination of cultures sitting together in obvious congeniality. He felt humbled by their smiles and their welcoming reaction toward him.

"I noticed the nurse did not call you Jews but Hebrews," Dougham said.

"The term *Jew* comes from the Southern Kingdom of Judah," Yaakov explained. "We are from the Northern Kingdom, Israel. So we were called Israelites. One of our ancient Levites prophesied the capture of Israel by the Assyrians and led us out of Israel to our new home in Scotland over two thousand years ago."

Dougham's eyes were wide with excitement and wonder. "Then you are part of the lost tribes. Which tribe are you? No, wait—*Ben Yosef*. You are either of Manasseh or Ephraim."

"We are both. That is to say, both tribes are here. While our first leader, Talmai, was of Ephraim, he and his wife, Miriam, were crowned king and queen by the Levite that led them to Scotland. Our tribes, Manasseh and Ephraim, have fussed and feuded over the years. The Manasseh tribe crowned their own king. But we came together to journey to this land. The king of Manasseh and the queen of Ephraim married. Their twin sons were named Manasseh and Ephraim, and when the twins' parents died, they each led the tribes they were named after.

"We have stayed very close because of the hostility of some of the natives of this land. About a hundred or so years ago, we gave up the trappings of royalty. We who are, or have been, leaders are now elected. We take on the name of Ben Yosef to be impartial to both tribes. Tell me, do you know what the word *Hebrew* means?"

"Yes, it means 'to cross over' or 'one who crosses over' and is used most often in the Torah to mean 'to cross over a river,' such as the Jordan. It also refers to those of us who have crossed over from the worship of a pantheon of gods to the worship of the one true G-d."

Yaakov and Maria smiled at the knowledge of this fervent young man. "We have crossed over many rivers, even seas, and an ocean to flee our enemies. It sounds like we must still cross more. Tell us about these folks who once again believe we killed their god. How many of them are there, and how close are they?"

Dougham bowed his head. He hated to once again cause these people to be uprooted. "It seems that almost all of Europe has decided to come settle these lands. There are already people from Spain, Portugal, and England here. All are of one flavor or the other of Christians." Dougham broke off, feeling he must have been terribly insulting to those Christians sitting around him showing him so much respect.

"Dougham, my lad," Dr. Eriksen said, "we are aware that Christians have taken on many different ways of following Christ. Some are tolerant of other faiths, some totally intolerant. We also know that they have colonies. We were, however, unaware that their number is growing. Your courageous efforts have given us warning in time to prepare. Thank you. This lets us know the reason for so much unrest in our native brethren." He smiled at Chief Chicogou.

The chief spoke very little Hebrew but knew enough to follow the conversation. He said in broken Hebrew, "This does explain the problems we are having with our warring tribes."

Dougham was beginning to feel quite faint, and his pale features showed it.

"It is time for you to get back to bed. I know this has been a strain, and we are so appreciative of your warning to us," Dr. Eriksen said. "Ask Nurse Dinah to meet us in his room, and we will help him back to bed," the doctor told his wife.

When Dougham reached his warm, clean room he was met by one of the prettiest girls he had ever seen. And he had seen quite a few since waking up this morning. Nurse Dinah was dark like the Ben Yosefs. Her eyes sparkled a deep brown, and her black wavy hair hung down her back to her waist.

"What tribe are you from?" he asked.

"My family are Levites. You just met my parents, Kohen Levi and Eve," she said.

"My family believes we are also Levites," Dougham said. "Perhaps we are distantly related."

She smiled at him and went about fixing his pillow and lifting his leg into the sling. He went about falling in love with his gentle caretaker.

Back in the meeting, things became very serious as the people there, most of religions other than Christianity, took on the serious discussion of what to do now that they had been warned. The thought of once again becoming nomads threw a veil of dysphoria over the room.

Only Dr. Eriksen was hopeful. "You forget, my dear friends, there are already Christians here, and we shall very simply deal with the new ones flooding in. We will move our clinic to the front of our settlements and build a large building. We will place a big sign over the gate which leads to all the tribes with the new clinic up front. It shall read—*Mission Hospital.*"

It was almost three months since Dougham had reached the land of these diverse people. The cast was removed, and he was now able to walk, though with a cane. Nurse Dinah had him up walking as soon as the doctors saw fit for him to do so. Dougham and the nurse took many strolls about the gardens behind the hospital. He had grown very fond of her. He felt it was mutual, though neither spoke of it.

It was weighing heavy on him that the prophecy that sent him here insisted he return to the Roanoke Island colony within two years. How would he ever make it back in less time than it took to get him here, through hostile native territory and with a bad leg? He sought the advice of Kohen Levi. After telling the kohen his concern, he fell silent, knowing he might be stricken dead for disobeying G-d's command.

"When did you arrive here? And exactly where did you land?" Levi asked.

"It was the twenty-first of Tevet, 5344. We landed on Roanoke Island with Sir Walter Raleigh. I explained to the Ben Yosefs that I came with my brother as his assistant. I pray he has not been harmed by my absence."

Levi thought this over carefully. He was converting Hebrew dates to Christian dates. He was also considering the news he was aware of that affected Dougham.

"Dougham, you have been gone for three years. Between your travels without benefit of calendar, your injury and illness, and…" Levi hesitated with a grin on his face. "And the distractions of a lovely young lady known well to her mother and to me, you have lost a whole year in your calculations."

Dougham was stunned. He stared at the kohen with horror. "My brother, my brother!" he said with heartbreaking sorrow.

"Dougham, you must not mourn," Levi said. "Your brother returned a year ago with Sir Walter Raleigh and the other scientists who came to this land with you. This was due to the severe unrest of the natives of that area. The rest of the colony has had to go into hiding. As far as the natives here and the rest of the world is concerned, they have just disappeared."

"How do you know this?" Dougham asked with astonishment.

"After several hundred years, we are still considered as mystics or even gods to many of the natives. This comes from our saving the villagers of the diseases their rulers had from eating unclean foods. We could not save the leaders. But the people actually were glad to be rid of those oppressive folks. We have also built relationships with many tribes over the centuries. They let us know of the unrest and helped us hide the colonists with tribes who are not violent. This proved advantageous to both the natives and the colonists who were so desperate for supplies."

"Can you tell me where they are?" Dougham asked, now less concerned of being left behind and more fascinated by these people who cared for him.

"No, my son, even though we have trust in you, we cannot betray, even to one of your honor, the trust the colonists have placed in us."

As the months passed by, Dougham and Dinah grew closer. On a warm summer day, Kohen Levi pronounced the Ashkenazi Jew and his daughter man and wife. This was on the banks of the great river known as the Mighty Mississippi. Hundreds of descendants of the "travelers" looked on as another nationality was added to the group.

Chapter 37

Illinois, United States
Hebrew year 5776 (2016 CE)

Nan McIntosh arrived at the airport the following Saturday. It was agreed that Nan would be told that the archeologists were working on the location of a Native American tribe who disappeared mysteriously centuries ago. The people with whom they were staying had some information about these people. Dunc would never lie to his sister. However, that did not mean that he had to tell her the whole truth. He took Kate with him to meet his sister.

"Now, she's a bit of a talker. You won't be able to get a word in once she starts. Anyway, she'll ask a million questions, but don't even try answering them. I've found it best to just nod and smile," Duncan said as he pulled into the pickup lane at the airport.

"Oh, Dunc, she can't be that bad."

"You'll see," he said with a laugh in his voice. "There she is now. She's the one waving furiously at us."

Kate looked and saw a very thin woman in her middle thirties. She was waving with one hand while clutching a small rolling suitcase in the other. A raincoat was draped over the case. She was almost as tall as her brother. She had her brother's coloring of brown hair and fair complexion. Her hair was long and straight and was pulled back at the nape of her neck by bobby pins. She didn't wear makeup.

To Duncan, the term *old maid* always came to mind when he first saw her.

The term *strong woman* was Kate's impression.

Dunc told Kate long ago that, though she could be quite exasperating, he loved her dearly. Their parents were killed in an automobile crash when Dunc was seventeen. Nan dropped out of her freshmen year at Hammond and enrolled in part-time classes at the local state college. Although she was only three years older than Duncan, she did this to care for him and make sure *his* education was paid for. She worked part-time at night to accomplish this.

Dunc pulled the car over, hit the button that opened the trunk, and climbed out. Kate also climbed out. Nan, leaving her suitcase for her brother to handle, ran to Kate. She gave Kate a quick hug and began right in.

"I'm so glad to finally meet you. Dunc is so short with his explanations of what people look like and do and are. Well, I just couldn't get a good picture of you. Does he do that to you? I'm sure he does. You couldn't get a good picture of me either, could you? Of course, you couldn't. I understand I'm going to be an auntie. I'm not sure how good an auntie I'll be, but I'll try. Are you an auntie? You'll have to tell me how it works."

"Nan, let Kate answer one of your questions," Dunc interrupted.

"Oh, I'm sorry. I do go on, don't I? I just can't help myself. I—"

"*Nan!*"

His sister closed her mouth and covered it with her hand.

Kate took hold of Nan's other hand and said, "No, I've never been an auntie, but if you are as good an aunt as you are a big sister, you'll do great."

Dunc watched with a smile as the two women he loved most in the world became sisters.

During the drive back to the Josephs', Kate sat in the back with Nan, and the two conversed with each other very comfortably. Nan talked, and Kate nodded and listened.

To Dunc's delight, when they arrived at the manner house, Moira treated Nan the same way Kate did, putting his sister at ease. She personally took Nan up to her room and got her settled in.

"You're right next to Kate and Mary's room. And speaking of Mary, she can't wait to meet you. She's been talking all day about getting an aunt. She's a wonderful little girl. Now I'll let you freshen up.

Dinner will be ready in a half hour. You can meet the whole brood then." With this, Moira left Nan, who was wondering if she could possibly measure up to the child's expectations of an auntie.

When Nan walked into the grand dining room her brother rushed to her side and steered her around the room, introducing her to Joshua, Jacob and Miriam, the Bruces, Henry, and a dozen or so other Josephs. Each greeted her warmly, especially Jacob. Finally, Dunc turned to Mary. "Mary, this is your Aunt Nan. Sis, this is your new niece, Mary Kathleen Wallace, soon-to-be McIntosh."

Mary shyly walked over and reached out her hand. "I don't use *Kathleen* a lot," she said. "Sometimes I forget that's my name."

Suddenly Nan became the teacher she was with the sixth-grade class she taught back in Boston. "Middle names are often forgotten. They are usually just names to remind you of someone else in the family. My full name is Nancy Margaret McIntosh. Margaret was my mother's name," Nan said, immediately putting Mary at ease.

The conversation was kept light. Nothing was mentioned about the real reason Dunc and the others were staying with the Josephs. After dinner, Henry, Miriam, and the other young people went outside into the warm summer night air to play frisbee. The Bruces took the rest of the group into the sitting room where the wedding was to be held in the morning.

"I thought we would just run through the ceremony so everyone would feel at ease tomorrow," Paul Bruce said. "Is anyone going to be standing with you? And, Kate, are you going to walk in alone?"

"We wanted Mary and Nan to stand with us," Duncan said.

"And I haven't asked yet," Kate said, turning to Jacob with a slightly embarrassed look. "But I would love to have Jacob stand in for my father, walk me down the aisle, to give me away. That is, of course, if he doesn't mind."

"*Mind?*" Jacob said. "I can't think of any greater honor."

Kate kissed him on the cheek.

With this decided, Paul went about having Nan, Mary, and Duncan come into place and Kate walk in on Jacob's arm. He went over what he would say and what the couple and Jacob needed to respond. This was done several times until Paul felt everyone was comfortable.

While this was going on inside, the frisbee game was getting very competitive outside. It was a surprise to all when Henry took his mind off the game and turned away. The frisbee hit him in the forehead, knocking his glasses askew.

"What made you do that?" Miriam asked, a bit irritated.

Henry put his finger to his lips. "I saw someone run to the side of the house," he said. "Something is wrong. Everybody, get over behind those trees." His voice was a whisper but carried a threatening tone to all the young people.

Behind the trees, they saw three more people move stealthily to the house from the road. Henry turned to one of the Joseph girls. "Is there a way to get inside without anyone knowing?"

The girl nodded and pointed to a darkened area of the manor house.

Inside, everyone was relaxing while champagne was being passed around.

"Oh my, I completely forgot. I have a bundle for you, Dunc," Nan said. She ran to the chair in the foyer where she left a bag of envelopes on her way to dinner. She rifled through it, completely unaware of the slim metal instrument being worked into the lock of the massive ancient front doors.

She came back into the sitting room and handed about a dozen envelopes to Dunc. Nan said, "The one on top is that letter from Lady McIntosh you said was about your thank-you note to her. It's crossed the ocean so many times that it has probably traveled more miles than your ancient Hebrews."

Duncan opened it while the others gathered around him. His smile quickly turned to concern when he unfolded the letter. His mouth fell open in surprise, and his brow creased.

"What's wrong?" Kate asked, attempting to look over Duncan's shoulder.

"What is wrong"—came the voice from the sitting-room door-way—"what is wrong is that I forgot what a sentimental bloc Duncan

McIntosh is that he would send a thank-you note for a tour of Moy and a copy of Lady MacKintosh's book."

Everyone in the room whipped around to see three men in Muslim attire and one woman in a burka with a head scarf that showed only her eyes. They all had guns pointed at the group. The shocked men in the room all pulled the women and girls behind them.

Dunc realized immediately why the voice from Scotland that he and Kate heard in the submarine was familiar despite speaking in Arabic with a Far Eastern accent. Jacob realized what had bothered him for so long about seeing Mamun Al-Khaldi when he came out of the cave in Skye after the bombing. Mamun was fiercely angry—not sobbing in grief as *Will Elder* had told them.

Kate glanced at the letter Dunc still held in his right hand. It was not from Lady MacKintosh but from her barrister, inquiring who had taken Duncan on a tour of the MacKintosh museum.

Will Elder was dressed in the same Muslim attire as the other men, which included black skull caps. He had grown a long thin beard since this group had last seen him.

"Your sister was very helpful to me when I checked with her to find out what you were up to as I do now and then. I do this to get hold of the blasphemous junk you collect. I thought you couldn't possibly leave these wandering Jews alone, not having the definitive end to their story. I didn't believe that they were just lost savages, and the front door assured me I was correct."

"Dunc, I'm so sorry, I never…" Nan wept behind her brother.

"*Hush!*" Dunc said. His anger was boiling over, but it was toward Elder. He kept quiet because he had a room full of people he loved and wanted to protect. He and Jacob wanted to tear this traitor's head off but had to figure a way to disarm him and his cohorts.

"Sorry, Dunc, old chap, but you will need to show me all the blasphemous garbage these filthy Jews have stashed while my people hold your group hostage. Any wrong move, and they all die."

Suddenly a colorful object flew out of one of the passageways to the sitting room. It slammed into Elder's hand, sending his gun flying. It was followed by a barrage of the objects, which hit the other guns and the terrorists themselves. In an instant, the floor was littered with guns and frisbees.

Mary, seeing the frisbees and being unaware of danger, pulled away from Kate and ran to pick up one. At the same time, Elder dove after his gun, grabbing it in one hand and Mary's wrist in the other. Duncan threw himself on top of Mary and tried to pull her out of Will's grasp. Suddenly a gun was fired, followed by screams of horror. Duncan waited for the pain of a gunshot wound. It never came.

The intruders had dropped to the floor, covering their heads to avoid the frisbees. Doing this revealed five people standing behind them. The four men and one woman were all in Western clothes. Each one carried his or her own gun. To the archeologists' surprise, the man in front was Dr. Mamun Hakeem Al-Khaldi.

When Will Elder dove for his gun, Mamun raised his gun and fired. Elder was now dead.

Three of the men behind the terrorists began gathering them up and snapping on handcuffs. As the woman terrorist was pulled to her feet, Kate saw her scarf had been pulled off. Just as quickly, Kate cried out. Duncan, now on his feet with a terrified little girl in his arms, ran to Kate. "What, dear God, what?"

Kate sobbed, "I thought for a moment that woman was Bonnie McGregor. It was not. Oh, Duncan, will I ever be able to trust again?"

Dunc caught Jacob's eye. They had both, at one time or another, thought they could not trust Kate. Jacob nodded in understanding of Duncan's thoughts.

"Yes!" Dunc said emphatically. "Yes, *we* will be able to trust again. Possibly never as freely as we once did."

Duncan also needed to assure Nan, who was cowering close to him, that none of this was her fault. By then, the Joseph young people, Miriam, and Henry were streaming out of the hallways into the sitting room, quite proud of themselves for saving the day.

"Henry knocked the gun out of that man's hand. He really is good at this frisbee thing," Miriam said, showing pride in her competitor.

Mamun, the woman agent, and one of the men walked over to Dunc, Jacob, and the others.

"I have been working with the Bureau of Investigation in Riyadh for almost five years now," Mamun said with his anger seething just below the surface. "I got in touch with you to try and bring these terrorists to light. Joodi got in touch with me to get to you. All the agencies have been working to find these people ever since the killing at the Kilmartin Museum and the bombing on Skye. This is Lieutenant Brody and Lieutenant Ogden of the Illinois Bureau of Investigation."

Lieutenant Ellen Brody took it from there. "MI6 tracked it to Elder through his contacts with some terrorist groups. They knew something was up when he contacted your sister, Dr. McIntosh. They contacted us, and we picked it up as soon as Elder and his group landed here." She nodded at Will's body.

Other agents, who had verified that Will was dead, were placing his body on a stretcher. Kate blocked Mary's view of the body and pressed her forehead into Dunc's shoulder.

Lieutenant Brody turned her attention to the young people. "You guys did a great job. We didn't have a good advantage with the terrorists between us and the others. You deserve medals for disarming them. If you guys ever go pro, I'll write you commendations."

The young people, rather proud of themselves, smiled back at the lieutenant. She spoke her appreciation to everyone there, as did Lieutenant Ogden. They even spoke to Mary to comfort her.

Everyone gave their statements to the agents. After they gave theirs, Duncan and Jacob walked over to Mamun. He was sitting alone, staring at his hands.

"Mamun," Jacob said, "how can we ever thank you?"

"You need to know that I never suspected you of being involved, and I thank you also," Duncan added.

Mamun thought for a minute and said, "I don't deserve thanks. I just killed a man. Am I any better than they are?"

Jacob leaned over to Mamun and quietly said, "Mamun, you saved many lives tonight. It is to your credit that you grieve over having to take even one life to save so many. When you can again think ahead, I want you to consider joining us once more to find the secrets of our past."

Mamun looked at this man, whom all the world labeled as his enemy. Instead, Jacob had shown him friendship and a chance to get back to his greatest love, archeology. Mamun smiled for the first time in over a year. "I would like that. Thank you."

At the same time, Reverend Bruce approached Kate. "One thing we must not allow this terrible incident to do is to stop the most important event of your daughter's life so far. That is, of course, her receiving a father tomorrow. I am asking you to go ahead with your wedding, with the minor change of having it in the garden rather than the sitting room."

Kate thought this might ruin her marriage. She realized the minister's clever psychology in making it about Mary, not the shock and terror she had just gone through. "Yes," she said. "Yes, this will not interfere with our wedding. We will be married tomorrow in the beautiful garden."

The next day, with all present, Kate and Duncan McIntosh, along with Mary, became a family. Right after Jacob gave Kate in marriage, he returned to his seat by Moira. She leaned over to him and whispered, "May I ask a huge favor of you?"

"Anything, my dear lady. Ask away."

"When you return to Israel, may I accompany you? It has been my lifelong dream to see Israel before I die."

Jacob smiled at this. "I would be honored to accompany you to our sacred homeland."

Moira smiled with the thought of realizing her dream.

Chapter 38

Edinburgh, Scotland
Hebrew year 5778 (2018 CE)

On Kate and Duncan's first anniversary, they were settling in with a glass of champagne. It was literally *a* glass. And it was for Dunc as Kate had just a month before announced to him and Mary that she was pregnant. Duncan had taken a position teaching at Edinburgh, though he kept ties with Hammond. To everyone's delight, both Henry Campbell and Miriam Rubin had enrolled at Edinburgh.

The McIntoshes—Dunc having formally adopted Mary within weeks of their wedding—were celebrating alone. The phone rang, interrupting the quiet celebration.

"Duncan, my lad, I want to visit Illinois again."

"And hello to you, Dr. Rubin." Dunc laughed. "Just why do we need to return to Illinois?"

"To answer some questions I have and see my lovely daughter. How soon can you leave?"

"Well, we're coming up on summer break. As soon as grades are out," Dunc said. "Did you want Kate, Mary, and Henry to join us? We'll have to hire a bus."

"Yes, yes, everyone. I'll take care of the costs."

"Is Moira joining us? What a joy to see her again."

There was hesitation; then Jacob continued, "Yes, she'll be there."

A very few weeks later, the group from Scotland met Jacob and Moira's plane. Jacob walked out to the sidewalk. Miriam ran to her father and hugged him. Something then dawned on her as it did to the others.

Miriam looked to either side of him and asked, "Where is Mrs. Joseph?"

Jacob's smile wavered as he reached into his carry-on. Quietly, he said, "She is here." He pulled an ornately carved cedar box from his baggage.

Miriam and Kate covered their mouths with shock. Henry and Dunc stared, mouths open and wide-eyed.

Jacob realized he should have said something earlier. "I'm so sorry I handled this badly. Moira was terminally ill when she asked me to take her to Israel. It had been her lifelong dream. She died only a few weeks ago. She explained that while she knew and understood the Jewish restriction on cremation, she deeply wanted it. She asked that she be forgiven, but her heart was torn between Israel and the land where her people lived for nearly a thousand years. She asked I place half her ashes in Israel and half here."

Jacob expected criticism, but instead Dunc came to him and put his arms around him. "You two became close friends, didn't you?"

Jacob nodded. Kate came and hugged him, and Miriam put her arm around him and led him to the rented van. Henry followed, having no idea what to do. Somehow Mary hugging his knees was the most comforting to him, despite her not understanding what all this was about.

As the van arrived at the location of the Josephs' compound, it occurred to all that everything had changed. The iron fence was gone, and there was a manicured lawn that led all the way back to the hospital. This was now a much expansive five-story building. In front was a sign that read *West Side Hospital*. There was nothing to be seen of the statue of Jesus.

Further down was a divided road with two signs: one very elaborate on a brick wall that read *Cahokia Acres*; the other was on a metal traffic sign with the word hospital and an arrow.

Dunc drove the van down the entrance road. After the turnoff to the hospital, they began to see tennis courts, a clubhouse with a large swimming pool, and farther off, the greens of a golf course.

"Wow, do you think the Josephs came into some big money? This is a real upgrade," Dunc said.

"Yes, I do," Jacob answered. "They came into that money when they sold their home."

A real sadness came over the van. They would not see their dear friends. Jacob knew they were gone. He did not know where.

They stopped at the gatehouse and, hoping against hope, told the guard they were there to see the Josephs. Expecting to be denied entrance to this posh gated community, they were surprised to be asked their names.

"We are Drs. McIntosh, Wallace, and Rubin. This is Mr. Campbell, and these are our children," Duncan said as he pointed to each of the van's occupants.

The guard smiled and said, "Welcome all. You may tour the grounds all you want. We only ask you stop here on your way out." He nodded and opened the gate.

The group, still a bit in shock at this invitation, followed the road, though quite changed, that they felt would lead them to the manor house. The street was lined with huge elaborate mansions, each on several acres of land. To their surprise, they came to the spot that should have led up the mound to the manor house. They found not a manor house but instead a park the area of what used to be the mound. The biggest shock was that the park was on flat ground. The mound had been leveled.

It was obvious that Jacob knew this would be the case. He asked Miriam at the airport if she brought the item he asked for. She smiled and told him she had. She handed him a garden spade. Jacob now took it and walked to the center of the garden. He knelt and began digging.

"I'll do that," Henry offered.

"No," Jacob said gently. "I thank you, but I promised Mrs. Joseph I would do this."

When the hole was the right depth and breadth, Jacob picked up the carved box with Moira's ashes and held it in his hands. Even Mary could tell how much the contents of the box meant to him. She walked over to him and patted his shoulder. Jacob smiled, but he didn't dare look at her for fear of weeping. So he pressed his cheek against her tiny hand, took a deep breath, and placed the box in the tomb he had just dug. He covered it over, murmured an ancient Hebrew prayer for such an occasion, and stood.

All were quiet in the drive back to the entrance, as much for reverence as grief. When they reached the gatehouse, the same guard smiled and handed Duncan a plain white envelope. "Have a safe trip home," he called as Dunc pulled away.

When they were down the road a bit, Dunc pulled the van over. He opened the envelope and read it. A strange smile came over his face. He read the letter out loud.

> In the words of Father Jacob:
> His glory is like the firstling of his bullock, and his horns are like the horns of unicorn; with them he shall push the people together to the ends of the earth; and they are the ten thousands of Ephraim, and they are the thousands of Manasseh. (Deuteronomy 33:17)
> I saw the sorrow in your eyes when I couldn't tell you anything about the Picts. Does it help to know that each of you met with and shook the hand of a full-blooded Pict?
> Think about it.
>
> Joshua

About the Author

M eg is a clinical social worker. She and her husband, John Duly, work as a team in writing and editing her books to present to the publisher. Meg grew up in Atlanta as a minister's daughter. In *The Ox, the Horn, and the Sheaf,* she draws on both her love of history and her fascination with biblical mysteries with the hope that you, the reader, will enjoy this book as much she enjoyed writing it.

CPSIA information can be obtained
at www.ICGtesting.com
Printed in the USA
FFHW020602221119
56113897-62200FF